THE TECH-NIGHT 1.0

THE TECH-NIGHT 1.0

by AAJ

AAJ WRITING

Publisher: AAJ Writing Ltd.

www.aaj-one.com

First published in 2024 by AAJ Writing Ltd.

First Edition: 2024.

AAJ asserts the moral right to be identified as the author of this work.

Copyright © AAJ, 2024.

Copyright © AAJ Writing, 2024.

Cover Design and Illustration by AAJ.

Copyedited by Gary Budden.

Typeset by Andy Harwood.

Set in Garamond.

Printed and Bound in the United Kingdom using 100% renewable electricity at CPI Group (UK) Ltd.

ISBN for 420 First Edition: 978-1-7390908-6-9

CONTENTS

PROLOGUE

The Secret-Special-Service Agency.
Fergus-Sundar.
Malabar Jones.
Devonte Lacy.
The League of Shottas.
Mike da Silva.
Shackleton Nair.
The Global Hub of Extraterrestrial Exploration.
Elisabeth Cervantes.

$\cdots \quad \cdots \quad \cdots$

What did they all have in common?

$\cdots \quad \cdots \quad \cdots$

Their paths were irrevocably linked with another, though they did not know this at this moment in time. This is the tale of how their fates would coincide.

One can read this story in the order that the respective stories have been arranged. Or one can read this story by reading each person's respective stories individually. The choice is yours as the reader of this story.

For ultimately it does not matter; the end result of the story is the same regardless. What's happened has happened; the only nuance in life and stories is perspective.

This is the start of the Tech-Night Epoch, the 1.0.

From 2025, to Non-Theorised-Time, to 2065, and beyond.

IN MEDIAS RES

BOOK 1
MALABAR JONES

Thursday 5th November 2065

In 2065, the Secret-Special-Service-Agent 4, Malabar Jones, is chasing Brian Harrison who is a prospective terrorist. Though he halts his pursuit as he sees a man who went missing forty years ago – the SSSA4 before him, Fergus-Sundar.

15:32: Piccadilly, Mayfair, London

And so, Malabar Jones looked up from the gum-splattered streets of London and initiated the protocol to apprehend his target, for he knew if he did not, then the man would evade him once more. His target, Brian Harrison, had evaded him for far too long, longer than any man had previously evaded the young spy. Malabar Jones was the Secret-Special-Service Agent 4 (SSSA4) and was the greatest spy in the world by decree of his case history; successfully capturing every target set before him. He had never failed and was ten years into the job, a lifetime in the vocation of a SSSA. Never before had an espionage agent gone so long without a failure and still be in service to the SSSA.

As he stalked his target, he saw a man who he never thought he would see with own eyes; a man who he ought not be able to see with his own eyes. The man in question was the infamous SSSA4 Fergus Sundar, the agent who went missing forty years previously in the year 2025, in unexplained circumstances. Now here he was in front of Malabar. How could a man who had disappeared in 2025, reappear four decades later, without having aged? This question gripped his mind, in a ferocious and unflinching manner – he feared this would distract him from his current case. The truth behind the disappearance of Fergus-Sundar had never been discovered. Fergus-Sundar was the SSSA4 before Malabar.

The title of SSSA4 was not one easily inherited. They were special not only in their discerning ability to apprehend a person outside of the view of the law and government agencies, but also uniquely specialised in their knowledge of technology and science alike. For the SSSA knew this world was no longer the world of the past, where guns and traditional espionage was king. It was a new age, a new threat.

And so perfectly apt was Fergus-Sundar for the job, they created the agent category of the SSSA4 specifically for him, and it took another thirty years before this specific SSSA category was filled; Malabar Jones was the successor.

Fergus-Sundar had been an espionage agent with freedom entitled to him beyond what the espionage agency typically offered. It was due to the decree of Queen Elizabeth II, and reaffirmed by King Charles III, that Fergus-Sundar became a SSSA4. For it was known that there were certain things, regarding technology and science, that a typical government agent and especially an espionage agent could do. Fergus-Sundar went beyond the scope of what was possible, or thought to be possible, with his first-class distinction in quantum physics along with the incredible natural aptitude to be able to fight, alongside the other intricacies needed to be an espionage agent.

Though the SSSA were also not the typical espionage agency. The SSSA were not like MI6 or MI5, or any other government agency in the world, for technically they did not have any legality in any sense; they did that which needed to be done off the record entirely. They operated in the shadows, where cruelty decreed that there ought not be record of their actions and findings, for sometimes the harsh reality of the world of crime, had to be matched by the captors of the perpetrators. The SSSA operated under the guise of the Royal Office. Though if one were to ever ask of its existence or ever acknowledge its existence, the response would be nothingness; this was not something that could be admitted. And thus, everyone who was a part of the SSSA operated under these same shadows. For to catch those who linger in the shadows, the underground organisations needed an agent capable of understanding those same shadows. And though the SSSAs were versed in the art of the underground, they were also versed in the art of aristocracy. Their agents needed to possess the specific decorum required of those who considered themselves to be a part of the upper echelons of society, along with the ability to operate in the shadows and in the under-ground – meaning adaptability was of paramount need; the ever increasing crowds of the city required one to be malleable to their surroundings. And thus, it seemed to be so that the SSSA were made up of what seemed to be ordinary people, nobility or poshness was not a prerequisite for this type of espionage agent – in fact typically it was the opposite that they sought after.

Malabar looked upon the face of Fergus-Sundar as he walked aimlessly with his brown cheeks growing purple due to the cold air. Fergus-Sundar was not meant to be in this year, in this space, in this spacetime. Fergus-Sundar was unaged in his appearance, forty years on from whence he had first evap-orated from the face of the earth and this anomaly was too far gone from the norms of this world, that Malabar knew he had no choice but to follow Fergus-Sundar. He looked down the road and saw his target Brian Harrison click on the side of his MobiGlasses and knew that if he did not initiate his apprehension of this soon-to-be-terrorist, he would evade him once more.

Malabar had struggled to find Brian Harrison the Elusive thus far; he had his face blurred from the database of the Facial Recognition Scanning Centre (FRSC) and the algorithms embedded in the system meant this could not be undone; a downside of a rigid and hyper-secure system. It had taken him weeks to track Brian Harrison and he did this by rummaging through the vast data on the FRSC database, and using statistics such as his height, his walking stride length, and a knowledge of his physique, to locate him – a tedious endeavour. However, he knew that Brian Harrison was within his grasp; this had been the closest he had ever been to him in terms of physical distance.

He knew that he could continue his chase of Brian Harrison as soon as he had, at least, gotten a visual confirmation of his identity, and perhaps questioned him. For if it was indeed Fergus-Sundar then likely, whilst it was highly abnormal and confusing that he was here in 2065, that he would come in for questioning and be cooperative. The mind of Malabar Jones had deviated from his duty to his case and he was the last man who wanted to abandon his case. So committed and stubborn was he, that he lost the ring finger on his left hand whilst being tortured on a case. He had not needed to endure that torture session for he had already apprehended his target, he had his target exactly where he wanted, on that 36th SSSA case of his. Though he endured the pain from the torture, for his knew that he could gather information from his target who boastfully spoke about events related to a previous case and organisation that Malabar had been looking into.

The curiosity that Fergus-Sundar's appearance in front of him had created was now indisputable within him and the curiosity needed to be satiated. And so, he was left with no choice but to temporarily abandon his current target and set his sights on Fergus-Sundar. And thus, he spoke into the microphone embedded within the TechSuit that had been specifically designed and integrated in accordance with the synapses on his body.

"Keshawn Braun, please note I must take a detour from this case for something has come up that I simply cannot ignore. Bring about the eFile of one Fergus-Sundar. You shall find it in the Archived Files of the SSSA Employee Database. Bring this up for me ASAP; time is of the essence. If this is the man who I think it is, I will be left with no choice but to follow him; for he is a former agent; the agent who came before me. The first SSSA4," said Malabar Jones as he clicked the button the side of his AirPol mask which defogged his tempered glass AirPol mask, as snow fell around him and onto his AirPol mask.

"Yes Malabar, I'll do that now. Are you sure though g? 4Honcho is gonna be vexed if you do this. Imma have to file that you deviated from the course of action," Keyshawn Braun replied through his earpiece.

"Do it now. I won't ask again. Do what you have to do Keshawn. If this is the man I think it is, then 4Honcho won't give two sh*t's."

"Aite say no more. I just hope they don't send Yonige-Ya after you for this. The eFile is up on your DigiLense right now. Lowkey though be careful. Looking from these notes now, if this guy really is this Fergus-Sundar don then you gotta be careful. I doubt its him though innit. My man went missing forty years ago, why the f**k would he be there now? And if…" replied Keshawn Braun as he was interrupted.

Malabar Jones responded without hesitation, "I didn't ask your opinion Keshawn. It's him. And I know what you are thinking. Wouldn't he be an old man? Wrong. He is unaged in appearance forty years after he disappeared, and thus I am left with no choice but to follow and question this man; this is highly irregular and you would do well to make note of that in your report to 4Honcho. Now put yourself on mute while I do this. I need silence while I work," he replied as he began to walk briskly; time was of the essence.

He saw Fergus-Sundar in the distance. Malabar, with his quick feet, managed to hide behind one of the many terrarium enclosed trees on Piccadilly as he saw Fergus-Sundar turn his head nonchalantly. Malabar observed Fergus-Sundar as he initiated the Retinal Viewing System in his DigiLense. He looked through the eFile of Fergus Sundar and his memories flooded back to him, like a country experiencing a frequent flood due to rising sea levels. Malabar had seen the eFile of Fergus Sundar on many occasions; this was a mystery within the SSSA that was a part of their studying, it was an example of an unsolved anomaly that they tried to avoid. It was a rare occurrence to see a case go unsolved, and to see their agent go missing with no reason or indication as to where he went; the SSSA had immense resources at their disposal.

Thus, Malabar believed this may be the chase which would determine the legacy of his career as a SSSA4. He did not know whether this man, who seemed to be Fergus-Sundar, was a threat or simply a confused and lost man, somehow displaced in time. He thought to himself, *is this the missing SSSA4 Fergus-Sundar or is this a clone of Fergus-Sundar?*

He smoothly slipped away from behind the terrarium and continued to slip through the crowd of people walking. Though as he gained ground on Fergus-Sundar, he saw Brian Harrison in the distance enter Green Park station, and he knew now that he had no chance of apprehending Brian Harrison in the next couple of hours.

And then he saw Fergus-Sundar enter the Burlington Arcade. Malabar himself knew the Burlington Arcade well; this was where he received his bespoke and SSSA4 purpose-made suitcase, from Globe-Trotter. He knew if there was anywhere that Fergus-Sundar would be comfortable within the city, it would be within the Burlington Arcade as the SSSA4 had gotten their cases from Globe-Trotter for a century. But Malabar himself was comfortable with the location. He quickly reacquainted himself with the eFile of Fergus-Sundar as he walked.

If this is indeed a clone of Fergus-Sundar, then why did they choose him to be a clone? He pondered on this as he entered the arcade. *Unless it is the case that whoever cloned him, knew specifically that he was a highly trained and resourceful SSSA — meaning that we are at potential risk of a security breach.* To Malabar, this was a concern as it was certainly a possibility considering the SSSA tended to deal with highly intelligent and highly resourceful criminals whom regular law enforcement operatives could not catch. This would mean that this potentially cloned version of Fergus-Sundar could be an enemy of the state. He then saw the following note in the eFile through the Retinal Viewing System in his DigiLense:

Fergus-Sundar is currently working on a formula for the feasibility of interdimensional travel through using primordial black holes (those black holes which were created as a result of the Big Bang) as a wormhole (portal) to other dimensions/worlds. – Though it appears to have been unsuccessful as FS has been working on this (officially and to the knowledge of the SSSA) since 2016, with no meaningful progress.

Thoughts now ran through Malabar's mind as he turned his head to look around the Burlington Arcade, hoping to see the silhouette of Fergus Sundar once more. *Did Fergus-Sundar achieve what he had set out to do? Did Fergus-Sundar complete his formula for interdimensional travel and if so, how could he have possibly travelled between dimensions; this requires advanced technology and space travel equipment to do so?* However, this could not have been done without the knowledge of the SSSA. And so, the questions running through the mind of Malabar Jones remained present as the answers were not deducible. Thus, he had no choice at this point but to question Fergus-Sundar; his questions needed answering.

He took off his AirPol mask as he looked to get a visual on Fergus-Sundar. He did not know how this encounter would go down for he did not know whether he even wanted to physically approach Fergus Sundar; he did not know what was going on exactly. And so, he decided to merely scope out his new target so that he may know how to proceed to apprehend him moving forward. For no matter what transpired and what he would find out about Fergus-Sundar and the mystery of him being present before him, unaged in appearance forty years after he had gone missing, he would have no choice but to apprehend and question him eventually. For technically Fergus-Sundar was a property of the SSSA, and Fergus-Sundar had sworn an oath to the SSSA.

He instantly assessed the number of people there in the arcade. It was not a busy day in terms of tourists; instead it seemed to consist of the regulars and if anything, this was much worser for Malabar Jones. For it meant if he did feel a need to detain or chase after his new target, his face would be exposed to these regulars of the arcade; he did not want to chase him here, it was too bait a location. And so, he proceeded down the arcade as the beadles – the private security of the Burlington Arcade – reverted their eyes away from their security duties for a moment as they gave him a nod of acknowledgement. Malabar was one of the faces those beadles knew as a special face, for he had special access in this arcade to any facility on-site if he needed it, a special treatment typically reserved only for select few people, such as the now deceased, Sir Paul McCartney. They knew well enough to not disturb or approach him if they saw him in the arcade unless he approached them; for he was a man who did not legally exist, a man of the shadows, operating outside of the law.

He tread slowly, in as inconspicuous and unassuming a manner as he possibly could. Though as he looked at Fergus-Sundar from behind, the man turned his head and locked eyes with Malabar. He felt a sudden shrill go through his body; this man felt familiar despite the fact he had only known him through images. Upon locking eyes, he felt as though Fergus-Sundar had looked at his soul; a feeling Malabar had not felt since his own mother and grandmother last put eyes upon him. And it was because of this that Malabar Jones knew that his cover, with just one brief but raw look, was blown within minutes of him following his target. This was not a usual thing he experienced. In fact, he had never experienced this before. Never before had his cover been blown in even a day, let alone minutes. Malabar, uncharacteristically, froze for a moment for this was an uncomfortable situation for him, one he had not prepared, or trained for. It was now SSSA4 vs SSSA4.

Fergus-Sundar squinted as he regarded Malabar, looked him up and down and then pivoted his neck and scoped the Burlington Arcade, making calculations in his head and planning his next steps. He darted and weaved in and out of the incoming traffic in the Burlington Arcade like a prime Lionel Messi. And so, Malabar had no choice but to do the same. He leapt over the man at the shoe-shining station who hurled a flurry of insults at him for Malabar's disregard of his work station.

Fergus-Sundar glanced back as he powerwalked through the arcade as the Beadles attempted to follow the two suspicious men. Though they were hopeless in this endeavour, for the people who were disregarding the rules of the Burlington Arcade were not ordinary people. The Head Beadle knew this as he knew who Malabar Jones was and gauged from the way that Malabar Jones was negating his standard protocol of blending into the crowd as a nobody, that the man he was chasing was not ordinary himself, and that this was an extraordinary situation. And so, the Head Beadle spoke into microphone embedded below his knuckles on the exterior of his hands.

"Leave them boys. It's above the paygrade," he said.

The other Beadles adhered and instead proceeded to apologise to anyone who had been brushed aside or been nudged by both men.

He quickly found himself at the end of the arcade and departed onto Burlington Gardens. Malabar turned to his right, his head upright and on the pivot, and suddenly his eyelids instinctively closed shut. A brown fist, with skin-broken knuckles, came towards his face at so fast a pace that he couldn't evade it. As he fell to the ground, he placed his hands by his side and felt the gravel beneath him rub and grind against the callouses on his palms. Fergus-Sundar stood above him now as he threw a short, but sharp, straight left hand at his face, and then placed his right knee on the chest of Malabar Jones with his left foot planted above his right shoulder. Fergus-Sundar threw two consecutive right elbows onto his face; the two blows felt like one to him due to the speed and precision of the strikes. He had now mounted Malabar and continued to land blows on the head of Malabar Jones as it hit the concrete beneath him. Then suddenly the two SSSA4s felt flashes on their faces as a crowd had amassed; taking pictures and videos of the fight. Fergus-Sundar for a brief moment turned to look at the crowd, and then as he looked down upon his opponent once more, he found himself blinded; Malabar from the bottom position had spat blood from his mouth into the eyes of Fergus-Sundar who now stood up and scrambled frantically at the discomfort caused by this dirty move.

It was valuable recovery time he had gained from that move and as Fergus-Sundar shouted profanities, Malabar blew out of his nose and blood dripped onto the gum splatted streets of London as it created a violent painting on the pavement. He had been caught off guard and felt cheated; for he had not been given the opportunity of a fair fight. *So that's what that feels like*, Malabar thought to himself. It was a tactic he employed success-fully on many an occasion himself and thus respect had been earned. He smiled as blood lined his teeth, and his smile was met with a clean faced smile from Fergus-Sundar who hopped from side to side on the balls of his feet with his body perfectly balanced still like a brawling ballerina, like a world champion boxer. *Who is this this guy, and why is he chasing me?* Fergus-Sundar thought to himself as he saw Malabar smile at him with his blood lined teeth. *Whoever it is, I like him.*

Malabar threw a jab followed by another. Fergus-Sundar slipped both the jabs and moved in tandem with Malabar as the two L-stepped and moved across to the side. Fergus-Sundar this time threw a jab which he missed, and instead of resetting, he cut the distance with a step forward, ducked down to his left and landed an uppercut to his opponents kidney, before finishing with a half-second delayed left hook up to the chin of his opponent, like the hall of fame fighter Caleb Plant. The punch dropped Malabar, but he quickly got back up. He saw Fergus-Sundar's face drop as he made his way back to his feet. Malabar realised then that he was on very unsteady legs, which felt like jelly.

Malabar knew from this sequence that Fergus-Sundar was not a man who he could challenge to a standard boxing fight; his gauge of distance and his precision and his timing was better than his own. He threw another jab which Fergus-Sundar evaded, before faking with a jab and unleashing a front kick to the face with his left boot which met the jaw of Fergus-Sundar and closed it shut for a moment, his teeth rattling like bowling pins from the impact of a strike. Fergus-Sundar's legs went beneath him and he now felt himself in a state of discombobulation as he tried to regain his equilib-rium; he had almost faceplanted. And so, Malabar seized his opportunity and swiped the legs of Fergus-Sundar beneath him. As Fergus-Sundar tried to get up again, Malabar saw him move into a freestyle wrestling position but could see that he was still dazed, dazed and confused. Thus, he took his chance, feinted a takedown and within the blink of an eye, reached over to his right side and pulled the left wrist of Fergus-Sundar back towards and down to his opponent's right ankle and watched him fold over – Malabar had successfully executed a Russian tie snap. Malabar had seriously buzzed and dazed Fergus-Sundar, and so he readjusted and took the back of his opponent. Malabar locked his legs and tightened them around the rib cage of Fergus-Sundar, squeezing from his legs. And then, he fully seized his opportunity and like a snake, slipped his arms under the neck of his opponent and locked in a rear-naked-choke. He had gotten rocked early on in their encounter and nearly lost the fight. Though he had come on top despite this, and he could now apprehend and take in this mysteriously vanished and unaged SSSA4 from 2025. He squeezed on the neck of Fergus-Sundar who was doing his best to pull the arms of Malabar off of his neck. Malabar was now comfortably in control and spoke his first words to Fergus-Sundar.

"Who are you? Are you Fergus-Sundar?" said Malabar. Fergus-Sundar did not answer, and so he had a feeling that he would not get an answer from him. He continued, "Listen here. I know you are him, or at least you are a version of him. I'll give you two options. One, I loosen my grip, and you and me talk like men, as two SSSA4's and you can tell me your story. We'll go to the SSSA together. Or two, if you do not cooperate, considering the situation, I must consider you an enemy of the state and I sleep you right here, right now."

"You're SSSA4?" Fergus-Sundar replied as he struggled to breath.

"Yes, I'm SSSA4 the second. Make your choice."

"I choose option three."

"Option three?"

"This is option three," Fergus-Sundar replied as he let out a deep breath, activated his core, and sat up with Malabar still latched onto his back with viper-like grip. Malabar tried to tighten his grip around the neck of Fergus-Sundar; he had to complete this rear-naked-choke now. Though through a feat of extraordinary strength and balance, Fergus-Sundar made his way to his feet with Malabar Jones still on his back. And then, it dawned upon him what was about to happen. The once missing SSSA4 leapt off the floor and dropped onto the concrete with Malabar Jones latched onto his back like the shell of a tortoise. The impact on the his was great. Malabar winced in pain as he lay on his back and as he eventually found himself turn onto his side, he could only watch the back of Fergus-Sundar's shoes as he walked away. Malabar was lucky, for he managed to come out of the fight relatively unscathed despite the attack from Fergus-Sundar; the fight safety setting on his TechSuit ensured his spine was protected on impact.

"I will find you. This isn't over. I know who you are. I will get you!" Malabar screamed out.

And so, he lay on his back as the onlooking crowd were stood like motionless statues, with their eyes transfixed viewing the events through the screens on their phones. He knew as he looked on them that he had to clear the data, and so Malabar spoke into the microphone embedded in his TechSuit.

"Keyshawn. Activate Data-Clearance-Protocol. I need everything in a two-mile radius of my location cleared for the last thirty minutes to be safe. Any pictures, videos or messages."

"Say no more. DCP initiated, it'll be confirmed and then checked across, full Web3.0 wide within the next two minutes. Did you get the guy though? I couldn't see the last bit".

Malabar replied with a bruised voice, "Not yet Keyshawn. Not yet."

BOOK 2

FERGUS-SUNDAR

Wednesday 5th November 2025

18:52: SSSA4 Provided Home of Fergus-Sundar,
South Kensington, London

Fergus-Sundar tried to concentrate as he finalised his set of weighted pullups, though found that his mind strayed back to the formula; the formula which he had worked on for near ten years now as for one reason or the other, intuition told him he was close to completing the formula but did not know if this meant he was to complete it today or tomorrow or in two months or perhaps in a year. Fergus-Sundar strained as he finished his set of deps, with the twenty-kilogram weighted vest draped across his body, before sliding it off over his neck as he strained and let it drop onto the concrete floor, with the thud of the vest causing the machines and weights to vibrate and cause a reverberating sound of vibration. Fergus Sundar knew he could not rest until this formula for interdimensional travel was complete. However, he knew that he would perhaps not rest until he died; for he had committed himself to the SSSA, and his duty meant he was committed to a lifetime of servitude to the SSSA.

He dropped down and squatted to lower his body close to the ground to reduce his heartrate. Sweat dripped onto the floor. He looked down on the puddle of sweat as he closed his eyes and brought his breathing back to his average resting heart rate of forty-five beats per minute. He had become accustomed to registering this as this was customary as part of his training to become a SSSA4. Fergus Sundar stood back up and took a piece of paper out of his pocket, which was now was on the brink of withering away due to sweat, and looked at his exercise plan for the day. He had a third of the workout left to do and he relished it; this was the only way he would better his mind and better his body. He completed the workout and groaned as loud as he needed to, for he was in the comfort of his own home and this enabled himself to push himself to limits one could not normally do in a public gym; especially a man like him who had to remain anonymous. He was a SSSA operative and thus he operated in the shadows of society; as such the SSSA provided him with this home with a gym facility which included every piece of equipment he desired and need. Though his home was not a home in the sense of it having home comforts or anything of the sort, instead it was more like a training facility worthy of an Olympian. As an SSSA operative, he had no choice but to live in the facility they provided for him. For this was the way that an underground government operative needed to operate; there was no switch off, not truly. Money was of no concern to Fergus-Sundar for the house was provided for free of charge as a result of his service to the SSSA and all expenses were paid for, and his salary also was six-figures If this home were on the market undoubtedly it would have gone for millions of pounds; due to the fortress like facilities and security systems in place, alongside the gym, the lab and the abundance of space.

He wiped away the sweat from his face and walked straight from his basement gym to his basement lab. It was a rare day off from his duties, as he had just completed his thirty-third case as a SSSA4. He did not have a life outside of his work as a SSSA. This was both a gift and a curse for a man like Fergus-Sundar; he had to give up everything in order to work for the SSSA. It was a life of servitude that required sacrifices that ate away at ones soul; one's personality would be voided.

Fergus Sundar had lost all family that he had known, and on his twenty-sixth birthday he was pronounced dead in a plane crash. From that moment he was alone in the world with nothing but his career as a SSSA operative, a life of risk but a life where his skills would be best utilised. He left behind everyone he knew and watched his friends cry at his funeral from a distance. It was on a day like this where occasionally he would find his mind gravitating towards memories of the past, memories of his mother and his friends and family whom he had not seen for at least fourteen years. He was forty years of age and he was alone on this day, a day others would be celebrating. However, he was working and preparing his mind for the next case. One could argue he was brainwashed. But Fergus Sundar lived with the knowledge that he was amongst the few in the world who could do what he could do as a SSSA4 and that was why he had to live this life that he lives. Few had the fighting ability, the ability to blend into a crowd and operate in the shadows, the intellect to piece seemingly random pieces of information together like a puzzle, and the knowledge of quantum mechanics, physics and computing; that placed him in an unique position to deal with national level security threats that the modern day criminal organisation operated with.

Though he did have a life before the SSSA. He was a professional boxer who also had a masters in Quantum Physics. He was 16-1-1 as a professional boxer with the majority of his fights taking place in Mexico and Panama. He had been nearing a WBC Interim title fight before he was approached by the SSSA, shortly after completing his Master's degree. Thus, when he committed his life to the SSSA and swore before the Queen to enact his duty to the country and the crown, he lost all that made him who he was; family, friends and passions. He thought of his mother as he quickly ate his spinach, kale and turkey salad, as he thought of what she would think of him now. He knew she would likely not approve of the man he had become, no matter how many terrorist plots he had foiled and how many people he had saved. He knew this because, despite the fact that he had surprisingly never killed someone, he had done many things he knew was not good. How many kneecaps had he obliterated and how many tongues had he removed as part of his 'duty'? He had lost count after the first fifty of each and ceased to count as reflection upon his actions only made his work harder to do and reduced his coldness required to do the job.

He shook his head as he found himself ruminating on the past, something he rarely did as he trained his mind to always remain in the present so that his senses were attuned and ready for anything that might come his way. He took in a deep breath as his lungs filled with the clean purified air in his laboratory. He was strong of mind and rare was it that he found himself distracted from his day-to-day life, though his birthday seemed to be the kryptonite to this.

He stood up and walked across to his basement gym and swung away with near perfect technique at the water bag he had hanging from the ceiling; for this was the only way he could let off steam and vent his frustration. This enabled him to bring his mind to a present moment in a situation whereby he was unable to focus on his duty; the catharsis this eventually brought him was like a person fasting taking their first sip of water after a day of drought. He hit the bag for twelve rounds.

Fergus Sundar now found himself once more grounded in the present as he slowly walked back over to his lab. He thought now of what he wanted to do with his day considering it was a rare day with time on his side, a choice of what he could do. He looked upon the whiteboard standing at the back of the room and saw the incomplete formula for interdimensional travel lying on the board. He faced a dilemma now that he had faced for near nine years. He looked upon the formula and thought of pieces he may have missed out on, and suddenly the missing element of the formula hit him, like the apple with Isaac Newton.

He wrote this down on the whiteboard and looked upon it once more and tears rolled down his eyes, the first tears that had fallen from his eyes for years now; he knew this was an extraordinary achievement, but one he would never get the credit for, and one he could not celebrate – they were solitary tears of joy. He did not exist anymore in the world; he was an agent of the shadows. He knew on the morrow he would have to lose this formula to the SSSA and that they would likely give it to a person who would perhaps go on to achieve a Nobel prize for his own work – this was too important not to be shared with the world.. Though he knew of the perils of his work and knew that he could not leave this formula written down anywhere where it could be found or used against him or the SSSA or the nation of the United Kingdom. Thus, he wrote and rewrote the formula on the whiteboard over fifty times till his fingers grew sore and blisters formed, for this formula needed to be etched into his mind like carvings of an Egyptian into the great pyramid's walls. He had to guard this until he brought it to the SSSA4, and they could do with it what they please.

And so, now the formula was stuck in his mind and imprisoned like a rat in a trap, only allowed out if Fergus Sundar decreed it. This was a dangerous formula if it fell into the wrong hands and thus he prepared to give it to his Honcho, 4Honcho, as now his role with regards to this was done. This formula, in theory, was a big break in the world of science with its value near priceless; the possibilities were unbound if one were able to harness and use this formula to actually physically travel between dimensions.

"4Honcho I'm coming in tomorrow. Make sure you are there. I have something for you," Fergus-Sundar said into the phone.

"Fine. Come for eight am. I have meetings after with members of the RO (Royal Office) from nine onwards so I will be preoccupied. Can you give me any hint as to what this is about?" said 4Honcho.

"I'm afraid not 4H, I can't speak about this unless it's face to face. This is information of the highest level; might even have to get 1Honcho in the meeting if you can. Actually yes 4H get 1Honcho in the meeting if you can, this can't wait," he said, pacing in his lab.

"Well alright then FS. This best be worth it lad. If I call 1Honcho in and this ain't worth his time then it's gonna be my f***ing ear that's gonna get chewed off not yours," said 4Honcho.

"Trust me it's worth your time. I'll speak tomorrow 4H".

"Alright I'll leave you to it. Be here for quarter to."

"I know," he replied. He slid his back down the cold concrete wall. He had done it, he had completed the formula for interdimensional travel enabled through wormholes found in Primordial Black Holes. He thought of the formula once more as he breathed in deep though his nose and exhaled through his mouth, calming himself and getting to grips with the reality of his success. He looked his watch, noting hours had flown by as he worked on the formula. And so, he went to bed.

He lay in bed and thought of the formula again, and knew it was entrenched in his mind now. And so, he could rest. Fergus-Sundar closed his eyes and soon enough, found himself drift into sleep.

The Dreamworld and The Astral Plane of Fergus-Sundar

The location was the Promenade de Anglaise in Nice. Fergus-Sundar knew instantly that he was dreaming as he reached his default state of auto-noetic-consciousness, albeit within the dream state of mind. He recognised the location instantly as he had been here with his mother. He walked down the riviera as he counted the number of fingers he had and felt the sensation of every part of his body, in line with his confirmation that he was lucid dreaming. And thus, he became fully conscious he was dreaming and now controlled himself and the nature of his dream. To confirm the nature of his reality and to ascertain he was in fact lucid dreaming, in line with his training, he reached for his phone but could not find it anywhere and looked upon his watch to see that there was no time; and thus verified that he was in the dream world. He continued to walk down the promenade as he looked upon the sun reflecting off of the water, before looking around to see it was just him, alone. *How am I the only one here,* he thought. Then he remembered he was in the dream world and that this was merely a figment of his imagination. Fergus-Sundar continued to walk down the isolated path and his SSSA4 lucid dreaming training taught him that he ought to follow the path of the dream; for oftentimes the storyline of the dream would occur as it would, as a way for the mind to register something occurring within the deep recess of his unconscious mind.

And thus, Fergus-Sundar knew not to deprive his mind of its inner desires as he continued to walk down the lonely path. He tried to walk slowly but could not control himself as he found himself revert to his brisk walking pace; he grew impatient to see the end of the dream. His mind was already fixated with keeping the dreamworld before him intact, whilst consciously choosing which course of action he would take in this dreamworld as opposed to blindly following whatever storyline his consciousness had predetermined – this was the difficulty and crux of successfully navigating lucid dreaming. He was well versed in lucid dreaming, but even for one versed in oneironautics as he was, he still had to consciously adhere to the integral principles and rules.

And finally, after walking for what seemed like forever, a grand wooden door appeared in front of him, seemingly from nowhere. It was designed like one from a Victorian-styled house and he was perplexed. He did not know why this was here or what lay behind the door. It eight foot tall, and before entering the door, he stopped himself as he found his mind was at this moment in time fully embedded within the dream world. Fergus-Sundar thought of his life in the real world and realised he could not lucid dream too hard or for too much longer; it might result in him forgetting the interdimensional travel formula he had just completed, if he became too entrenched in the dream, due to the drowsiness he would feel in the morning.

And so, Fergus-Sundar, still waited in front of the plain but grand door, closed his eyes and tested himself by thinking of the formula once more. He picked the memory of the formula out of his mind like a man picking a book from his bookshelf, and opened his eyes. As Fergus-Sundar looked upon his door with his chocolate brown eyes, he found the lengthy and complex formula written before him on the door, which looked like a fresh inscription with wood carvings hanging off of a few of the numbers – the formula was correct. He knew it would be correct as he would not forget it so quickly, considering the efforts he went through to remember it and the efforts he went to complete it over all these years.

And then below the formula appeared a passage of text, once again looking as though it had just been carved upon the wooden door before his very eyes. It read as follows:

Here lies the Wormhole-Maze.
Enter at your own peril.
For once you enter, you cannot leave until the maze is completed.
If the maze is not completed, consider yourself forever lost.
If there is an entry, there is an exit.
For you enter as one man, you may leave as another.
Prepare your body and mind as you enter this spacetime.
One will cease to exist as the other expands beyond the simple
confines of an ordinary human mind.
I warn you again to enter at your own peril.
For what is done can never be undone.
And whatever time has gone by, you can never rewind.
Whatever has choice you make has already been made.
And whatever choice you will make, once was already made.
Enter at your own peril.
Here lies the Wormhole-Maze.

He raised his eyebrows and instinctively raised his left hand to brush across chin; the bristles of his beard rubbed together and made the faintest of sounds, barely heard. He re-read the passage of text, and felt curiosity overcome him. Fergus-Sundar would normally hesitate to open such a door in the real world as he knew that behind such doors never lay anything good, though the text upon the door caught his attention. He simply had to enter the door. He felt content knowing he was dreaming and thus safe from any real physical danger should he enter this door which warned him of entering; this was simply existing within his consciousness and thus he was safe from peril other than psychological peril – which he had faced plenty of, through his line of work and from the torture he once had to endure.

And so, without a second of hesitation, Fergus-Sundar opened the door and looked in to simply see a chasm of nothingness; a profoundly abnormal absence of light.

As he stepped through the door, the door slammed shut and the ground disappeared beneath him, and he felt himself falling as tried to jolt himself awake but could not do so. This was highly irregular. He tried to compose himself mid-fall but was unable to do so as it felt as though he was actually falling. His cheeks flapped like the wings of an eagle, as his body felt as heavy as a boulder - he continued to fall at a rapid pace, with gravity feeling stronger than it normally did. He attempted to stop the falling, but to no avail.

Suddenly, after what felt like minutes, he stopped descending and now gravity seemed to cease to exist as his heartrate slowly came down and his cheeks felt less hot, no longer hurting from the impact. He now floated in nothingness and he could see nothing but the silhouette of his body which seemed to be illuminated from within him as though his DNA itself was illuminated.

The absence of light negated the possibility of sight and only a glow somehow permeating from deep within him, allowed him to see the outlines of his own legs and arms. Then in the distance he saw a hedge floating in the black space. He propelled himself to the hedge that, peculiarly, was shaped like a tunnel that perfectly shaped for him to fit through. On the side of the hedge lay a plaque. It read as follows:

Here lies the entry to the Wormhole-Maze.
A final warning: once you enter you cannot go back.
You must complete the maze or lose yourself in the maze.
Turn around and propel yourself upwards if you choose to live yourself as you

previously lived your life.
Alternatively …
Propel yourself into the hedge, and enter the Wormhole-Maze.
This is your last chance, make your choice.
I already know what you will do for as you are here, all that follows has been
determined, but in this moment the choice is yours alone as free will still
dictates that which occurs now and has occurred, and that will occur.
Choose now Fergus-Sundar, for once you enter, you cannot un-enter.

He could not control himself. He grabbed the top of the hedge with both hands and propelled himself through the tunnel as he fell through, unaware of what would come before him now.

··· ··· ···

And thus, Fergus-Sundar entered the Wormhole-Maze – the portal to another dimension which lay within Primordial Black Holes – whilst lucid dreaming, transporting his consciousness from the Earth to this Primordial Black Hole based Wormhole, with the interdimensional travel formula being the access code to enter the Wormhole-Maze.

Contrary to the beliefs of Fergus-Sundar and the scientific field of knowledge, space travel was not needed to travel between dimensions; instead, the key lay within consciousness itself. As now Fergus-Sundar had the formula for interdimensional travel, his consciousness through lucid dreaming transported him to the door of this Wormhole, which presented itself before him in the form of a maze.

With this, the body of Fergus-Sundar evaporated from the face of the Earth, for now he existed within the Wormhole-Maze, in a time non-theorised by humanity. Thus began the journey of Fergus Sundar from the year 2025, to Non-Theorised-Time, to the Wormhole-Maze of a Primordial Black Hole.

BOOK 3

FERGUS-SUNDAR

Non-Theorised-Time

Non-Theorised-Time: The Wormhole-Maze

And as Fergus-Sundar entered the hedge-tunnel, he let out scream so silent, that the lack of noise was paradoxically deafening. He felt a pain he had not felt before and looked at his skin; the glow permeating from beneath it. He watched as his body slowly withered away; the skin and flesh ripped off his bone like rust developing on metal, and his bones crumbled like rotten wood. He looked upon his skin and bones as they ceased to be a part of him and watched as he saw it cling to the hedges around him like a magnet. His body seemed to no longer be his, but instead property of this maze; he was simply cohabiting in this space and thus his body adhered to the nature of this domain he was in, to the rules of the wormhole. Though what remained of Fergus-Sundar, was his soul. His soul was still his and this, as well as his consciousness, seemed to be all that remained. His physical body no longer existed in this place, except from within the confines of his consciousness. And so, his consciousness created a body for him only so that he could fathom that which was happening to him; the brain and soul could only perceive true reality to an extent, for it the limitations restricted on it from whence Fergus-Sundar was on Earth. This wormhole was not designed to be inhabited by a human being. Though deep within him, ingrained like molten lava in an inactive volcano, was something protecting his soul and consciousness from being ripped apart like his body had, and this kept him alive in the Wormhole-Maze.

He had not been entirely ripped apart because of what lay within his consciousness and soul, creating an extraordinary and peculiar glow that was dark and as black as the black hole itself. This thing allowed him to exist in a place and time in which he ought not be able to exist, in this Non-Theorised-Time of the wormhole and in this space of the black hole. The answer lay within his very being, the DNA within him and his genealogy that had been illuminated by this black glow; it was dark energy and dark matter – a mystery to science.

The dark matter and the dark energy within him ensured that when the gravitational pull from the edges of the wormhole eviscerated all of his physical being by pulling his physical body apart and towards the edges – that he was able to still exist; the dark matter and dark energy was embedded within his soul now, and thus he was unknowingly as dependent on this as a human being is to water, gravity, and oxygen.

Once again, he descended as he now walked in this tunnel of hedges. Gravity worked against him once more and he felt the whiplash as his body dropped from the pathway he was on; the floor beneath him vanished. Fergus-Sundar landed on a boat with great force, feeling the water around him swish from side to side, as the boat braced the impact of his body cascading onto the hard and dark walnut wood. He looked around. It was pitch black. He looked around and could only see the light of the jungle in the night, the naturally occurring light. The jungle was loud in its stillness and he felt the hairs on his now non-existent transparent body, stand up. He felt a level of petrification that he had not felt since he was a child. And then it dawned upon Fergus-Sundar as to where he was. He looked around and could see that he was surrounded by mangrove trees. He was all alone. And on either side of him, all he could see were mangrove trees, with their long and wiry grey and white roots shooting from beneath the water up into the sky, with the leaves draping down. Fergus-Sundar realised where he was and he could not quite believe it. He found himself overwhelmed for the memory of this place was buried deep in the recesses of his mind.

He had not been to this place since he was just five years old and now he was a forty year-old man, with many years of experience under his belt. His surrounding was a familiar one, but not one he was comfortable in. His surroundings took himself back to a holiday he had as a child, one of his earliest memories: a holiday with his mother as he went with her to her homeland of Trinidad and Tobago. He had found himself in an organically grown pathway of mangrove trees mimicking a tunnel, in the Caroni Swamp.

There were no oars in the boat; it was moving by itself and it was going down this path on its own. The course of action had already been set; he was simply on the ride. The boat was rocky, as the waves of the water crashed against the boat and made him feel uneasy, his stomach feeling queasy, and his head beginning to hurt due to the stress of the situation he found himself in. He looked around him and up into the trees and could see things he wished he was not able to see. He felt eyes on him. And he knew then that there were things in this jungle around him watching him, that he could not see. But what he could see, petrified him. And he could only see these things because he had been taught to look out for them. His mother's younger brother, his uncle, was a tour guide for the Caroni Swamp in Trinidad and their family had done this for generations and generations before them. This was their domain and so they knew what animals to be conscious of. He saw the snakes who so cleverly blended into the multiple shades of green of the Mangrove Tree's leaves, as they perched on their branches above his head. He saw the glimmer of the water as something moved beneath the water, invisible to the untrained eye – Caimans moved stealthily underwater, he felt as though they were ready to pounce on him, simply biding their time. His heartrate rose, immeasurably.

And then he heard the birds and other animals quietly chitter chatter between themselves. But alongside this he heard the silent cries, a sound he did not recognise from his childhood, but one that he could not avoid hearing in this moment. These voices too came from beneath the water. It was not a loud noise, but rather it felt like white noise. Fergus-Sundar found curiosity overcome him and he zeroed in on this white noise. The silent cries were unavoidable in this kind of an environment; there was no other stimulus other than the unnaturally devised natural environment around him. He tentatively peered over the edge of the boat and into the water. He expected to see his own face in the mirror of the water but could see nothing but the trees above his head and this stunned him – for he remembered again his physical body was no longer a physical body but rather a metaphysical element that only he felt. He was not meant to be here, and he was not really here. This was all a figment of his imagination. That which he saw was not real; he remembered he had entered the Wormhole through the Primordial Black Hole, accessed through his lucid dream. He was losing himself already and not seeing his face in the reflection of his water, reminded him of the unnatural nature of his situation.

He shook his head and looked at the water, for his curiosity had not left him, he wanted to see what was beneath the water, for the silent cries persisted like white noise in the background, at a frequency of sound that he would not be able to hear in the real world – though it was unavoidable here.

This time he saw a body floating beneath the surface. And then a hand reached out to grab him and instinctively Fergus-Sundar threw himself backwards and he hit his head onto the wood. He moved his hand to the back of his head, expecting to feel blood, but of course there was none. He slowly sat up and peered over the side of the boat once more. The white noise of silent cries screaming in the pitch-black dark of night, were the cries of men and women lost to the swamp. The hand had reached out to him to ask to be pulled back up and onto the boat. Though he knew in his heart that this was a trap for once he grabbed the hand, the hand would drag him down into the water again.

He was petrified, his mind going back to one of the the most traumatic experiences of his life. It was the cause for his petrification at the sight of the water. However, he reverted his attention away from this memory, he was already confused and slightly lost as to where he was and he did not need to delve into this dark memory, not now. Then he felt the pain once more and he fell onto his back and screamed soundlessly. He did not know what was occurring. He was lost.

What is happening? He thought. *I thought this is a dream. I am not to feel like this. I need to wake up.* Fergus Sundar tried to get himself to wake up but he could barely think for the excruciating pain His skin and limbs and bones were piece by piece leaving him as they stuck on to the sides of the maze and were seemingly devoured by the hedge. He screamed in pain and thought of what was going on. Suddenly it clicked. This was the dreamworld and thus anything was possible. He thought of the formula once again. He thought of what a wormhole actually was. He knew that science had yet to come up with something that could physically allow someone to even pass through a wormhole, as one would find that the edges of the wormhole would rip their very being apart due to the intense gravitational pull of all the edges of the wormhole – just as it had done to him. Thus, whilst his formula proved it is scientifically possible for a wormhole to exist if they were to be located in the right primordial black hole – it was not scientifically possible for this to occur yet. Fergus-Sundar then thought of what this ripping apart of his body felt like. Fergus-Sundar then thought of what the door itself said when he entered it. *Surely I am not inside a wormhole?*

He thought back to where he lay and as he closed his eyes he pictured his body lying motionless on the bed. Though as he looked on at his motionless body, he saw it wither away. Fergus Sundar ceased to exist in 2025. He was indeed in a wormhole between dimensions. There is no telling what time and place this is. What spacetime this is. Thus, it can be said that Fergus Sundar now exists in Non-Theorised-Time. As it said on the entrance door of the maze; Fergus Sundar had to pass through the maze. He had to complete it as otherwise his soul would also be taken by the Wormhole-Maze. Something kept him alive. He knew he would find out how. Perhaps in the maze. He was in it now. There was no going back.

Fergus-Sundar realised then he was stuck on this boat. He looked out to the sides of this mangrove tree pathway and realised there was no opening on the sides, nowhere for him to dock or leave. He then fathomed jumping into the water and could think of nothing worse for he knew there were caimans swimming in the water and he knew there were people who had been lost to the Caroni Swamp who were residing in the water. He looked upon his hands once again and recalled that they were not even really here; he had forgotten. His physical body seemed to be no more, and Fergus-Sundar pondered upon this.

Perhaps it is the case that reality, and how I perceive reality – the lens upon which I see the world – is not as it truly is. I know that my physical body has been ripped apart. I know this because I have felt it. Never have I felt such a pain. This has occurred because my body dared to exist inside of a wormhole. I did not ask for this, yet here I am. Perhaps in a roundabout way I did wish for this, not overtly though, through my actions of constructing a formula for wormhole travel. It seems the universe has manifested this for me in some way. I do not know if it was God, but if God exists he certainly has this planned for me for I cannot be here by mistake – this must be through design.

From what I understand of quantum physics, one cannot exist in a wormhole and not have their entire being ripped apart to shreds – because the gravitational pull around the corners of the wormhole, demand that I am pulled into every direction towards the edge of the wormhole.

This is how I know I am in a black hole. I do not know how I got here exactly though it seems that my consciousness has transported me from the dreamworld – reality existing inside of my own consciousness – into this black hole. Again, I do not know how this has happened exactly but it has. I am near certain of this now for what else could this be? I see nothing but nothingness and that which I do see, seem not to be real; but rather a figment of my imagination, constructed so that I may not lose my mind and lose my sanity in this dark, lifeless place.

This black hole (this primordial black hole?) has ripped apart my physical body and now I am but mere consciousness. Though within this consciousness it seems I am able to feel physical things, without the physical effects. This makes no sense, I know. I believe as a result of me losing my physical body, my consciousness has instead created the sensation of existence and of a physical body, so that I may pass through this wormhole. And I believe, rather I know, that my consciousness has created pathway, so that I may find a way to the exit of this place. I have entered, and so there must be an exit. For otherwise I will be lost into oblivion and nothingness. I must pass through this maze, one way or another.

He now watched his physical body as he began to stand on the boat and he realised that his body seemed to be a mere hologram, not a true physical body, but one that he could work with and feel nonetheless.

There was no one else, or no other boat in sight. He was all alone. This path ahead was lonesome and he felt lonely and knew this feeling would only be exacerbated the further the boat travelled. There was no end in sight. He did not know how much time had elapsed thus far, and he could not fathom how much had elapsed or how long it would take him to continue on this path and reach the end. He was tired. And now he was anxious as he realised he may be stuck here in perpetuality. He felt hot. He knew he could not really feel this as, of course, he no longer had a physical body. However, his consciousness' manifestation of his body felt the heat. He was losing his mind. He was forgetting life before this, and the fear of what he faced before him overtook him.

Every movement I make seems to deplete me of whatever energy my consciousness and soul has. I must do something else for I know if I simply continue through this pathway and this maze, as though it were like any ordinary maze, likely I will find myself lost and losing myself and my mind.

I must find a way to navigate this terrain. I cannot lose my sanity.

This Wormhole-Maze is not like any ordinary place. Though, I do not believe I can fathom the true nature of what this is like and thus I must try to imagine that this is like any ordinary maze. This way perhaps I will pass through, as unscathed as I possibly could be.

He noticed that whilst on the boat, the only thing accessible to him were the roots and branches of the mangrove trees. He looked at the mangrove trees and looked at the prop roots which allowed the trees to sit in the water.

This must be accessible to me for some reason.

If in fact I am in a primordial black hole, and this is a wormhole between dimensions; there are certain things which I know to be true. The boundary of the black hole – the event horizon – has caused my physical body to be ripped apart due to the gravitational pull. Though why has my consciousness and my soul survived? I have a few theories, but I must address this heat I feel before doing so because I believe time may be of the essence.

At this point I guess I must accept that I am in a primordial black hole, and I am in a wormhole. Thus, I must think of what this primordial black hole is. It is a black hole, likely created as a result of the Big Bang. It is thought that whatever falls into a black hole, can never escape. Nothing is thought to be able to pass through the event horizon of a black hole due to the gravitational pull; yet here my consciousness and soul still lives? There can be only one reason why. One unaccounted for element of science and quantum physics, that I have hypothesised in my formula, that would allow one to survive the event horizon of a black hole or wormhole. This is dark matter and dark energy. Could negative energy be present in this? In this dark matter within me, negative energy?

Much is unknown about these two elements though it is said they comprise of 95% of the universe. Perhaps it is the case that I have dark energy within my consciousness and soul that is allowing me to survive this event horizon. It is hypothesised that there may be a negative gravitational energy that permeates within this dark matter – only this would explain why my consciousness and soul were not ripped apart as soon as I entered this 'Wormhole-Maze'.

I believe this to be true and if it is not then I certainly hope to find out how I have survived, for this is something beyond the knowledge of science.

Further, if I am in a primordial black hole, and inside a wormhole, then I know that this will soon shut. By soon I don't really know when this is, for time is not governed by 12am to 12pm in a place like this. Spacetime does not exist as I think it does here. Come to think of it, I don't know what time or space

I am really in. Am I the first to ever exist in a space and time like this? I do not believe there is a word for it. Thus, is this non-theorised-time? It was not thought it was possible to exist here, yet here I am. Perhaps I am the first to exist here and even fathom that there is a space and time here. Though now I am here I know that the concept of spacetime does not really apply to a place like this. Though, for the sake of my own sanity and clarity I must use the notions and my own understanding of spacetime to categorise this. Yes, this is non-theorised-time.

From what I understand of black holes, my very being here is uninvited and I am a foreign being. I feel the heat around me and this tells me a sign. This black hole is soon to disappear. Thus, whatever time I have left here, however it works, is limited and I will continue to feel this heat get stronger until eventually this black hole shuts forever and this wormhole, this portal between dimensions is shut forever. As it said on the door to this wormhole-maze, I cannot go back and thus I must pass through this wormhole-maze to the other dimension, and I must do it quickly.

I need to get to grips and understand this terrain and determine how it is I will pass through him. I don't have time to mess about. The absence of time as I know it, is an illusion and a farce. For I believe this is a trick of this maze inside of this wormhole. Time must matter here. the walls of this wormhole can close in. And if I do not understand this terrain and figure out how to pass through here, the event horizon will likely rip me apart. Simply sitting on this boat is doing nothing for me, the path is not changing, and my energy is being depleted nonetheless by me sitting here. These prop roots of the mangrove tree are visible to me for some reason. I need to do something about it. I can see a vibrational energy radiating off these mangrove trees. I do not know if my eyes deceive me, but I know there is something to it. It is all there is. And so, it must have reasoning behind it. I must grab it. Perhaps in these mangrove trees lie the key to my departure from this Wormhole-Maze. I am going to grab it. Let us see if this does anything.

Thus, he reached out to grab the prop root and much like how upon entering the door on Promenade de Anglais had transported him to this place, grabbing the prop root of the mangrove tree did something similar, something he could not imagine.

As he grabbed a hold of the white mangrove prop root, he found himself attacked by a snake which emerged out of nowhere and went straight for his face. He felt as though he had pissed himself and again screamed a silent scream. Though the snake did not bite him; the snake was not even real. In fact the boat was not even real, this water was not even real. This fear he was feeling was not even real, though here he was, and he could feel it one way or another. He had to accept that which he was seeing and feeling around him and take it for what it was. He had to keep an open mind. And so, Fergus-Sundar found himself transported to another time.

He looked beneath his feet and realised he was standing on water. He lifted his foot and placed it back down on the water beneath him and realised in this moment he was not truly on the water; he was merely a bystander. He was merely a watcher of this memory. He looked around himself and found himself once again in the Caroni Swamp in Trinidad. He looked at the boat and saw himself, a five year-old Fergus-Sundar. He watched his younger self, look into the water as his mother and uncle bickered, as they seemed to always do and he watched himself put his hand onto the water. And then he saw his small body fall into the water. He remembered the sensation of sinking deep into the depths of the Caroni Swamp. What he did not see as a child, was the panic of both his mother and uncle. They looked around frantically and screamed out his name to no avail. And then he felt it. He felt what his younger self felt as he transported into the body of his five year-old self, the old Fergus-Sundar. He felt the water enter his lungs again as though it were happening to him now. He panicked. He flailed his arms around and flapped them like a helpless fish flapping its fins as though it was naked on a rock, not immersed in water, struggling to breath. He attempted to call out to his mother. But she could not hear him. She could not see him. Fergus-Sundar the five year-old attempted to open his eyes amidst the algae which impaired his vision in the water, but as he looked up all he could see was the underside of the boat.

He tried to grab up to reach the boat, to hold on, but he could not. Water entered his lungs again. He couldn't swim but pure adrenaline and the intrinsic will to live, had allowed him to survive underwater until this moment. And then in one last push, before Fergus-Sundar the five year-old began the final ascent to death by drowning, he kicked and kicked and propelled himself slightly, enough to reach out and whack on the underside of the boat. Then he felt the energy escape his body and the air leave his lungs as water filled them. And he began to descend towards the bottom of the swamp. In this moment, Fergus-Sundar of the Wormhole-Maze became conscious of where he was in spite of the fact he was reliving this moment as a five year-old version of himself. And he realised that death, whatever this was, was around the corner. Whence he had experienced this in real time, there were no thoughts in his mind at this moment in time for he was unconscious, barely holding onto life. Though in this moment, he was conscious and highly aware that he was helpless, lifeless. And he took comfort in this paradoxically for he felt his life was already over. He was all alone here at the bottom of the swamp. What was the point of his existence in this moment? There was none. He was stuck in this moment for an eternity, and had always held this pain. He had carried it with himself subconsciously, shackled by it, since he was a child and it burdened him greatly for the loneliness he felt in this moment, stuck at the bottom of the swamp had never left. The guilt had never left him.

Fergus-Sundar of the Wormhole-Maze, stuck seemingly perpetually in non-theorised-time, remained conscious in the lifeless body of his five year-old self as he watched, being unable to move, his mother swim towards him at the bottom of the swamp. He wished in this moment she would not continue swimming towards him. He wished he did not slap the bottom of the boat. For the guilt pained him as he felt her small hands grab him as she propelled herself and her son back to the surface. This guilt never left him. For when she jumped into the water to save her son, inadvertently it marked the beginning of the end of her journey on Earth as mother to Fergus-Sundar. She entered the water with an open wound which she had developed in the frantic and panicked moments whence her son had entered the water. The mother of Fergus-Sundar received a deep gash on her back near her spine on the side of the boat, in the hubbub of attempting to locate her son. Whence the boat received a thump from underneath, she was left with no choice but to jump into the water. She did not even think about it. She didn't have to. The maternal instinct kicked in and within moments she was swimming towards her son. Both adrenaline and euphoria was pumping through her veins; she was feared if he was alive, and felt euphoria from seeing him,. The open wound and the water of the swamp resulted in her getting Leptospirosis, a blood infection. They did not know of the infection until it was too late. And by the time he was six years old, he was without a mother, and thus an orphan.

He awoke again on the boat, conscious as his older self, but trapped in the body of his five year-old self and he stared at his mother who looked deep into his eyes to see if he was okay. He feared this would be the last time he would see her again. He had not seen her face for so long, not so vividly. She felt real. In this moment, time did stand still for Fergus-Sundar as he wished he could have this moment for life. He wanted to remember this moment and live in this moment perpetually. It was a moment filled with pain and guilt, but the respite was that he could see his mother's big brown eyes, and feel his mother's touch.

And then he awoke again on the boat. Though now it was not as a five year-old. But rather he was his forty year-old self once more. He wished to transport himself once more to this moment. And so he grabbed onto the prop root of the mangrove tree again, and again a snake attempted to bite his face. Fergus-Sundar relived the moment again but this time as he found himself in the water. He tried to stop himself from touching the boat. He was conscious as his current self, though entrapped in his five year-old body, and so he attempted to simply allow himself to drown under the boat without fighting, without causing his mother to die by her saving him. But Fergus-Sundar could not help himself, and he found that amidst the fear of death he reached out again and fought to live once more, and again he managed to touch the underside of the boat, and began his descent to the bottom of the swamp. He attempted to scream out to his mother to tell her not to enter, as water entered his lungs and his five year-old body began to lose life and sink to the bottom of the swamp. But again, he saw his mother swim towards him and pull him out. Again Fergus-Sundar looked at her as she looked down on him as he lay on the boat, and he felt her hands on his face. And just like that, the moment ended once more and he was awake on the boat, back where he started.

He felt aged and far older than forty years-old. This was aging him, not physically, but spiritually and emotionally; his soul felt as though it was withering away like his physical body had. He felt the wormhole begin to eat away at his soul and he could do nothing. Now he lay on the boat in the dark of the night and felt tears run down the side of his face and past his ears. It was going to happen again, he knew it.

Please end; I can't take this pain; I am lost – I wish this for this to be the last time.

Fergus-Sundar reached out once more and grabbed the mangrove tree and experienced the same fate again, and again, and again. Though nothing changed. He was stuck and he was unable to change it. Though still he tried. But whatever he did, he could not change this moment. What had happened, had happened. Nonetheless he tried once more. He reached out to the mangrove tree once more and grabbed a hold of the prop root and found himself transported again to that memory.

He did not know how many times he had relived this memory now. Fergus-Sundar had lost count, and lost care. It was inconsequential. Truth be told, at this point, he had forgotten why he was there. He had lost sight of what he was attempting to do. He knew not what to do.

He was a lost soul in the Wormhole-Maze.

The Maze had consumed him, and it seemed he was fated to be stuck in the Wormhole-Maze, perpetually living in this moment until fate determined it was time for him to die.

Though he knew not when, and cared not for when this was. He had lost his mind. The absence of time as we know it, was causation enough for one to lose themselves and to lose the importance of existence. On top of this, guilt had consumed him, guilt over his past mistakes had gripped his essence and this was all he could see. He wished to change that which had already occurred – forgetting the ways of the world and of cause and effect, of action on the time continuum. He found himself transported to the memory once more and he looked upon his five year-old self as he sat on the boat whilst his mother and uncle bickered.

Fergus-Sundar saw something though this time, which he had not seen in the countless times that he experienced this moment. He watched his younger self look into the water and reach out. And Fergus-Sundar saw now why he had reached out to the water. He saw a hand under the water reaching out to the young Fergus-Sundar. The young Fergus-Sundar had reached down into the water, for he saw a hand in the water. How could this be? He did not reach out and grab the hand as an old man in this Wormhole-Maze, for he knew it to be a trap and that he would be dragged down and unable to be saved by another as he was saved as a child. Though he did not know the perils of this as a child. He had been lured to grab the hand as a child.

Though he watched as the invisible hand grabbed Fergus-Sundar the five year old and pulled him into the water. It did not seem to be done with malicious intent behind it. The hand from the water grabbed him because he had to do so. The action was unstoppable, the event unchangeable. History had occurred exactly as it was meant to occur. It seemed as though the hand was the same hand that had reached out to Fergus-Sundar as an old man in the Wormhole-Maze. Fergus-Sundar felt in the depths of his soul as though it was because he was here in this Wormhole-Maze now, stuck in this pathway, that he grabbed the hand as a child. The younger version of himself grabbed the hand and entered the water, because his future self would find himself in this same swamp, stuck in a Wormhole-Maze.

A part of Fergus-Sundar died that day, and it was that very death which had allowed him to go on the path that he did in his life – it was why he found himself travelling between dimensions stuck in non-theorised-time in this Wormhole situated in the primordial black hole. His very existence in this wormhole meant that a part of him had to die that day in the past, his connection to the real world had to die. His connection to the real world was his mother. That was all he had. He cared for no one else, not really. It seemed as though his future had been the cause for the actions of his past. He came to understand and accept his actions and past for what they were. His guilt cessated. He took accountability. And this time when Fergus-Sundar found himself transported into the body of his five year-old self and in the water, with water filling his lungs and himself fighting for life – he chose to fight. He consciously chose to fight and he slapped the underside of the boat as he felt life beginning to leave his soul.

And this time, he did so knowing that this was the beginning of the end of his mother's life and connection to him. He let history take place as it was meant to take place. And Fergus-Sundar this time, when being resuscitated by his mother, truly took in the face of his mother and the moment. He looked upon every part of her face and cherished the memory of it. He was overcome with serenity and happiness. He knew this time it was different. This was the last time he saw her.

And so, Fergus-Sundar awoke on the boat once more, as though he had never left. Though whence he arrived on the boat this time round, he was different. He was changed inside. And then the thought dawned upon him. He closed his eyes as he entered a meditative space. The effects of the Wormhole on his energy seemed to dissipate.

I believe I now know what it is that I ought to do here in this place. I believe I know the route of my escape, if that is a possibility. This moment seems to have been a keystone to my journey, to my essence as a human being. And I have let this moment go now. For guilt had me trapped under the water. though I recognise now that every moment of my life was caused by actions of my future, and it has caused me to be here and make my choices in the here, in the now. My actions in my life, and the events on my path seem to have been somewhat predetermined I feel. I had the choice to choose these actions and to walk down this past nonetheless. Because my future self was and is only in existence because of what has occurred before me. And so now I can see that my future has caused my past. And this comforts me now for I see that life and how I had perceived and thought to have experienced it, is not entirely as it is. This life is set, my path already determined by my future, though ultimately there was free will, necessary free will in all my actions, and this has resulted in my guilt inevitably. For I have chosen to do things in my life as a SSSA4 that ultimately are intrinsically wrong. But it had to be done and I knew of the future that it would cause, and of my inevitable existence in that future.

And that future version of me, and the future I ended up living – was already written and existing in the space time continuum. Thus, my future has caused my past, and is causing my present. For this present moment must exist as it does for the future to occur. Though one could argue what if one has done a terrible thing in the past, what good can occur out of a past mistake. And I realise now here in the Caroni swamp as I relive a tragedy of my life. That even in tragic events, it is knowledge and understanding of a tragic event, that helps prevent it in our future.

The future needs tragedies of the past, in order to better its own future. For tragedy is embedded within the essence of our humanity. It is ingrained within us through our ancestors and our DNA and our history as people, and from this has come wisdom. And it cannot be changed, it can never be undone. I know this now and accept this now. And as I lay on this boat, even in the pitch-black dark of night in this jungle, surrounded by caiman infested waters, with mapepire snake hanging from the branches of the mangrove tree – I can see the beauty of the world in all its complexity; the fauna around me, the fact I am surrounded by water, on a boat man-made from wood taken from the trees of the jungle.

I exist in the moment and I come to be through my mother and father and their mothers and fathers before them, and I breathe and live here now and pass through this wormhole in space, situated in a primordial black hole, and accessed from a metaphysical portal I have accessed by lucid dreaming and having discovered the formula for Interdimensional Travel, and facilitated by the suspected Dark Matter and Dark Energy infused within me, perhaps through my DNA – this is a miracle, and the miracle of life itself, has me realising my blessing.

I have died today, as I died as I entered that water in Trinidad when I was just five. And I have in this wormhole, in this maze, countless times. My soul and ego have died a million deaths and I now find myself humbled and blessed to be here. I was here to die, so that I may relive. I must live. For to live is the ultimate blessing no matter what life presents us with in our fortunes in this world and in life. So, I must pass through this Wormhole. It is time to live. I wish to facilitate others to see the beauty of this world as I can see it now. This world and nature is all that we have, and it is through this miracle that we find ourselves to live, we must care for it. And thus, I must live. No longer am I purely a spy, a SSSA4.

He opened his eyes and felt a serenity overcome him. He lay on his back for a while and watched the branches of the mangrove trees as the wind pushed the leaves from side to side. He sat up now and watched the ripples on the water, and he saw the hands beneath the water. The bodies lost to the Swamp were the ones moving the boat for him. They were guiding the boat through the path, through the maze. He looked up in the distance and saw the path narrow; there was less water in the river. And in the distance, for the first time, he saw light beginning to emerge; he was coming towards the Event Horizon. He realised he ought not fear the jungle or the natural environment or animals around him. What once caused fear within him, no longer was a cause for fear. He had learned to detach himself from this fear. For he realised the world and natural world was occurring around him regardless of whether he liked it or not.

And then out of nowhere, a caiman disrupted his peace. The back of his boat had been bitten off. And then chomp! Again, the caiman bit into the boat. Fergus-Sundar stood towards the front of the boat and looked down at his boat as it began to sink. He had to jump. He was about to drown or be eaten for lunch. Fergus-Sundar turned around and saw the pathway of water begin to close in, the tunnel was closing in and the boat would not fit through the gap anyhow. And then snakes dropped from the trees above. They gathered at his feet and some of the snakes began to stand. They were ready to pounce. Fergus-Sundar had no choice. He looked back down at the water. *If I jump will the people lost to the swamp let me back out,* he questioned. *F**k it*, he thought to himself. He dived into the water to evade the caiman and snakes who had taken over his boat; he had no choice.

Though once Fergus-Sundar found himself in the water, he began to drown – just as he had done so years before. History was repeating himself. He panicked. Water filled his lungs, and fear gripped him once more; he could not swim. He felt the hands of the people lost to the swamp bring him down, and soon enough he was stuck. Fergus-Sundar remained conscious, but he was motionless. His energy began to leave his soul and he floated lifeless. He felt then the pain grip every essence of him. He felt it within his being, his internal organs and on his skin, even though his physical body was no more. His very being was being torn apart; he was in the midst of the Event Horizon.

His eyes remained open, and instead of seeing the foggy green water with caimans and fish and the hands of the lost people beneath his feet in the water reaching up towards him, his vision began to switch to a white light, and Fergus-Sundar knew what this meant. This was his chance for respite. He would be free of his pain and all that he felt. It was right there for him. It was within his reach. When he closed his eyes and opened them once more, the white light grew in strength, it began to cover more and more of his lens. He knew all he had to do with close his eyes for longer and then he would be free of the pain.

And then he heard a voice. Fergus-Sundar looked up above. He heard his name. He remembered himself once more and realised where he was as he moved in the water. The white light began to fade. He had a choice. To live, to fight to survive. Or to die, to succumb to pain and the weakness within him. He heard the voice once more calling his name and he realised this was all he needed to fight. For even if there was one person who called his name, he would fight to live.

And so, Fergus-Sundar battled through the Event Horizon as it attempted to rip apart every bit of his soul now so that he was unable to pass through the Event Horizon, the edges, of this Wormhole situated in the Primordial Black Hole. He opened his eyes again and began to swim back up to the surface – the white light disappeared. Though as he continued to swim and swim up, it seemed that the surface was no nearer. He was beginning to lose air and again water entered his lungs. He was stuck again, and it seemed lost once more.

But then it dawned up him that the prop root was visible once more to him. Within his reach. It seemed nature was once again the answer to his woes, and so before he passed out, he managed to reach out and grabbed the prop root once more.

And once more, he found himself transported to a memory of his. Though this time it was the purest and happiest memory he had, one locked away deep in his subconscious, seemingly inaccessible before this moment, the moment when he needed it most. Fergus-Sundar watched on as he watched his mother sit on The Englishman's Bay in Tobago, with the sand beneath her feet and a book in her hand, as he played football with his uncle and his uncle's friends on the beach. It was a simpler time. This was the day that his mother had reacquainted him with the sea as he overcame his fear from the incident where he fell in the Caroni Swamp just a few days prior. It was one of the last moments his mother was still healthy before they returned to their home in Inverness and her health quickly declined. He had indeed gotten to see her once more.

Though this time Fergus-Sundar did not need to see her again. He looked around him and saw the beauty of the Earth once more. He was blessed. But he knew this was not real. He had to leave this place. He wanted to see it again with his own eyes, his real eyes, and to do so he needed to escape this place, to escape the Wormhole-Maze. He closed his eyes again, and he returned to the Wormhole-Maze, though now on the surface with air once again entering his lungs.

He turned his head and saw the half-eaten boat – an allegory for his former self, the death of his past self, an ego death. Fergus-Sundar kicked in the water as he kept his head just above the water and looked in the distance, with a light beginning to appear on the periphery, and saw a crisp white boat, larger than the dingy wooden boat he was previously on, in the distance. The boat in the distance represented his new self that he would emerge as and aim to leave this Wormhole as. His journey had been tough in the Wormhole-Maze of the Primordial Black Hole, in Non-Theorised-Time, but it was not yet over and he still had a way to go before he would reach the end and evolve as this newer version of himself. He began to swim and he swam hard and fast. Caimans swam behind him. In a normal world, in the real world, he would have been caught by the Caimans and his legs would have been chomped off. However, here Fergus-Sundar managed to outswim the caimans like an Olympic swimmer. It was sheer determination and the will to live, which was ingrained in his soul that allowed him to preserve in the direst of circumstances and against odds which seemed unfathomable for him to overcome – this will to live was ingrained within the soul of all human beings.

He continued to swim, as the waves came at him hard and fast and slapped him in the face and for a brief moment it slapped him so hard that he felt himself be overturned by the waves. And as he gathered himself and pulled his head above the water, the waves slapped him in the face once more and Fergus-Sundar found himself losing the battle. And then he brought his face above the water once more and he saw the gap between either side of the mangrove trees continue to become smaller. It was almost collapsing on itself. The Event Horizon was closing in and Fergus-Sundar would have to swim hard and fast to pass through. As he swam, he felt himself be pulled from all directions. Gravity was attempting to pull him into the event horizon in all directions and it succeeded in doing so as his physical body existed no more. Though within his very being, lay the Dark Matter which had interacted with the Dark DNA within him and so his soul was saved, and able to pass through the Wormhole without being entirely ripped apart. As a result, a Negative Gravitational Pull occurred due to the negative energy being generated by the Dark Matter and Dark Energy infused within the essence of Fergus-Sundar – and so the soul of Fergus-Sundar could pass through the event horizon without being ripped apart. He now just had to fight and fight he did.

The waves continued to crash against him, but he did not give up. Fergus-Sundar had realised, in the midst of being slapped hard by the water, that the waves crashed the caimans behind him also, and slapped against the mapepire snakes which were dropping from the trees attempting to reach Fergus-Sundar. He realised in this moment, that the adversity and struggle he was facing from the event horizon of the Wormhole in this Non-Theorised-Time, was not personal. It was occurring because this was the nature of the Event Horizon. And he had the tools ingrained within him to survive. The caimans and mapepire snakes were there already and they too were being slapped by the aggressive waves of the water. Mid swim he turned his head further this time and looked once more to see the caimans struggling to chase him. And he realised his fear was withering away.

The Caimans and Mapepires were allegories for the fear he had within him, and they too were struggling to exist. He realised not to fear his fears, and rather to accept and recognise their existence around him. For he had the tools within his being to survive, and the Event Horizon was merely testing him if he were simply to be patient and to realise the impersonal nature of the struggles he faced. *This is simply the way it is;, it is not about me or against me, this is just how it is and what it takes to get through – get through it Fergus-Sundar,* he thought to himself.

And so, in a final push, he continued to swim and swim and this time he pushed through the crashing waves against his face and Fergus-Sundar found himself battling against the pull of gravity as it attempted to rip his soul to the edges of the Event Horizon.

He made it. He reached up and grabbed the rail as he found himself next to the boat and pull himself up and over the rail and collapsed onto the wooden deck of the great white boat. And just like that it was over. He could breathe once more; he could relax. He sat up and looked back at the narrow pathway behind him and the caimans and mapepire snakes stuck behind this narrow pathway of Mangrove Trees, representing the Event Horizon – they could not get through. And then Fergus-Sundar realised he had to shed this fear and angst of his to pass through this event horizon. He had to transform and leave his former self behind. He had completed the Maze. Though as he looks back at the waves crashing behind the boat, and as he recounts the memory of swimming through it – suddenly it doesn't feel as though it was that tough, it was just in the midst of it that he felt as though he could not survive it.

Fergus-Sundar looked forward and saw the sun come up; Flamingos and Scarlet Ibis flew the crisp blue skies, with the sun creating a ineffably beautiful glimmer on the water around him – the beauty of the world and nature around him, was unfathomable to him in that moment. He found himself enamoured with the beauty of the natural world, and tears of joy rolled down his face. Never before had he felt a euphoria and serenity like this. He felt completely content for a moment, and this moment felt like forever in the best of ways. But then it dawned upon him, that there was no one for him to share this moment with him. He was all alone, and he had been alone for many years now. The nature of his work had forced him to isolate himself.

He had left his former self behind on other boat. And he was open and ready for a new chapter. He realised the follies of his former ways and Fergus-Sundar would commit his life to something else now other than a life of fighting and chasing after danger. He saw the sun in the distance and drove the boat into the light.

As the boat drove into the light, Fergus-Sundar left the Wormhole-Maze of the primordial black hole, and left non-theorised-time. And in doing so, he became the dimension travelling spy; he entered a new reality, and to the year of 2065, a changed man.

BOOK 4

FERGUS-SUNDAR

Thursday 5th November 2065

14:26: Green Park, Mayfair, London

And so, Fergus-Sundar found he reappeared on Earth, the world he once knew, in the year 2065. Though he knew not the year. His reappearance was as instant and as unexplained and as unflamboyant and sudden as whence he had first disappeared.

The world around him appeared to be different on first inspection. As he looked around, the colours and everything he looked at all blurred into one with a visual residue almost as his eyes moved around. He felt over-whelmed and this resulted in the sensation of a brewing migraine.

The Fergus-Sundar who walked in 2065 for the first time, was much changed from the man he once was – though he did not know whether this was a good thing or not. A lesson he had learnt in the Wormhole-Maze was that all happens as is meant to happen and thus he did not fret on this change he felt in himself for this was meant to happen and no matter what he thought or did, he could never go back to the man he once was or to his perception of reality that he was previously accustomed to and familiar with.

The Wormhole-Maze had changed the genetic makeup of his body; his very essence had changed, his thoughts and perception on the world and way he viewed and saw images had changed. Everything had changed. In a way, this drastic change that he felt comforted him somewhat as he felt the snow numb his bare toes and he shivered, his head on a swivel as he looked from left to right, like a squirrel. For he was forced to accept the nature of life and existence: perpetual change occurring in the world, for time only moved forward and was only ever felt and experienced in one given moment by any one person – as such the world and people were forced to constantly accept and acclimatise to change, for every moment is new with all elements changing.

Fergus-Sundar felt the sensations in his feet as he shivered on the spot and felt the hairs on his arm stand up like an upright solder. He looked around and recognised the area after struggling for a moment. He was in Green Park amongst a bush in a secluded area and, as he now became more aware of himself in the present moment, he realised he was wearing the exact clothes he had been wearing whence he disappeared when sleeping on his fortieth birthday on Wednesday 3rd December 2025. He did not know what the date was, or when this year was. *What year is this? I need to find out.*

He looked around as he attempted to make his way out of this park and to find a person whom he could ask the date and time; he desperately needed to know. His head was not feeling right, and his sensations were all over the place. Everything seemed more vivid than what he previously remembered, and Fergus-Sundar felt as though upon everything he looked, there was a trail of colour or particles in the air that he could see radiating from it almost, like the visible steam coming out of a hot cup of coffee.

Though as he walked through the thick sheet of snow covering the ground and felt the falling snow come into his eyes, he noticed something peculiar. The trees in the park were enclosed in a huge glass container and it seemed as though air was coming out of the glass container. Fergus-Sundar stopped in his tracks and observed the glass. He walked up towards it and knocked on the glass as though he were knocking on a front door. He could not fathom it, but he believed this to be a terrarium, a self-sustaining enclosed ecosystem which was usually in a glass dome or container of some sort.

Why was this here? Why were all the trees in this park in terrariums? Why is the nature here in an enclosed, self-sustaining ecosystem. None of this makes any sense. And why can I not remember how I got here or what just transpired?

There are too many questions. And there is too much stimulus from that which is around me. I need to walk around. I need to acclimatise. My brain is adjusting to this time and reality. I must give it time. I must be patient. He thought to himself.

Fergus-Sundar knew that it was certain this was not the year 2025 and this could not have been a year within even ten years of 2025, for a massive change like this in the landscape of a City like London, would take years of planning and development. If he had not already been curious and confused, he was even more so now.

Have I travelled forward in time? What and when is this spacetime? For I know now this reality is not the reality that I know. This is something strange. He thought to himself.

He walked out of Green Park and on to Piccadilly. Instantly he noticed the difference in his surroundings and the people on this famous road, for they did not look like what he remembered them to look like. He looked upon the people on the street, bemused at this contraption they all had on their head. They were all wearing masks, not like a covid mask that he remembered – instead this was a high-tech contraption that seemed to be a breathing apparatus of some sort, covering the eyes, nose and mouth and in some cases, the person's ears as well. Fergus-Sundar found himself staring at these people and further realised that everyone was staring at him because he was the only person on the entire street who did not have one on.

He needed some answers. He had too many questions, questions he could not fathom the answer to. He saw a man standing outside Green Park station looking at his palm. Fergus-Sundar approached him because he seemed to be relaxed and because his mask did not cover his facial features completely and so Fergus-Sundar felt comfortable approaching him; he seemed more human than the others on the street. As Fergus-Sundar grew closer to him he realised that there was a digital screen of some sort embedded within the palm of the young man and he realised in this moment that this was a society and time far beyond the one he knew. For this meant that society had now found a way to establish a symbiosis or connection between the body's synapses and with technology – these people all seemed to be somewhat in tune with technology, one with technology.

"Hi there, excuse me. Sorry to disturb you, young man. I was just wondering whether you have a moment. I just wanted to ask a quick question," said Fergus-Sundar.

"F***ing hell mate aint you cold. Its minus twelve degrees right now and you're barefoot and wearing a t-shirt," the young man replied in astonishment.

"Yeah I' very cold. What's the date today?"

"Wait you're a crackhead innit. Bruv, you aint even got an AirPol mask on. F**king hell. Go away man I ain't got time for this sh*t."

Hmm AirPol mask. Fergus-Sundar made a mental note of this so that he would look this up later. He assumed it was something to do with air pollution.

"Please just tell me the date."

"It's Thursday."

"No, the full date please"

"Fifth of November innit. Thursday bruv. Now f**k off before I spark fam. F***ing crackhead. Imma ring your jaw if you come near me."

"Fifth of November? Today is the fifth of November?" *How peculiar,* Fergus-Sundar thought to himself – it was his birthday, the same day he vanished from earth, the same date he had reappeared on earth.

"Alright thanks. Sorry for disturbing you," he began to walk off before he remembered, "Oh wait one second. What year is it?"

"What year? Mate what are you on," the man replied in a confused manner, then the confusion turned to shock as he realised Fergus-Sundar was not joking and – he let out a sigh of frustration, "It's 2065".

"2065?!" Fergus-Sundar replied in astonishment

"Yes, 2065. You don't even know what year it is." The man walked off with a look of disgust. "F***ing clapped crackhead," he said as he spoke to himself, disgusted at Fergus-Sundar for wasting his time and disgusted at his manner, having assumed he was in fact a crackhead.

It's the 5th of November 2065, which means I'm 80 years old, he chuckled to himself. However, looking upon his hands and feet, it seemed as though he was in the same body and thus, physical age, as the one he had vanished from earth with in 2025 on his fortieth birthday.

Fergus-Sundar then felt the harsh cold once more as his bare feet could scarcely hack the cold any longer and realised he needed to get some clothing that was made for this weather.

Wait why is it snowing and so cold right now? Its early November. He saw another person, this time a woman in her thirties and he approached her. As he approached her, Fergus-Sundar could see she grew extremely fearful, perhaps coming to the same judgement about him as the man before, assuming he was a crackhead.

"Hi ma'am, sorry to disturb you. Can I just ask you a quick question? Don't worry I'm not asking for money," Fergus-Sundar said, playing into the role which it seemed people were judging of him, to ease their angst and make his approach more successful – a spy technique he had mastered, playing into the stereotypes of a target. "Why is it so cold and snowing here right now?"

"Erm yeah sure. Because its November and it's a SuperWinter right now," the lady smiled hesitantly and clicked a button on her AirPol mask to put the privacy screen on. However, she saw that he wanted to speak again. And so, being kind, she gave him more of her time.

"Sorry ma'am I should've said. I've just come out of a coma so I've not been awake for twenty-five years, London doesn't seem to be what I remember it. Can you explain what a SuperWinter is – if you can spare the time that is. I totally understand if you can't," he replied without hesitation, speaking as though this lie was in fact the truth.

"Oh wow, I'm sorry. Yes, you should've started with that," she replied, breaking into laughter as Fergus-Sundar visibly saw her body language significantly change as her shoulders opened up. "Okay so basically, right now we're in the middle of what you call a Super-Winter. I don't really know what exactly it is? So I don't really know the actual science behind it, but basically every three to five years we get a pretty wild winter where it's like super cold and snows a lot. If you go on Web3, so whenever you have access to a device, I'm sure you can find more information on it. I just know it's because of like climate change. But for more context, it's been like this as far as I can remember, and I'm only twenty-two right now so like I'm guessing the Super-Winters have been around I guess like for the last twenty-five years at least then maybe if it didn't happen when, well you know, when you were awake before I guess," the woman replied with curiosity in her eyes, "but yeah that's, wow, yeah super interesting. So you've been in a coma for twenty-five years? That's mad. I've never met someone who's been in a coma before. How do you feel if you don't mind me asking? Do you need help? Oh sh*t your feet. I can see you aren't dressed for the weather. Are you okay? Do you need some help?".

Fergus-Sundar could tell this woman was a genuinely kind lady and so he could not engage for too much longer, for he did not like to deceive or interact with nice people – only where necessary. His time in the SSSA taught him this, and it was standard operating procedure for him now. For the more he encountered good people and the closer he became to them, the more chance there was that good people would get hurt around him. This was the nature of his work as a special agent, dealing with the type of things that he dealt with.

"Ah okay thank you ma'am. Yes, it's all a bit crazy; it's a different world now. Anyways, thank you for your help; I really appreciate it. You are a good woman. Have a good day!" he said as he quickly ended the conversation, and darted off in the opposite direction as the woman stood in the same spot, bamboozled. The woman dropped her head once again, to the now natural body position of humans – with her neck firmly arched down looking at her technological device.

Super-Winter's? I need to do some research. I need to find myself a computer. Much has changed. I should check in with the SSSA, what I've done is unprecedented. Come to think of it I don't actually know if they are still around. I must go to the SSSA HQ now. Perhaps I should check in at the Burlington Arcade and see if the suitcase shop we are affiliated with is still there. But first I need some clothes.

He proceeded to walk down Piccadilly and found a crowded store. He knew this would be the best place to go for he had no money and thus he had no choice but to steal and this store seemed to be the best option; considering it was crowded, more variables which he could use to his advantage to steal when the workers were not looking. However, he knew this may be reasonably difficult to do as he was without an 'AirPol' mask and without shoes.

Fergus-Sundar slipped through this crowded store and did his best to avoid the attention of those around him despite his attire and how he found himself. Slowly but surely, he picked up bits of clothing which he systematically put on when the moment presented itself, starting with socks and then shoes and then a jumper and then a jacket. And in the space of just ten minutes, he was looking like an ordinary citizen minus the AirPol mask which seemed to now be a staple of social norms in this society of 2065. Though as Fergus-Sundar looked around the store, he saw that perhaps out of a hundred people, there may have been one to three people who were also without this mask or helmet. And so, if he were questioned upon this, he now knew it would not be so out of the ordinary for him to be a person who did not wear an AirPol mask. Though Fergus-Sundar knew that it was far better for him to blend into the larger percentage of the crowd for there was greater scope for success at avoiding attention this way.

He did not like to steal, and this was not something he had even done or had to do before today, and it was something he was hoping he did not have to do for very much longer. It seemed he would have to do this for a while longer still though until he sorted out his finances and came to grips with this peculiar situation and sorted out a resolution or explanation with the SSSA. He realised it was likely he would now be subject to many tests and his freedom would no longer be his. Though arguably he'd had no freedom since he joined the SSSA. He knew his success potentially time jumping or dimension travelling or wormhole jumping, or whatever it was that he had done – would raise many questions with the SSSA.

What do they know about me? Is this time a continuation of the time in which I was in before, from the spacetime that I knew and was a part of? Or is this another reality completely whereby I did not exist and so I am merely a completely odd person, out of place, non-existent in this history, not from this time? Or is this an alternate reality from the one I knew, whereby things are different in the sense that I was different – could they think I am a threat to the protection of the realm?

There were many questions Fergus-Sundar had himself. He did not know the answer to these questions but took comfort in knowing that as time elapsed, the truth would be revealed. And so, Fergus-Sundar for the first time since his entry into 2065, felt a sense of calm.

No matter what would happen now, he would live in the moment. This is something which he felt now more so than ever. In his previous life, he was a pawn to the demands of the SSSA. But things were different now, for he had travelled, between what appeared to be dimensions and a wormhole situated in a primordial black hole? Suddenly that momentary serenity Fergus-Sundar found just minutes ago dissipated as his mind, for a moment, attempted to fathom and truly deep the reality of what he had experienced; his memories were slowly flooding back to him. It was impossible and unexplainable on most levels of logic and science. The science was there, though it was underpinned and supported by what could only be deemed as being the supernatural, that which is unexplainably by science, and so Fergus-Sundar feared he would become an enemy of the state for his story would be unexplained and thus highly suspicious. There was a chance that they would believe him, but he knew that humans were obsessed with power – and a formula enabling one to travel time between dimensions, could bring out the worst in humanity, and they could view him as a threat for having successfully done this.

Though having experienced what he experienced and been on the journey he had been on, Fergus-Sundar knew he had to follow the path of his life now wherever it took him, for ultimately there were lessons to be learned along the way and whatever was meant to be, will happen as it is meant to be. Fergus-Sundar knew now his life was no longer about merely trying to capture people for the SSSA, for whilst his work was undoubtedly important, his vision and perspective had changed. He felt as though he had left that life of violence behind.

And so, he walked down Piccadilly towards the Burlington Arcade as he was enroute to the HQ of the SSSA. No matter whether they wanted to keep him in for either intense questioning, otherwise known as torture, or keep him for a never-ending stream of tests, or perhaps simply get him to explain to them how he did what he did when he travelled through the Wormhole – he would oblige.

For now he knew that, despite his state of discombobulation, he had changed. He was not the same Fergus-Sundar that he himself knew. He was far removed from this. The overwhelming sea of information and the truths of the nature of spacetime and human beings, that he encountered in the Wormhole-Maze, had changed him. He thought now once again of how he should not have been able to enter, pass and survive this Wormhole-Maze situated in the Primordial Black Hole. Even as he thought this, he realised the ludicrousness of it.

And for a moment, Fergus-Sundar contemplated to himself whether perhaps he was dreaming this all. He knew from his experience in the Wormhole-Maze that anything and everything was possible in this life; reality and consciousness was not as it seemed – he had a filter on as did everyone else. Could it be that he was still in that very same lucid dream, and he would one day wake up in his bed back in 2025? *Did I ever wake up?* At this point he could not say for sure, though he was 99% sure this was not the case. However, whatever had occurred, was outside the realm of what was deemed possible and ultimately seemed to be an amalgamation of science and the supernatural. And in that moment, Fergus-Sundar did not have an explanation or proof or formula for the supernatural element which made his travelling through dimensions a possibility. He hoped he would find this one day.

He thought now to a specific element in his formula, and of a thought he had in the Wormhole-Maze. He thought of Dark Matter, and the dark matter which may be in his DNA and perhaps through all his cells and every element of his body, brain and perhaps his consciousness and soul, if that were event to be a quantifiable or tangible element. This dark matter and the dark energy, if it existed, would have ensured his survival and altered him. He was left now feeling uneasy with this thought of what this could mean, and so now realised that whatever the case, he would have to get checked up; for the answer to perhaps even the supernatural may lie within his dna and his cells. He had to go to the SSSA's HQ and he would have to be honest with them and hope they were open to hearing him out.

And so, Fergus-Sundar entered the Burlington Arcade feeling free of his past and ready for the future ahead, for whatever lay ahead.

BOOK 5
MALABAR JONES and FERGUS-SUNDAR

Thursday 5th November 2065

18:08: The River Thames, Victoria Embankment, London

Malabar saw Fergus-Sundar approach a lonesome bench, scarcely seen due to the thick veil of snow it was coated in. He wondered to himself why the missing SSSA4 had stopped here and realised that it was likely that he knew Malabar was tracking him. If he was in fact this man who the SSSA eFiles claimed him to be, if his case history was accurate, and considering the fight he put up – then certainly he would know that he was being followed. And so, he was dumbfounded as to why Fergus-Sundar was now sat upon this bench, with his back turned to the road behind him and thus his vision of any incoming attacks blinded. The man seemed not to have a care in the world for what was going on.

And so, Malabar decided he would have to change his approach regarding Fergus-Sundar for this was not like any other target he had encountered before. This man was truly unpredictable and had no recent or contextual intel on the spy who vanished intel. For it appeared that the notes that the SSSA had on the eFile of Fergus-Sundar was undoubtedly outdated considering it was from 2025. The urgency that a SSSA4 would have in a situation such as the one Fergus-Sundar was in, was not showing in his actions. *He doesn't seen to be sane.*

Instead of stealthily tracking him, with the intention of apprehension, decided to follow and mimic Fergus-Sundar for he needed the intel on the man – there needed to be something he knew of Fergus-Sundar, something he could use, something tangible, if he was to catch this man. And so, he walked further down the Thames and saw on a bench which was slightly out of the view of Fergus-Sundar. Malabar could see him and that was all that was need-ed. If he were to have an advantage over him, he needed to get inside his head. Fergus-Sundar, from their first bloody encounter, evidently had the advantage of unpredictability. This had to change. This was the first step to that.

· · · · · · · · ·

Now seventy-four minutes had gone since Malabar Jones had been sat on this bench with snow falling on his face. He grew tiresome and frustrated at this lack of movement. *He's moving very stiff, almost not like a human. Is he human? Is this a clone of the Fergus-Sundar from 2025? It would explain his seemingly confused state also. It would explain his unaged appearance. Perhaps it was GHEE who cloned him (the Global Hub of Extraterrestrial Exploration),* Malabar thought to himself. However, Malabar then remembered his fight with Fergus-Sundar and remembered the feeling of the punches landed on his face and realised he couldn't be a robot; the blows felt as though they were from a man. Fergus-Sundar was not the biggest of men, perhaps he fought between Lightweight and Middleweight at most as a boxer, but he hit like a Cruiserweight or Heavyweight. Though he still hit like a man. But Malabar knew that GHEE – under the tutelage of Elisabeth Cervantes, the billionaire tech extraordinaire, now a celebrity adored by millions – were certainly capable of making a clone made of human flesh. Even still, this possibility was perhaps less complicated for Malabar and the SSSA to deal with, than the potential of this Fergus-Sundar being the Fergus-Sundar from 2025, having completed interdimensional travel. For a truth like this was perhaps too much for the world to bear, considering that Malabar knew the technology did not exist for a man or any object to be able to pass through a black hole and come out on the other end, unscathed. And so, as he looked upon this man who appeared to be the vanished spy of 2025, who still sat motionless and looked out upon the Thames, he found his hairs stand up. Though for Malabar, this was not goosebumps of joy or eager anticipation, rather it was fear and unrest that lay within him.

• • •   • • •   • • •

"Mind if I join you young man?" said a voice behind Malabar. He turned his head and saw an old man standing behind him.

"No not at all, have a seat," he said reluctantly; there were so many other benches around. However, he felt obliged to say yes as he did not want to cause a scene.

"It's okay son, I know you probably don't want an old baldy like me sitting right next to you, but I felt I had to come sit down. How are ya?" the old man said as he slowly lowered his body, before plonking on the seat, with the seat shaking a bit as the old man's full weight dropped onto the bench; he was a very large man and if it were not for his cane, he would scarcely be able to move around.

"Erm, I am doing well. Just embracing the elements, taking in the sunshine," Malabar replied as he shuffled his hands through his pockets, preparing himself to move away.

"Please don't go. Come on. Don't be so antisocial. Your generation never want to have a conversation, only through bloody technology. Come on, let's have a little chin wag. What's going on? I gotta be frank here. Forgive me if I'm being forward but I was just on my afternoon walk, ya know before rush hour and that, and I couldn't help but notice you've been sat here and staring at that man for at least twenty minutes now. And I don't know how you been here, but something tells me from the look on your face as I'm saying this, it's been a long time. I don't mean to overstep but I'm just curious is all. Why are ya sat here looking at that man? Youse both haven't even been looking at technology all this time and I tell ya what, that is a rare occurrence these days. Are youse both gay? Is that your ex or something? This ain't no stalker thing is it?"

This caught him off guard for he did not expect the man to be so blunt. However, he was surprised because the man was not far off with the stalker statement; it was not far off the truth. Malabar was stalking Fergus-Sundar, and stalking him like a cat stalking a rat. Despite the fact Malabar could not tell the man the truth, and did not want to answer the man – the man was here in front of him and asking him this. And so, Malabar felt he may as well use this to his advantage.

"No I'm not gay. But it's for the same reason you came and sat down next to me and asked me that question. I am just curious is all. I was doing the exact same thing. Walking down the embankment, and again, enjoying a rare bit of sunshine in this SuperWinter, before I saw this man sitting and staring out to the Thames, not looking at any technology and so I figured I might do the same and simply do what he's doing," said Malabar as he sprinkled in some truth with the lie. For it was true, he was curious as to why Fergus-Sundar sat here, especially considering that he had a bloody fight just a few hours before.

"Ah so it seems we are all not to different from one another then, are we. The name's Andrew by the way but Andy for short. What's your name son?" said Andy the Bald Old Man.

"Arjun, pleasure to meet you," said Malabar as he smiled and reached over for a handshake.

"Alright then Arjun well what's your thoughts on the lad sitting over there then?"

"I don't know. I'm confused. I haven't seen a man like this before. He's almost like a movie character, proper broody but I dunno, just an observation," said Malabar as he looked out towards Fergus-Sundar.

"I mean fair play. I can empathise with that for sure. You wanna hear my thoughts?" said Andy the Bald Old Man in his scouse accent.

"Well, that's why you sat down isn't it?" replied Malabar.

"You're a cheeky sod ain't ya. But yes, you're right. Whatever drew you to come sit down here, the curiosity – I guess I was drawn in to that too.

Something about the lad, got this magnetism or something I don't even know. I know that sounds gay but I'm not. I've got me missus at home she's gonna be fuming if I don't come home soon cos I've got to take the dog for a walk with her but I gotta buy the dogs f***ing AirPol mask as well before cos the muppet chewed into his one. But anyways, like I was saying, this lad ain't your usual lad. I don't know obviously what he's got going on but he seems old. From here it looks about your age, but he seems like an old fella. The way he's sitting there and not looking at technology, actually living in the present moment, weirdly reminds me of meself and my friends. All us old boys. We're all born in the twentieth century, so late nineties. Obviously I know I am old. Look at me bald head. I know I'm f***ing old but I don't feel old inside. But then you come outside and you see everyone and how everything's changed nowadays with modern technology and all that and you just feel out of place sometimes. I mean that's why I walk down here sometimes as well and just look out on the Thames, to get some f***ing peace and quiet away from everyone and everything. Everything is so fast paced nowadays in this city. This lad you been staring at over there looks like that. He reminds me of meself. Just an old man out of touch with the world. I don't know f**k all about the bastard though, he might just have something wrong with him as well but ya never know," Andy the Bald Old Man said as he was sat with his hands clasped together and was also looking over at Fergus-Sundar. "F**k that though I dunno why I'm talking all soft with you now but anyways I'm gonna love ya and leave ya now lad. Have a good one yeah Arjun. I best get going or me missus is gonna have a fit."

"Wow, well. Thank you for that Andy. Pleasure to meet you. You're probably right with those observations. I'm going to sit here for a while longer and mull over those words of wisdom from you. But have a good one yourself," said Malabar as shook the old man's hands.

"Alright lad settle down. Stay safe, catch ya later," said the Old Man as he shook Malabar's hands and walked away, carefully placing each foot in front of the other to manage the weight onto his knees accordingly.

And so, the old man walked away from him. He thought of their conversation and now that the conversation was done, he was grateful for the old man's insight. He looked at Fergus-Sundar, as he was sat alone motionless like a robot, and recognised the truth in his words. Fergus-Sundar did seem like an old man; like a man from another era. For he did seem to be peaceful in this moment and perhaps it was true that this was what he was seeking; tranquillity, that the life of a SSSA4 did not offer.

Malabar thought of the potential reality whereby Fergus-Sundar had indeed travelled between dimensions from 2025 to 2065 and attempted to think what this might feel like. He could not imagine it. However, he knew that it would certainly be uncomfortable and perhaps very stressful. He then thought of the possibility of this Fergus-Sundar being a clone created by GHEE and realised that it was unlikely he would simply be sitting here for this amount of time; likely he would have been coded to cater to the assignments given to him by GHEE. And so, in this moment he concluded that Fergus-Sundar had travelled from 2025 to 2065 and so, he was likely not a threat. Regardless of whether Fergus-Sundar was a threat or not, he had to approach him as he was curious to how he had travelled between the dimensions. For Malabar, being a SSSA4, was knowledgeable in Quantum Physics also and so wanted to know how this was a possibility. *Fergus-Sundar is not a threat to this reality*, concluded Malabar Jones. *But how did he get here?*

He figured it was perhaps best if he were to approach him now, whilst they were in this scene, where it was not such a threatening environment, and they were not in an enclosed place. The best way to approach the man would be to peacefully do it and simply engage in a conversation. Their last encounter began with him running after him; this did not set the tone for a peaceful conversation.

He looked back up at Fergus-Sundar as he shook himself from the deep thought he had just been embarked in, which left him staring into space. Though things quickly became complicated, for Andy the Bald Old man was now just steps away from the bench on which Fergus-Sundar was sat upon. Malabar stood up as he contemplated whether he should move away. However, he thought about it and realised there was nothing he could do about it. The man was speaking to Fergus-Sundar. It was inevitable and now he may have to change his approach. Malabar Jones sat back down, and watched.

• • •   • • •   • • •

"You alright there lad? Ya mind if I sit down here?" asked Andy the Bald Old Man as he put arm on the bench of Fergus-Sundar.

"Yeah sure mate have a seat. You from Liverpool yeah?" said Fergus-Sundar as he slid across the bench.

"Sorry lad. But yes of course. What gave it away? The accent? You can always tell a scouse" said Andy the Bald Old Man as he ascended into laughter which resulted in a cough erupting from deep within him like a dormant volcano dying to come out.

"You okay? How's things?" said Fergus-Sundar as he let out a deep sigh and placed his hands in his pockets and outstretched his legs, still looking out onto the Thames.

"I'm all good lad. Name's Andy. What's your name fella?"

"Mo mate, nice to meet you," said Fergus-Sundar as the two then sat in silence for a moment.

"Alright lad I'm just gonna be upfront and say it straight yeah. That man back there on the bench has been sat there and watching you for at least half an hour. Now I don't know what the deal is between youse but I thought it was only right of me to let you know. Cos God knows that if I had a man stalking me, I'd like to know about it. And looking at the state of you as well as him over there, I'd guess youse two are brothers or friends or something. Cos the lad said youse weren't gays. And come to think of it, youse do look kinda similar," said the Bald Old Man as he pulled out a TasteVape, the a vape version of a cigar.

Fergus-Sundar could not fight his urge to turn and look at Malabar. Though as he looked around, he could not see him and quickly realised he likely had changed vantage point. *I'd have done the same*, he thought.

"Thank you, sir. Really. I appreciate you telling me. Not many would," he said as he tilted his head slightly and looked at the large man hold the TasteVape to his mouth. He realised he needed to get some things off his chest. It was why he was sat here. He did not know really what was going on. He had a piercing headache, being still slightly discombobulated from his arrival in this world. And he was attempting to piece together what he ought to do. He looked the Bald Old Man up and down once again and decided to trust and confide in him. Technically Fergus-Sundar did not exist in this world, and it was highly unlikely that in this packed city, they would ever cross paths again. This Bald Old Man was clearly not a threat and Fergus-Sundar needed someone to voice his thoughts to; the serenity of the Thames was a welcome help to him in this moment, though there was only so much silence and serenity could do – sometimes an avenue to vent down was what was needed to help cleanse the soul of angst.

"But yes we're not gay and we're not friends and we're deffo not related. I only met the man today. As you've pointed out. Yeah, we did have a fight. I don't really wanna say why exactly but just know it's to do with a woman," said Fergus-Sundar as he spoke a lie. It was the best he could come up with so that he could gain the trust of the man without revealing too much of the reality of the situation.

"Well ain't it always. As boys we fight over girls, then as men we do the same but with just more muscle and anger inside us. That's what happens when you get older. You'll realise when you get to my age lad. You either get older and don't give a sh*t about everyone and everything. Like me. Mate. I don't give a f**k what anyone thinks of me no more. I know there's more to life than what some random twat thinks of you. They don't know what you been through. Same way I don't know what another man, woman or trans been through in their life. But when you're young, that's all you f***ing think and worry about. What others think of you. Especially everyone nowadays. It's more about appearance than real substance. Thank you Social Media. But anyway. Or you go the complete other way and you become an angry old f**ker I know so many men, and women you know, that get f***ing angry about everything. They sit and watch the news all f***ing day, cos that's what the government tell you to do and all the politicians and everyone makes you think you gotta do or else you f***ing miss out or something. Yeah they sit and watch the news all day and become depressed and angry at everything and think they have a f***ing right to be angry at every little thing and certain types of people – and it causes hate and anger to build up. For what? So you're in the know. You tell me lad. Cos you're old enough now to have seen enough in the world. What f***ing say and impact on the world and the wider scheme of things have me and you got, sitting here doing our normal day to day jobs?" Andy the Bald Old Man ranted.

Well I think I've had quite an impact on the world Old Man but I hear your point.

"Exactly lad. F**k all. So why the f**k am I spending my whole day worrying about that? Because that's what they want you to do. So you don't worry about what you actually got going on in your day to day life. Don't get it twisted lad. it's important to know what's going on round the world. But I don't need to be reminded every f***ing day. That sh*t just makes you angry and then the anger comes out in random places in your own life. Like you and that Arjun lad other there. I bet the girl was good looking but it probably weren't worth them marks youse both got on your face and the energy. But that's what it f***ing does. She weren't worth your anger but youse both still got angry over her," said Andy the Bald Old Man as he now sat forward in his seat and let out a sigh. "F**k me sorry lad. I don't know why I just went into little rant there. Don't know what it is," said Andy the Bald Old Man as he now turned his head, the sweat between his neck rolls trickling down onto his chest.

"It's okay Andy don't worry. I understand. Did you say his name was Arjun?" asked Fergus-Sundar.

"Yes lad, he said Arjun. Do you actually not know him?"

"Nah. Met him today," replied Fergus-Sundar as he looked into the distance once again. He knew that whilst this man was supposedly called Arjun, it was unlikely this was his real name – for if he was in fact a SSSA4, which was no longer a doubt to him due to the nature of their fight and the fact this man had managed to keep up with Fergus-Sundar, he would have lied, just like he himself had done.

And so, he stood up and reached down to touch his toes with ease. He was still loosening up and only just acclimatising to his body. Fergus-Sundar had become so accustomed to moving, operating, and existing without having his body physically there in front of his eyes and able to feel his senses, existing as consciousness alone in the vast unimaginable void of space – that having his real physical body and senses with him was something that he had somewhat forgotten about. *That SSSA4 fella would never have caught me if I didn't have this Wormhole hangover*. He felt if the two were to meet again, and Fergus-Sundar was in tune with his body once more, himself again, the fight would have ended in his favour, as opposed to the stalemate it had ended in.

"Alright well you off then lad? Sorry if I was ruining your peace and quiet," said Andy the Bald Old Man.

"Nah mate don't worry. I just needed to get up and stretch. Besides I probably should get going anyhow. I need to stretch and get my legs going again. Everything really. Even speaking again to be honest. Thanks for the convo ... lad," said Fergus-Sundar as he smiled to Andy who once again had his TasteVape to his mouth.

"It's alright fella. What do you mean speak again mate? You been in a coma or something?" he replied. Fergus-Sundar chuckled to himself.

"Yes mate as a matter of fact I have been. Funny you say that. Been twenty years and I just got out today," said Fergus-Sundar as he smiled. He had forgotten the joy of conversation. It was something he had stopped doing for a while even at the time of his disappearance from the world in 2025, due to the nature of his work.

"Wow lad that's mad you know. I said it as a joke. I never thought you'd actually have gone through that. How ya doing lad? You alright? Since we're sat here I'm happy to offer ya my ear? It's better than keeping it all locked inside lad, trust me on that."

Fergus-Sundar sat back down as his stretching had finished. He realised this was probably a good moment to come to grips with what he was feeling. *Why not? I won't see this man again. London's probably still the most crowded city in the world, so chances are slim that I'll see him again. Get it off your chest FS. We need to move on.*

"Thanks Andy. Sure. Why not eh. Give me a minute though, it's been a while since I've done something like this," said Fergus-Sundar as he now sat forward. He looked up down at his feet and then up at the sky.

"I know how I got here, but at the same time I don't. Man, I really don't know how to explain it. I can't explain it. It wouldn't make any sense if I did explain it and I don't need to either. It doesn't make a difference. F**k it, the end of the day, all that matters is that I am here. I've reached this stage regardless. I. I just don't know. I don't know what's real anymore. I feel like I am lost Andy. One minute I was with purpose. I knew who I was. What I had to do. What I am. And then you go to sleep and you wake up and it's a completely different world. I'm different. My body feels different. My mind is different. Everything is just different. The world is different. Like I look up at the sky now and I don't see any stars. I can't see the stars Andy. And it's snowing. It's f***ing snowing in November, early November. I just. I just don't know. I don't know who I am anymore Andy. I don't know this world. I don't know what I am meant to do. Everything I once knew, is no longer. Everyone's wearing Air Pollution masks. I. I don't know. It's all just too much. Everything's changed you know. And me man. I've changed. I am not the man I once was, and I don't know what to do about it. I wish things would go back to what they once was you know. When I knew wagwan. It all seemed to be better before you know? Anyway. That's. I mean that's all I got. I dunno how to compute this and take it all in Andy.

Forgive me for this explosion. I, I just haven't spoken to anyone in quite a while now."

Fergus-Sundar let out a deep breath from his mouth. In this moment he felt comfort, he felt a weight lifting off his shoulders and a synergy and sense of peace with himself; tears welled in his eyes. Never did he think he would ever be in this situation.

"Well lad. I'm an old bastard. The way you talk though you sound like an old bastard too. I respect you for your honesty. For real. I really do lad. It takes f***ing balls to sit and be truly open and vulnerable like that, and so I respect you for it. But I'll just give you one bit of wisdom that I've learned over my lifetime. You listening yeah lad?" said the old man said as he nudged Fergus-Sundar's knee with his own knee.

"Yessir?"

"Accept it mate. Whatever life throws at ya, you gotta accept it as it is. Don't be feeling f***ing sorry for yourself lad cos once you let that energy come in lad, it takes over like a virus and it clouds everything in life lad. You don't want that. I know that's not you anyways just speaking to ya. You gotta accept the hard times as they are. And if you get tough times coming your way, then f***ing stand up and look it in the face and f***ing accept that it's there and that it's f***ing happened. Cos if you don't accept it and try fight it before you've accepted it as a thing. Then lad you can't fight it properly and it'll f**k you up. You gotta show it the due respect. So you gotta accept things as they are in life so that you can actually get on with things, strategize and f***ing move on," he said as Fergus-Sundar listened to him intently. "Cos I tell you what lad. Change is permanent. It's the only f***ing constant in this world. For a long time in my life lad I couldn't get to grips with the changes in this world, with what the youth of today are doing and how it's all; changing. I mean I was f***ing born in 1998 lad. I'm an old bastard now. Sh*t's changed since I grew up. Course it has. It always does and always will. I remember my dad and uncles talking about things changing from when they grew up as kids way back when. And now the same f***ing things happening again to my generation and we make the same mistakes trying to fight it. But it's done in vain and just makes ya unhappy cos you end up tryna fight something you have no control over. Its already happened. What's done is done. The change is done and its constant anyways. Only thing you can do, and the best way to move in my opinion. Accept the change lad. Cos once you accept it, then you take control of the change within yourself mate. That way you aint governed by it. You can do what you want to do then. So chin up lad. You'll be fine mate," said Andy as he slapped the back of Fergus-Sundar with his chubby calloused hands.

Fergus-Sundar nodded his head as he kept his gaze to the floor and suddenly jumped up and moved his arms and legs in tandem with one another as he bounced from side to side like a boxer, loosening his limbs, before shouting out into the sky.

"Andy. You are a top, top, lad. I wish you all the best in your life," Fergus-Sundar replied as he smiled and shook Andy's hand.

"Mo it's been a pleasure. But anyways lad, I gotta get going, or the missus is gonna have my balls for dinner," said Andy as he lifted himself from his bench with difficulty. "Catch ya later yeah lad? Keep yourself well kid."

"Cheers Andy," said Fergus-Sundar as he watched the bald old man slowly tread through the snow

Fergus-Sundar had become accustomed to not speaking, to dealing with things himself. It did not trouble him or hinder him for his focus was always unwavering and he was always ready and clear in his mind. However, he had changed. Fergus-Sundar no longer had his time scheduled and designated to anything really. He felt simultaneously free and lost. For whilst he was now free to do as he pleased with his time – for he was no longer in servitude to the SSSA and the crown and country – he was not accustomed to choosing to do what he pleased with his time, for this was something he had done for years within the confines of each case he had to work on. Thus, he was now in the unknown, and without purpose. For he no longer had the duties of a SSSA4, and as such no longer knew what to do. It was liberation that came with a loss of a sense of self, for the SSSA and the duty of a SSSA4 meant he had lost himself as it was not about him.

Though this chapter of his life was over, and it had dawned upon him as he sat on this bench and looked out at the River Thames and watched the waves of water move from side to side. He thought again of the Promenade in Nice, his time there in his formative years and his time there in the lucid dream which brought him to the Wormhole-Maze, which had in turn brought him to this present moment.

A part of Fergus-Sundar wished he had not opened that door on the Promenade in Nice, for he could never go back, and he lost that life behind him; he lost it all. Though even still as he travelled through the Wormhole- Maze and forty years in the future, to this year 2065 – his past life still haunted in the form of this man chasing him. He was not the same Fergus-Sundar who entered the Wormhole-Maze. In the Wormhole-Maze, he had seen too much, known too much about the truer nature of the world and time now – that what he did before no longer was of interest to him. For once he was completely and utterly directionless and Fergus-Sundar felt the worst he had ever felt. For being devoid of purpose, meant he did not know who he was.

And then it clicked. This was exactly who he was. He had lost his ego in the Wormhole-Maze and so he was somewhat without what made him, him. Fergus-Sundar remembered what he had experienced in the Wormhole-Maze and decided that instead of moping, he had to be positive. The glass being half full or being half empty was a choice one could make, for it was about how you choose to see that which is in front of you. He had a choice. And Fergus-Sundar had a choice now in front of him to do as he pleased with his life, in this world.

Fergus-Sundar knew he could travel between dimensions again if the conditions were right. Though, he did not want, or need to do this as of yet. For what would he do if he travelled to another dimension right now? He knew he could explore different cultures and see different times in history, but what would this do? For what he would do if he went back in time would simply be to alter and change the future of the past, to change a reality which existed and Fergus-Sundar did not know why he would want to do this now. Before doing this, he had to fix his home first. He had to pattern where he was right here, right now, the world in which he grew up with and knew, this reality and the people that come from it – before he could move outside this. For Fergus-Sundar knew now that he only wanted to do good upon the world now and change things for the better – for what else was there for him to do? He had accomplished much already in terms of achievements – regarding the formula and interdimensional travel – and fighting and chasing cases no longer interested him. For his scope and view of the world had changed now he had travelled between dimensions. And like the old man, surprisingly, wisely had told him – change was the only constant in this world and so Fergus-Sundar no longer felt scared or uncertain and trapped by the extreme change in the world which he had felt discombobulated by since his arrival in 2065. He decided to embrace the change in the world, and within himself, so that that he may help guide this perpetual state of change perhaps in the right direction, a direction he chose.

But first, before he could do what he wanted and now needed to do, he had to get the other SSSA4 and now the only SSSA4 – as Fergus-Sundar from this point on no longer considered himself a SSSA4 – off his trail so he could go on about his life in peace. Fergus-Sundar knew he was lurking around somewhere. Though he could no longer see this man around him, he knew he was close, hiding in the shadows. Fergus-Sundar had a plan, he knew where he could lose him. And so, Fergus-Sundar walked through the snow and made ways to the tube station, to lose the SSSA4 on his trail, underground.

BOOK 6
MALABAR JONES

Thursday 5th November 2065

20:17: The Underground Tube Network, London

Malabar-Jones peered between the gaps in the large crowds which had amassed in the Underground Station. This was simultaneously a strength and weakness of the man. For his short height and slender frame allowed him to blend into many a crowd and be relatively ordinary looking, though this also hindered him because it meant he did not have the naturally high vantage height in situations such as these that his taller counterparts had. However, this was why the SSSA demanded that all SSSA's were between 5ft 7 and 5ft 10, and weighing between 145lbs to 165lbs. For all SSSA's had to have a high degree of athleticism and agility on top of their other skills of the mind. For the SSSA and its agents were not like your standard government agents. These agents often had to act outside of the law and without the support or knowledge of other government agencies and law enforcement, in places where agents did not typically work – their speciality was in public places and as such, being a large hulk of a man was not conducive to this niche. What Malabar lacked in height, was made up for with athleticism and inconspicuousness.

And as such, Malabar-Jones was slender and quick enough on his feet to keep up with Fergus-Sundar despite the speed of the man. *Fergus-Sundar certainly has the speed of a SSSA4*, he thought. For every time he tried to get close to Fergus-Sundar and close the distance between them, amongst the

81

overcrowded sea of people which inhabited the rush hour of the Underground System, Fergus-Sundar would find a way to two-step and swivel his shoulders so that he could fit between a gap of people that most would not be able to do in such a smooth and seamless transition. Fergus-Sundar also seemed to have an ability to time his movements in such a way that Malabar-Jones was always one step behind, his speed of thought made it seem as though he was a few steps ahead of everyone else and it seems he had a visual map of the area ahead of him. The unpredictable nature and smart movements of Fergus-Sundar was something Malabar recognised, as he had this himself. *So this is what it's like. He was smart to bring this here.*

• • •   • • •   • • •

Malabar continued to follow the once vanished SSSA4 and he looked down at the digital time embedded in the skin on the back of his hand, to see that the two had been in the Underground network for near forty-five minutes and had barely travelled any distance at all – Fergus-Sundar was moving in circles hoping to confuse the man and lose him in the busy areas. It was a smart ploy, but it was not smart enough to lose a man such as Malabar Jones.

He walked onto the platform behind Fergus-Sundar and received the TrafficText on his TechSuit which notified him that the tube was delayed and only to be on the platform in four minutes time. Malabar turned his head around like a meerkat looking from side to side, to try to spot Fergus-Sundar. His eyes flickered from side to side as he scanned the room; and all he could see was the impatient fidgeting of the crowd on the platform as they waited for the Tube. Malabar walked down and suddenly locked eyes with Fergus-Sundar who was at the end of the platform and Malabar knew that at the very least, he would be able to get on the same carriage as Fergus-Sundar now for there was no way he could be able to pass him without him knowing.

The two patiently waited with their legs both shoulder width apart and their heads held high on their shoulders. Malabar could feel Fergus-Sundar's gaze turn towards him on occasion during this wait, and could feel the tension between the two which radiating off them, like the radiation in Chernobyl. Then surprisingly, he saw Fergus-Sundar move closer towards him. *Is he challenging me?* Malabar thought to himself. It certainly felt like a challenge; he felt he was being goaded.

The tube then arrived and the two both slid onto the tube amidst the crowd and, customary to an experience in the tube during rush hour, felt backpacks hit them from nearly every angle as no one seemed to care for social etiquette, or human connection anymore in the overcrowded London – the concrete jungle had truly become a jungle.

This was the first time Fergus-Sundar had been on the tube since 2025 and Malabar could see him process what he saw around him. Despite the height of the two SSSA4s, Malabar could see Fergus-Sundar with ease as every person, bar the two of them, had their necks fixed looking downwards, like a lamp, at their technology devices of some sort. Malabar looked in the direction of where Fergus-Sundar was looking as he saw a pregnant lady with what looked to be her mother, standing and clinging onto the rail above them as a group of teenage boys laughed together as they all respectively looked down at their technology whilst they talked through their headphones with music also simultaneously playing as a residue of sound echoed through the otherwise silent tube, unaware or uncaring of their surroundings. This had been the first time he had seen a glimpse of an emotional response, other than when he had induced pain on Fergus-Sundar outside the Burlington Arcade, on the face of Fergus-Sundar. *He is definitely human*, Malabar thought to himself as he squinted his eyes at Fergus-Sundar who continued to scan the tube and the people on it.

The two then locked eyes and Fergus-Sundar smiled at Malabar who remained unwavering in his stare. Fergus-Sundar then pursed his lips in his direction before raising his eyebrows together, and then doing so one by one. However, Malabar did not budge and give in to Fergus-Sundar's goading. Malabar had undergone training, mental training, of the highest order and so it would take far, far more than this for him to flicker or flinch. Fergus-Sundar then smiled once again and chuckled to himself as he looked from side to side, observing the silent passengers of the tube as they either had their eyes transfixed on technology, and or had their minds fixed by their music, with some even dancing to the music despite being surrounded by others. They locked eyes once more, though this time it seemed to be a battle of will as both were unwavering and did not move their eyes from one another. The silence continued on as the train stopped between stations due to the effects of the icy weather of the SuperWinter of 2065 on the Underground network. Near five minutes had passed and still there was silence on the tube. Malabar continued to receive TrafficTexts through his TechSuit as others around him received their TrafficTexts on their own respective technology, which buzzed each time – causing a slight echo of reverberation through the carriage which seemed to not be noticed at all or bothering most people.

However, Fergus-Sundar certainly heard it and his ears instinctively flickered as it did so – he was not accustomed like everyone else to the constant buzz of technology which captured the attention of the human being, like a drug addict. This had almost distracted Fergus-Sundar from this contest of the gaze he was embarked in with Malabar. *I can't cave first*, thought Fergus-Sundar as he readjusted his feet and braced his core once more as the train got moving. He never held onto the rails for support as the trains moved at high speed. His balance, core strength and stabilising muscles in his abdominals and legs were near unmatched. Malabar saw this through the corner of his eye as he continued to stare at the face of Fergus-Sundar, and followed suit.

In this moment Fergus-Sundar knew he had already won this mini battle for he was now leading the dance; he was controlling proceedings. Fergus-Sundar was from a time before and his time in the Wormhole-Maze had aged him mentally far beyond the age of forty, despite his physical appearance having stayed at forty. Thus, Fergus-Sundar remembered this and sensed the fear of the unknown within Malabar. This was a fear which had eroded from within Fergus-Sundar in the Wormhole-Maze, but one who had briefly reemerged within him upon his arrival in 2065. And so, Fergus-Sundar felt the tide switch as he led the dance with Malabar Jones in the tube.

"I just want to talk that's all. Just talk. Why don't you come in?" said Malabar as he now grabbed onto the rail above him while Fergus-Sundar still stood upright with his hands clasped together and resting on his chest with his elbows tucked in.

He waited a moment for Fergus-Sundar to talk but realised quickly that he was not going to talk, not here. Fergus-Sundar simply smiled back at him and closed his eyes for a moment. *What's he playing at?* thought Malabar, as Fergus-Sundar now stood with his eyes closed in the tube carriage, which was now less crowded.

21:21: Hampstead Tube Station, London

"This is Hampstead Station. Please mind the gap between the train and the platform. Change here for the Northern Line."

Suddenly, Fergus-Sundar darted and made his way through the crowd in what seemed to be a split second. *Damn he's fast*, thought Malabar. He followed swiftly but again found himself to be lacking in speed as he did not want to cause a scene, allowing those less able to continue upon their walking path. He continued to follow the stream of people as they make their way to the lift. However, he couldn't see Fergus-Sundar anywhere, until suddenly he saw Fergus-Sundar from behind, with his peculiar rhythm of walking.

As Malabar approached him, he felt this was the moment. The moment the two would come face to face again and speak to one another since their bloody battle earlier in the day. Malabar, though hopeful of resolution and bringing Fergus-Sundar into the SSSA HQ, was conscious that

Fergus-Sundar had no problem with ending him. If it were not for the Tech-Suit, his spine would likely have cracked on the pavement due to the backdrop by Fergus-Sundar. The Tech-Suit had activated the tortoise shell as he was dropped onto his back and saved his life, saved himself for this moment.

Malabar turned the corner and saw a plaque on the wall of the Hampstead Tube Station which read as follows:

This stairway has over 320 steps
Do not use except in an emergency

Peculiar, thought Malabar as he read the sign. He had never seen such a sign in a tube station before. He turned the corner and walked into the entrance of the staircase. Though as he turned the corner, he was met with a stiff leaping jab to his face and felt himself stagger back as the leaping jab was followed up with a clean right hook to his temple. Malabar, mid stagger, brought his arms together and tucked his elbows in close towards his ribcage as he covered up while Fergus-Sundar unleashed a barrage of punches towards his ribcage. A few of punches landed but the majority were caught by the elbows of Malabar.

Suddenly Malabar realised Fergus-Sundar had L-stepped and created some space for himself. He looked through his tight and high guard he had up and saw Fergus-Sundar slightly shake his right power hand and wiggle his fingers slightly. Instantaneously, Malabar grabbed his left wrist with his right hand and held his two index fingers onto the outer side of his wrist for two seconds and repeated the process with his right wrist – this brough out the hand wraps out of his Tech-Suit.

Fergus-Sundar, as he shifted his weight from one leg to the other and dipped slightly, trying to find his angles and the optimal striking range against his opponent in front of him – for a brief moment looked at the hands of Malabar and saw the hand wraps appear out of the Tech-Suit which covered his body. *Hmm that's useful. Resourceful little thing. Seems to connected to synapses somehow,* thought Fergus-Sundar. Fergus-Sundar had broken skin across near all of his knuckles and had his hands loose and fist unclenched as he rested his hands. He was in desperate need of hand wraps; the bones in the hand could only take so much impact as it impacted with the dense bones of Malabar Jones.

"Good jab. Gazelle jab. Technique used by Marvin Hagler. You know how to box," said Malabar as he slowly circled around Fergus-Sundar on the small landing before the staircase.

"Yes I do. By the look of your face, it seems quite well."

"Yeah it seems that way doesn't it. Now. We just gonna keep doing this? Or you want to come with me. I have no problem with you Fergus-Sundar. Just want to have a little chat."

"Shutup. No chance. I know what you want. I'm not coming in mate. That's the last thing I'm doing,".

"Why? What's the harm? You've been gone for forty years Fergus-Sundar. We need to know what happened. I think I know but I don't know for sure. That's why we need to talk. I want to do this peacefully but I will bring you in the hard way if I have to. It's my duty."

"What's the harm? Listen kid. I've worked at the SSSA as well. Don't forget that. You're only here because I'm here. I know how they operate. And for your information. You don't know sh*t. What do you know about me? About where I've been? You don't know f**k all so don't presume to know wagwan. You read something on a file and think you know everything about me. I'm done mate. No chance. I've had my death mate. I died forty years ago. I don't owe anything to the SSSA. I'm going to go my own way now. So you can either let me go, or you can follow me up and we can have a good f***ing fight. I don't need to fight you kid and quite frankly I don't want to. You mean f**k all to me. You're just some guy following me. So if you wanna go down this path, say no more I'll happily give you a good beating. But know kid. This ain't gonna end well for you. This staircase is three-hundred-and-twenty steps. Steep. Uphill. I've fought men on these stairs before. This ain't my first rodeo. You're fighting a SSSA4. The SSSA4. I'm your f***ing daddy. There ain't no you without me. You ain't a SSSA4 without me g. So know I am that guy. S you let me know if this is how you wanna go," said Fergus-Sundar with venomous intent.

"Well if you want to go then we can go. I will do my duty and do what I must to protect this nation from any poten…"

"Oh, spare me the f***ing bullshit *I protect and serve my country* bollocks. Like I said. I've been in your shoes before mate; I know what you're on. Just tell me if we're gonna have a scrap or not so I can time myself as we go up these stairs. I might as well have some fun and track my time as I f**k you up. I ain't gonna make it easy for you going up here. Let's see what the SSSA are hiring in 2065," retorted Fergus-Sundar.

"You're … you're just. Fine you want to go then let's go. I'll do what I must," said Malabar as he bounced on the balls of his feet and brought his right hand up and kept it tucked under his chin, and felt his left shoulder blade go loose as his left arm hung low.

"Now we're talking. Let's go b**ch," said Fergus-Sundar.

Fergus-Sundar leapt with the gazelle jab once more and once again he found his target as the jab landed clearly on the nose of Malabar. Fergus-Sundar side stepped and turned Malabar using his tightly tucked elbows and teed-off on him with a fast combo of a left hook to the solar plexus, followed by a straight overhand right hand which found its way through the guard of Malabar, before unleashing a leaping left hook which Malabar swiftly ducked under with Fergus-Sundar missing his target by mere inches. He was rocked. Fergus-Sundar was fast, much faster than any criminal or target he had ever fought before and so he knew he had to approach this differently, he could not allow Fergus-Sundar to control the action and range. He had to do something to change this for Fergus-Sundar had already found his range. He was right – he was not an ordinary fighter.

Fergus-Sundar stepped back and then released, another jab which was followed by a straight jab and again it met his target and Malabar felt his large nose shift slightly out of position. Malabar could not track or predict the punches coming at him from Fergus-Sundar as it seemed he punched off rhythm, in his own tempo. He was certainly dictating the tempo and proceedings. He was terribly hard to read. Fergus-Sundar through punches which were untelegraphed and again he flicked out a double jab towards the head of Malabar and even though Malabar moved around the landing and moved his head around off the centre line, still the punches landed.

Fergus-Sundar then stepped in once more and this time instead of releasing a jab which Malabar expected, instead threw out a feint which Malabar ate, like a fat kid eating cheesecake. And Fergus-Sundar dipped down slightly to his left and unleashed a sharp and short left hook to the ribcage of Malabar. His left foot was firmly planted to the floor and allowed the power to travel through from his plantar fascia through his legs and into his strong abdominal and through into his serratus anterior and latissimus dorsi, and unleashed the ferocious left hook through his left shoulder and through his bulky forearm which delivered the blow through his toughened fist.

Malabar winced and felt the weight under his legs go and his body instinctively curled up and he fell to the floor and rolled around, with his clothing gathering dust from the dirty and old tube floor, of this seemingly ancient tube staircase. As he winced, he could for a moment see the undersoles of Fergus-Sundar's shoes as he glided up the stairs. Malabar had fallen like the former Super Lightweight World Champion Marcos Maidana had fallen against the former Super Lightweight World Champion, Amir Khan. It was a picture perfect punch by Fergus-Sundar who set the punch up perfectly with his constant flickering off beat jab, which allowed him to feint and level change as Malabar brough his high and tight guard up to his face, creating the space for the body shot to land. The smart footwork and boxing IQ of Fergus-Sundar was proving to be the difference and Malabar rolled on the floor still. If they had been in a boxing ring then Malabar would have been counted out as close to fifteen seconds passed as he finally managed to bring himself up off of the floor.

As he regained composure and was able to bring his consciousness back to the present moment he looked up and could not see Fergus-Sundar. He had escaped. However, Malabar knew that this was a long staircase and so he could catch him still if he sprinted.

Malabar took in a deep breath as he was finally able to regain his breath as Fergus-Sundar's liver punch had severely winded and incapacitated him. However, there was no moment to spare. It was no telling how far Fergus-Sundar had gotten. He sprinted up the staircase, surprised by how steep the stairs on the staircase were.

"Fergus! Fergus-Sundar!" he shouted. However, as Malabar shouted this out he realised there was no chance he could hear him. Malabar could not even hear himself shout out. *I can't even hear myself think*, he thought to himself Malabar continued his ascent up the staircase as he felt the burn in his vastus medialis and vastus lateralis in his thighs.

"Fergus-Sundar!" he shouted out again.

Malabar, after a minute of running, saw Fergus-Sundar leisurely walking up the stairs and as he navigated himself on the sharp corner, which had little real estate for his footing he pushed into his back.

"Wow. You came back for more? I'm impressed," said Fergus-Sundar – though Malabar did not hear him over the deafening sound of the tube on the moving tracks.

"Let's go then," said Malabar as he tried to shuffle up closer to Fergus-Sundar on the staircase. However, Fergus-Sundar threw a sharp counter check left hook which landed clean on the jaw of Malabar.

Though this time it was Fergus-Sundar who winced as now his left hand was hurt from the impact of his fist hitting the skull of Malabar from the force he had swung with. And though Malabar was buzzed from the left hook of Fergus-Sundar, he knew this was his opportunity.

Malabar threw a jab to the midsection of Fergus-Sundar, as his head was at the height of his opponent as they stood on the narrow and steep staircase. He followed the jab with a strong push up the stairs and Fergus-Sundar fell back and tried to readjust his feet as he found himself on the landing. *Perfect, some actual space and even footing*, thought Malabar. Malabar threw a jab with his right hand again neatly tucked under his chin. The jab was parried by Fergus-Sundar who at this stage was firmly on the defensive; he knew his hands needed a rest.

Fergus-Sundar knew he could quite easily threw a knee to the midsection of Malabar but did not do it or even think to do it. The same applied to Malabar, as it seemed the two had an unspoken and unconscious agreement to allow for their duel to simply be one of the fists. A battle of the oldest martial art.

Malabar thew the jab again but this time followed it up with a huge haymaker right over the top and Fergus-Sundar, in a defensive manoeuvre perfected by Niccolino Locche and James Toney, dipped from his waist and moved his shoulder into Malabar to evade the punch. He did so successfully and the two engaged in a clinch. Fergus-Sundar knew that punch had come close to landing as he felt the dust particles from this old underground staircase move as Malabar's fist flew over the top of his head.

"What's your name kid?" said Fergus-Sundar as it seemed Malabar, despite not landing a significant strike as such, had earned his respect or at least gained his curiosity.

"The names Malabar. Malabar Jones. And I'm not a f***ing kid. I'm a thirty-nine year old man," said Malabar as he broke the clinch and through a sharp and short lead uppercut off the break of the two SSSA4 agents, which rattled the teeth of Fergus-Sundar.

"Interesting name," replied Fergus-Sundar. *My family were from Malabar, Kerala,* thought Fergus-Sundar. He threw another gazelle jab which this time Malabar saw coming. As Fergus-Sundar leapt, Malabar in a split second took a slight step to his left and threw a blind overhand right which landed clean straight under the right eye of Fergus-Sundar and immediately his skin tore and blood began to seep out.

Huh, thought Fergus-Sundar as he took a step back and darted up the stairs. *The kid can bang. I need to switch it up – we're nearly at the top now*, thought Fergus-Sundar.

"Why you running for? Thought you wanted to fight," shouted Malabar as he chased after him.

However, Fergus-Sundar could not hear Malabar as the noise in this particular section of the staircase was too loud, only in fleeting moments could they hear one another.

The two met on the landing once more though again the space was limited and the two were within arm's reach of one another. Reach did not matter in this fight, though ultimately in terms of physical appearance there was not much between the two men anyhow,

"Why Malabar?"

"What?"

"Why are you called Malabar? Interesting name," asked Fergus-Sundar who seemed genuinely intrigued. He threw out another jab but this time Malabar slipped it and countered with another lead uppercut from an awkward angle which again met the chin of Fergus-Sundar though this time grazed it as Fergus-Sundar straightened his bent knees which brought his chin up and out of position just enough so that the punch did not land clean on him. *Unload while he's defending, take advantage of his high guard,* Fergus-Sundar thought.

"My mum named me Malabar."

The two then danced moved around in tandem with one another as they exchanged jabs and head movements and both landed some clean shots. However, at this stage it was Malabar who was landing the better shots as he could throw more due to his protected hands and counter punching. Though Fergus-Sundar was coasting and knew that he did not need to win every encounter in this battle of the 320-Step staircase. *I just have to win the right moments,* he thought to himself. He ran up the stairs again and stopped once more on the small landing, and like every previous time the two engaged in a mutual reset as they both appeared to re-strategise and gain their breath, for the staircase was steep and long and the two were trading blows. Fergus-Sundar looked at Malabar as the two of them seemed to be stood in front of each other and feinting and could see the open mouth of Malabar. Fergus-Sundar knew he himself was tired but it appeared Malabar was even more tired than he was. He had not exerted as much energy as Malabar had done in this middle portion of the fight, and Fergus-Sundar remembered the blow to the body he landed early in this battle and the fact that Malabar had to run up the flights of stairs to catch him.

And so, in this moment Fergus-Sundar took advantage of this and again began to target the body of Malabar before again grabbing the elbows of Malabar and manoeuvring him around to create a more optimal punch angle – a technique of the late great Roberto Duran. Fergus-Sundar landed a few good body shots, and then, to the surprise of Malabar, he ran back down the staircase.

Alright then, why's he running back down? I'll definitely catch him now.

However, as Fergus-Sundar felt Malabar closing in on him he quickly turned him as Malabar was about to grab his shoulder, and ran back up the stairs and felt his leg muscles pulsate like a heartbeat as he leapt up two steps at a time.

The two reached the penultimate landing to the top of the staircase and again Fergus-Sundar lunged with a gazelle jab again, but this time after doing so, for the first time in the fight, switched stance effortlessly and using the famous but dangerous technique of the V-Step, used by the legendary Willie Pep, he landed a crushing right hook which crept around the high guard of Malabar. Though instead of follow up with punches, as Malabar was still in front of Fergus-Sundar and ready to go – Fergus-Sundar decided it was time to end the fight and swiped the legs of Malabar and pushed his shoulder at the same time which sent Malabar Jones tumbling down the staircase and it seemed once again his Tech-Suit was the only thing saving him from death.

Fergus-Sundar knew he was the better fighter but also knew that Malabar and him could have continued boxing for some time. But it was time to end the fight and so he had seized his moment. This was the difference between the two. Fergus-Sundar was not afraid to get his hands dirty, especially when he knew of his opponent's capabilities.

"I hope you've learned your lesson now. Leave me alone. Tell the SSSA to leave me alone. I'm done. I don't want any trouble. Good fight kid," Fergus-Sundar shouted to the incapacitated Malabar Jones.

And so, the SSSA4 lay on his back as he struggled to move around, and thought about how he lost the fight. *How did I get here?*

This was now the second time in a day that Malabar was left lying on his back by his SSSA4 predecessor and it did not feel good. He was not accustomed to defeat like this. And so, Malabar saw Fergus-Sundar stand at the top of the stairs, turn and walk away. He knew he could chase after him but what good would it be? It was unlikely that he would be able to catch Fergus-Sundar, not in his current state and not without significant resources and intel on the man, for he was a formidable opponent. Though Malabar knew Fergus-Sundar was likely going to his old apartment which was a now abandoned government property in Hampstead. But he had already wasted much time.

And, so he would end his pursuit of Fergus-Sundar for the time being and revert his attention to his actual case … to apprehend the man behind the prospective terrorist plot on the Dala Electricity Hub's around the country, which the SSSA had identified.

The start and main target was the Dala Electricity Hub of London and it was Malabar Jones' job to stop Brian Harrison, the leader, from enacting the terrorist plot. And so, he picked himself up from the floor and had purpose once more. He was now also behind schedule on his mission and so the drive behind his purpose, was tenfold.

Right Malabar, let's go catch this Brian Harrison f**ker, he told himself.

BOOK 7
DEVONTE LACY

Thursday 5th November 2065

16:00: A Mega-Terrarium owned by Jarred Lane Johnson,
Belgravia, London

And so, Devonte Lacy took off his gardening gloves and carefully treaded over towards his buzzing phone as he prepared himself to answer the call he was simultaneously dreading and excited for. For what he was to hear was to be either terrible or amazing news.

"Hello this is Angela calling from the National Basic Health Service. Is this Mister Devonte Lacy Junior I'm speaking to?" said Angela from the National Basic Health Service (NBHS).

"Yh this him. So what's up. Give me the news. I ain't tryna partake in no small talk," said Devonte as he wiped sweat which lathered his forehead, like butter on toast.

"Well Mister Junior, I'm ..."

"Don't call me Junior please. I don't like that. Call me Devonte or Mister Lacy. Ain't nobody called me Junior since my pops."

"Oh okay. Well I'm afraid to say that I've got some bad news for you Mister Lacy. Our consultants have advised that there is nothing we can do about your aunt's situation at this stage. Quite frankly it's just too late for any of our treatment to have any effect on her health. So I'd advise you and your family start getting prepared and making the necessary funeral arrangements because it's most likely her last few months now. I'm really,

really sorry to have to deliver this news Mister Lacy. If it's any consolation, your aunt has lasted much longer than most people with her condition and it's a testament to her strength. Please let me know if you have any questions," said Angela.

"Say less Angela. Well if it's any consolation to you. I know this is bull-sh*t. You and your doctors could do sh*t if y'all wanted to but I know you technically can't cos this is the NBHS so if I wanna get some legit treatment y'all gonna make me pay and go to the other side. So knowing that, do you know if the National Superior Health Service will have all my auntie's details on record? I was finna call them after I heard news from y'all but I wasn't sure if they'd have her details. I read something online about having to pay for access or some sh*t but I didn't think that was legit," he replied whilst pacing, watching his step to ensure he did not step on the plants around him.

"Well Mister Junior. Apologies I mean Lacy. It says Mister Junior on our records. I do apologise. So yes the National Superior Health Service does have access to your auntie's details but you are right. There is a file access transfer fee of £300 for them to be able to access these files as this will currently be locked or, I should say, hidden on their system. If you would like I can help you process this payment now as long as you have your Dala Device next to you. To do this I would send you an NFT, which will pop up on your Dala Device and you would need to verify this of course with the Retinal Verification Scanner on your Dala Device to confirm the £300 payment and enable the National Superior Health Service to have access to the health files for a Mrs Shonda Miller. Please confirm if you'd like to proceed with this or if you need me to clarify anything?"

"Okay so I'll have to pay £300 for the NSHS access to her files?"

"Yes Mister Lacy. Do let me know if you'd like to proceed with this. I can send this over to you now."

"Ah. Okay hold up one minute. Imma put you on hold for a minute, don't end the call please I just need to check something. I'm at work right now," said Devonte.

"Yes certainly. I'll be on the line. Take as much time as you need."

Devonte put Angela from the NBHS on mute and went onto his online banking app. He looked at the screen and saw he had £600 left in his account for the month but knew he had a total of £300 which was scheduled to go out of his account in the next two days; loan repayments. He knew he could not really afford this £300 fee the NBHS were asking for so that the National Superior Health Service (NSHS) could access his auntie's health files, as it would leave him with nothing for the rest of the month. Devonte was already overdrawn and had maxed out his overdraft on all his bank accounts, and so it was unlikely he could get another overdraft to cover him for the month. However, the health and potential life or death situation with his auntie went above his own financial security – he closed the app and unmuted Angela from the NBHS.

"Okay Angela, yes please send the NFT now. I got my Dala Device here," he replied as he went down to sit on the grass.

"Yes Mister Lacy. So this has been sent now, you should see the NFT on your Dala Device. All you'll have to do, as I'm sure you're aware, is accept the NFT from us and complete the payment with the Retinal Verification Scanner. Then your auntie's, Mrs Shonda Miller, health files will be instantly accessible on the National Superior Health Service's systems across the board. Do let me know if you have any questions about this."

Devonte stood up as he accepted the NFT and confirmed himself as the recipient with the Retinal Verification Scanner (RVS), placing it to his eye as the RVS scanned his retina. He then received another notification on the Dala Device, prompting him to confirm payment, before then confirming his purchase using the RVS. Devonte, as he usually did when confirming a payment using the RVS, felt a slight tingle through his body and cracked his neck from side to side to stop the sensation – it was more comfortable to do standing up for him.

"I can confirm that has come through on our system already. Thank you for doing that so quickly. So the health files will now be on the National

Superior Health Service's systems across the board. Please let me know if there is anything further I can help you with," said Angela from the NBHS.

"Can you put me through to someone from the NSHS please. I don't wanna have to call and wait on the line to get through to someone," said Devonte.

"I don't have a specific number, I'm unfortunately unauthorised to do that. But because you've paid that £300 file access transfer fee, the National Superior Health Service call switchboard will automatically pick up your number on their system as someone who's paid their fee, because it is the emergency contact number on your auntie's file, and so you should be on their priority list which means your call will be fast-tracked on their system. You'll only be behind other National Superior Health Service users, so you shouldn't have to wait too long at all. Please let me know if any of that needs clarifying or if there's something further I can help you with today Mister Lacy."

"Aite. No that's all. I think we're done here thank you."

"Okay well if you think you've had good customer service today please leave me a rev…"

"F**k man!" shouted Devonte in as quiet a manner as he could, as he ended the call, and controlled himself from breaking his phone in rage.

"F**k man. F***ing bullsh*t NBHS man," said Devonte Lacy to himself as he looked online to find a number for the NSHS.

He called the number and expected to have to answer all he questions on the automated service, to be able to get through to a human. Though as Angela from the NBHS had told him, he was surprised to hear a human voice on the other side of the phone.

"Hello this is Shannon, Health Administration Assistant at the London Branch of the National Superior Health Service, how can I be of assistance. I take it this is Mister Junior on the phone? Your number and name came up on our system as the emergency contact for Mrs Shonda Miller. Is this correct?," said Shannon from the NSHS.

"Hi Shannon. Yeah it's Mister Lacy. Please don't call me Junior. I go by Mister Devonte Lacy. Before I get into things, can you first take the name Junior off the file please? I don't like that name" said Devonte.

"Hi there Mister Lacy. Unfortunately, I am unable to edit personal details on our system as these are linked to your passport details. But I can put your preferred name on our records. This is something we do offer through the National Superior Health Service and is something you would not have been able to do through the National Basic Health Service system. Please confirm if you'd like me to change your preferred name to Mister Devonte Lacy?"

"Yeah. Change the preferred to Devonte Lacy please. Anyways. Now reason I'm calling is cos I just been told by the NBHS that they can't do no more treatment for my auntie and that she gone die in the next few months. Now I know that be some bullsh*t and there deffo gotta be some treatment for her condition. You got my aunties files there in front of you now I'm assuming. Can you confirm if this the case, or do I gotta speak to a Consultant for that? I don't mind coming in for an appointment or something. Oh and as soon as possible as well ideally. I finish work at 6pm everyday but I'm good to come in any time after that. I work all across London."

"Well Mister Lacy you actually wouldn't need to book an appointment or wait for an answer. You are right, I do have Mrs Shonda Miller's file in front of me and I can see that she would be eligible for three different treatments here at the National Superior Health Service. These treatments would not have been viewable by the team at the National Basic Health Service and so they would not have been aware of them. Now regarding the treatments and life expectancy. I'm very pleased to say that if you were to proceed with any of these treatments, the success and subsequent recovery rate would be guaranteed at hundred-percent for all three of them, with the cheapest option having a full recovery time of six months and the most expensive option having a full recovery time of just one month. Now, if you'd like Mister Lacy I can run you through the details of the treatments and then advise the next steps. However, I have to tell you that this hundred-percent success rate is only guaranteed if she gets treatment within the next three weeks. Any time after that and our algorithms show based on the data we have available from other people that have had her condition and these treatments with the stage of her cancer she has and the spread of the cancer, that the success rate goes down to fifty-percent and it goes down sharply after date. Please let me know if you'd like me to run over all of that again and clarify anything."

"Nah nah it's all good, I got all of that. So f**k the details of the treatments. I ain't gonna know what all the operations and potential treatments are even if you describe them right now. We can sort that out later. Just tell me how much the treatments is. Tell me the most expensive one first then work down from there please. Oh and sorry for my language. It just been a stressful day you know," said Devonte as he felt reassured knowing that his auntie would live. His auntie had an eleven year-old son, Shakur, who would become Devonte's responsibility if she passed away. Devonte didn't want her to die. It would only be himself and Shakur left from their family if she passed away. She was all they had left.

"That's okay Mister Lacy. Totally understandable. I'll just stick to the prices at this stage then. So, for the Highest-Tier treatment available for your auntie at this stage, it is £30,000 and as I said before, has a hundred-percent success rate with full recovery being just 1 month. Our Mid-Tier treatment available for your auntie at this stage, is £15,000 with a hundred-percent success rate and full recovery time of three months – our data shows this to be the most popular option. And finally the Standard-Tier treatment available for your auntie at this stage, is £8,000 with a full recovery time of six months. Now these are fantastic rates and we are proud to say that this is around fifty-percent less than the rates than our partners over in the United States of America. The only reason we are able to offer these health-care rates at such a good price here in the UK is because of the past history of the National Healthcare System, going back pre-Isolationism Act and pre-Privatisation of our Healthcare system, which was a free service and highly inefficient and underfunded system might I add. And so these really are fantastic rates. Further, I'm very happy to tell you that if you decide you'd like to proceed with any of these treatments today – I can offer you a forty-percent discount on whichever treatment you go for. So that means the Highest-Tier treatment goes from £30,000 to £18,000, the Mid-Tier goes from £15,000 to £9,000 and the Standard-Tier goes from £8,000 to £4,800. Now if you'd like me to go into further details, I would be more than happy to do so. And if you need me to repeat anything I've said, I'd be more than happy to do so, and would be happy to answer any questions you have," Shannon replied.

Devonte's felt his heart rate rise as he attempted to process all that Shannon from the NSHS had told him. He had never known anyone, in his ten years in this country, who had gone through treatment from the NSHS and those that he did know, had always kept quiet about the treatment and prices. Now Devonte knew why. He could not afford it. He could not afford any of those treatments, including the Standard-Tier treatment. And so, Devonte felt tears well up in his eyes as he feared what no treatment for his auntie would mean, as he feared what a life without his auntie would mean. She was everything to him. She accepted him with open arms to the UK when his mother passed away back in Atlanta when he was seventeen and left him an orphan, alone with no family in the States; for Devonte did not consider his father, his father. Devonte imagined the face of his cousin Shakur when he would have to break the news to him that his mother would not live. He did not want to have to have this conversation but knew he would have no choice but to break the news to him.

His thoughts now reverted to *I need a zoot man*, as he struggled to keep himself composed. He pondered on the idea of being ignorant and not knowing that there were treatment options for her. For he felt it was almost better to be oblivious, rather than knowing he could not afford to get treatment for her; this was more heart wrenching, knowing there was a way for her to live. *I wish I had the ps for this.*

"Thanks Shannon, I guess we'll go with the Standard-Tier treatment. Let me know the next steps on how to proceed with this. I can't pay today but can I pay in three weeks. And can I split the payments?" he replied. *Why the f**k I done said I can pay for it?* He did not plan to say yes to the treatment but something overcame him in that moment, perhaps instinct. He knew now that he was going to have to find a way to pay for this, and he knew getting a loan or overdraft was not an option; his credit score was not good.

"Unfortunately, we would require payment to be made in full prior to the treatment. Would you like to take advantage of the sixty-percent subsided offer today for the Standard-Tier treatment? I can send an NFT to your Dala Device now and have this confirmed for you?"

"No Shannon. I can't pay it today. I'll pay in three weeks? How do I get a hold of you?"

"I understand. Okay so you can either call or email me. I'd prefer that you first email me at shannon@nationalsuperiorhealthservice.com whenever you are ready to make payment and then at this stage I will send you an NFT to your Dala Device to confirm the payment of £8,000 to proceed with the Standard-Tier treatment for your auntie's cancer. Alternatively, you can call me at 07*******69. Now I will send you an email follow up with the details on everything we have discussed today and include an information package on the Standard-Tier treatment you may be opting for. Please do let me know if you have any further questions," said Shannon from the NSHS.

"Okay thank you ma'am. But since you're offering us £4,800 if I paid for the today; can I not just pay this amount in three weeks' time?"

"No I'm afraid not Mister Lacy. It's company policy that I can only offer this on the first day you are aware of our treatments."

"But it's the same treatment. So why y'all gotta charge me more later on just cos I don't pay straight away? That don't make no sense? What the f**k? That mean y'all straight up just overcharging for the sake of it. Just for money. Don't make no f***ing sense. Come on Shannon y'all gotta understand that's a lot of f***ing money," he replied.

"I'm sorry Mister Lacy but there's nothing I can do I'm afraid. As I said before, it's company policy. I'm just giving you the information is all. Is there no way you can make the payment today? I am happy to extend this to tomorrow if you'd like. I can cause a delay on our system for a day but anything after that our systems would see that a phone call has been made today and so the records would show that the treatments have been outlined to you today."

"Nah I can't pay today lady. Ain't you been listening. But cool I get it, ain't nothing you can do. Is what it is. Say less, I'll drop you an email in about three weeks. Hopefully the success rate stay at one-hunna by then. Thank you for your time. Bye," said Devonte as he didn't wait for her to respond before ending the call. As he ended the call he sat down on the ground once more, but this time with his knees close together and his arms folded.

He did not know what to do. What had he gotten himself into? On one hand he knew he could not afford the £8000, but at the same time he simply had to find a way. It was either £8000 and debt, or losing his auntie, one of the only two family members he had left. Devonte Lacy knew in this moment that he had limited time to find the money and thought about which of his friends may have been able to help him. His mind drew a blank as truthfully he didn't have too many close friends anymore. It was few and far between as he kept his circle close. He had lost many friends back in Atlanta and had left that life behind him all of those years ago. He didn't want to have to contact some of those people he once knew, for he knew if he asked them for a favour, he would be in their debt and they were not people he wanted to be in debt to. He had to find another way.

And then a message popped up on his phone. It was the one man he was close to and did trust, and it was a man who he knew dealt with large amounts of cash. It was his dear friend Bixente Lemaire, who he and many others knew simply as Bix. The message read as follows:

Message Delivered: Bixente Lemaire to Devonte Lacy:
16:42 – 05/11/2065

Wag1 my bro
  You tryna burn one tonight?
  I got some 10/10 cali there
  I was gonna sell this pack but lowkey it was too dank I had to hold onto this one still loool
  Lmk innit. You can roll through mine after work. Hopefully I still got some there when you get here lool

---

Bix was a weed dealer, aka a Shotta, a highly lucrative profession in this current era of Marijuana Prohibition. Ever since the Psychedelic Riots of the late 2040s, following World War Water, and after the United Kingdom officially entered Isolationism in 2045 – Marijuana was strictly illegal and was classified as being a Class A-Star drug in the UK. This meant that those who were able to successfully sell Weed in the UK, typically dealt in big numbers as it was a limited resource, with a high demand. Thus, it was known that the numbers in the Weed game were extremely high, and all of this was underground money, non-taxable. Devonte Lacy had heard stories from Bixente Lemaire about what he had seen in the game, though Bix could only tell him so much as he was somewhat bound to secrecy – a small price to pay considering the benefits it gave Bix. Bix was big time in the weed game; one of the top streamers in the world, friends with all the rappers and athletes, and was always seen with a few loud packs on him.

And so, if anyone would be able to help Devonte front the £8000 that he needed for his auntie's cancer treatment from the National Superior Health Service, it was to be Bix.

Though despite the fact Bix would likely have and be more than happy to loan him the £8000 – he did not want to accrue any more debt to his name as he already had far too many on his name, and he did not know if or when he was going to be able to pay Bix the £8000 back. He already had enough debt to pay back, which was eating away at his otherwise healthy monthly salary. Any more and he would be destitute, for with his current loan and debt repayments he was on a month-by-month expense situation, with no comfort room at all.

And so, he knew he would need to find a way to get the money himself. He looked at Bix's message again and thought, *I do really need a zoot right now.* Though he didn't reply instantly as there was much on his mind.

Amidst all of this going on in his mind, he had forgotten he was at work, which told how much of a state of disarray he was truly in. He loved his job; it provided him with the finances that he needed, but more than all it provided him with a level of catharsis which seemed to be lacking elsewhere in his life and in London. Devonte Lacy was a Mega-Terrarium Executive for the City of London and as such was trusted with decision making on all the private Mega-Terrarium's in London, the only places in the city where large amounts of Ecology and Fauna truly existed in a healthy manner, unaffected by the pollution. It was a haven for nature, and he took comfort on a daily basis that he could be around nature and be entrusted with its care in these Mega-Terrariums. He had gained contacts with the wealthy nought-point-five-percent of the City of London. and was Head Mega-Terrarium Gardener for several of the wealthy elite.

This provided him with access to these beautiful Mega-Terrariums, a haven away from the concrete jungle and polluted air that was London in 2065. Though the caveat was that he had to speak to these people who were out of touch with the reality of the masses and often had to overhear conversations riddled with pomposity and a blatant disregard for the everyday man. In the grand scheme of things – this was a small price to pay. Devonte sometimes felt imposter syndrome as he felt guilty for rubbing shoulders with the rich and pompous, but knew that if he chose not to do this job simply because of them, then someone else would, as these circles of people existed regardless and these Mega-Terrariums also would still exist.

And so, he went back to work assessing the quality of the plants around him and found for a little while he had no stresses as he was completely in the present moment. Then he heard the door crank open and turned his head as he heard the thundering voice of his boss.

"Devonte! My man! Tell me. How's it looking? How's my babies doing?" said the man.

"Ah they looking good Mister Johnson. Same as last week which is good. I did adjust the temperature slightly though. Just cos it was too cold, and …"

"Devonte! How many times have I told you, call me Jarred. I don't call you Mister Lacy do I? You've been working for me for just over a year now. Just call me Jarred," said Jarred Johnson.

"It's okay Mister Johnson. Imma keep it a stack. I call all my clients Mister or Miss or Missus. Ain't nothing personal. Its's, it's just good manners is all."

"Ah well in that case, call me Mister Jarred Lane Johnson, CEO of Johnson Pharmaceuticals!" he said as he puffed his chest up before guffawing uncontrollably, stepping nonchalantly on the plants around.

Devonte's eyes flicked down to the plants and he took in a deep breath. This was a pet peeve of his, one that seemingly all privileged owners of Mega-Terrarium's in London seemed to do. *Bitch ass, if only he knew how precious that plant is in a place like this, he don't know the value*, he thought.

"Alright, well Devonte. Let Reginald know if you need anything. I'm off now but … oh wait a minute. I need to answer this," said Jarred as he went to answer his call. Unaware of his surroundings, he stepped on all the plants again, further vexing Devonte.

"Yes Elisabeth? Yes, darling I'm on my way. No, no. I've already left. I'm in the Rolls right now," said Jarred displaying a cheeky grin and winking at Devonte. "I'm about ten minutes away. No, I'm not lying, I'll be right there. And don't worry. Just tell them my name at the door, they won't shut the doors on us, you've nothing to worry about. They know me," he continued on the phone as he hurried and skipped across to the exit of the Mega-Terrarium.

He wylin' man. Thank f**k he gone, he thought to himself. And so, Devonte went back to his work as he heard the door crank shut behind him, with the sweet familiar hiss of air following the closed door.

Though as soon as he bent down to pick up the device which he used to measure the healthiness of the soil, he heard the door crank open and this time it was the unsweet familiar hiss of air which he heard as he saw Jarred Lane Johnson again trample over the precious plants, as he ran towards him.

"Ah Devonte. One thing. On the weekend I was watching this streamer on the Dark Web 3.0," said Jarred.

On my mama I already know this mother*****r gone ask me about Bix and the weed man. F**k I don't need this sh*t dawg, for real. He done got the game f**ked up boy if he gone fire me for this sh*t dawg.

"This guy called Bix3.0. And well, I'll just be honest and say it openly Devonte. I saw you on there and don't worry I'm not bringing this up to question you or anything. What you do in your personal life is up to you young man. But I was wondering. Considering the status of your friend, and well, what you both were doing. You wouldn't happen to be able to get your hands on any, well, you know, marijuana would you? You know the old Mary-Jane? You see I've got a bunch of business associates coming over from the States next weekend and quite frankly I didn't know who else to ask. It's difficult getting your hands on some," said Jarred.

And just like that, the golden ticket presented itself to Devonte. Without a moment of hesitation he replied, "Yessir Mister Johnson I can get that for you. How much you need?"

"Oh well I don't know. What's like a lot? It's a group of ten of them and I know they all like to partake," said Jarred Lane Johnson, CEO of Johnson Pharmaceuticals.

"Deadass you probably need like a Z then I guess," he replied, with his face unwavering and emotionless. He wanted Mister Johnson to think he knew what he was talking about and did not want him to realise he was getting him way more than he needed.

"What's a Z? Come on Devonte. I don't know what lingo you people use," said Jarred. Devonte knew there was racial connotations behind this comment, but knew he could not call him upon it and instead felt it was the opportunity for him to make use of the racial ignorance of this wealthy white man in front of him.

"Well a Z is twenty-eight-grams, or an ounce. But. You can't buy anything like that from suppliers. It's gotta be like a big order. I ain't even gone cap. Like at least four Z's for them to sell it to you. Cos I mean it's very illegal you feel me. On God I ain't tryna get bagged for being no weed dealer you feel me?"

"Well fine let's get four of these Z's then. And I know the risk you'll be taking. So I am more than happy to pay you handsomely for it. What does a typical Z go for then?".

"A Z go for like £1000 so four Z's be £4000. But that's a lot of weed man. If I get caught with that much then imma be jailed, potentially for like you know. I dunno if I can really be doing that Mister Johnson," said Devonte, as he used the element of truth to his advantage. He knew that for Jarred Lane Johnson, money was not something he had to worry about, and that his concept of what was a lot of money – was far different to him. And he knew that Jarred needed this and would pay, as he said, handsomely for it.

"Well fine. I understand. For your troubles, I'll pay you £8000. Double. That seems fair to me. Does that sound fair?"

"Yessir that sound good. When you need it by?"

"By next Sunday. Can I trust you with this Devonte?"

"Yessir Mister Johnson I can get that bud for you. And don't worry. I'm from South Carolina Mister Johnson so aint no motherf****ng way I gone open my mouth. On my mama I aint ever snitch on nobody bruh. I ain't no snitch man. Snitches get wacked."

"Good man. I knew I could rely on you for this. Well. I'll send you an NFT for the 8K once you bring me the *Bud*. And I'm assuming you'll sort out transport and smell proof storage and what not? I can keep it all here of course, but getting it across here – I can't have it smelling or anything now."

"Yessir Mister Johnson I got that for you. But with that being said, if I get my hands on it earlier, I'll let you know so I can sort the necessary arrangements to get that to you here swiftly you feel me"

"Yes sure. Now well Devonte. I'm glad we have that agreed. Keep well. I'm off now, Miss Cervantes is going to be very annoyed with me if I don't get going . I'll see you next week. Bye now!" he said as he again darted off, stamping on all the plants on his way to the door.

He felt relief as Jarred Lane Johnson left the Mega-Terrarium and left Devonte alone with the plants and trees. He looked down at the ground with his hands on his hips and then up to the top of the glass dome as he saw the tallest tree's longest branch wrestle against the dome. *On my mama, I wish they could be free*, he thought to himself as he looked upon the tree which seemed to want to grow beyond the glass dome of this Mega-Terrarium.

He now took out his phone and proceeded to reply to his Bix. Devonte hadn't the slighted clue how he would go about to get this weed and how he was meant to store and transport it and if he could even get it in such a short space of time. Though he knew Bix would know, and he knew it was likely he would have to speak with The League of Shottas to be able to deal with this large a quantity of marijuana, whilst being protected legally. He texted Bix the following:

Message Delivered: Devonte Lacy to Bixente Lemaire:
17:46 – 05/11/2065

Yo dawg. I'm down. Imma head outta here in like 20, I'm in Belgravia right now. So I'll catch u soon
  But question.
  U think you can hook me up with ur LoS link? I need some real nice bud n I need like 4 z's of it n I need it fast dawg. Already got someone who gone buy a lot of it …

Devonte sent the message and put down his phone. Though as soon as his phone sat down on the brick wall, it buzzed as Bix replied; he was fast with his replies, a part of his occupation being a shotta.

Message Delivered: Bixente Lemaire to Devonte Lacy:
17:46 – 05/11/2065

Snm I can do but you sure you wanna fam? I can do it for you if you want? And I can split the money with you?

Devonte didn't wait a moment to reply.

Message Delivered: Devonte Lacy to Bixente Lemaire:
17:47 – 05/11/2065

Nah dawg
  I appreciate it but u aint gotta
  I finna do this myself
  My time to get into this sh*t you feel me
  Hook me up tho dawg fr. I need the bud by next Sunday. 4zs

Bix instantly. Devonte could tell he was dialled in to the conversation. Whenever it was a conversation related to his job, being a shotta – Bix was always dialled in. Some of it might have been down to his ADHD but he also knew that being a shotta under The League of Shottas gave Bix stability and secure income, meaning he never reverted to the criminal life he had before he was a shotta.

Bix had been in jail and heard of The League of Shottas whilst he was in the pen. He had worked with them ever since he got out of jail. Bix had never been violent ever since and left his darker days behind him.

Message Delivered: Bixente Lemaire to Devonte Lacy:
17:48 – 05/11/2065

Snm bro. I'll message my Honcho today and get a meeting set up for tomorrow if that's good for you? They gotta put you on their books if you sell their sh*t innit

Cos they run sh*t legit there at LoS innit. Obvs its all underground, but they run it like it's a legit ting innit. Mike be strict with it you know

You're gonna have to have a meeting with one of the Honchos innit who'll basically be like your boss and then they gonna give you like documents and codes of conduct etc which you're gonna have to follow

And legit bro. You gotta follow that sh*t as well otherwise they'll f**k you up or they'll give you up to get bagged if you don't

I'll explain more when I see you. I aint gonna say too much now. And you'll see wag1 at the meeting as well

But yh that's why if you want I can just front you the ps now and you can buck me back later. Its all love

---

Devonte read the message and was not surprised to see Bix offer him the money. However, he did not want to rely on anyone else anymore. He was tired of loans and debts, and with this expense; it was his auntie's cancer treatment and so there was something inside him which told him it'd be better if he paid for it himself. For one day he could look back and say he paid for it on his own volition, no matter the method through which he got the money.

I gotta do this for her man, for the family, he thought to himself. It was a pride thing for Devonte Lacy and it was something that likely he could not shake off so easily; it was a calling within him.

AAJ

Its all good dawg. I wanna make this sh*t myself
Let me know wag1 widdit
As long as they can get me 4zs by next Sunday then we good
You know me dawg. Jus setup the meeting.
But anyways. Ill catch u soon. Imma leave here asap. I need a zoot dawg.
Been a longgg day loool

Cool bro. Ill setup the meeting with my Honcho. Lowkey good for me too cos
each time I bring in another shotta to my honcho I get a quick 1000 but dw ill
split that with you lol
And loool dw bro. If they say you're good tomorrow and put you on the books.
Then you can get the 4zs tomorrow even loool
Say less. We can smoke a fat one today then lool. Catch you soon g

A part of Devonte felt ashamed of this path he was to go down, but he felt
he had no choice. He did not want to go down a path of crime, especially
considering this was the path that his father went down. He was ashamed
that he was going down this stereotypical and somewhat antiquated trope
of a brownskin man going down a path of crime.

But he had to follow this path to care for his family and this to him was
more important than anything. He had a BSc in Ecological and Environ-
mental Sciences, an MSc in Plant Biology and a PhD in Terrarium Science.

And now, he was to be a shotta under The League of Shottas. *What a
strange life man,* he thought. He was uncertain of the future ahead, but
regardless, ready for whatever the future held.

112

BOOK 8
DEVONTE LACY

Friday 6ʰ November 2065

*18:11: The Warehouse aka The League of Shottas HQ,
Ilford, Greater London*

Devonte pressed the button neatly tucked away on the left side of the open door of the car, and watched the door slide in swiftly.. Devonte had noticed that he was more in his head than usual. He could feel the rumination in his mind. He could almost visually see, through his feelings, his thoughts moving in and out of focus in his brain, as his internal monologue felt erratic and overactive like a volcano of thoughts. This was anxiety. This is what he felt in this moment as he stood of the soon to be departed e-Cab – the electric cab of choice in the City of London – and looked up at The Headquarters of The League of Shottas.

"This is it bruv. We call it The Warehouse. It's mad innit. Looks like a dump. Like there ain't nothing in it. But real talk. When you go inside your mind is gonna be like *what the f**k, this is a mazza*. Real talk bruv. Oi," Bix stopped his sentence so he could laugh, clap his hands together and then bump shoulders with Devonte, "Nah I'm gassed for you to see this still. I been telling you about this place for a minute now. You gonna see for yourself now bro but obviously when you're inside just act like I ain't told you nothing. Cos slyly I ain't meant to be talking about this place outside of here. Unless I mention it inside there. Obvs then it's calm. Cos lowkey like, the streets know about The League of Shottas cos people talk about it innit

But obviously we're not meant to innit. So it's like one of them things where you don't talk about it, but also everyone does talk about it, but like in a chill and like a respectful way innit. Kinda lowkey innit. So yeah just don't say too much innit. Follow my lead. You'll be calm don't worry." said Bix.

Whilst Devonte was anxious, so too was Bixente Lemaire. However, they were anxious in two different ways. Bixente faced what was positive anxiety as he wanted his friend to finally see his place of work, the place that inspires him, the place that changed his life, the place that gave him an opportunity to be a better man and have a better life. The League of Shottas was somewhat of a university or a trusted establishment for Bixente. When Bixente had been to jail and come out, he did not want to follow down that same path he had been on which got him to jail – though his opportunities for change had dwindled now he was an ex-convict and Bix was okay with this for he knew his actions prior had warranted this categorisation and limitation that society had now put on him.

And so, Bix knowing himself, knowing he would still need money to live in the world, was going to have to find a way to still make money and a life worth living. He had heard of this Underground Corporation, this Underground MegaCorporation which controlled, or at least played a huge part in running and controlling, the weed business in the UK. He had heard of them in prison, and the organisation was The League of Shottas. Bixente still remembered the conversation. He remembered why The League of Shottas were even brought into conversation. However, he could not remember the name of the man who had told him about The League of Shottas, for it was a brief conversation when he was in the yard with another inmate who seemed to only be in the prison for a short time, not long enough for him to make a mark in Bixente's mind. The conversation went a little like this.

The Tech-Night 1.0

The Courtyard, Prison: Bixente Lemaire and the Unnamed Convict
— Sunday 20ᵗʰ November 2063

20:27 – Bixente Lemaire: *Man I'm excited for this one. Youse gonna watch it? The Khan of the Kumite Final. It's in like an hour, I can hook it up to my phone still.*

20:27 – The Unnamed Convict: *Let me check me schedule mate. I don't think I have anything planned? But what the f**k is Khan of the Kumte? Kumite? I dunno how you f**king say it.*

20:28 – Bixente Lemaire: *Bruv Khan of the Kumite? Ayy you know this sh*t man. You probably just didn't know the name of it but real talk you probably seen something from it before. I know you have. Definitely. It's that MMA tournament. You know the that one on the Dark Web, where they allow killings in the quarters, semis and the final. They use weapons as well in the semis and the finals. You've probably seen clips of it before.*

20:28 – The Unnamed Convict: *Yeah rings a bell. But I don't know though. I don't know about that fighting sh*t. Ain't really my thing. That is sounding violent as f**k mate, pretty f**ked up.*

20:28 – Bixente Lemaire: *Yeah but it's like some gladiatorial sh*t, it's mad bruv trust me. Too sick, they man sign up for it innit so why not, you can make p's from it. anyway Anyways though, this year the final got Mike da Silva in it. You know, the IFL 5-Weight and 8- Time World…*

20:28 – The Unnamed Convict: *Ay I know Mike da Silva. The Black Tiger. He, yeah. Fine, yeah, I get it now. He is the f***ing man. Ruthless. I met him like 5 years ago. He Head Honcho of The League of Shottas. Probably still is. Actually he definitely still is, it's his TING. Yeah man fine I am definitely down to see that. He's a f***ing beast. Mike, Mike a good guy too for real.*

20:29 – Bixente Lemaire: *Rah swear you met him? That's sick. Yeah he's hard bruv. He's f**ked I can't lie. Probably greatest fighter of all time. But what's The League of Shottas. That's sounding like some comic book sh*t.*

20:29 – The Unnamed Convict: *I ain't know too much 'bout it. But it's this underground weed organisation. My man runs the whole game in the UK.*

Mike da Silva, League of Shotta – that is the government of Weed. Guaranteed any of the weed you smoked after 2054, yeah that was Mike's. That sh*t most likely, especially if its any good or regulated, that's The League of Shotta's bud. They keep the shit running now. All regulated, and he taxes. But he keep you safe if you with The League of Shottas. As long as your still to Mike's rules – you good.

20:29 – Bixente Lemaire: *Swear down. Why ain't I heard of it then?*

20:29 & 20:30 – The Unnamed Convict: *It's one of them ones when you won't know until you know but then once you know, you see it everywhere. They in the shadows but once you clock the shadows, you realise them shadows be everywhere. The streets know, and the streets respect it cos The League of Shottas respects it. Mike runs that sh*t legit as f**k man. That's why I got a whole lotta respect for that man cos he about his morals and he won't let anyone f**k with that compass. That compass stays strong and it stays looked at and listened to by Mike and by The League. And that's how I know Mike ain't a man to be f**ked. I seen how he deals with people who don't conform to the Compass of The League of Shottas. That's what he called it. What they called it. The Compass. I think it meant like Moral Compass, like the regulations but I aint know for sure. So yeah. Tell me when you're gonna watch that. I'm down. Mike a real one. Cold mother*****r, but he a man of principle and I can always respect that.*

And so, this was how Bixente Lemaire discovered The League of Shottas. And from this moment on his life was changed; through The League of Shottas he found a better path despite the fact they were technically a criminal organisation. He found a vocation in which he could use business acumen and skills, at a company where, surprisingly, morals and rules existed as though it were not an illegitimate industry or product he was invested in. They ran the show like a legitimate business with regulations and safety testing on the weed that was being grown and sold, and tax on the sales of the product.

For Bixente, The League of Shottas were dear to his heart, in a way he could not quite articulate to his friend; being a Senior Shotta and Global Ambassador at The League of Shottas satisfied him on multiple levels. And so, this was positive anxiety for Bixente, entering The Warehouse with his dear friend Devonte Lacy, for it was two parts of his life coinciding.

For Devonte Lacy, it was consequence-based anxiety. He did not know what was to come from his visit to The League of Shottas. He was not sure of what the outcome of him joining was going to be. Was this to be a long-standing relationship? Was this to be a temporary situation? Was this even going to come to fruition? Him being a Shotta? He did not know what the future was to bring with regards to him being a part of The League of Shottas and this is what stressed him as he stood outside of this dilapidated building, this Warehouse. He could not believe that the inside of this building, that Bix had previously described to him, was like a Palace. He did not believe it; his eyes would not allow him to believe it, for logic stated it could not be possible. However, this is why The Warehouse was the perfect Headquarters for The League of Shottas. It was in plain sight, and as such it blended in so well with the environment that people walking by would never think an operation as vast and rich as The League of Shottas would be operating in a building that looked like this Warehouse.

They walked up to the door of the Warehouse and Bix took out his phone and placed his unique QR code to the scanner, neatly tucked on the underside of the letterbox next to the entrance of The Warehouse. *This is it dawg. No matter what you gone need that bread. You gone need that 8k so you gone have to go through with this thing,* Devonte thought. The successful scanning let off a ping on Bix's phone, and the door unlatched and made a grinding sound from the multiple locks, much like the door of the Mega-Terrarium of Jarred Lane Johnson.

"Oh, this QR code gives us access innit. Everyone in The League of Shotts got one innit. They send you an NFT of it, and that QR code is your specific access code, so they can edit it as well and give you access depending on clearance level and sh*t. It's quite a certi system" said Bix. "Well, you'll see inside innit."

"Cool dawg. Let's go inside then. We gone be late for the meeting."

"It's good bro don't stress. My Honcho, the one we got a meeting with, Jamal Pitcher. He's one of the seniors here. He's a Honcho Management Executive. So basically, he's always a bit behind schedule innit. He got bare meetings and sh*t to do, so we good. Plus, we already like five minutes early. Relax bro," Bix replied as he turned to Devonte and swung his arm around him and gripped his shoulder, as he could see the tension in him. Devonte was standing stiff and upright, with his shoulders pushed back and chest saying hi to the sky.

The two walked through the door, which very quickly slammed shut behind them, not allowing sunlight to enter the corridor and not allowing the door to be ajar for any longer than it needed to be. Devonte followed behind Bix as they walked down the dark corridor which eventually seemed to cascade into a somewhat steep staircase going down. It was like a dungeon. Devonte walked down the staircase and towards the light, which seemed to reflect off the white stone which felt rough on his palms as he let them run across the walls to ensure he walked down the stairs safely. They reached the bottom of the stairs and before Devonte and Bix met the man at the bottom of the stairs, guarding the entrance, they encountered the large eerie shadow of the man in front of the door in question.

"Stop. Let's see some ID," said the eerie shadow of the door. He was a true hulk of a man, as tall and wide as the door.

"Come on Samson. Really? I mean obviously I'll get it out but why we gotta do this every time. You know me," replied Bix.

"Protocol Bix, you know how it is. How you doing though fella?" replied Samson, the eerie shadow of the door, as he unclasped his hands which had rested on his solar plexus and raised his left hand into a fist in front of him, met by the comparatively small fist of Bix.

"I'm good man. Can't complain innit. This is Devonte. I sent his details in a doc to Seniesa earlier today innit. So he should be on the Visitor Register," replied Bix as he opened his stance up to allow Devonte to enter the conversation.

"Wagwan," said Devonte as he stood forward and offered his closed fist to Samson, the eerie shadow of the door, expecting it to be matched by his scarily large fist. However, it was not; he was left hanging.

"You American?" Samson asked.

"Yeah dawg. But I done lived in London for years now though," Devonte replied.

"Where you from? Atlanta?" Samson asked.

"Nah I'm from South Carolina, but I get why you thinking Atlanta. The accent kind similar still. I lived in Atlanta for a bit too"

"Alright. One second mate," said Samson the Eerie Shadow of the Door. He took the glasses which sat in the front pocket that was on the chest region of his suit and put them to his eyes. He clicked a button on the side of the MobiGlasses which brough up a screen. Devonte and Bix stayed somewhat motionless but both looked at one another and met eyes for a moment, as Samson navigated through the home screen of his MobiGlasses before finding the handover notes for Friday 6th November 2065, sent to him by The League of Shottas' Administration Assistant, Seniesa Sanches. "Alright. ID please mate. You'll have it back when you leave. And don't worry. I'll be here. One way in. One way out."

Devonte had no follow up questions or anything to reply to Samson. Instead he simply obeyed and nodded his head. He felt it wasn't a choice and so there was no point questioning it.

"Looks fine. But alright now. So, Bix. I've been told your Honcho is running slightly behind schedule. Jamal's pushed youse back fifteen. So you'll see him at 6:45. Oh and just for your information, the big boss is in today, so he'll probably be in on the meeting with the kid alright. But they'll be done by 6:45. I'll shout you when they're ready alright. Now bout this kid here. You know the rules here Bix. You can wait in the café, or you can take your pal on a little tour. Choice is yours fella. Yeah. Sound good. Alright good. Off you go now son," said Samson as he moved out of the way of the door and placed his hand on Bix's head as he walked past and endearingly pushed his head as he walked.

And as Devonte walked into the entrance room of The League of Shotta's Warehouse, he realised Bix had not been lying. The Warehouse was indeed a Palace in disguise, a Palace of Weed. As they walked around, as Devonte smelt the weed, he also smelt the fear of the people who sat with smiles on the faces as they smoked. He was not too sure whether these smiles were genuine or whether it was all a façade; to him it felt like the latter as he gauged the energies in the room. However, he realised either way, this did seem to be a cool organisation to be a part of.

Despite the fact that Marijuana was a Class A-Star drug, here all these people were hotboxing in this vast palace with a deceptive floorspace and in this vast palace which was like a museum hosting some of the seemingly rarest items in the world. Bixente led the way through the palace as they walked through, nodding his head and slapping hands and bumping his fist with many a people along the way. The light from the chandelier, on occasion, blinded Devonte as followed Bix, with the light reflecting either directly from the marble floor or reflecting from his grills then back onto the marble floor and back into his eyes.

A few years back Devonte would have felt out of place being surrounding by so many lavish and expensive things. For he was just an ordinary boy from South Carolina, accustomed to seeing things not quite like this; he had seen pain and struggle. Then he was forced to make his way and become accustomed to the streets of London due to the loss of his mother and father. Since he moved country, he had graduated and worked his way up to being a Mega-Terrarium Executive for the City of London – it meant he had been forced to rub shoulders with some of the richest and most successful people in London, with some of the richest people in the United Kingdom. Because of this, he was used to speaking to people with a lot of money. And so no more did he feel out of place in places like this; he had made his way here, it was his journey here, and he felt he earned his way. He had made his way here, despite everything. Any build of imposter syndrome within him, slowly withered away for Devonte Lacy. *I'm here now.*

And so, Devonte did not feel out of place walking around this palace situated inside a warehouse. Further to this point, Devonte's best friend Bixente Lemaire had found fame just over a year ago.

Bixente was famous online. He was one of the top thirty Streamers in the World and was a Global Ambassador for The League of Shottas. Bix3.0 was his name online and he openly smoked weed on his stream on the Dark Web and had over 10million subscribers for his primarily weed channel. Though Bix, or Bixente or Bix3.0 depending on how you knew him – was friendly with rappers and fighters; the hip-hop, the fight and the weed game were intertwined with one another. The synchronicity between the three industries was ubiquitous regardless of where it was in the world, and Bix3.0 epitomised that on the web. This meant he was a huge asset for The League of Shottas and so once he hit the 500k subscriber mark, The League of Shottas promoted him from Shotta to Global Ambassador.

This meant he was one of a current staple of ten Global Ambassador's for The League of Shottas. He was a big name in the weed industry and culture worldwide and was seriously pushing p. This meant that Devonte had also become accustomed to seeing his friend with a large amount of bread, and Bix frequently bought things he did not need and should not have splashed so much money on.

This was why Devonte was here on his own accord now though; for he needed this money for his auntie's treatment, and he had taken too much from Bix, on a financial level, till this. He no longer wanted to rely on his friend and wanted to make the money for himself. Devonte knew he could make money in this venture too if he committed himself to it, for he had clients from his job as a Mega-Terrarium Executive and Private Gardener that were supremely wealthy and in need of a plug like him who was discreet and well connected.

I ain't no bitch bruh, Imma get this bread myself now. This mother*****r too connected man I aint even gone cap – I gotta step out myself now too bruh, thought Devonte to himself as he saw Bix approach a very familiar group of people who were all sat with zoots in their hands and laughing together, before standing up and each greeting Bix.

"Bix bro! What you telling me fam? Been a minute cuh!"

"I'm good gangy how y'all doing? I ain't even gone cap. I gotta keep it a stack y'all. Narsaying. I gotta keep it a stack" started Bix as the group began to chuckle. It seemed whatever he said the people would laugh. Devonte stood behind Bix, slightly hesitant as he did not know all of those in front of him on a personal level, and so was untrusting to say the least – he did not like fakeness, and he was used to people jumping on the clout of Bix; a caveat of his fame. "Lonza. Girl you looking fire I aint even gone lie. We need to chill sometime," they laughed. "I'm deadass," continued Bix, not allowing the group's guffaws to put him off his game. He was used to laughter and attention, such was the life of an internet sensation. Lonza tilted her head to the side ever so slightly, with a smile on her face, and instinctively pulled down on her skirt with one hand and took in a puff of her zoot with the other hand.

"Bix. You always playing I swear. You know I'm too boujee for you. We ain't ever gonna get it on. But anyways. How you doing though? You look good. I like what you done with your dreads," said Lonza.

"Stop it girl. You gassing me. I knew you and your fine ass BBL was gonna be here," said he said as the group laughed. "I knew the mandem. Hah. I knew the mandem would be here too, so I had to switch it up for y'all."

"L rizz Bix. L rizz, just allow it. You're moving simply g," replied another man, his name was Fyter.

"Bruh you an NPC for real. Why you ain't let me cook dawg?," the group laughed again as Bix spoke in his trademark animated fashion, playing up to the crowd around him as usual – this was standard operating procedure for him, now. Devonte just stood back with him arms folded and chuckled to himself – he had known Bix for a while now and one thing he respected about Bix was that even before his fame, he was as he was now, though now everything he did was simply exaggerated, it was all tuned up to 100 now. "You got no rizz. You wylin telling me I ain't got no rizz. Y'all tell me when you ever seen Fyter spill some W rizz. F**k that actually. Tell me when you ever seen Fyter, Ryter or Wyzer spit some rizz bruh. I'm listening. Don't be questioning my rizz bruh. I'm rizzaldinho for real," said Bix as he turned his body side on and put his hand to his ear

"Ay boy, they all rappers. They all get hella girls bruh. They ain't like you. You gotta spit some game to make up for your face bruh," said Devonte as he entered the conversation. The group laughed.

"Man shutup. Why y'all pressing me?" "F**k you Devonte, what you doing bruh. To be honest though, I can't even say nothing bout my slime's rizz right here. He the rizz king. Y'all probably seen him on my stream. Sh*t man, I ain't even introduce him. I'm glitching what the f**k. I'm bugging no cap. I think some of y'all probably already met. But this my boy Devonte. He's from South Carolina so excuse the accent, but he been living here in London for a minute now innit. With the mandem in the ends. Narsayin, with the mandem in the ends bruv" said Bix as he mocked his British friends with his exaggerated accent and hyper-focus on the British slang.

"Bix shutup bruv. Always mocking the ting. Man's always tryna do the fake London accent. You been here like five years now bruv, you're bait in these ends now. Dunno why you're violating the accent. Anyway though, enough about this jokeman. What you saying Devonte? Nice to meet you bruv. I'm Ryter. These my boys Fyter and Wyzer and you probably already know Str8 Abe, Lonza, Forrest, Fillipa and Sophocles. Sophocles? Bruv sorry I never know how to pronounce your name innit," said Ryter as he shook hands with Devonte.

"Nice to meet you man, and all y'all too. I done seen some of y'all on Bix's stream and on the internet. And you know, things of that nature. Obviously he talk about y'all all the time too," said Devonte.

"Hi I'm Lonza. Nice to meet you," said Lonza as she extended her hand out to Devonte, accidentally looking him up and down.

"Nice to meet you ma'am," replied Devonte.

"Aite what the f**k's going on?" said Sophocles.

"F**k sake she's already claimed him," said Fillipa as she flicked her hair from one said to the other.

"I told y'all. My man's got that W rizz. That unspoken rizz you feel me," said Bix.

"So, what y'all all with it? You know. Y'all all on the books?" said Devonte as he looked around inquisitively. Despite the fact his good friend Bix was a Shotta on the books of the The League of Shottas and was still famous – he struggled to believe these other famous and wealthy people were also on the books of The League of Shottas, as shottas. He couldn't understand why they would need to be considering their status and their profile.

"What you mean as a shotta? You ain't gotta be so coy about it mate, it's all good here," replied Sophocles Tsmikas, he was a former Professional Foot-baller who had played at the very highest level. "Safe space fella. But nah not all of us. So me personally I'm not a Shotta like some of these guys but I'm a Global Ambassador for The League of Shottas. Same as Filipa, Wyzer, St8 Abe, and obviously Bix as you know. Then some people just hang here you know. As long as you got a membership to The League of Shottas Café like Lonza, and Mister Hollywood, Forrest Giles, who's being all quiet for some reason. Then obviously you got some people yeah who are on the books as a shotta, like Bix and Ryter, and obviously like Fyter who used to be one."

"Don't assume g. I can speak for myself innit," said Fyter.

"Cmon man it's all good he don't mean nuttin by it," chimed in Wyzer.

"But yeah man it's a spot here for sure. So yeah, I guess we are all on the books one way or another," said Sophocles.

"Aite bet. Say less. But what y'all ain't worried bout, you know, being famous and open with the weed and all that," probed Devonte.

"Bix check your boy bruv. Asking too many questions. You're talking too much g. Don't even know man like that," said Fyter.

"What? You gone do something about it? You ain't gone do nothing boy. You done got the game f**ked up boy thinking you gone step to me. Step if you bad bruh. Do something," replied Devonte as his face dropped and intensity rose. Fyter was a man of his word, the rowdy one in the rap trio of Fyter, Wyzer and Ryter – he calmly dotted his zoot and stepped up as he said he would before the group quickly stepped in front to stop a brawl from occurring.

"Chill bruh. What the f**k y'all playing at? We in The Warehouse right now bruh. Samson gone come f**k all us up if he see how we moving right now. F**k man. God damn," said Bix.

"Forget Samson. Leroy or Mike will come do the job bruv. They're all here today too. Chill out," said Str8 Abe.

"I don't like his energy bruv. Mans come in thinking he's some big man," said Fyter.

"What I done to you bruh? Why you pressing me bruh?" said Devonte.

"You're asking too many questions bruv. I don't know you g."

"Cos he's tryna get on the books as well man. Devonte's my gangy bruh. Let him cook. He ain't come here on no bad vibes. You pressing him Fyter, Imma keep it a stack. He just curious is all. You feel me? Obviously I done told him how it be round here, but I'm his dawg, so I'm assuming he just wanna hear it from some of y'all too," said Bix as he attempted to ease the tension.

"Real talk bruh. I dunno why this guy getting intimidated by me for," replied Devonte.

"Intimidated?" replied Fyter.

"Cool, cool just leave it. Say no more. Just leave it yeah. We're all chilling and relaxing having a good time. Look around now, everyone else is looking at us now too f**k sake. Samson is deffo gonna come over now. But yes Devonte to answer your question, we all good here. Mike … you know who Mike is right? Mike da Silva?" said Sophocles.

"What The Black Tiger? Yessir, I done seen all his fights. Mother*****r just won the Khan of the Kumite for the second time right? 2063 and 2065 now. Yeah he different gravy dawg. He a legend bruh. Course I know Mike da Silva bruh. He the MMA goat. He a violent mother*****r though

I swear. Mother*****r got something wrong with him. Five-weight world champion man."

"Well yeah that Mike. Mike da Silva, the Black Tiger, the reigning Khan of the Kumite – he's the Head Honcho of The League of Shottas. He owns the whole thing. He started it in 2054 and obviously since then it's grown like crazy. He controls and owns all this, worldwide. That's why we all good here. Mike's connected man. It doesn't matter if we're League of Shottas and famous; Mike got us protected. I mean sh*t, Mike gets all the celebs their stuff. So yeah we're good man, nothing to worry about," replied Sophocles.

"What the f**k? You telling me Mike da Silva is the Head Honcho? What the f**k Bix, why ain't you tell me this before?"

"What you mean? I thought it was obvious. It's like an unsaid thing. Everyone knows man. What you getting onto me for? I didn't realise you was a stupid ass," said Bix. "Bruh you watch his streams what you talking about? Who you think I been talking about when I say Mike? Bruh you seen me on stream with him."

"Yes I watch his streams dawg. He top five in the world bruh. Number one on the Dark Web, obviously I watch them bruh. He a violent mother-*****r. And I don't know. Mike a popular name bruh, could be anyone. That guy on the other said of the room probably called Mike for all you know. Plus I just thought y'all was friends" said Devonte.

"Bruh them streams when he being all violent with the swords and them old ass weapons. He does that here," said Bix.

"So what you telling me when he be fighting them motherf*****s and then killing them, deadass killing them – he does that sh*t here? What the f**k? I thought that was his house or some sh*t? It be the fancy ass basement right with all them weapons and his trophies and sh*t all on the wall?"

"Yeah man that's the Basement here bruh. We call it The War Room. Or just the Basement. That's like Mike's office. Mike and all the other executives have their meetings and disciplinaries there. That's who he be fighting in them streams bruh. It's people who break the Rules and Regulations of The League of Shottas. Mike a violent man bruh."

"Why you think he gets away with all that on the streams? The obvious violence and murder? It's cos he owns all this sh*t man. Mike's powerful as hell. That's why it's all good for us. He's got everyone in his pocket. Police, judged, everything man. But yeah I'm sure they'll tell you all this later," continued Sophocles.

"Anyway though you gonna see it yourself big man. That's where all the introduction meetings with The League of Shotta's take place. He'll probably tell you all about it as well since he's here today," said Fyter. "Hahah you ain't talking so much now are you big man."

"I ain't scared bruh I'm just confused. I'm surprised I didn't know this sh*t bruh. And man f**k. Mike da f**king Silva. Imma be a little starstruck though for real, I aint even gone cap. Lowkey I'm scared as hell now," said Devonte as the group chuckled at the final statement.

"That's all good but you will be scared. Soon enough," said Fyter.

And so, it seemed game was run by the International Fight League (IFL) Hall of Fame fighter – Mike da Silva, endearingly known as 'The Black Tiger'. In the IFL MMA promotion, the World's premier MMA promotion and fighting competition, he was a five-weight World MMA champion from Welterweight to Cruiserweight. He was the consensus greatest of all time (GOAT) in Mixed-Martial-Arts.

Mike da Silva was now, in pop culture, more known for being the back-to-back Khan of the Kumite and current reigning Khan of the Kumite – a no-rules underground MMA tournament run by the wealthy elite of South and South East Asia, strictly shown on the Dark Web. Mike was not a man to be trifled with and was running the biggest underground Marijuana operation in the UK – The League of Shottas.

The League of Shottas was somewhat of a myth in the streets, though all knew it was real. Any shotta who was around for a significant amount of time in the UK, was likely under their ranks. And anyone who had been bagged for being a shotta, was likely in jail because they had disobeyed or gone against the organisation, which went to show the power that Mike da Silva and The League of Shottas had.

"Alright Bix. Come on let's go. I got Sheila by the door for now so come quick fella. Bring the yank," said Samson, as he startled the group, he had seemingly appeared out of nowhere, a commendable feat considering his size.

"I ain't from New York dawg. I already told you …," replied Devonte.

"Cool. I don't care. Come on now yank."

They followed suit, Devonte noticing that Bix was not talking quite as much or being quite as animated and energetic as he was before; he appeared nervous.

Samson led the way and just about managed to squeeze his frame into the stairway which lead down to the basement, or "The War Room" as it was affectionately known. He knocked on the door three times, and this was followed by three knocks on the other side of the door.

"Alright you're in boys. I think the disciplinary is still going on but Mike's wrapping up in there so enjoy the free show," said Samson as he opened the door slightly ajar for Bix and Devonte to enter.

Disciplinary? Devonte mumbled to himself as he remembered what he saw on Mike's live streams on the Dark Web – he was not ready for this. Prior to coming to The Warehouse with Bixente Lemaire, he did not realise that the man he was to be answerable to was Mike da Silva. He stood motionless as he pondered whether he wanted to do this. However, this ponderation had come too late. Samson pushed Devonte through the door and slammed it shut.

And so, it seemed the time had come. Devonte Lacy was to meet Mike da Silva, Head Honcho of the League of Shottas.

BOOK 9
DEVONTE LACY

Friday 6th November 2065

18:45: The Basement / The War Room in The League of Shottas HQ

"Well, well, well. Look what the cat dragged in! Bix. The man himself. The top dawg himself! Come here little man, been a while … oi shut the f**k up blud. You keep your mouth f**king shut till I tell you to speak mother-*****r. You lost your right to speak. That's why I'm shutting your mouth for you," said Mike da Silva, the Black Tiger.

He was wearing a crisp white shirt with splatters of blood it. Mike stood over a beaten and bloodied figure whose face could hardly be recognised even if you had known who he was. It was irrelevant who he was. His fate at this stage was inevitable. He would not be making it out of this room, not alive at least.

"What's good Honcho. It's cool, I ain't tryna come near you right now dawg. You got blood and sh*t on you. I ain't … I ain't too good with blood dawg," said Bix as his short frame stood tall with his hands clasped and rubbing together as he spoke.

"Hahah of course, of course. I forgot you too p**sy for this shit," said Mike. "Is you a p**sy Bix?" he probed, erupting into manic laughter.

"Well … I … ," Bix stuttered. Devonte stood tall behind Bix and kept his pose and stance straight, though his eyes flickered quickly as he scanned around the room and looked at his best friend Bix, who he had never seen so flustered and lost for words. Devonte's eyes now found its way to Mike da Silva, the famous Mike da Silva who he had watched growing up and continued to watch now as a grown man. The man was frightening to watch online, amazing but frightening – though his presence and aura could not be felt truly online. He was an entirely different beast in-person.

"Hahah don't worry Bix I'm playing. Hold up one minute though yeah. Let me get back to this sucker. My guy here broke the first, second, and third motherf****ng Commandment of the Compass. The first, second and third. So of course, of course, he just had to have the trial. He had to. He's legally entitled you know. And we're in the middle of his Trial by Combat right now. But hold tight Bix imma be with you in just a minute. We're just about at the end of the Trial now," said Mike with a smirk on his face.

Devonte, as he typically did, scanned the room and saw the faces of those sat around the room and sensed the fear, or respect, they all had for him. Though he recognised that some of the people seemed to be completely contented despite the violent beating to death this man was evidently receiving – this must have been normal for them, they were desensitised completely. Devonte watched Mike's streams on the Dark Web and watched most of the fights he would have with people in this Basement – he had never realised they were disciplinary meetings for the League of Shottas. *Mike be taking the piss for real,* Devonte thought to himself. The fights started off as direct combat between Mike and his opponent, each with a weapon in their hand, before Mike disarmed his opponent and then chose to fight hand-to-hand combat; and Mike always won for he was simply too good.

And now Devonte focused his attention on Mike da Silva's energy and presence, to gauge how he himself should behave. He saw how seamlessly Mike switched between being cordial with Bix, to then be thumping this utterly pulverised, bloody, and now defenceless man. He looked at the face of Mike and looked at his large dark brown eyes which were laser focused on his target. He continued to pummel the beaten and bloodied figure with more straight right hands as blood launched from the man's nose and latched onto the hair on the knuckles of the Black Tiger's left hand, which was clasped onto the man's rather large left trap (the muscle between the shoulder and the neck) with ease, like he was holding down a piece of paper with his left hand and writing with his right hand.

Mike's eyes did not move from the pulverised man and he continued to throw right hands on his face, but now changed the position on his face that he was launching those clobbering shots onto and kept his eyes locked on the man. And then, for a brief moment, he looked up and locked eyes with Devonte Lacy who was in a state of petrification.

He stopped punching and dropped the man like a sack of potatoes. His eyes were now fixed on Devonte who stayed motionless and firm in his stance, despite that fact that he took in a deep breath through his nose and gulped. He felt his Adam's apple move in his neck and realised he had never felt his Adam's apple feel so heavy in his neck before. Mike, astute as ever, saw the slight movement in Devonte's neck. The Black Tiger attempted to rub the blood off of his hands by rubbing them on his now already bloodied shirt and walked towards Devonte, disrespectfully stepping on the torso of the downed man. He stood directly in front of Devonte and looked him up and down. They were both the same height, though their frames were far different. And much to Mike's surprise, though his expression did not show him, Devonte did the same and looked Mike da Silva up and down.

"Cigar please Seniesa," said Mike as he outstretched his left hand. Seniesa Sanches stood up from between the group of men who sat on the velvet and leather sofa, with gold detailing between the wooden frame of the sofa and walked towards him. He took the lit Montecristo Linea 1935 Dumas Cigar from her hand – this was his favourite cigar. She quickly looked up at Devonte as she backed away from the two; Devonte kept his eyes on Mike, as Mike did to him. Mike blew the smoke in Devonte's face, who felt his eyes sting, squinting due to the discomfort.

"What's your name kid?" said Mike.

"It be Devonte sir," replied Devonte.

"Devonte," said Mike as he looked Devonte up and down one more time. "Proper American name. You Bix's boy?"

"Yessir. I done known Bix for a long ass time, long ass time."

"Well, if you're a friend of Bix, then you're a friend of mine," Mike outstretched his hand, which Devonte shook instantly. "Have a seat young man. You too of course Bix. We'll get to your business here in a moment. Sit down between Mister Weah and Mister Raushanfikri over there in the corner please. I'm sure you know who they are."

Devonte nodded his head and proceeded to walk over to the corner to sit between Terry Weah and Zion Raushanfikri. However, Devonte awkwardly stopped in the middle of the room, right next to the dropped combat weapons and next to a pool of blood as he saw Mike embrace Bix. He lovingly put an arm around Bix and lifted him up with one arm as he held onto his shoulder. The whole room laughed.

"Don't worry Bix I'll buy you some new clothes. I know you're scared of blood," said Mike.

"You big, but you a dumbass for real. I beat your ass if I wanted to I ain't even gone cap," Bix replied as Mike and the room let out a guffaw. Devonte's lip dropped as Bix dropped this line to Mike da Silva, the Black Tiger, and observed the room as Bix said this. His eyes flickering from left to right, and back again. Devonte was astonished at how Bix could get away with saying such a thing to a man such as Mike in a room and scenario like this. *I guess that just be Bix man,* though Devonte to himself. Bix walked towards Devonte with a smile on his face as he was now at ease, his body language was in stark contrast as to when he had first entered the room. Bix walked towards Terry Weah and Zion Raushanfikri and lifted his head up before slapping hands with the both of them as they shuffled across the luxurious sofa to make room.

"Sit down young man," Zion Raushanfikri said to Devonte, in his patented and instantly recognisable deep voice, as he tapped on the seat next to him as he kept his legs crossed; he was very relaxed in this environment.

Devonte, despite feeling slightly uneasy due to the extreme violence he was witnessing, was strangely put at ease by Zion Raushanfikri and Terry Weah. Zion was the announcer and lead presenter of the Khan of the Kumite, whilst Terry was the President and Promoter of the International Fight League (IFL), the leading MMA promotion in the world. Devonte had seen them both countless times online and so it comforted him to see their faces in the flesh, a sense of familiarity in this unnatural environment was welcomed.

Devonte through his periphery looked across to Bix and recognised that Bix too was not looking comfortable. He seemed to have warmed up slightly, but still he was not relaxed; and he realised then, that this was likely the first time that Bix had seen a disciplinary too, despite the fact that he had been with the League of Shottas for a while now.

"It's aite young blud. He had it coming," said Terry Weah, as he looked straight on ahead at Mike da Silva taking care of business by applying his fists to the already battered face of the downed man, unflinching, unwavering & emotionless, as he took a puff out of his cigar. "You wanna smoke? We got zoots, blunts, or even roll-ons like they smoke in the Caribbean. Or we got vapes as well, if you're a b**ch like Bix," he continued, as he winked to Devonte. "Or if you're a real man we got cigars too."

"I'm good bruh thank you," said Devonte. He wanted a cigar and he wanted a blunt; but he did not feel comfortable taking one. He was overwhelmed by the situation. Terry made a face and shrugged at Devonte's response, for Terry always offered to share a smoke.

And finally, Mike da Silva stopped. It was not to take a break because he was tired. It was not because his knuckles were swollen from the impact of his fist directly hitting the skull of the man, with the velocity at which he was throwing his punches; a velocity that could have broken his hands had he continued at the rate he desired to do so. He stopped punching because the man was no longer responding to the Black Tiger's thudding blows. Unfortunately for the man, he was conscious still. Through what little facial tics the man was still able to make through the soft tissue which was swollen irreparably, the Black Tiger could see his prey was still alive. His prey was still there for the taking. There was more punishment yet he could deliver.

However, the Black Tiger did not simply want to catch his prey as a normal predator in the food chain would. Mike da Silva was an apex predator, and one with a sadistic stream; one with a penchant and near insatiable craving for violence. This man in front of him did not test his abilities in the slightest, and so he toyed with his prey and enjoying doing so. The sadistic nature deep within him, driven by something burning deep within him that he could never quite understand himself, was never satiated but seemed to be as close to being satiated either when he was in the midst of a fight that was testing his abilities, or when he could toy with the prey in front of him; the competitiveness or helplessness from his opponent gave him satisfaction.

Mike da Silva had taken losses in combat before. His record in Mixed-Martial-Arts was an exceptional one, though not without losses. He was 60-8 across five weight classes – he was the only five-weight world champion in MMA history; a champion from 170lbs to 230lbs across a nineteen-year career. Though those eight losses were against the highest calibre of opponent, and he had avenged all but one of those defeats. However, outside of the octagon, outside of the case, with no rules – he was the king. The Khan of the Kumite tournament consisted of combat without rules, with the usage of weapons, and where death was the final outcome – and in this domain, the Black Tiger was undefeated, for this was his domain. This was the closest thing to the gladiatorial venue of ancient times; and this was where he thrived.

Mike walked from the near lifeless corpse on the floor and walked past Seniesa Sanches, who stood with a digital clipboard in her hand in her stunning red dress made of polyester, over to one side of the basement and allowed his calloused and blood splattered palms to brush over his assortment of antique weapons. It was one of the greatest collection of antique weapons of war and they were all in the possession of Mike da Silva.

What once started as a hobby and fascination for history and combat, had evolved and become something else entirely. Mike da Silva had brought these weapons of war back to life through actually using them in these Trial-by-Combats at the League of Shotts, and now also at the Khan of the Kumite in both 2063 and 2065.

Mike da Silva looked through his collection for a moment, before gravitating to an ornate but slightly rusted dagger with the jaguar head handle, made of jade, and grabbed the dagger – allowing the dagger to move around seamlessly between his hands, and within moments it seemed the dagger was now a part of his arm; he was at one with the weapon. Considering the nature of this act was that of a sadistic and violent one, Mike found his heart rate drop as he tightened his grip on the dagger and tread carefully towards his prey, almost like a ballerina or a thief walking on a creaky wooden floor, towards the near lifeless body. The Black Tiger flung the dagger from his right hand to his left hand as he danced across the marble floor. However, somewhat to the chagrin of the Black Tiger, the man managed to make his way to his feet in a final act of defiance, and as such his method of death had been determined by this final act of bravery from the man who was soon to meet his death. The Black Tiger saw this as a challenge to himself, or as a sign that he had not inflicted the type of damage that he thought he ought to have, and was capable of; he was now angered, for he had high expectations of himself, especially so with combat.

The Black Tiger, kicked down on the front of the man's left knee and Devonte Lacy could not help but instinctively shriek aloud as he saw the man's bone protrude through the back of his knee and through his jeans; the man was now on the floor and in excruciating pain, a pain so unbearable, he could barely scream.

"Don't be a bunch of p**sies. Shutup, watch, and enjoy it. Be present you know. See it as it is. That's a master at work right there. You don't know how privileged you are seeing this man, this warrior, in front of your very eyes, working. Working this man. A private showing, live in the flesh. And learn. Learn from this guy's mistakes and you'll never have to worry about this aite. This is what happens if you don't abide by the Compass of Commandments," Terry Weah said to Bix and Devonte as he sat forward on the sofa, eagerly watching. Terry's look did not waver as he said this.

And in one swift motion, in a moment which seemed to pass by as quickly as a shooting star would pass through the sky, the Black Tiger firstly slashed across the back of both knees of the man, before then slashing across the back of both Achilles of the man. Blood seeped out the man like water out of the Trevi fountain. To Devonte this was merciless and unnatural, ungodly even. Though to the Black Tiger, it was poetic; a violent work of art, and the Black Tiger smiled with pride.

"He dared walk around here knowing he supplied unregulated, unchecked, unsafe marijuana in my domain. He dared walk around here knowing this is the first Commandment of the Compass of the League of Shottas. He knows the history of this organisation. Everyone hears it day one. They know why I started this sh*t. Breaking the first was enough for me to end this man. But then the mother*****r disobeyed the third Commandment too. The mother*****r used knives. He carried knives. A weak weapon when not used in direct, organised and predetermined rules of combat. A b**ch uses a knife. He used knives on a man whilst on my books, our books, as a Shotta of the League of Shottas. And then he broke the second Commandment and he killed a man. And still, he had the cheek to walk in here. So that's why fool. That's why you die today. This is why you die from blood flowing from your Achilles as though it were the river Nile. This is why I use the dagger on you. You have lost your right to live and I am pleased to provide you with your sentence," said the Black Tiger in his final sentence to this man; the Trial was over.

"Seniesa. Tell Samson to send the cleaners in. Let him bleed out first of course, then get his ass out of here. Burn him," said Mike da Silva who had now returned. He turned into the Black Tiger whence he engaged in combat or violent activities. Though now he had purged, and somewhat satiated his intrinsic desire for violence, and given the man the right to his Trial-by-Combat for disobeying the Compass of Commandments of the League of Shottas – he was Mike da Sila again.

"Sorry boys. Let me just clean up quickly alright. I'll be right back. I appreciate you all waiting. Thank you for your patience," said Mike as he bowed to the group with both hands by his side, a custom he learned in Japan, before leaving the room to clean himself up and change clothes. He seemed a different man to the one who had just murdered the lifeless corpse bleeding out on the floor. Remorse now showed on the face of the man; a single tear rolled down his face.

The men and women around the women muttered on as usual to one another as Mike had now left the room. Devonte and Bix watched on at those in the room as they expected more of a reaction at the sinister act of violence they had all witnessed. However, instead this group of people seemed to be completely contended with what they had seen.

Devonte Lacy and Bixente Lemaire had previously seen the violence of Mike Da Silva only through a digital screen, but even the hyperreality that the digital viewing experience offered them – could not truly prepare one to witness the act in real life, for there were far more factors at play rather than the brutality in itself. It was seeing the blood ooze out of the man in real life, it was the invisible but still very tangible energy and vibrations that Mike Da Silva was radiating as he took out this act, and then there were the sound of the thumping punches from The Black Tiger landing on the man's body, as well as just being able to physically see it in front of them. Viewing something through the digital lenses offered a distance and thus protection from the act; for it seemed to be something other and outside of the realm of reality. Devonte Lacy thought of how he had grown up idolising Mike Da Silva. He no longer idolised him.

Devonte previously had only ever seen one man die in front of his very own eyes and this was a man he saw his father kill. He wished he had never seen this and neither was he ever meant to see it. It had fractured his relationship with his father beyond repair. He did not want to become his father. And so, he hated being called Devonte Lacy Junior, because he did not like Devonte Lacy Snr. And for a moment, he forgot where he was, as he pondered upon the trauma of his past.

"Yo he coming back bruh," said Bix, as Devonte's wandering mind jolted back to the present moment.

Mike walked back into the room with a swagger that was hard to put into words. He oozed presence and commanded attention and control wherever he walked – it was a self-assuredness. Mike adjusted the cufflinks on his shirt, ensuring this was showing slightly under his dark navy, tailor made, suit which was pinstriped. Though the pinstripes were not lines; instead it read 'The Baddest Mother*****r'.

"Alright let's get straight into it," said Mike as he now stood directly in front of Bix and Devonte who were sat down between Zion Raushanfikri and Terry Weah. Mike offered his fist out to both of them, who met his fist with their own as they chuckled to themselves.

"So you're a friend of Bix," he continued.

"Yessir," replied Devonte.

"How can I know I can trust you? I don't know you. We trusted this man you saw die today. I trusted him. And here we are now. I had to dead the man. Now you know why I did that?"

Devonte took a gulp, not meaning to. "No Sir."

"Cos he broke the Commandments of the Compass. And it weren't just any of the them. He broke the first, second and third – the most sacred of commandments. Without these commandments we'd just be like any criminal organisation. This ain't no mafia ting. This is legit. It's as legit as we can get while still being underground technically. This is a business. And without our principles in life, we are nothing. Now do you know what the Commandments of the Compass are? Has Bixente here told you about them?"

"No sir," replied Devonte.

"Good. That's a good thing. Better we don't talk about our business to outsiders. But you ain't an outsider no more. You wanna be one of us," replied Mike as he folded his arms and smiled. "So tell him Bix."

"Well. I ain't gone lie I don't know what they be word for word. But imma paraphrase if that's aite with you Mike," said Bix.

"Go on then," Mike replied, taking a puff of his cigar again.

"Well. The first one be all weed we sell as a Shotta under the League of Shottas, gotta be regulated, tested and grown to comply with the Marijuana Regulation and Safety Protocols. It gotta be League of Shotta's certified innit. League of Shottas created all of that," said Bix.

"Yes that's correct," said Mike. "Now why is that? What you thinking?" Seniesa passed Mike da Silva a Digi-Pad. "Mister Lacy Junior."

"It's Devonte. I'd prefer you call me Devonte. I don't go by Junior."

"Why not Junior?" said Mike.

"Cos I don't like it. I done already told you," replied Devonte.

"Why Junior?"

"Bruh, cos I said so," said Devonte as he took in a deep breath and let out a sigh as he tried to control his rage.

"Yo chill dawg," muttered Bix as he sensed the tension rise out of nowhere. He nudged Devonte, attempting to remind him of where he was and who he was talking to.

"It's okay Bix. Its aite. Why can't I call you Junio? Junior."

Devonte stood up.

"Cos I done already told you bruh. I don't like being called Junior. Why you need a reason for?"

Mike stepped forward and laughed to himself as Devonte squared up to him. Zion Raushanfikri and Terry Weah puffed on their respective Cuban cigars, a Partagas and Ramon Allones, as the smoke crossed over across the front of Bix's face, in a weirdly intimidating way.

"Okay. Devonte it is then. Sit down young buck. Chill out.."

Devonte sat down.

"I just asking you not to call me Junior is all. I ain't trying to cause no disrespect. I'm just asking you respect me is all. And I can respect you too if you feel me. I ain't see why that's such a problem," said Devonte.

"I feel you. Damn kids got a bit of bite ain't he. But listen Devonte, just tell me why?" said Mike. Devonte had shown a part of himself and Mike had sniffed it out like a shark drawn to blood. He had now his full attention and curiosity. "Is it cos of your dad? Says here he's in prison right now?"

"I beg you stop talking about this bruh. I ain't finna talk about this sh*t. I ain't even know you like that dawg. I understand this be your establishment but I ain't talk about this sh*t like that."

"Leave then kid. Remember you walked into my office. You sought after me. I don't need you. You need me. And now you've seen what you've seen, I cannot let you walk out of here like that without anything. So Devonte Lacy, if you're gonna be a part of my establishment. I need to know who you are bruv. You came here okay. You came to me. To my crib. And you want an opportunity from me. Don't get sh*t twisted here and know your place. Look around you kid This is my shit. I have been respectful to you. If anything you ain't been respectful to me stepping in my face like that. But, I like you and so I've let it slide. And frankly, you ain't nothing to me. See, I find you stepping in my face funny; cos I'd snap you like a motherf****ng twig. But I can tell you got balls and I respect any mother*****r that got balls. So you got me on that. Now you just need to tell me wagwan with this Junior sh*t. Cos I'm curious now. Terry curious too; I can see. Look bruv, he's f**king laughing at you right now. So be a f**king man and say your sh*t. Don't let that sh*t control you young buck. You came in here and I just said Junior and you got your little knickers in a twist, about to lose yourself one of the biggest opportunities you got in front of you. You know who I am. You're speaking to the Head Honcho of the League of Shottas. Not everyone gets to do that for their introduction. And I like you. That's why I'm tolerating your sh*t. So go ahead now. And own your sh*t. Step up, be a man. Don't let your insecurities or past control you kid. Own it."

There was stone cold silence. All eyes were on Devonte. All that moved in the room, was the smoke from the cigars and zoots.

"Aite. I don't like being called Junior cos I don't like my father. I don't like that mother*****r, and I ain't him. That's it bruh. It's my bad if I came across disrespectful like that. I ain't mean to. I just stand up for myself wherever I go sir. It ain't nothing personal. I ain't a violent mother*****r or nothing and I ain't aggressive. It just be instinct. But I do got a temper sometimes. My bad Mister da Silva. I got respect for you for real," said Devonte as he humbled himself. He felt at ease and realised the opportunity he had before him and realised where he was. Sometimes it was better to sit back and listen. He had to be careful and Mike had a point. He had exposed himself and shown weakness, and now it was out in the open.

"Cool. Is that it? Weren't so hard now was it? I respect your honesty. That was some vulnerable sh*t and I can respect that. I don't like my pops either; man never f**king believed in me, but here we are. King of the f**king castle. But see. Now we have an understanding and I respect that you held your own. We can move on now. So the question still remains. Why do you think my weed, that all my shottas sell, has to be safe and regulated? Cos this is important. This is what separates us from everyone else, from the criminal underground weed organisations of all other countries."

"Well I'm assuming cos it means then all the weed y'all sell goes through your systems, so you keep the profits and so that they all have some similarities and ways of verifying your sh*t compared to other people's sh*t," said Devonte.

"That's smart thinking but that's not it. Now that you've shared a bit about yourself to the group, I'll share a bit about myself – the whole reason why I started this organisation. I did not start the League of Shottas because of money. I had hundreds of millions in my bank account before I started the League of Shottas. Money is not a concern for me. And it's not because I love weed. Well I do love weed, but that's not why I started this. I started this because of the first commandment. My daughter died Devonte. My eldest daughter. My only daughter died. She died in the year 2053, twelve years ago now. And to be honest, I still haven't recovered from it. She died from a bad batch of edibles. Can you believe that? She was sixteen years old man. She'd be twenty-eight now and I can never hold her, or see her face again. Ain't that a mother*****r. She had just finished her GCSE's and wanted to celebrate with her friends, and she died for it. That's why I started the League of Shottas. Cos the government, this country. They didn't care for her, or people like her. People smoke weed every day in this country. But this sh*t's illegal. People still do it. Think about how much money is spent on it, money that cannot be taxed. So why don't they just make that it legal? This way they could also regulate it so that it's being grown in a proper way, in a healthy way and regulate it so that people like Leyla won't be taking in bad sh*t that could f**k them up," teared rolled down the hulk's face as his face remained emotionless – no matter how stoic he was, his body could not deny the hurt he felt; he always cried telling this story.

He continued, "So they forced my hand. I lost the greatest thing in my life because of this problem. And so I took sh*t into my own hands. I killed for the first time after that. And ever since then this addiction has been something I gotta live with. I hate killing Devonte. I f**king hate it. But I'm addicted. In sport it's all good. In combat I got to. In the Khan of the Kumite I got to cos it's the competition, and its kill or be killed. It's the highest level of combat, and I am the greatest combat athlete of all time. I am not afraid to say it no more. But these disciplinaries. They kill me man. I lose a bit of Mike da Silva every time I gotta end someone, but I gotta do it. I'm addicted to it. And this is what it takes to protect the integrity of what we're doing – then I will do it. If someone sells unregulated weed, I have to punish them. This is who I am. This is what I'm here for. The government of this country couldn't protect the people from that dud weed, and so here I am doing it. I make sure that all the weed my company sells, is safe and regulated. And if it ain't, then I will be the judge, jury and executioner on anyone who doesn't abide to the Compass of Commandments of the

League of Shottas. And all my shottas abide by my rules. And they all pay their taxes. And they work hard. And drug related crime has gone down with me in charge. That's why the authorities don't f**k with me and it's why I got an agreement with them. Cos they know I got this sh*t on lock. I fill that hole the government left. This man I ended today, he broke our commandments. And so he met his death – this is what it takes Devonte. You understand? Now carry on Bixente," said Mike.

"Damn bruh. Okay Mike, you got it. So, the second one is no killing unless you got permission from a Honcho. Third one is no knives or guns. Fourth one is don't talk about The League of Shottas to anyone, even to the feds and to people tryna buy sh*t from you. Fifth one is you can't sell any other drugs if you a shotta under The League of Shottas, unless that sh*t be Magic Mushrooms, and even then that sh*t gotta be safety regulated and you gotta get approved to be selling that sh*t. And then finally the sixth one is you gotta pay the taxes on all the sh*t we sell which is 40% and this gotta be deducted from when you make the sale, ain't no pay it back later. That's the six Commandments of the Compass. Obviously they be a whole list of sh*t you gotta comply with cos you get a document and NDA (non-disclosure-agreement) you gotta sign and sh*t. But they be the commandments. I think I got all of that right," said Bix.

"Thank you Bix. Yep that's it. You got it, well done. So yeah kid, that's it. They're simple. Don't break them. If you sell unregulated weed, or if you kill, or if you use guns or knives. You will answer for this. You'll be entitled to a trial, and that's a Trial-by-Combat, which you just witnessed today. You saw the end of one today but I'm sure you've seen my streams on the Dark Web. That's what this was. I carry out all the Trial-by-Combats. Me. So you break any of the first three, then you gotta come to me. And if you break any of commandment four, five or six - you'll have a disciplinary hearing and you'll either get a suspension, permanent banning, or you could be a Headline Arrest for the police. A Headline Arrest, means we'll hand you over to the police so that they can reach their arrest quota; it's part of my agreement with the police. I own a jail and I got judges in my pocket, so we can really fast-track that process. All clear. You understand?"

"Yessir understood."

"Good. Easy. When you leave, Seniesa will send you all the files and details through to you as an NFT on the Dala Device so that it's unique to you and verified by you. Personally I don't use that sh*t; I got people who do that for me. But you gotta verify yourself using that okay," said Mike. "Anyway, I'm off. Me and Mister Weah got some business to discuss. Everybody, you've got my number. Let Miss Seniesa know if there's anything urgent. I'm booked for today but we'll get something in the diary no doubt."

"Yes sorry everyone; I'm taking the Head Honcho away for now. We've got important IFL stuff to discuss now. I'm trying to convince this man to come back to IFL for a Heavyweight season," said Terry Weah as he smiled and slapped Mike on the back.

"Well I'm there as long as it's a heavyweight salary," replied Mike.

"Well let's go talk Mike. You know we deliver."

$$\cdots \qquad \cdots \qquad \cdots$$

"Okay so as Mister da Silva said, please get your Dala Device ready please Devonte. I'm just about to send you the NFT of your NDA with the League of Shottas, Terms of Employment, and most importantly, the Compass of Commandments of the League of Shottas … which you should have now received. You will need to open the file and accept this using the Retinal Verification Scanner which will certify that this is your unique copy and that you agree to abide by all that is in these files. And as Mister da Silva said, non-adherence to this could result in varying degrees of punishment depending on the severity of your non-adherence. Now if you have any questions. Now is the time to ask," said Seniesa in an assertive voice; she was all about business.

"Yes Seniesa. I got a question. When you gone let me take you out sometime girl?" said Bixente with a smirk on his face.

"Never Bix," she replied.

"Why you still playing hard to get?," replied Bix.

"Don't mind my friend. He always be clowning for real. I'm Devonte. It's good to meet you ma'am.," said Devonte as he extended his hand out for a handshake.

Seniesa did not meet his hand with her own.

"Nice to meet you. Now any questions regarding what I've told you?"

"Rah girl. You just gone leave me hanging like that?" said Devonte.

Seniesa shook Devonte Lacy's hand. "Now any questions?"

"No ma'am we all good. Crystal clear. I'll verify that sh*t now," said Devonte. He opened the file up on his Dala Device, skimmed through the documents, saved it to his Web3 cloud, and initiated the Retinal Verification Scanner which as usual, made him shake slightly for a brief moment as he felt his pupils dilate due to the sensation. "All done b."

"Great. Now any future questions you have, you've got the contact details on the bottom of all the documents including my work email and work number. Please feel free to shoot any questions you may have regarding our League of Shotta's operations my way, but do note that there are several shottas on our books, so please only use my direct line if it is an urgent matter."

"Cool sounds good ma'am."

"Great. Bix mentioned to me prior to your introduction today that you wanted to place an order for four Z's? And for the sake of clarity, just so we're on the same page – a Z is twenty-eight grams of weed. Am I right in assuming this is the amount you'd like to order?"

"Erm yes ma'am if that's good. I need it asap, I ain't even gone cap."

"That's fine. We have plenty in storage. Our team will help you with safe transportation and we'll provide you with smell proof containers, and things to maintain the relative humidity of the weed. But please note that when you do make the transaction with your client, regardless of the amount you sell the weed for, you will need to deduct the forty-per-cent taxes at the point of sale, once you've taken it from the client, and have this sent over to our League of Shotta's account and this must be done within twelve hours of the sale or else you will be summoned for a meeting, which will take place as soon as possible. These details are now embedded within your Dala Device contact list, for your ease, and this is something that was done as you accepted and verified the documentation sent to you. Is that clear?"

"Erm yes ma'am all good. Crystal clear," replied Devonte. He tilted his head and looked around the room to see if anyone was watching their interaction. It seemed everyone was distracted with something else; though as he looked around once more, he locked eyes with someone who he had not seen on his first look around. Zion Raushanfikri had his eyes firmly planted on Devonte Lacy, puffing his cigar with his legs crossed, and with his diamond-coated-gun hanging from his waistcoat underneath his blazer.

"Okay well you're free to go now. You can choose the quality of the weed you're going to sell from our selection in storage, though do note that some of the strains come at a minimum sale price per gram; to ensure you're not selling below production or value. Samson will introduce to our in-house grower and regulator, Virender, who will take you through all the finer details and nuances. Any questions?"

"No ma'am you explained it all good for real. You a real professional. I'll ask Virender at the time if I got any questions."

"Great. Good luck and stay safe Devonte. Please for your own sake, ensure that you abide by our rules. Bix, I'll see you around here soon I'm sure," said Seniesa as she had her hands clasped together and bowed her head slightly before retreating from them.

"Bruh. I ain't even gone cap. She feeling you for real. I never seen that b**ch smile like that bruh. She always keep a straight face. " said Bix as he tiptoed and threw his arm over Devonte's shoulder.

"For real?" replied Devonte.

"Word to my mother bruh she on you."

"I thought she was feeling me too I ain't gone lie but I think she just professional as hell bruh. She probably just being nice man," said Devonte.

Their interaction with Seniesa had briefly distracted them from the heinous act they had witnessed.

"Aite lets go now though. F**king storage gone take a long ass time man. That mother*****r big as hell," said Bix.

The two walked towards exit of the basement and made sure to nod and acknowledge those that they walked past. They walked past as the cleaners threw heaps of bottled water onto the bloodied carpet, without a care for how much water was actually needed. As the two were about to walk through the door, a voice called out from behind.

"Oi wait up. Junior let me talk to you," said the voice, a voice so distinct, that the duo knew it could be none other than Zion Raushanfikri himself.

The duo turned around, and Bixente's shoulders dropped slightly; he was visibly slightly afraid of the man; Zion Raushanfikri was heavily involved in the Khan of the Kumite tournaments, and thus was accustomed to viewing violence on a regular basis. Rumour had it he had escaped a murder charge once upon a time, long before he went 'legit' and entered the world of ring announcing and presenting. His eyes told the same story of Mika da Silva, a man who had seen much violence, and alas revelled in it.

"Imma keep it straight junior. I don't like you," said Zion as the smoke from his cigar slowly gathered in front of Devonte's face.

"Is it? What I done to you?" replied Devonte as he folded his arms, moved his tongue across his teeth, and took in a deep breath through his nose before letting this out through his nose.

*I aint gone rise cos he know what he be doing right now. Hol' it together Devonte. Ain't no time and place to be beefin' motherf*****s. Think 'bout where you is right now bruh. Don't let this b**ch ass get to you man,* Devonte thought as he composed himself.

"I don't need a reason junior. I keep it real and so I'm just letting you know is all. Face to face," replied Zion as he continued to puff on his cigar and let the smoke dissipate into Devonte's face.

"Aite bet I respect that. Well I ain't got nothing against you sir. I respect you for real. I done seen you presenting the Khan of the Kumite and the IFL. I f**k with you, no cap. So, yeah bruh, it is what it is I guess. Imma get going now anyways. Nice to meet you Sir," said Devonte as he nodded his head at Zion and turned to leave the room with Bix.

Zion Raushanfikri grabbed his arm.

"Did I say you can leave? I don't remember doing so. I'm wanna tell you why I don't rate you," said Zion as he seemed to be challenged by Devonte's seeming desire to diffuse any tension. "I've been watching you since you came into this room. I don't like how you stepped to Mike. He might've respected that, but I didn't. I know what that man is capable of and I've seen first-hand what he's had to do to get where he is, and I think you disrespected him. I don't give a f**k who you are or think you are. But you need a humbling Junior. And I'm telling you to your face I'd be happy to provide you with that humbling. Don't forget where you are. I seen how you were chatting to Seniesa too. I seen you trying to rizz her, and I know you saw me see you. Don't act like you weren't," said Zion, as he and Devonte both turned to her. Seniesa Sanches was mid conversation, but curiosity meant she turned to watch the two's intense conversation; she felt their eyes on her. And she turned away as soon as she realised Zion was indeed looking.

"Say less bruh I hear you. But word to my mother I ain't tryna cause no problems. I get it though. I respect you. I'm just being me you feel me. I ain't let no man disrespect me no matter where I'm at. That just be what I'm like dawg. I respect you and everybody here, but you gotta understand I'm a grown ass man. Where I'm from, I can't let nobody disrespect me unless there be a reason for it. So if you don't like me, that's aite. We ain't gotta be friendly. But imma keep it amicable. I know I be here for business and I ain't want no problems. I ain't got no reason to be beefing you and I don't want to either bruh. I know who you is. I don't want no smoke. I apologise if I done came across disrespectful. But yeah you right with regard to Seniesa. I was tryna rizz her. I ain't got no shame in that either though. She fine as hell; I think that be clear to see. So let's not drag this out. Let's end it respectfully. Imma shake your hand and go about my business if that's cool with you sir," said Devonte as he extended his hand out to Zion. Zion took his hand and shook Devonte's hand with a viper like grip.

"Cool. Well you know wagwan from my side now kid. Before you leave here though. Just know, this is my world; you're in my world, my ends. I don't give a f**k if Mike likes you. I'll be watching. So don't f**k up; cos I will make your life peak. Off you go now; you have my permission. Get out of here," said Zion as he let go of Devonte's hand and stood standing in the same place, unflinching. Devonte looked Zion up and down, and backed away. And Zion did the same back.

Bixente and Devonte walked out of the door and out of the basement. What they had seen and experienced would stay with them, for this was not something that one could easily forget. This was the nature of this business and they had witnessed it first hand, albeit comforted by the fact they had seen that together. Bixente himself had always been somewhat sheltered from this side of the League of Shottas operations; he had always been an exemplary employee.

For Devonte Lacy, this was his first experience of the League of Shottas. He knew now of the harsh reality of what could happen to him should he stray away from the Compass of Commandments of the League of Shottas.

Though he knew he had no choice but to break the regulations decreed in the Compass of Commandments. For his reasoning for breaking the Compass of Commandments was greater than the potentiality of facing time in prison. The why for his actions were far too strong to stop him, despite the gravity of the consequences. His father before him had gone to prison and so Devonte, despite not wanting to meet this same fate, was somewhat unafraid of this prospect; it was his destiny and in his DNA. His father before him had walked his path and his father before him too. And thus, Devonte Lacy took solace knowing that if his ancestors had walked this path, no matter how unfortunate it was, he could do the same and live to tell the tale.

Family was everything to him and so protecting what little he had left of this was all that mattered. He had not the heart to tell Bixente his plans, for the actions were already set in motion and he was prepared to do what he needed to do. Bixente Lemaire would help his dearest friend had he just asked.

Though the ego is a mysterious thing upon time to time and for some reason or the other, Devone Lacy knew that he had to do that which he was to do. It seemed to him that fate brought him to this path and choice, and he felt something deep within him telling him to walk the path despite the angst it gave him. Fate had brought him here, and he would walk the path of fate.

BOOK 10
MALABAR JONES

Saturday 7th November 2065

*19:53: The Facial Recognition Scanning Centre London,
Kings Cross, London*

Malabar Jones patiently watched as the woman locked the building with the bleeping alarm barely being heard over the raucous laughter from the people with her.

"Julie, drinks on you today," said one of the men.

"No, no. No chance Julie is paying. Can't let the girl pay on her birthday now, can we?" one of the girls replied.

"Well, that's exactly why she's gotta. Come on Julie. Julie get some cans, Julie get us a couple cans," the man replied.

"Listen. I'll go with the flow, if you guys wanna buy me drinks, I'm not gonna say no!" replied Julie as her and the group slowly made their way through the car park.

"Yep, it's done. Drinks on us today!" the girl replied.

Malabar watched as they left the car park and locked the entry gates. He had expected to have waited for longer. The opening hours for the Facial Recognition Scanning Centre (FRSC) was supposedly 10am to 8pm on a Saturday. However, it seemed as though they had closed earlier today and Malabar was pleased by this. He was behind schedule. Brian Harrison had to be found. There was no time. He needed to be found as soon as possible. Or else Malabar Jones would have failed his mission. His pursuit of Fergus-Sundar had wasted precious and valuable time, time he could not get back. What made the time lost from his pursuit of Fergus-Sundar worse, was the fact that he had failed in his pursuit of Fergus-Sundar too; he had nothing to show for the time spent and his distraction from his existing case. And now he was desperate; it had already taken him some time and difficulty finding Brian Harrison. He was within touching distance of Brian Harrison just a couple days ago and was ahead of schedule and would likely have caught him with ease; were it not for the appearance of Fergus-Sundar.

Malabar's intel had told him that Brian Harrison was to attempt to shut down The Dala Electricity Hub London on Saturday 7th November 2065, and that day had now come. And Brian Harrison's terrorist organisation was to attempt to shut off the Dala Electricity Hubs across the UK after the London Hub had been turned off. The Dala Electricity Hubs were all connected and so, the London Hub had to be turned off first before the others could be turned off. He could not wait for Brian Harrison at the Dala Electricity Hub of London either for there were many potential entry points he could access the Hub from and Malabar knew Brian Harrison, the elusive, had a strong team.

And so, Malabar made his way into the FRSC and to one of the many desks inside the mind-numbing and characterless office layout of the FRSC. He put on his MobiGlasses, provided to him by the SSSA, and began looking through the database. He again looked through all the blurred faces of people inside of the City of London. Despite the fact that the FRSC was vast and had the overwhelming majority of the UK's inhabitants on file, there was still less than one-per-cent who had their faces blurred from the database. And the algorithm embedded in the system meant this blurring could not be undone. Although there was only less than one-per-cent of the population who had their faces blurred on the system – this was still a large amount of blurred faces which he had to go through; this equated to roughly at least ninety-thousand people in the City of London.

Malabar went through a process of elimination based on location and took out a large percentage of his pool of blurred faces out of the equation. He then used his knowledge of Brian Harrison's stride length, and physique to take more people out of the equation. After some time, he located his man and now the problem was getting to Brian Harrison in time, before he would move once more and become untraceable again. Malabar knew he would have to move quickly.

He left the building of the FRSC London and ran to his motorbike; he had to get to Brian Harrison fast. He knew he would have to speed if he was to get to his man, and thus run the risk of being stopped by the police. Though Malabar Jones was a Special Operative and somewhat above the law, the problem lay in the fact that he was in the shadows and thus not technically employed or given an official title – his Government and legal name was not Malabar Jones; it was Mahendra Jimothy. And so, it was best to avoid encounters with the law at all costs. However, if he was to be caught or had an encounter with the police, then the SSSA would instantly be notified on their systems that Mahendra Jimothy had ever been apprehended, and consequently bailed out. The SSSA had the power to forgo typical legalities. Malabar Jones could not afford to be caught as Mahendra Jimothy right now; he knew the SSSA would be watching him closely.

Malabar hopped onto his motorbike. *Go fast Malabar, we must catch him. Failure is not an option.*

21:35: Ilford Station, Greater London

Malabar Jones drifted around the roundabout and narrowly avoided an old lady who was about to cross the road as the TrafficTexts advised her it was safe to cross. Malabar let his bike drop to the curb and jumped off the bike as swiftly as it had dropped to the curb. He did not need to lock the motorbike away like a regular motorbike. For the bike had a sensor on the grip which meant only he could use and activate the bike – if someone else was to use the bike then he would have to grant them permission to do so through the bike's settings. Thus, it was safe for him to leave the bike anywhere.

Ilford Station was the last place that Brian Harrison was supposedly located from Malabar Jones' research, and he now somewhat frantically paced up and down outside of the former shopping mall in Ilford. He knew Brian Harrison was in and around this area somewhere, but he did not know exactly where at this stage. Malabar Jones was not sure why Brian Harrison was here but suspected that the man and their organisation may well have had a hideout or apartment here in Ilford, for it was a condensed area and somewhat riddled with crime and nefarious activities going on – thus he could somewhat hide in plain sight. Malabar continued to rush up and down the street but realised soon enough that this was causing him no good and likely he was attracting much attention himself. And so, he decided to plonk himself in a specific area and just watch people go by – he was sure that he would spot him at some point.

Instead of hanging out on the corner of the road, bored and with nothing to do – he figured he ought to treat himself with either some food or drink. Malabar Jones looked for a spot on the main road with visibility to the road outside, and somewhere nondescript, whereby he would aptly blend into the atmosphere somewhat. He was dressed in a casual way, as was typical for a SSSA, in black jeans and a black hoodie; so if looked upon by a stranger, his attire at least would never garner attention from onlookers. Though little did they know that he had a state-of-the-art, TechSuit on underneath – which was kitted out to the max and cost more than the majority of houses in the area even. Malabar had never been in this area before, but as he looked up and down the road, it seemed the highest percentage of shops were either off licences or chicken shops.

And so he walked into a chicken shop, for the first time since he was just a teenager, and proceeded to order the meal he had always ordered as a kid. It was a rare moment for Malabar Jones to enjoy and live his life somewhat like a regular person, weirdly in arguably the most stressful time of his life – the odds were against him at this point. He never had the opportunity, or licence, to eat out; it was not a privilege that was bestowed upon him or allowed by the SSSA. Distractions were not permitted, and he was typically not permitted to casually engage with the public, as per the SSSA regulations.

"Hi boss. Can I get a six wings meal please?" said Malabar Jones as a smile grew organically on his face, he could not contain it. He had not uttered those words in decades, and yet it came out of him as though he had uttered them, just yesterday.

"Hello mate. Sure that's £10 please," the bossman replied as he picked up the companies Dala Device, eagerly waiting to take payment.

And in that moment, as quick as he had become excited to order the meal, his excitement had dissipated for he realised he had no means to payment and thus would not be able to order the meal he now craved. He did not own a Dala Device. He had a fake one – that would remotely be verified by the SSSA without the Retinal Verification System actually working or being needed. The SSSA did not allow for him to use one; for it meant his details would be linked and on file then with the government. However, he would have to call in to the SSSA and authorise this first, and he did not want to do this now – not for chicken wings. He did not want to rouse suspicion at the fact that he did not have money on his Dala Device or one with money on it. Everyone had a Dala Device, or at least someone with them that had Dala Device; for it was from Malabar Jones' experience with the extremely wealthy in the UK, that they typically did not carry a Dala Device with them and instead had people in their cohort carry a Dala Device and make transactions for them. And thus, he continued.

"£10 boss? That's a lot. What's in the chicken?" he joked.

"Come on man. Everywhere same price," the bossman replied with a smile on his face.

"Okay no worries boss. Thank you though," replied Malabar as he proceeded to leave the Chicken Shop.

"Yo wait. I got you. What you want? Six wings meal yeah?" a stranger shouted out to Malabar's surprise.

"It's okay you don't have to," Malabar replied, suspicious of the man. He typically did not take charity from random men, especially considering his line of work. He noticed from his MobiGlasses that this man's face, and consequently his identity, was not recognised by the FRSC – he was a part of the less than one-per-cent not recognised by the FRSC. But even still, Malabar recognised the man.

"Don't stress bruv it's calm innit. Mo, pay for the guy's meal," the stranger replied.

"Thank you. You're very kind. You didn't have to do that," Malabar said as he continued to keep an eye out on the road outside.

"No stress. It's nice to be nice innit. You're moving stiff though. You're nervous. Looking out onto the street every two seconds. Relax bruddah. You're good here," the man replied as he erupted into raucous laughter, his friends following suit.

"No I'm good. Just not used to the area is all. I appreciate it," replied Malabar. He was indeed nervous and the muscular man – with two burgers, a large fries, four chicken strips and four chicken wings in front of him – had noticed quickly. Malabar was curious to know more about the man, but naturally was also hesitant; the man was now curious about him also and this was not a good thing. It was typically best to avoid conversations like this altogether, but the man had paid for his meal and so he had no choice but to engage. Malabar was conscious also of the fact that this man was with three others and their faces were all blurred from the FRSC – he could be anyone, Malabar had no intel on them as a result.

"Say no more. What brings you to the area then?" the man asked.

"Just come to see an old friend, guy I went uni with," Malabar replied.

"Nice. The name's Mike, Mike da Silva," the man said, before devouring an entire chicken wing in one bite. And then, it dawned on Malabar as to who this man was.

"Oh, I thought I recognised you. Mike da Silva, the MMA fighter right? Wow good to meet you. The names Mahendra.".

"Good to meet you Mahendra. Keep safe yeah. Just tell the bossman what drink you want," Mike da Silva replied.

"Yes sure thing. Thanks Mike, appreciate it. I'll leave you to it now."

"Hello man. What drink?" the bossman asked.

"Strawberry Mirinda please, and can I get chilli mayo sauce as well," Malabar replied. He proceeded to tuck into his meal, with full view of the road ahead. He had his back turned from the road for at least five minutes, as he had engaged in conversation with the stranger who turned out to be the famous fighter Mike da Silva. Malabar was also aware that he was the founder, owner and operator of the largest and most successful underground weed organisation in the world, explaining why his face was not registered on the FRSC.

And as he began to bite into the chicken wings, Malabar saw an unidentifiable person prop up on the screen of his MobiGlasses and recognised the man's face instantly – it was Brian Harrison. He finished the chicken wing, and hurriedly cleaned his rubbish.

"Rah you barely ate half of it bruv. Bad guy. Wasting food. Didn't even have the decency to finish a meal bought for him. F**king pr**k," Mike da Silva shouted out, as Malabar Jones rushed out of the door.

As he proceeded down the road, he saw Brian Harrison turn his head and look directly at him, with one hand on his MobiGlasses. And just like that, it became apparent to Brian Harrison that this man was following him. He instantly ran.

Malabar Jones stopped in his tracks and sprinted in the opposite direction towards his motorbike. And as he approached his bike, he saw a couple of local Police Community Support Officers looking at his motorbike which was incorrectly parked in a location it ought not be left – a rare mistake from Malabar. They saw the grip of his bike, as they could tell it had been modified – in a way which was not legal.

"Hi mate is this your bike?" the officer asked him.

"Sorry no time," Malabar Jones replied as he hurriedly hopped onto the bike and sped off.

He took his bike down the road and quickly saw Brian Harrison enter his car. It was close to 10pm now and Malabar knew that Brian Harrison and his team were to attempt to shut off The Dala Electricity Hub London after 10pm. He knew Brian Harrison now would be looking to get the job done as soon as possible; he had been spotted and despite the fact he did not know of Malabar Jones or the SSSA, he knew instantly that this man was after him.

Brian Harrison entered his four-by-four SUV and as he drove, Malabar knew he was in for a chase. The SUV looked like an old car, but it was clearly modified, and the aesthetic of the car was a delusion as to the true nature of the vehicle.

The two continued to drive through the streets of Greater London in a manner that Malabar was not fond of. He did not like speeding for he knew it attracted unwanted attention and he had personal bad experiences and a sour taste with driving. Prior to his time with the SSSA, when he was a regular civilian and had friends and attended social events – he had lost friends to reckless and erratic driving, either by them trying to prove their masculinity on the road, or through actions such as driving under the influence of either alcohol, balloons, or weed – it was an epidemic of the youth. And as such, he only engaged in fast driving as of when it was needed.

Brian Harrison was clearly a skilled driver and Malabar Jones would have lost him had he also been in a car. Though the manoeuvrability in small spaces that his motorbike allowed for, allowed Malabar Jones to cut through alleyways and other tight spaces and as such he kept up with the elusive Brian Harrison.

And then the two approached The Dala Electricity Hub London, and Brian Harrison parked his car a few roads away, before going the rest of the way on foot. A few moments later, Malabar Jones found himself in the same spot and left his motorbike before running after Brian Harrison, who was surprisingly fast considering his podgier frame.

Nonetheless, Malabar promptly caught up with Brian Harrison who was only a few meters ahead of him. He glanced back at the man chasing him, before pulling himself up and over the tall gates with relative ease, and Malabar realised then that whilst Brian Harrison appeared to be podgy; he was clearly still athletic and quite strong to be able to hoist himself up like that. And this excited him for he knew he would inevitably have to fight him – this was the part of the job as SSSA4 that Malabar Jones most enjoyed; the fights.

And so, the two were in the final stretch of their respective missions.

For Malabar Jones, this was Brian Harrison. And for Brian Harrison, this was The Control Centre of The Dala Electricity Hub London. Malabar looked up at the steep and seemingly never-ending staircase which led to halfway up the sustainably designed Dala Electricity Hub of London, and saw his target running up a couple steps at the time, but slowing in pace. *We got him, he won't make it,* he thought.

*22:33: The Control Centre Staircase,
The Dala Electricity Hub, London.*

Brian Harrison ran up the stairs and found himself almost half way up before he noticed the mysterious man closing in on him rapidly. Malabar had recently just travelled up a staircase even steeper than this one, and that too whilst fighting the formidable Fergus-Sundar. And so Malabar swiped at the feet of the running Brian Harrison, with a leaping left hand, causing the man to tumble and yelp. Malabar knew he would best Brian Harrison easily; he had already showed weakness. Malabar swiftly picked himself up and kicked the downed Brian Harrison once in the stomach to ensure he took advantage of his superior position. He could not allow for it to be a completely even fight; the stakes were too high, and time was of the essence.

"Brian Trevor Harrison. You don't know me, but you do now. I am hereby seizing you in the name of and for the protection of, the Crown and its People – for the act of terrorism. Note that anything you do say, may well be used against you in the future should you pose or continue to pose a threat to the security of this nation and of its people. Do you understand? You are being seized for terrorism. Do you accept the charges?," said Malabar Jones as he kicked Brian Harrison in the stomach again, he was lying on his side and breathing heavily.

"Hah, I'm the threat. Sure. You're as much of a fool as I was. Looks like we've all been f**king fooled man. Ahh man. F**k me man.. You kicked me proper hard man. Why'd you kick me so hard?," said the man as he rolled onto his back, before rolling back onto his side again.

Why is he not even fighting back? Weak, he's a weak man; a coward.

"I take your lack of a fightback as an admission of defeat and acceptance of the charges. Still though, I can't let you walk out of here unrestrained. Please roll onto your front."

"Sure mate whatever you say. I'm rolling yeah; don't shoot me. What are you though? A fed? MI6?" Brian Harrison said as he rolled over.

"It dooon't matter who I am. Your terrorist plot has been foiled. Hold still," said Malabar as he knelt with his knee on the back of Brian Harrison and went into one of the hidden and seemingly invisible pockets on his TechSuit for his handcuffs. "Now I'll be honest, I'm surprised you're coming along so amicably. I will remember it. I hope you have some remorse over your act…" said Malabar as he suddenly saw a person emerging at a rapid rate in his peripheral vision. At which point, whilst his attention wavered, Brian Harrison seized his opportunity and exploded, using the man's low and somewhat unorthodox and unbalanced position against him and pushed him off.

As Malabar readjusted his body position to face back up the stairs, he saw Brian Harrison's face in front of his own while his face turned forward; Brian Harrison had intrepidly thrown himself at the spy. The momentum was enough to send them both tumbling down the stairs. Malabar though was fast enough, both mentally and physically, to react mid tumble and click the button on his TechSuit which enabled Impact Protection Mode; protecting his body in the event of serious and immediate impact on his body, which this was.

However, mid tumble, he glanced up at the stairs to see two figures – a man and a woman – sprinting up the stairs, and in that moment he knew he may well have failed; they were almost at the top now.

As they landed, Malabar had the upper hand for Brian Harrison was bruised and battered from the tumble, he was visibly wincing. Though as they had landed in close proximity to one another, Brian Harrison again threw himself at Malabar, but this time with the intention to wrestle him. Brian Harrison immediately had top position and the double underhooks, which meant it was hard for the smaller Malabar Jones to wriggle his way out with ease from underneath; Brian Harrison had already gained a strong position and his weight was firmly on him. This battle for position went on for a brief moment before Brian Harrison moved quite neatly into a full mount position and unleashed a short elbow down at the face of the SSSA4. Uncharacteristically, the SSSA4 found himself irate, perhaps due to the predicament he was currently in; he did not like to lose, and was not accustomed to failing. Malabar threw an elbow himself before pivoting out by pushing off of his right leg and swivelling his body to reserve Brian Harrison's top position and taking the back of Brian Harrison. He punched him in the face with a few looping left punches which landed cleanly on the side of his face, causing a cut to emerge almost immediately; Brian Harrison evidently had a lot of scar tissue on his face and it alluded to the fact he had fought before. Malabar readjusted and attacked from the other side with more punches landing. Malabar looked up briefly and saw the two running figures at the top of the stairs. *This is being ended now.*

Malabar continued to land his shots on Brian Harrison and again proceeded to take his handcuffs out of his TechSuit; he had to restrain him. It occurred to the SSSA4 now, that Brian Harrison had waited for his team to arrive at the staircase before fighting back, and Malabar had fallen for the trick.

Though as Malabar Jones was about to take the handcuffs out, he felt a gunshot on his left shoulder which sent his momentum off. And if he had not already lost, Malabar Jones had now certainly lost. He had been shot and as he sat on the stairs, he saw a line of special forces operative approaching him with their guns pointed at him. He could not proceed. His mission was over; he had failed.

"F**k!" he shouted out in frustration. "F**k sake!" he was irate.

"It's for the greater good man. We've all lost our minds. You'll see man. It's all connected. You'll see soon enough now," Brian Harrison said to Malabar Jones as he began to sit up also. "This is a good thing fella. The country will be better for it."

"Shut up b**ch. You'll get what you deserve. You're not gonna get away with this. You'll be locked up for a lifetime and more. I'll make sure of that," Malabar Jones replied.

And so, Malabar Jones had failed his mission and was being arrested by the Police as Mahendra Jimothy. He went amicably and kept silent as they spoke at him. He would not incriminate himself or say anything that would reveal any information he ought not reveal. He knew within two days he would be out of jail and the case on Mahendra Jimothy would be erased from the records, and he would go free because of the SSSA. However, his failure would not be taken lightly by the SSSA.

What would come to transpire was now out of his hands and he would have to deal with the consequences with the SSSA, and likely the backlash from the ensuing attacking he failed to foil – but so would the nation and its people. He had failed. He failed the mission. Brian Harrison and his team would succeed. The Police ran up the staircase themselves, but judging from the building plan that Malabar had seen, he knew it was likely that the two figures would reach the Control Centre and shut down The

Dala Electricity in London regardless of the Police's attempts to stop them. He had failed. And so, he reverted his attention beyond the failure, and towards his next steps in the coming days. He knew the SSSA would not be happy about his failure. He feared they would send SSSA1, the Yonige-Ya after him. *If they send the Yonige-Ya I will accept my fate, and my termination into the night.* But in the meantime, he was ready and awaiting his release. He needed to fix this. *But I will complete the mission still, to the end.*

22:44: *The Control Centre, The Dala Electricity Hub, London.*

"Artur wait a minute. Do you think Brian's okay? Should we go help him?" the woman, whose name was Shonda Wright, said as she looked down from the top of the stairs.

"There's no time Shonda. We gotta go do this now. There's no time. We gotta go. He's fine. You can worry about your boyfriend later," the man, named Artur Turgenev, said as he attempted to hurry Shonda.

Artur was nervous about the task at hand, but Shonda was nervous for the love of her life. A part of her felt to run back down and help her love Brian Harrison against the much smaller man who was beating him up. But she knew she couldn't. Brian Harrison had only just reminded their team of the task they had at hand and the inevitable struggles they would face from the law when completing their mission. They had to shut off The Dala Electricity Hub of London if they were going to reveal the truth about the Dala Device, and if the rest of the population were to have a Realisation as they all had. *Brian would want me to finish the job, he started this all. It's his vision and his dream,* she thought to herself as she tried her hardest to stop herself from turning back. But she remembered Brian's rousing speeches that he had delivered, with such gusto and passion; was so committed to the cause. He had been the first to experience a realisation regarding the true nature of the Dala Device. And he had experienced this alone, whilst on a Government sanctioned trip in Paris, when both his Dala Device and backup Dala Device were destroyed. Stranded without it, he was forced to have his realisation alone – and remembering this made Shonda strong and her resolve grew. *If he could do it alone, I can finish this off now. Be tough Shonda*, she thought to herself. And so, Shonda and Artur continued, and used their intel and entered the access code.

The plan had not been for Artur and Shonda to be the ones who would shut off The Dala Electricity Hub of London off, for Brian knew that whoever would be the one to do it – would likely suffer the longest amount of time in prison for their direct involvement. Brian Harrison wanted this to be him. The plan was always for him to go alone. However, plans changed. When Brian Harrison spotted Malabar Jones following him in Ilford, close to their safehouse, he called Shonda Wright and advised her that Artur ought to follow him and complete the job if he couldn't. He had expressly told her that she should not come herself; Brian Harrison did not want her implicated in any way. Though Shonda had a mind of her own and was strong willed – she told Artur that it was both her and Artur that Brian had called for.

Artur and Shonda were now in the Control Room. This was it. The moment they had been building towards for over a year now. The time had come. The two of them looked at one another and were conscious that there were cameras in the room.

"I'll do it Shonda. Brian wouldn't want you to do it," said Artur.

"Well Brian isn't here Artur. It's me and you now. Let me," she replied.

"No. I'll do it. It's better if I do it. F**k. Here we go," he said as he took in a deep breath and accessed the system, again using his intel provided to him by Brian and entered the clearance codes and initiated the Emergency Shutdown Protocol. Once confirmed, the Dala Electricity Hub of London would shut down for a minimum of eighteen hours – it would be the first time it had ever been turned off since the system was first introduced, and it would result in the rest of the Dala Electricity Hubs of the UK to be turned off. It would be confirmed after the two-minute countdown. Shonda and Artur turned and looked at each other with anxious excitement and jumped up and down excitedly whilst hugging each other.

"We did it! We actually did it! Ahh the relief. What a year it's been. It's finally coming together Artur, just as Brian said it would," Shonda said. "Gosh I hope he's okay. Should I go check in on him?"

"I know right. Feels surreal to be honest. Still another ninety seconds to go officially but yeah its close now. Everything is gonna change now. It'll all change. But yeah go check on him. I'll see down the countdown. You know the code?"

"Yeah, I got it. I'll be right back," said Shonda as she left the Control Centre and walked down the short and narrow corridor back down to the staircase. As she pressed the door release button, she began to put one foot out of the door before seeing three Special Forces Police Officers running up the stairs with guns in their hands. She tried to close the door quickly but she knew that they saw her. She slammed it shut and looked down at the watch embedded within the skin on the exterior of her right hand. She knew there was only around sixty seconds left on the countdown. She stood in front of the door, at this point panicked, and felt her heart-rate rise exponentially; she did not know what to do. The Police opened the door and now all that stood between them and the Control Centre was herself.

"Ma'am put your hands up and don't move. You're under arrest. My colleague is going to approach you and put some cuffs on you now. Can you confirm if the shutdown has been activated or not?" the Police officer asked Shonda, with a gun pointing directly at her. Shonda did not reply. She was stuck. She did not know what to do. "Ma'am please. I'll have to shoot if you don't comply," the officer shouted out again with a hint of desperation. Shonda again did not respond and again glanced down at her hand.

"She's just checked her watch. He's activated it. Ju, we gotta move now," the other officer said.

"Ma'am please, just put your hands up," the officer said.

There's still time, if I comply then they'll stop it. It'll all be for nothing, Shonda thought to herself. *I have to delay them.* Shonda began to raise her arms, but ensured to do so very slowly. As she saw the female officer who was pleading with her, slowly lower her gun, Shonda ran towards the officer and screamed as she did.

"For the people!" she shouted. And so, the officer was left with no choice but to shoot, and Shonda took a bullet and fell to the ground. The officer, Juliette Palmer, attempted to stop the bleeding – but it was to no avail; the gunshot had hit an artery. Shonda had successfully delayed the officers and they could not stop Artur in time. The Emergency Shutdown Protocol had been initiated at the Dala Electricity Hub of London, and the other Dala Electricity Hubs across the country went on to shutdown too.

Electricity would go out completely across the country, and thus all systems would fail and falter as a result. The digital monetary system was down, trains would not work, phone signal was gone, internet did not work, planes would not fly, and the list went on – their society's dependence on technology-centric operations had resulted in a cessation of life operating regularly, in the absence of technology working. Though the focus of this terrorist organisation was not to cause the operational issues that it caused; their vision was centred on spiritual revolution, a cleansing of the mind and to recalibrate and fight the programming the Dala system had caused. They would succeed.

Artur Turgenev was arrested, Shonda Wright had died for the cause, and Brian Harrison cried at the sight of his dead girlfriend being brought down the staircase, as Officer Juliette Palmer spoke to him. His team had succeeded to shut down the Electricity Hub of London, and consequently the others across the country, but he had lost the love of his life for it. *Was it worth it*, Brian Harrison thought to himself.

And thus marked was the start of the night which would remembered in history as, The Tech-Night 1.0, of the year 2065.

BOOK 11

SHACKLETON NAIR

Saturday 7th and Sunday 8th November 2065

Saturday 7th November 2065, 21:45:
The Home of Shackleton Nair, Kent

Shackleton walked through his front door, expecting a warm welcome, but found an empty room with the lights turned off. His son was seemingly already in bed and his wife seemed to be in bed too.

"Claudia?" he called out. He walked through to the kitchen and opened the fridge to find it full of food cooked for him. *She really is the best cook.*

"Hey," she said as appeared out of nowhere and gave him a hug and a soft and short kiss on his lips. "How was the drive?" She came down from her bed to greet him.

"Hey, you look good. The drive was okay. So much traffic but yeah it was not too bad. How's Charles?"

"Thanks. Erm Charles is good. I've got him to do all his homework. But I think he's missed you. He asked me where you were and I said you were away for work. Then he said, 'but Pappa already works so much'. But yeah, it's all good. While you've been away, I've been holding it down here. You know. All alone out here. Like a good obedient wife," she replied with very blatant sass.

"Claudia, I've been back less than five minutes and you're already giving me grief. What do you want me to do? I hadn't been to this Conference, or for a work event in years. You know I didn't really want to go anyway.

I hate these things. Everyone is so pretentious. Their views are so limited. It's jarring being around them. I only went because I wanted to catch up with some old friends and because there are some people in the field who I wanted to meet; they've brought about some interesting theories and research".

"It's cool Shack. It is what it is. It would just be nice if you were around more is all I'm saying. Your absence is noticeable, and you should see that as a compliment. I need you around Shack; to help raise our boy. I didn't sign up to do this all alone."

"Listen we wouldn't have this life if I was always home. If I wasn't working so much. Do you think we got a home like this, with all this space and privacy, and the grandiose furniture that you love – if I didn't work so much? It's because I work so much and so hard and it's because I spend my time doing stuff like this that we can live like this. That's why you and Charles can live the life you do, and that we can send him to the school we send him to. So save it please."

"Cool you're going to play that card, are you? Real classy Shack."

"What? It's the truth. Do you think we'd have this life if I didn't make those investments into Vertical Farming? Or if I didn't do all the work I've done with mycelium, and all the years of hard work I've put into my craft? Don't be cheeky with me Claudia. Don't take the piss alright. Be a little grateful please. I can take criticism but not when you're chatting sh*t."

"Are you done being a pr**k, or have you got more?"

"I think I'm about done."

"Good because if you really listened to what I said and weren't such a insensitive wan*er; you'd have …"

"Why are you calling me names? There's no need to be rude."

"Rude. Oh Shack, give me a break. For someone who is so rude yourself, you've got a right f**king nerve to call me rude . But anyway, can I finish my sentence? Or do you want to whine a little more."

"Go on then. You're so feisty. I love it," he said as he leant back on the kitchen counter; a smile emerging on his face. He motioned for her to come to him.

"I'm trying to have a serious conversation with you Shack. Don't patronise me. Now back to my point. I'm not saying I'm ungrateful for what we have Shack. Of course not. We've got a beautiful home and family here. And I am grateful for all your hard work. You know I respect you for it and I love that you've supplied this life for us. I just wish you were around to actually enjoy it. We have it all Shack. But I don't have my husband around, and Charles doesn't have his father around. And what's sad is, that I think you're choosing this. It's like you run away from us and I don't know why. You're so distant. It's like you're trying to lose yourself with your work. You don't need to do as much as you do. You are self-employed now Shack. I need your help around here Shack. You can be at home, but it still feels like you're not here. It's now a problem too because it's not only me who's noticing this. Charles can see it too and he's only young. Do you get what I'm trying to say? Is this registering?"

"I understand babe. I'm sorry I'll be around more. Okay I'm going to make a conscious effort to do so."

"It's like even with this conference. It's a three-day conference. But you were gone for almost five days. Why did you need to go for five days, you could've been gone for four or three if you really wanted. You're just not present Shack and I need you. I don't just need you for money. That's not why I married you. I need you to be present emotionally for me. I'm being real honest here."

"You're right babe. I'm sorry okay. I'll be around more. I'm sorry," said Shackleton as he moved towards Claudia. "Look at me. Come on. I've been away a few days. Show me some love. I have missed you my love."

"I've missed you too Shack. That's my whole point," she replied. Shackleton Nair lifted her chin up and gave her a kiss. Though this time it was a longer kiss. The two hugged and Shack put his arms around her as he slid his coarse hands up under her silk pyjamas and caressed her soft skin with his coarse hands. "You want to have some fun tonight? It's been a while baby."

"Oh, I would love to. Just give me a couple hours. I'm gonna go out into the field for a couple hours; I've got some work to do," replied Shackleton. She withdrew from him immediately in frustration.

"Seriously? Seriously Shack? We literally just … okay go on. Go ahead. Goodnight, I'll see you tomorrow."

"Babe it's just a couple hours."

"Do what you have to do Shack. It's your life. Do what you want. You know what's important to you. Goodnight," Claudia said as she quickly walked out of the kitchen and up the stairs. She did not want her husband to see her pain in that moment. But Shackleton Nair knew she was hurt. They were in the same household, but he and his wife had never been more distant from one another.

22:35 *The Field of Shackleton Nair*

Shackleton opened the door of the conservatory and looked out over his garden, almost a whole field in itself. He had acres of land at his disposal. Shackleton had invested in Vertical Farming in his younger days, and this blessed with him a mini fortune to his name. Though he was an esteemed individual with a considerable name in the field of mycology, and had received awards for his work and contribution to knowledge – this was not where he made his money. However, Shackleton had been somewhat detached and isolated from the scientific field of mycology for some time now.

He had hypothesised years prior, whilst at the height of his success, that mycelium from different parts of the world could communicate and share information with one another, and mycelium that had existed in a location for hundreds or even thousands of years, could communicate and share and store the information that they had gathered regarding nature and the wood wide web, across time. Whilst grounded in legitimate scientific theory, much of his hypothesis was ludicrous and far reaching; ultimately speculation. The theory was laughed at and ruined the scientific credibility of Shackleton, who was deemed as being a hippie who had lost his mind. As such, a dark cloud gathered over his reputation, and Shackleton himself disassociated with the rest of the field of mycology; seeing his peers as being afraid to take chances and really advance the field, afraid of taking risks in fear of what it might do to their reputations.

And so, he left his university teaching role, and he isolated himself – reserving himself to private research conducted on his own property. Alas, he lived a peaceful life away from the limelight and no longer was burdened by the dogmatic nine-to-five lifestyle that he had grown to hate. However, in turn, he had lost himself somewhat; he no longer had any restrictions on when he had to work. The lines were blurred between his personal time and work time and his relationship with his wife suffered as a result. Shackleton Nair spent much of his days researching and studying and writing at any hour of the day he chose. One would assume that since his wife was at home, and now Shackleton had more time on his hands without the dogmatic nine-to-five routine – that he would spend more time with his wife and kids. Though it seemed the routine-less nature of his work meant he lost himself in his work, and perhaps lost the desire and need for socialisation from not having regular work; meaning he reverted into himself, into his work.

Shackleton Nair walked in the freezing cold with a long, thick coat towards his e-Van, powered by sustainable electricity provided by the UK government for free through the Dala Electricity Hubs. He checked his pocket to search for his gloves and was pleased to find them there. The Skintight-High-Sensation gloves were skintight gloves which thin and practically stuck to his hands using advanced technology and kept his hands warm – it meant he could work outside during the extremely cold winters that they experienced in the UK.

Shackleton drove his e-Van through the vast acres of land that he had at his disposal, and he felt contented as he saw greenery around him. He had grown up in the City of London and lived there for the vast majority of his life. However, he had always felt somewhat disillusioned in the City. Whilst it offered him vast opportunity in the sense that there was always much to do in terms of different opportunities and food to eat and people to meet from around the world. Something had been missing all of his life. He did not know what it was exactly until his studies. He had left the City and found that there was another type of life outside the Concrete Jungle. Life could be quieter, surrounded by nature and the loud stillness and serenity of nature. He felt contented whence out in his field and surrounded by greenery.

Granted what he saw before him was not a jungle or landscapes that were unbelievable to look at – it was nothing extraordinary, but it was nature and greenery undisturbed and unburdened by the modernistic and capitalistic desire to build housing or buildings. He was at peace once more. He continued driving through his field and was happy to see the different shades of green available for him to look at. The lighting installed and situated across his field, again powered by the Dala Electricity Hub, ensured he was able to work even when it was dark and Shackleton Nair was grateful for this; nature was different at night and through observation of nature at night, one could see things which they would otherwise be unable to see during the daytime – bioluminescent fungi was one of these things, only really activating its light emitting properties at nighttime in a bid to conserve energy.

Shackleton Nair was now deep into the field. He went to the last area which he had excavated and inspected. And when Shackleton arrived, he noticed something that was not there the last time he had looked at this very piece of land. He had only been there on Tuesday 3rd November, and it was now Saturday 7th November. And significant change had occurred in his field in just four days. And there was no rightful reason for this change. None at all. Shackleton Nair blinked a few times to ascertain whether what he was seeing was truly as it was appearing in front of him. He could not believe his eyes. He checked his bearings to see where he was in the field. *Is this the same location I was at on Tuesday,* he thought to himself. And when he checked he realised this was indeed where he was. And once again he looked upon what he saw; he did not believe his eyes.

The Mycorrhizae and Mycelium in front of his very own eyes had drastically changed; the Mycorrhizae was bioluminescent. This was not entirely uncommon in itself, as there were now just over hundred known species of bioluminescent fungi in the world. Though to his knowledge there were only two species of bioluminescent fungi in the UK – xylaria hypoxylon and omphalotus illudens – and this bioluminescent mycelium which he had stumbled upon was neither of these, for it was not large and orange or small and white.

And it was not the fungi itself which was bioluminescent, but rather the mycelium and mycorrhizae itself. The bioluminescent mycorrhizae were comprised of azure, baby and Egyptian blue – with each of the strands of this mycelium having different colours. *It has the colour of entoloma hochstetteri*, he thought. Though what was special and different about this, was the fact that the mycelium itself was bioluminescent – it was not the fungus. Further, Shackleton Nair knew that the entoloma hochstetteri was indegenious to New Zealand, and so this could not be that same species. Alas, there were many questions that came to his mind. He could not contain his excitement. He screamed out loud in joy. But upon inspection, Shackleton knew though this was not a new strand of fungi or mycelium. For it looked exactly as it was before, expect that now it was bioluminescent. *Has it evolved?*

He was at a loss for words. He would have to investigate this further. But some unfathomable theories came to his mind now. Again he blinked and looked back at the mycelium in front of him for he could not believe what he was seeing. *Am I seeing things,* he asked himself. He knew only six to eight per-cent of fungi in the world had been discovered, and perhaps he had stumbled upon a previously undiscovered element of the kingdom of fungi. *Is this dark fungi?* He pondered on the nature of the fungi he discovered; was this indeed dark fungi which he had discovered, and that was now visible to him suddenly? *What has changed in this environment for this mycorrhizae to become bioluminescent?* He knew that likely he would not find answers now or anytime soon; such was the nature of scientific discovery and under-standing of a phenomena. Mycelium, in itself, has more networks than the brain has neural pathways; the complexity of mycelium and mycorrhizae is unfathomable and somewhat ineffable – and Shackleton Nair knew this, and as such his brain could not compute that which he saw.

He decided he would need to isolate the mycelium from the mycorrhizae, and so he went closer. He noticed something strange. The mycelium, whilst still attached to the mycorrhizae, was buzzing. *This is abnormal.* It had a very high and visible vibrational frequency to it; one not typically visible to the naked and somewhat primitive and ultimately stunted human eye, despite the complexity, nuance and brilliance of human sight at its general fullest capacity. The mycelium, of course, was attached to the mycorrhizae, but it seemed to be levitating, trying to come free. He felt petrification come over him. *Seriously am I tripping*, he questioned. The only previous occasion whereby he could recall physically seeing a vibrational frequency or pattern radiating off of something, was when he had tripped on magic mushrooms the first time – he could see the unique vibrational frequency radiating off of every person around him, and it was then that it dawned upon him that everyone was different and unique in their own way, and that he ought to live his life and walk his own path and not be afraid to be his true self.

Though Shackleton could now see this in front of his own eyes with the mycelium and he was in complete awe and astonishment. He touched the mycelium and received a minor electric shock from doing so. It was as though the energy of the mycelium repelled upon touching him, like a magnet would and Shackleton Nair found this to be very curious. This was unlike anything he had ever seen before.

This cannot be real, he thought. He went to grab it once more, and this time isolated the mycelium from the mycorrhizae, and as he did so, he found that it levitated in his hands ever so slightly. Armillaria mellea also had luminous mycelium, but a nonluminous fruiting body – but that did not vibrate like this or levitate, and it was not blue. And thus he knew, this was something else entirely. Aristotle himself had first recorded bioluminescent fungi, and Shackleton Nair wondered how Aristotle would have perceived and written about this bioluminescent mycelium that Shackleton himself had in front of him.

He knew he would have to use DNA barcoding methods to look into this, but had a feeling that this mycelium in front of him would fall under the umbrella tree of dark fungi – dark fungi being something which sits outside the confines of traditional science of mycology, for there being no known understanding and legitimate theory upon the nature of it. And so, Shackleton looked again upon the levitating and bioluminescent mycelium that was vibrating in his hand and thought, *this is otherworldly – it cannot be from this Earth; something has occurred to the Earth itself for this to be occurring. The mycelium before me has changed in its nature in a matter of days – this vibrational frequency and levitation I see upon this mycelium is unlike anything I or, perhaps, any human has seen – this must be dark fungi I have discovered. Perchance, what is in it – something is in it for sure – could be dark matter itself which is resulting in these anti-gravitational and anti-known-physics-tendencies that I am witnessing upon my own eyes.*

Shackleton Nair came to his hypothesis in that moment; it was an intrinsic feeling; something that came from deep within him. He had his suspicions now that there was dark matter somehow infused within this mycelium. He did not know much about dark matter itself, other than the fact that there was much which was not understood or known about dark matter – but that it existed in this world without us even being able to recognise it, for it comprised of the matter which human's, limited under-standing of, science had not accounted for. But something within him told him it was this. The mycelium was non-adherent to the laws of physics. *This is certainly otherworldly,* he thought. *But how can I prove this? – is revolutionary; it will change science itself. But is this even science?* He thought. *But then truly, what is the difference between science and magic?*

He brimmed with excitement. He went to text his wife Claudia despite the fact he knew she was not happy with him. *F**k my phones out of charge,* he thought as he realised that his phone showed nothing but a black screen. He walked to his e-Van.

And then, it happened. All the lights went out and now all that he could see was the luminescence of the mycelium in his hand and in the ground in front of him.

Shackleton looked out across the field and could see nothing but the darkness of light. He looked up to the sky and saw that the imagery of stars produced by ArtificiSky was out too. He managed to find his e-Van and attempted to start it, but found that this too was out of charge; he had not charged the battery and so the battery was only being powered by the active Dala Electricity Hub. *The Dala Electricity Hub must be switched off, but why? This has never happened before. Is it only off here?*

And then panic began to sit in. *Sh*t how do I get back.* He realised he was very deep into the vast field. Without any light he would not be able to get back, and his phone was out of charge. And then it dawned upon him, *The Dala Device isn't working either.* He had nothing. He was not even able to arrange for a flashlight to be sent to him via same hour delivery by Rainforest-Prime. He was stranded, alone in the pitch dark of the night, deep in his field. *Sh*t Claudia and Charles,* he thought, *I've gotta get back to them – she's gonna be so annoyed with me.* Shackleton knew he had to get back home; his wife and son were all alone in the dark too, and again he was not there for them in their time of need, and was now not even contactable. He grabbed a handful of the bioluminescent mycelium he had discovered, and bunched this together in his hands to make a ball of light, and took this with him in a moment of ingenuity. And it did an ample job in at least giving him some light as he attempted to navigate his way back home. Shackleton decided to abandon the e-Van as he realised that needed to get back to Claudia and Charles as soon as possible. He ran through the field as he felt he would be able to figure out the tracks. Though without the field being lit up by the lights he had installed, he really could not see much. He could not even really see his house in the distance.

He now continued to jog with the bioluminescent mycelium giving him enough light to see where he was stepping. However, an hour went by fairly quickly as Shackleton jogged and soon enough he was out of breath.

And as he took a break to catch his breath, he realised that he had run in a circle. He was back at the same place. He was lost.

Another couple hours went by, and Shackleton was still unable to make his way back. He had given up hope as he realised he was going to be unable to find his way back in the pitch-black dark of night. The tracks on the ground could not be seen, and he was lost, without hope. The watch embedded within the exterior of his hand was not working either; he realised in this moment that this was connected up in live time to the Dala Electricity Hub. Thus, it stopped working entirely.

He was lost without his technology, with no map on him, and no way to contact his wife. He felt helpless and was unsure of how to proceed. He sat on the grass for a moment as he embraced his helplessness.

And then it happened, as it happened to everyone else in the UK of the early hours of Sunday 8th November 2024. As Shackleton sat on the ground, suddenly he felt lightheaded whilst his body simultaneously felt extremely heavy. He toppled to his side, like a sack of potatoes, and his face slapped onto the mud. Shackleton felt as though he was falling down a hole. This feeling of falling persisted for the entirety of the trip.

Though in this moment, Shackleton did not know what was going on, and he did not know he was about to embark upon a journey, which whilst would last for just a few hours, but feel like multiple days. Thoughts swarmed his mind like bees on honey. He could not control it, or even identify or isolate each one. He did not know what he was thinking, and yet he was thinking so much. His brain was on overdrive. But he could not tell himself to get up. He was stuck with his body feeling stuck completely, each limb feeling like a hundred kilograms.

And then he felt a pain come over him. It was a type of pain that was ineffable in nature, for it was not exactly pain that you would feel like one would feel with a broken bone, rather it was a pain which was deep inside of him, beneath the surface of his skin and bones. He groaned and he screamed aloud, but ultimately the scream could be heard by no one. For the scream was not even a sound said aloud. His larynx was not working even though he wished for it to work. A scream would have provided him some catharsis to his pain. But whatever this feeling was, whatever it was that had gripped him, was not allowing him to feel catharsis from the pain which he felt. He had no choice but to feel the pain in its complete entirety. Then rain slapped his face and for a moment, Shackleton thought he may have been imagining this.

But it was happening. And Shackleton began to feel sensations once more and his limps felt looser than before, the heaviness dissipated as the rain thudded on his cheeks, with what felt like rocks raining on his face – yet it was merely rain. Though now the heaviness of the limbs turned into an extreme looseness, and he felt like jelly, melting into the ground now, not falling due to the weight of his limbs.

This continued for some time, that felt like forever, and Shackleton eventually realised he had been tossing and turning and yelping and groaning in pain. He was curled into a ball on the ground, and wished for the pain to end.

With time the pain eased slightly and Shackleton Nair found he could recall his thoughts a bit better. He began to hyperventilate slightly and breathed out as he tried to breathe the pain away and take the negativity out of his lungs. As he did so, he calmed his breathing and soon enough Shackleton Nair recognised the feeling and his symptoms.

He was undergoing withdrawal symptoms, and these withdrawal symptoms were coming hard and fast at him with a vengeance. He could not control it till now but his experience having taken drugs, and his knowledge of the mushroom allowed him a relative ease and tranquillity that others who were undergoing this on the same morning of Sunday 8th November 2065, were not afforded.

What is this? Why am I experiencing withdrawal symptoms? I am not taking any drugs? What am I experiencing withdrawal symptoms from? These withdrawal feelings I feel are extreme too – as though I have been on a drug and addicted for some time now, he pondered.

He began to shivering. It was cold outside, but the shivering was from the extreme symptoms of drug withdrawal he was experiencing. Though as Shackleton has come to terms with his situation, his knowledge of drug withdrawal and psychedelic experiences – allowed him to be more calm and he practiced meditation techniques to relax his breathing and be grounded and centred with where he was and what he was going through. The rushing thoughts were suddenly not coming at him as fast as before and instead he felt his vision impaired. The clump of bioluminescent mycelium he had been carrying around with him through the field, now lay beside him – he had forgotten about it till now, unable to remember it or recognise its value to his current situation – but it did not look as it did before.

Shackleton looked at the bioluminescent mycelium which glowed, but then as he averted his gaze to and from it, he found the light to be carrying like a reside trail almost from light to light. He was seeing things. His vision and perception of light was off, it was as though he could see the light travelling. And now he felt even more so than before, that he could see the energy radiating off of the bioluminescent mycelium, and he could see it very clearly now. *I'm tripping*, he thought, *did I take something,*. But he knew he had not taken anything. *Is this from merely touching the mycelium that I am feeling this – I think not for no mycelium does this but ultimately I do not know because I have never seen mycelium or fungi like this before and so it could be.* However, whilst Shackleton had an open mind and he would entertain possibilities with mycology that other intellectuals in the field would not, these were grounded still within scientific fact – and the notion that by touching this mysterious mycelium alone would give him psychedelic like feelings; was completely improbable to him. And then it dawned on him. *Could this be from the Dala Network being down – is this because the electricity is down – it's the only thing which has coincided with this trip?* Though Shackleton himself knew that this was not grounded within fact or reason either –it certainly felt as though this was linked. *It feels to be true.*

And then for a brief moment the sensations stopped. Thoughts no longer rushed his mind. The light was no longer carrying and dragging as he looked from left to right. His vision was back to normal. The pain had gone. And so he stood up. He stood up, he was lightheaded once more. Headrush, he thought. And then, Shackleton Nair dropped to the floor. He blacked out.

The Astral Plane of Shackleton Nair

Shackleton awoke and lay flat on his back. And for a moment, he did not want to get up. He was rested so comfortably in the bed. And then he realised that he was on a bed of cloud. He looked directly ahead and saw a crisp blue sky, with clouds slowly moving above around him.

Is this a dream, he thought. *This cannot be real – it isn't real. Am I dreaming – am I dead,* he pondered. Shackleton slowly brought himself up to his feet and he looked around and realised he was in the clouds. He looked on his feet and found them embedded in the cloud as it looked as though the cloud was like candy floss. He laughed heartily; he could not believe that which he was seeing. *If this is death then I am in heaven and I do not think I will be making it to heaven,* he thought *And so I am not dead – I cannot be – this is a part of the experience – I am indeed tripping – and if I am tripping then this is the spiritual and introspective part of the trip and I must take this simply as it comes – I have done magic mushrooms before and my trip with Psilocybin gave me three truths the last time I did it – three truths on myself – three realisations and so I will look to find these three realisations of myself.* Shackleton had done Magic Mushrooms before and so he recognised that something was waiting for him here in whatever place this was he found himself in. He was deep within his consciousness, or perhaps his consciousness had reached another dimension or part of himself – he never quite knew or understood what happened to the consciousness when it embarked upon a psychedelic trip. Though Shackleton Nair knew that he was to learn about himself today, if he were open to the message and experience and he certainly was. The neural pathways of the brain expanded and connected with different parts of the brain when tripping on psilocybin and whilst he knew this was not psilocybin – he felt as though he had been transported to a place or state of mind whereby he was experiencing a psychedelic experience and so the effects were somewhat similar at this stage. He was ready. His spiritual and psychologically introspective part of long night, this night with no technology – this Tech-Night – had begun.

He knew what he felt and saw was real in some regard, in relation to his consciousness and his deep subconscious, but not real in the physical sense – it was a metaphysical reality he was experiencing. He began to have fun and tested the parameters of this reality he was in; he ran across the candy floss clouds and leapt from one cloud to another, and felt like superhero. He did this for some time before then coming to a sudden halt. A large wooden door with a hand for a doorknob appeared in front of him just five clouds ahead. And then in front of that door, just another five clouds ahead stood another door. And then in front of the second door, just another five clouds ahead stood a third and final door.

This is there for a reason Shackleton, it is time to face your truth.

And so, Shackleton now treaded more carefully across the clouds as he strolled toward the door, preparing himself with conscious breathing to see what lay behind the door for him. Shackleton grabbed the hand on the doorknob, and at first attempted the pull the door, but it was a push door. He turned the hand to the left and heard a click, then pushed. But as he pushed the door he felt himself pulled as the hand grabbed him and propelled him through what felt like a tunnel slide on a playground, and he felt himself catapulted and transported to another place and time.

Door 1 in the Astral Plane of Shackleton Nair

Shackleton Nair opened his eyes. He saw the red, dust filled carpet beneath his feet, and instantly he knew where he was. *It cannot be*, he thought, *why here.* He began to look up, but as he was about to look his up, he looked back down to his feet to see he was hovering above the ground beneath him; he was floating mid-air. He looked up and saw the cocoa brown quilted sofa in front of him and saw a younger, slimmer, beardless version of himself sitting on the sofa. He saw the black suit and white shirt he was wearing, the solemn look. His mother was on the sofa next to him. *I miss her.* His brother, Archibald Nair pacing up and down the room. This memory was from after his father's funeral, whence everyone had finally left the house. It was the last time he had seen his brother, years ago now. They had not spoken since. Shackleton did not want to relive this moment, but he knew he had no moment. He could not move from this position. He stood there levitating. He was not there, but he was there and he was stuck. A part of him was always stuck in this moment.

"Respectfully you have no right to be angry with me. You cannot tell me how to behave; I'm the older brother," said Archibald.

"Well, you should act like the older brother then. We represent the family now. You represent the family. Do you think people aren't watching us and making comments under their breath when they see you acting up?" Shackleton replied.

"Oh, I'm sorry Shack. Am I not behaving cordially enough for you, or to your standards? I'm sorry I am not behaving like your friends at Cambridge. I do not care what other people think. I'm the one who's been here. You have not. How dare you question me? You don't know what it's like to be the older one. You don't know what we've been going through."

"Darlings please. Don't fight. Please stop. You're going to say something you'll re…" their mother interjected.

"I don't care anymore mum. It's his fault. He needs to hear it. He's got the f**king cheek to tell me how to behave and deal with my grief. My f**king grief, when he's not even been here. You don't know the struggle or sacrifices I've made, or the pain we've seen with Pappa being ill. You were at uni the whole time doing your precious work. And while you were at uni

I was holding sh*t down here. So don't try question me and tell me how I should be acting like an older brother. I don't care what other people think when they look at me. I could not give a flying f**k. They weren't here for me when we were looking after dad. They didn't pick him up out of bed. They weren't there for that. They don't have the right to judge me. They don't know what I've sacrificed or lost. You don't know Shack."

"You gonna hold that against me Arch? The fact I was at uni? That's what Pappa wanted. You wanted me to stop my studies?"

"You could've been around more. I know what f**king sh*t you get up to there. Don't act like you were studying all the time."

"What do you want from me?"

"I don't want anything from you. Not anymore. I needed you before."

"Then why didn't you say?"

"I shouldn't have had to ask you Shack. You're my brother. You're there son. You should've wanted to be around."

"I had to do what I had to do. I couldn't put my life on hold for it. Pappa's been ill for years now. You wanted me to stop? It's not my fault you didn't have anything worthy going on in your life?"

"You think I didn't have sh*t going on? You think I've not sacrificed stuff. You're not the only one with stuff going on Shack."

"What do you want Arch? You want me to say sorry huh? Is that it? I can't undo what's happened. What's happened has happened. Get with the programme and stop crying. Be a f**king man Arch. This is life."

"You know what. You're a right piece of work. And you aren't a brother. You ain't my family. Not anymore. Not from today. You abandoned us. You left me and mum here to pick up the pieces as everything went to sh*t. You abandoned us Shack."

"I'm not … I'm not listening to anymore of this sh*t. This is just toxic at this point, and I don't need this. I'm going."

"Great. Walk out. Like you always do."

"I'm leaving. We're not getting anywhere with this conversation."

"You're running away again, like you always do. You haven't got the balls to stand here and talk like a man or to face your problems like a man. Walk away then. Always running from problems. Once you leave, we ain't chatting again – I hope you know that. It's done."

"Boys please," their mother pleaded as tears ran down her face. She grabbed Shackleton's hand before trying to grab Archibald's at the same time. Once Shackleton caught wind of what she was doing, he removed his hand quickly.

"It's done then," said Shackleton as he looked into the eyes of Archibald, for what would be the last time. They never spoke again.

· · ·   · · ·   · · ·

Shackleton felt himself catapulted back to cloud and he laid his back on door one. He felt a tear drop down his face. He had relived the moment a few times before, but had he seen it so clearly, without his personal bias. He watched it as a bystander, somewhat uninvolved. He realised that the way he recalled the encounter was different to how it actually occurred, and he recognised that his memory was based upon his personal emotions and his ego. He had run away from the situation, and he did not take responsibility for the breakdown in their relationship. He had been stubborn. His ego had gotten in the way of reconciliation. *He was sad – he felt alone like I left him and he too was grieving – why did I not apologise, why did I not just hug him and say sorry*, he thought as he dropped his head back onto the door, *so many years wasted man.*

He sat with his head on the door for some time as he cried a little. The lesson and message had been taken in and Shackleton knew he had to do something about his relationship with his brother. He looked ahead now and saw door two in the distance. He got up from the cloud-floor and proceeded towards door two. He was ready now for his second realisation. He walked up to the door and again felt the doorknob hand yank and transport him.

Door 2 in the Astral Plane of Shackleton Nair

Shackleton opened his eyes and again found himself to be hovering over the ground. Though now the ground beneath him was crisp cream sand. He looked around him and saw the sea and heard the soothing crashing of waves. He saw himself, a few years on from the experience of the previous door, now bearded and slightly stockier than before, sat on the side of the beach with Claudia next to him. They were on a beach in Trivandrum, Kerala after their wedding ceremony in India. Shackleton Nair could not recall the name of the beach but he knew it did not matter. Even at the time he had forgotten which beach they were on in that moment. Much like how he had been transported to another place from the field to the clouds to this memory, Shackleton recalled instantly how he felt with Claudia in this moment. They could have been anywhere in the world, feeling her body in his arms – he felt as though they were separate from the rest of the world, transported to their own world.

"Ahh, this is so beautiful Shack," said Claudia.

"You're beautiful," he replied cheesily. Claudia turned and kissed him on the lips. She first kissed his bottom lip before moving to his top lip and gently biting his lip. They stopped for a moment as he lifted her chin up and the two looked not at each other's eyes, but rather into each other's soul. They were lost in the moment and in each other. They leant in to kiss once more, but this time went in for a more passionate kiss as their tongues connected, much like their souls had connected, as they were now legally and spiritually tied through the union of marriage. This went on for a few minutes in what felt like mere seconds to them; they were lost in the moment.

"I wish we could be here forever Shack."

"We can if we want baby. We could afford a mansion here," he replied.

"Obviously not actually here. I don't know what I'd do for work here. And my parents are back home in London. I can't move here."

"I know what you meant. I just mean to say. We can go wherever you want. I'm just happy with you Claudia. I'll go wherever you want. Forever and always baby. You got me," he said as she turned and looked up at him once more before giving him a peck on the lips again.

"You're such a sweetheart. Let's just sit here for a while. It's really nice. Just bliss. Pure bliss."

"I can't wait for the future. For everything. To have kids with you. For forever. You're mine now, ain't no running away," he said.

"I'm yours baby. Forever now," she said, falling into his arms as he cuddled her with the sand gathering between their toes. They both looked into the distance and spent the next hour watching the sunset.

· · ·   · · ·   · · ·

Shackleton Nair sat in front of Door two now, but he sat cross legged and looked down at the ground as he took in a deep breath before letting it out. He beautiful and peaceful that moment was. He then consciously took himself through their whole journey together as a couple, all those years spent together. And he felt a tremendous amount of guilt overcome him, a guilt which led to him feeling a pain inside of him that was heavy on his heart and more painful than whence he was laying on the ground, sinking in the mud with the thudding raindrops on his cheek. The guilt he felt in this moment was unbearable. He was not there for his wife. He thought back to what she had said to him earlier in the day back at their house before all of this. And whilst he had heard what she said to him, he did not feel it or really listen and understand it. He had been disassociated from it.

But he felt it now in this moment. He had been selfish. He was not around enough for his wife. And she had been there for him, for what now felt like forever. He was at home, but he was not there for his wife or his son, and he had only himself to blame. He had everything he could ever want, everything a man could want or need from their life and here he was ungrateful for it and not seeing or valuing it even though it was always within touching distance. He had pushed her away and he was losing her. And his actions of this week would only push her away more. He had planned to lie to her and not tell her the truth. But having seen that which he saw, the good times and trust and devotion she had promised and acted upon, in their times spent together after their wedding – he had to tell her. His infidelity was not something he could avoid. He had to be honest, but he knew it would break her. *She deserved better than me and she deserves the truth – how could I be such a fool, I'm sorry Claudia – what have I done*, he thought.

He sat there and pondered on his infidelity and of how the knowledge of it would break his wife's heart and only solidify and further exacerbate her frustration with his actions in recent times. But having seen this memory they shared so clearly, the guilt he felt was unfathomable and utterly un-avoidable. He had been dishonest and not conducted himself with honour for far too long now and he had to change no matter the consequences. *These decisions were mine and so I must face the consequences*, he thought. *I must win my family back*.

Shackleton Nair stood up and walked up to door three. He wasted no time. He was ready for whatever was in front of him now. He did not know what it could be. For nothing could have prepared him for that which he saw behind door one or door two. But this was no surprise, for these were realisations that had to occur for things which lay in his deep subconscious. *I'm ready*. He grabbed the doorknob and initiated the process – his body transported again.

Door 3 in the Astral Plane of Shackleton Nair

Shackleton Nair opened his eyes once more. He blinked, looked around, and blinked again. *Have I returned?* He was back at the field. However, as Shackleton Nair looked down at his feet, he saw himself to be hover-ing over the ground once more, much like the bioluminescent mycelium. And then Shackleton saw it once more. He watched himself discovered the strand and place it in his hand and he looked on at his own astonishment at his discovery.

As he watched on, he ensured to look once more at the bioluminescent mycelium. He looked on again at the vibrations which were visible to his naked eye and of how it levitated in his hand – and it solidified the notion that this mycelium is from another world. Shackleton did not know how it came to be or why, but he knew for a fact that it was not from this world and that something had occurred to make it as such. *I know this is other-worldly, and it is something like dark matter that is infused with this mycelium, or else there is no explanation for this phenomenon – there already is no explanation for this, and this is why this must be the only explanation.*

. . .   .

Shackleton now found himself back on the clouds. *Why was this one shown to me – I have only just experienced this. Why this one?* For the first two were in his past, and there were clear and obvious reasons to him as to why they were moments he ought to relive; he had guilt attached to both moments and the people involved. But that which stood behind door three, was nothing obvious to him. And then it dawned upon him, The first two doors had shown him something he needed to work on, and things which were very personal to him. Door three had shown him this bioluminescent mycelium, and perhaps this was something he ought to work on; it was personal to him now. This was something that was unique in its nature and it was truly extraordinary. Seeing that moment again reminded him of just how ineffable and magnificent that strand of mycelium was. This was his purpose and had to explore and look into this more, whatever the cost. *I could have been shown anything amidst the vast experience and memories I have in this life, and it is this discovery of mycelium that has come to me – that must mean something – I must look into this no matter the cost – mycology is my everything,* he thought.

He closed his eyes as he pondered on this. He looked around once more as he figured this was the cue for his departure from this place. He remembered again the nature of how he found himself in this position and wondered if others would have navigated through this as seamlessly as he had. *Probably not*, he thought. And then he blacked out. His consciousness was ready to return to the normal world.

Sunday 8th November 2065, Early Hours of the Morning:
The Field of Shackleton Nair

Shackleton Nair was back to reality. Though things were not as he saw them before. His vision had altered. His sensations had changed. He felt as though he was in a daze. When he looked from left to right, his sight was blurred but more real than ever before. It was as though the ultra-high-definition image he was seeing in front of him, with all the intricacies of light and the subtle movements he saw, such as the rain droplets hitting the floor – was too intricate for his brain to process. Shackleton watched as the droplet of rain hit the floor and he felt as though he could isolate this image and concentrate highly on it, and it felt as though while he was looking at this, this was all there was in the world. He stood up and felt slightly woozy instantly. He looked upon his hand and felt a glow permeating from him; *I can see my energy radiating off my skin, this must be the aftereffects of the trip. I wonder if others are experiencing that which I am experiencing – they must have – but have they taken from this experience that which I have taken and understood – I am somewhat of an experienced psychedelic user and so perhaps they will not have been able to navigate that reality and state of consciousness as I have. But what has caused this? Either it is because I have touched and been in direct contact with this bioluminescent mycelium that has appeared in my field from seemingly nothing – or it is because the Dala Network is down – but why would the absence of technology and this network of electricity and technology have caused such an impact as though I am withdrawing from a drug – it does not make sense – or does it – either way I know that the these two things have occurred at the same time that I have had this experience, and it cannot be a coincidence – I suppose I shall have to wait to see if others have experienced what I have experienced before making my judgement – but regardless of whichever is the cause, both are phenomenal events with potentially longstanding consequences of which we do not know at this stage how far reaching and impactful these consequences are – but oh how I wish I could have used my Dala Device, for I would not have been stranded otherwise and so helpless – though this feeling I have now, these sensations, is something I must cherish and embrace and enjoy in this moment for the serenity of the nature around me is all that has gotten me through this, not being in the concrete jungle – I do not envy people if they have experienced what I have experienced in the city – God forbid – surely not – it is probably because of the bioluminescent mycelium, it must be – it can't be because of the Dala Network, it can't – for everyone is dependent and connected to this in the UK and so I don't believe it – ah we shall see – but for now I will enjoy this moment, and I need to see the mycelium again, especially with these sensations.*

He was amazed at the sensations he felt. *I can see it all clearly*, he thought to himself. He spent the next hour or so walking around and found himself inevitably gravitate back toward the bioluminescent mycelium he had discovered previously, and he marvelled at that which was in his hand. *I will be conducting a significant amount of research on this, and I will have to release a paper or article on this at the least – I can't not do it – this is bigger than me – and I care not what the consequences are or what others will say on my thoughts – this is bigger than me and it is bigger than them – this will revolutionise our thought on mycology and who knows what this means for humanity – there are so many questions about this and this magical mycelium is in front of me – it is in front of me and I cannot waste this opportunity – God has put this in front of me,* he thought to himself.

Another hour went and soon enough natural light began to come through the polluted sky as the sunshine was just about visible to Shackleton Nair. And then the reality of his situation dawned upon him as the sun came up, for he had forgotten in lieu of the trip and it's impacts on him both during and after the trip. *Crap, Claudia and Charles*, he thought to himself. *I must get back to them.*

Shackleton could now see his house in the distance and he ran. He ran as hard and fast as he could, for he recognised again the value of family and his devotion and duty to Claudia and Charles as a husband and father – his trip had exposed this to him and reminded him of who he was; he had neglected this part of himself. He looked down to his hand to see watch as he ran, but the network was down still – he had no clue what time it was but knew that likely it was after six am as the sun was out and they were in the midst of winter.

He went to unlock the door from the outside but realised in this moment that he could not open it; it was electronically sealed. He placed his hand on the sensor, but it did not detect his fingerprint – with the electricity gone, so to was his access to his home. He attempted to ring the bell but the button did not work; this too was connected to the Dala Network. He knocked on the door and knocked and knocked and knocked, for what felt like forever – his wife and son did not hear him. With the electricity down, and thus technology not working – he was stuck and unable to do that which he wanted, to access his own home.

Then soon enough he saw a shadow move past inside and Shackleton knew it was his wife, for his little son's shadow would not have been so large – not that his wife was large, as she was a petite woman. And so, Shackleton continued to furiously knock on the door and he knew that his wife would have heard it. However, the door did not open from inside and he was left perplexed. *Why is she not answering – I know she can hear me – perhaps she thinks it is not me – is she listening to music?*

And then the door unlocked finally. Shackleton smiled and his grin went from ear to ear; she was a sight for sore eyes, his sore eyes, the only face he wanted to see in this moment. *Forever,* he thought. Though the smile was not reciprocated. She scowled at him for a brief moment before rapidly pivoting and walking towards the sofa. She had given him the cold shoulder. Shackleton thought she would have opened her arms so that he could hug her but he was sad that she had not done so.

"Hey babe. I'm so happy to see you. Are you okay? How's it been here? Did it happen to you too?" he asked. She sat on the sofa and looked down and stared at the floor even though he had spoken to her. It was like he had spoken a different language to hers and she had not registered that which he said. But Shackelton knew his wife and he knew what she was like when she was annoyed; she either swarmed him with a barrage of insults, or she gave him the silent treatment – and Shackleton knew that the latter was the worser of the approaches.

"Talk to me. Are you okay? How's Charles? It happened to both of you too didn't it. I'm sorry I wasn't there. I hope you're okay."

"Shack. I'll be honest I think I need some time. I can't look at you right now," she said as she continued to actively avoid eye contact with him.

"Claudia. Baby please. Don't do that. Talk to me."

"Why Shack? You weren't here when I needed you. Again. Charles and I needed you. Do you know how hard it was going through this night without you there? It's the middle of the night and everything went out. And Charles was so scared. He was having a panic attack Charles. I mean so was I but I'm a grown woman. I can look after myself. But our son. Our son was in pain too and it was just me there. He's fine now and he's fast asleep. But you could have been there. If you just stayed inside. You were gone for four days and then you come back home and the first thing you do is choose to go be outside in the middle of the night, alone in your field and with your precious mushrooms. So yes, Shack I am pissed off with you. And I do not want to see you or talk to you right now. I just don't need it. I don't need your sh*t."

"I'm really sorry Claudia honestly. You are right. I should have been there. I was thinking about you when I had those realisations. I'm not sure if you experienced them too. From the sounds of it, I think you probably did go through it as well, but I am not quite sure in what capacity exactly.

I'd love to hear about it if you want to share and talk about it. I just wish I could've been there for you. But ultimately, I wasn't. And that is on me, and I've gotta live with that …"

"Yes, but it's not only you who has to live with that Shack. It's me too. I live with that already. Maybe you've only just realised that you aren't around. But I've known this for a while now. And yeah, I did see some things today as well. I wish I didn't see it but I think I needed to see it and it really did hurt me. This is a regular occurrence now and it seems like things have been like this for a while now and to be honest I really don't think this is working out as it is Shack. I'm all alone out here and you are just not present. Not anymore and it hurts me Shack. I'm not happy Shack. And I don't know if you're just blind to it or if you don't care. But either way, that is not a good sign because you should see that in me. I'm your wife."

"I'm sorry. You're right. I really do need to fix up. And I know my sorry doesn't mean anything right now because they're just words. But I am going to change. I saw things too. I relived a moment in our honeymoon. You know that beautiful beach in Trivandrum. When we were just sat on the beach for hours. I saw that and how serene it was. The promises we made each other. And somewhere along the way, I've lost my way. And this is on me. And I am truly sorry for this my love. I want to get back to where we were," he said. She patted down on the sofa in the empty space next to her as she ushered for him to come and sit down next to her. "I'm so sorry baby. I wish I was there for you. I am going to change now and that is a promise. Things will be different, and I swear it on everything I love."

"Ughh you're forgiven. How can I stay mad at this face? With those eyes looking at me and this beard. Come here," she said as she kissed him. This was a problem that Claudia had: she could never stay mad at him long enough because there was a part of her that could not resist him; the chemistry between them was undeniable.

"But you're okay though yeah. I really was worried about you Claudia. I was stuck out there. My phone died and I was deep in the field and the lights went out. I was running around in circles at one point and then I got stuck in the field and then the effects of whatever it was that happened, happened. And I was lying on the ground and the rain was hitting me and I couldn't move. And then when the effects eventually wore off, after the experience, I ran to you as the sun came up. So yeah I'm also very sorry about the smell because I was definitely sweating like crazy," he said. She pulled him close and wiped some mud off the side of his face before pulling him in closer and smelling his neck.

"You still smell good to me. Yeah, I'm okay though. The visions were a little bit mad though. I saw three things that I remember but I really don't remember too much about it. I just remember seeing us on our wedding night, and then when we first met, and then a moment when my parents were holding Charles as a baby when we spent Christmas around theirs. It was kind of beautiful to be honest and that's why it was worse that you weren't here babe. Because if you were here then I think it would've been strangely nice and kind of cathartic to see you and wake up from that to your face."

"That makes sense," he said. Shack thought on this as he realised that his wife has just seen and thought of him through here realisations. She was so committed to him. *I don't deserve her*, he thought to himself as he remembered his infidelity. "Well a positive from being out there was that I discovered something which I really think is something special Claudia. It's something out of this world. I've honestly never seen anything like it, and I don't know how it got there. This mycelium was bioluminescent, and it was levitating. It was just so beautiful. It is something out of this world I'm telling you Claudia this is something greater than I am. It's one of the greatest things I've ever seen. And I think this is going to be huge. Potentially what this can mean in the mycology world but also the physics world, if this is what I think it is, is groundbreaking and potentially will change everything. It had me in a trance Claudia seriously. It was just astonishing. I found myself looking at this mycelium as it sat in my hand, just in awe. I was stuck; it was just something you know. I can't wait to run tests on it.

I still can't quite believe what I've discovered. But yes, it is truly something special. This is the start of something truly special, and it's greater than me – but I am grateful that I am the one who's been blessed and bestowed with the duty to discover this mycelium and bring it into the world, that it's in our field. Everything happens for a reason right, so I know that this is on our doorstep for a reason. Seriously Claudia it was beautiful, I was just staring at the thing for at least an hour – it was so serene," he said as he looked into the distance with Claudia in his arms.

Claudia once upon a time found his devotion and commitment to his passion as a mycologist fascinating and somewhat attractive, for it showed her that he had a purpose in his life other than his family. However, she no longer really felt this way. For it had come to a point now whereby he was lost in his work, and it to her, it felt as though he chose his work over her and Charles.

"That's nice. I'm happy for you Shack. Good to hear though you were just thinking about your mycology all night though. Even now you're just thinking about that. Some things never change I suppose right," Claudia said as she bit her lip and stared into the distance, with tears welling in her eyes. Shackleton Nair looked down at his wife as she said this for he knew what she was thinking. *I just can't win,* he thought to himself. *I have to tell her about Cheryl, I'm going to have to – I can't do this to her – it's going to break her but I can't live with myself if I don't – she deserves to know – she is too good for me*, he thought to himself.

"You must be knacked babe. Shall we go to bed?" he said.

"Yeah, let's go."

"I'm going to have a shower quickly and then I'll join you in bed," he said. "I need to tell you something as well, but it can wait till tomorrow."

"You sure? We can talk about it now if you want? Everything okay?" she asked.

"Yeah babe, it's been a long night. I'm going to head up now though."

"Alright I'm just going to get us some water, maybe make a tea too and then I'll head up. Hopefully the electricity will be back soon too. Do you think it's just us or do you think it's everywhere? It's been out for eight or so hours."

"I think it's everywhere. What happened with those visions and everything was not normal. I don't know what happened exactly, but it was strange and if the Dala Network and electricity did go out across the entire country, and everything we went through and felt, happened to everyone else – I fear what the impacts could be on the country on a human and logistical level. But I guess we'll see what they say on the news tomorrow."

Shackleton made his way upstairs and as he did, he felt a tremendous amount of guilt overcome him, he felt it almost permeate through his skin and the guilt was so heavy on his soul he felt he could not look at her with a straight face; the reality of his infidelity weighed on his mind.

Shackleton Nair would not wait till tomorrow as he had initially intended. He would sit on the end of their bed after his shower, still sat in his wet towel, and wait for his wife and the love of his life Claudia Nair to enter the room. Tears fell down his face as the shower could not clean his sins off, as he felt dirty still leaving the shower. He would tell her of his infidelity. Shackleton Nair would not sleep in his bedroom that night, as his confession would break his wife's heart, and potentially their marriage and love story,

BOOK 12

FERGUS-SUNDAR

Friday 13th November 2065

*10:18: The Bedroom of Fergus-Sundar's old SSSA4 Provided Home,
now an Abandoned Government Building*

Fergus-Sundar decided that enough was enough; he was not able to enter
the Wormhole-Maze again, at least not at this moment in time. It had
been over a week now since he had been back at his old SSSA4 provided
home and he had tried and failed every day, multiple times per day, to enter
the Wormhole-Maze through lucid dreaming and from his knowledge
of the Formula. Something was wrong. There was a blockade preventing
him from accessing that same door which had teleported him out of his
origin reality and into the Primordial Black Hole, which allowed him to
pass through a wormhole and enter this reality of 2065 that he now found
himself stuck in.

Fergus-Sundar perched on the side of his bed. In the last week he had
barely moved. He had slept more hours than were healthy, but he had done
so with purpose. For he knew that one of the conditions which facilitated
his travel from the previous dimension to this dimension; was the fact
that he was an oneironaut, a man who could navigate the dream world in
a self-conscious manner. He was experienced at that, for the practice of
oneironautics was a part of his training as a SSSA4. For it allowed him to
tackle the traumas at the depths of his subconscious, and it allowed for
strength of mind to be developed in the potentiality of being tortured by

an enemy; he could escape the real world and inhabit the dream world. Though it was a dangerous thing, for one could lose their mind if they strayed in the dream world for too long, literally losing touch with reality – and Fergus-Sundar had really pushed the limits in this week.

Though he had grown desperate. He had been trying to recreate the exact conditions of the true reality in which he slept and went into the lucid dream, and attempted to recreate the lucid dream which he had found himself in. It was to no avail. Fergus-Sundar was well and truly stuck in this dimension. He got out of bed and moved his lethargic body and mind to proceed with his daily routine.

And as he brushed his teeth, the mission condition he had not been able to recreate dawned upon him. It was his birthday on the day that he had lucid dreamed. He guffawed to himself as toothpaste splayed from his mouth and was caught by his full, black beard. Could it be that his birthday was the missing component which allowed him to enter the Wormhole-Maze? It seemed improbable and frankly stupid to him. However, at this stage Fergus-Sundar pondered upon the reality of the situation he found himself in. He had at several points in the last week hoped and believed he was simply still dreaming. Yet him entering the dream state on several occasions during this time reawakened him to this ludicrous reality. It was unfathomable that he had left one dimension through a lucid dream, and then travelled through a Wormhole which was situated in a Primordial Black Hole, and then awakened in another dimension, unaged in appearance.

He had seemed to accept the nature of his reality whence he had first appeared in this dimension, though this ease of acceptance of knowledge and understanding seemed to evade him now. He looked at himself in the mirror and he found himself, for a moment, perplexed. Whilst he was unaged in appearance from forty years previously, he noticed for the first time that he had shown any physical signs or marks from his fights with Malabar Jones. If this was true, then it was possible that this somewhat magical condition of it needing to be his birthday for him to be able to access the Wormhole-Maze whilst lucid dreaming and with the Formula for Interdimensional-Travel – was a real possibility. Anything was possible.

Fergus-Sundar thought of his journey in the Wormhole-Maze and how time seemed to be non-existent. He thought of how he had experienced and seen his life at once. Of what he experienced. Suddenly he felt faint. His brain and soul were forced to accept and feel all of this in the Wormhole-Maze. The dark matter which existed within him, alongside his real memories and experiences in those specific timestamps of those specific moments of his life, were all that kept him from being ripped apart when passing through the event horizon of the wormhole, and it was what kept him sane and allowed him not to be lost in the maze of the wormhole.

However, now he was grounded and existent in a timestamp and dimension such as the one he was in, it was too much for his brain to process. In the wormhole, time did not function or operate as one experienced it on Earth and in an ordinary human life and experience; the human brain cannot see all of reality as it may very well exist. The Non-Theorised-Time of the wormhole meant his brain and soul had to adapt to that unique way of seeing and experiencing time. However, here he could not process and fathom that experience; he feared it would rip his brain apart and the angst of it all was too much and sweat now dropped profusely from every possible place on his body. And so, he decided to do something he had not done in quite some time, for he had not had the liberty, luxury, and paradoxically, the time to do so – he decided to sit down and write a diary entry. He had to bring himself back to Earth, metaphysically and literally.

He made his way to his desk and begun to write with his Ivory coloured Mont Blanc pen, which had the inscription *SSSA4 FS*.

I bring myself to the page for I find there is no choice but to. I cannot go on like this. What have I been doing? Where do I find myself? Truly, I think I have not been able to process this all, and I suppose it only makes sense considering the circumstances. But let me be honest with myself now. Let me be honest to the page.

For else there is no point in me even bothering to write. Why should I write this out if I cannot be true to myself and how it is I feel deep inside of me and if I cannot be honest. For writing is not important if it is not true and it would defeat the very purpose of me sitting down and writing if I cannot be honest.

So that brings me to the topic at hand here now. Why is it I need to be honest to myself? What is it I am looking for? I suppose with me trying to recreate the circumstances that brought me to this dimension, I need to understand why I am even trying to recreate those circumstances. Why am I doing it? Why am I? I suppose I no longer know. I thought I knew who I was. I did. I used to have purpose in this life. I was a special agent. A spy. I was at the top of my game, and I've served my country for years. I've saved lives. I uncovered lies. But what am I now?

I'm alone. I was alone before as a SSSA4 but now I am even more alone. I am alone and without purpose. I don't know why I came to this time. Why is it I landed in 2065? And if I landed here in 2065, why is it I've landed in a dimension in which I supposedly previously existed? Have I just travelled forward in time, or have I travelled to a parallel dimension of sorts. I don't know. I don't know and its hurting me. And there is no one for me to discuss this with. I am all alone. I am lonelier now than I ever have been before because at least before I shared loneliness with my fellow operatives, there were others like me. Though now, having experienced and seen the true nature of time and life and the realities of time as a construct – I find myself hurting inside for I am isolated by this wisdom.

I am afraid. I did not know it before. Though now as I find symbiosis from the pen to my fingertips to my wrist to my forearms to my shoulder blades to my neck to my head and to my brain and to my heart – I know I am laid bare and vulnerable to the page, as writing always does to me. It opens my heart and mind. I cannot do this. This is the angst I have at the deepest recess of my mind. How can I do this? No one knows and has seen and felt that which I have seen and felt and know to be true. And I have no one to share this with, no one to share my pain with. Though I must say I find some catharsis here having written down this hurt and pain onto the page, for at least I am giving this angst an avenue to breath and be seen. It is always better out than in. When alone and hurting from pain it is always good to write. This must be why I have been drawn to the page today.

I have never felt this loneliness and the pain that comes with it before. Or more pertinently, whilst I have known isolation and loneliness before, it was self-inflicted and a desired course of action for me – it was a choice. At this point now I am lonely and my experiences in the Wormhole-Maze have left me perplexed. It was a lot. As simple as that, it was a lot. And I have not family to support me. Even if I had not been a Dimension Travelling Spy, stuck in the year of 2065, I would still not have family for they have all died before their time. Quite simply I have no one to share this with, no one to tell. I find myself stuck in a time that I am not from, and I don't know what to do with myself. I have lost all that made me who I am. I held onto it vehemently and my job comprised who I was as a man.

Though now I do not have this, who am I? What is it I want to do? I wish to go back to 2025 and be a SSSA4 once more. Perhaps I could still do this now if I just get into contact with the SSSA. I know they search for me and are aware of who I am, Malabar Jones, my successor as a SSSA4 hunted me and failed to catch me.

But could I return to the life I once knew? I feel too much has transpired since then. I am not the man I once was. I don't think I have the strength and cold-heartedness to do what needs to be done as a Special Agent to protect this United Kingdom. Even if I could go back now, would it be enough for me? Really and truly, it would not. I think I am clinging onto something true that I once knew, though am past this point. I have grown and evolved into something else. Once your mind has seen a truth, it is impossible to unsee this truth. Would I even want to unsee a truth? What kind of a life would I be living if I was living a lie and living in ignorance?

One thing the Wormhole-Maze and the Non-Theorised-Time showed me, was that what's happened has happened and I cannot change it. All that has happened has brought to me where I am, good or bad, and I can try to fight this truth and try to disregard the reality of my life – but what will this achieve apart from adding to the discomfort and angst I feel inside of me right now.

I need to get with the problem, and stop feeling sorry for myself. I am where I am now, and it is what it is. This is the nature of this life. If I truly look at my life at this current moment in time, things are still well. I have life and breath. I have food and I have water. What more really is there to it? It could be so much worse. And truthfully, to achieve what I have achieved so far, travelling between dimensions, is a great achievement and I ought to be proud.

I don't like to sit and ponder and reflect on the good things I have done for typically I find this can make one complacent and I won't chase the next thing or accomplishment this way. But recently I have not been myself. And when one is not themselves and feeling low as I have been feeling. One must be kind to oneself. You must be kind to yourself Fergus-Sundar. Having written this out now I know some things to be true and I know which foreign thoughts do not have worth, value and truth in them in my mind. I am rid of these doubtful, intrusive thoughts.

I do know who I am. I am Fergus-Sundar, a Dimension Travelling Spy. Though I am no longer a SSSA4 And truthfully, I never want to return to this. I was clinging onto a reality and previous experience of mine whereby I felt safe .

I am an Interdimensional Traveller now.

I now know there is no point on clinging onto the past. I must move forward, much like how my physical body has seemingly moved forward in time. I have been ruminating on the negatives this last week or so and hoping to return to what I know. Though I cannot return and that is okay. I have accepted this now and I know from my experiences in the Wormhole-Maze that everything happens for a reason, and truly there is much to be hopeful for. I have been given a chance to change myself and my life for the better. And perhaps this world.

Upon my arrival into this world, I see that much is different.

This world is gripped and destroyed by the impacts of Climate Change. Perhaps I arrived in this specific time for a reason. Regardless of what the reason *is and what the future hold – I do not want to kill anymore. In my line of work as a SSSA4 I have killed too many even if they did need to die for the safety of many. I do not want to be a part of this anymore. There are others who can do this. Though there is no other who has done what I have done and travelled between Dimensions. I need to contribute to good to this world and to enacting positive change if I can. I need to work out what this is, and how.*

You are yourself once more Fergus-Sundar. No longer a SSSA4.

And so, Fergus-Sundar sat back and closed his eyes. He felt a tranquillity he hadn't felt in some time. The reflective writing had healed the angst in his heart and opened up the door for a new future.

13:42: The Basement Gym of Fergus-Sundar's old SSSA4 Provided Home

He had just completed his workout, and now he sat and quietened his mind as he attempted to be still, and focused on the sensations he felt in each part of his body, starting with his feet and gradually moving upwards. He entered a meditative state and listened to the thoughts which entered his mind.

I don't want to be a SSSA anymore. I don't want the SSSA to chase me. I want to be rid of this part of my life. But how do I reach this place? They know my face. If they know me and know of the situation – they will consider me an enemy of the state and forever I will be a target unless I check in with them. But I do not want to check-in with them. I need to move on. I am free to live my life; I have the right.

And then it dawned on him. He made his way to the shower and once he was cleaned and rid of the sweat from the workout – he wanted to test a theory. Malabar Jones had landed several hard blows to his body and head, and whilst he felt the pain from the blows, he had not a mark on him from the fight.

It seemed to Fergus-Sundar that another person or object could not inflict damage on this physical body of his he was inhabiting in this dimension.

Did this mean he was invincible? Was he unkillable? Was he now an immortal being? Fergus-Sundar did not think so, but truthfully he did not know. He did not know the parameters of his Dimension Travelling. He certainly hoped he was not immortal for the prospect of this scared him to the core and made him uneasy.

And so, he took a knife and nicked himself on the outer part of his forearm. And it made him happy to see blood trickle from his body. He let out a sigh of relief. And thus, the theory had been tested and proven right – he was not immortal, though it seemed only he could cause serious harm or inflict damage to his own body in this dimension. He wondered if this was a nuance specific to this dimension or if this was simply how it would be moving forward in his life and through his prospective future travels. He did not have the answer to these questions now but knew that one day he may very well find out and he would be happy to wait till that day. Though for now he would extend the testing of his theory to his real plan of action.

Fergus-Sundar had found a way to ensure the SSSA would no longer know his face. He took the knife, slashed his face, yelped in pain, and watched the blood trickle down into the sink. He had defaced himself. He was no longer looked as he once did – gone were his looks. But he did what he had to do to secure the future which he sought. The SSSA would recognise him no more. He was now the scarred.

20:02: The Lab of Fergus-Sundar's old SSSA4 Provided Home

Fergus-Sundar touched his face and felt the freshly applied stitches on his face. He was still in slight pain from applying it and having done it himself, it was certainly not a perfect job and thus it would perhaps leave some unnecessary scarring on his face. Though he was okay with this, it was the objective. He did not care for how he looked as it was not important to him and had not been important to him for some time. He ran his hands over his jaw and felt the bristly stubble on his face, he could hardly be recognised now with the slash across his face and untypical for him, freshly shaven aesthetic. It was a mission accomplished; he looked like a different man. And so, he went back to his SSSA first aid kit and applied the FastHeal steroid gey solution, specially made by the SSSA, to his fresh scar and stitches. Suddenly, and painfully, the stitching melted away and the scarring turned from a fresh scarring, to the look of an old scar. The job was done and Fergus-Sundar had bled for the cause. And so now, all there was for him to do was to figure out what he was to do and where he would go.

Time to do some research, he decided.

• • •   • • •   • • •

Some time passed, and he had scoured the internet. There were some benefits to still having access to the facilities of the SSSA as he had access to information which was otherwise hard to find. He found a company on the records of the SSSA as being a corporation to look out for and be wary of. This should have deterred and steered Fergus-Sundar away from the them, but it did the opposite and drew him in. They had his curiosity now. The company in question was that of the Global Hub of Extraterrestrial Exploration, more commonly known as GHEE. For it was from his experience, that those companies on the radar of the SSSA, were the ones which were either involved in some very shady business or just doing something which was extraordinary and potentially groundbreaking. Fergus-Sundar knew from experience that it was likely a company could be both extraordinary and shady at the same time. Thus, he was to be cautious in his movements but wanted to scope the place out for himself and make his own judgement based on what he could see and figure out. There was a chance that GHEE were engaged in nefarious activities. Though from accessing the SSSA database and what little he could see on here – they tended to keep written and logged information down to a minimum so as to avoid a leak of information in case of hacking – nothing had been proven and he realised that a certain SSSA4, Mr Malabar Jones, had been on the case on two separate occasions.

GHEE were heavily involved in Quantum Physics and the exploration of space and seemed to be interested in discovering whether interdimensional travel was possible. Their founder and CEO, the young Elisabeth Cervantes, seemed to also be committed to improving the world through her huge donations to people and countries affected by World War Water. GHEE were committed to helping the world be a better place and better at dealing with Climate Change. It was up to him now to look into this further and determine the truth behind the matter. He was no longer a SSSA4, though it seemed he could not truly escape his roots; he seemingly had another case on his hands.

Using the Quantum Computer in his home, he hacked the database of a London University and added his credentials to their staff and research team, whilst fabricating a history for himself. He then hacked into the calendar of Elisabeth Cervantes of GHEE, scheduling a meeting with himself. With the resources at his disposal and his skill with Quantum Computing; this was relatively simple for him to do.

But Fergus-Sundar had decided to leave his life as SSSA4 behind and so it was only fitting to leave this place he once called a home and properly vacate. He gathered a few things, the bare necessities only and a few handy gadgets made for him by the SSSA.

He hoped the GHEE and Elisabeth Cervantes were not engaged in nefarious activities; he wanted to believe they were not. For it seemed if there was anyone who may help understand his situation, and whom looked to contribute to a better world – on paper, it was GHEE.

And so, begun a new chapter for Fergus-Sundar, a new case.

BOOK 13
DEVONTE LACY

Friday 13th and Saturday 14th November 2065

*Friday 13th November 2065, 17:24: A Mansion of
Jarred Lane Johnson, situated in Belgravia, London*

"Well, well, well Mister Devonte. I suppose it's time to get this deal finalised then ain't it!" said Jarred excitedly as he rubbed his palms together, hardly controlling his excitement. "I must say I am surprised at how quickly you managed to get this to me. I am assuming this is the best quality stuff you got there. I am paying top dollar and when I pay top dollar, I expect top dollar product," he continued, with his tone changing slightly as the sentence carried on.

"Yessir Mr Johnson. You know I ain't play like that. If I done told you this gone be some good sh*t, then you know with me it's gone be some good sh*t. I always deliver you feel me? I mean that why you hired me right? Ain't nobody gonna look after your plants the way I do sir, and you know you got my word on that sh*t. That's why I'm an executive with this and so I try to my best to conduct myself as an executive with whatever it be that I put my name on," replied Devonte Lacy.

"Now that's a f**king sales pitch! That is a f**king sales pitch right there Devonte. If you spoke with a better accent and better English and like some hood guy, I'd hire you for Lane Johnson Pharmaceuticals immediately. You could sell my legal drugs for me, let alone this Mary-Jane!" he replied, slight condescension in his tone. Devonte took no notice to it; he had worked under Jarred Lane Johnson for some time now and he knew what he was like. He knew Jarred meant no offence; this was simply his demeanour and it was ignorance. For as much of a self-entitled, pompous and arrogant man that he was, he was calculated. Thus, if Jarred had the intention of being rude or demeaning, you would feel it with the ferocity of his words. It seemed extreme money and privilege could make a man feel as though they could get away with speaking to people as Jarred did, and his experiences taught him that he could get away with it.

"Thank you sir, I appreciate that. So shall we confirm the sale? I got all the bud loaded up in the Mega-Terrarium's shed with all the garden supplies and that, and I got my Dala Device all ready for you too."

"You don't play around do you. Alright let's do this then Mr Lacy. I'm nervous using these Dala Devices now ever since that night. I'm still recovering myself."

"Yessir I feel you on that one. I ain't finna try use that sh*t that much no more, but we got to" replied Devonte.

"£8000 we agreed on yes?"

"Yessir. £8000. I got you hella nice weed too by the way since you paying me nice. This sh*t gone last you a while. But then again I dunno how, how crazy you and your guests gone go," said Devonte as he prepared the Dala Device for the large transaction.

"Oh, we're crazy Devonte. Crazier and wilder than you could imagine," said Jarred as he brought his personal Dala Device to his eye and confirmed the sale. Devonte found the sale request on his Dala Device and verified the purchase from his side of the bank account. And boom. Just like that the money arrived into his account and for a brief moment when Devonte looked down at the number he felt like a rich man, or how he imagined a rich man would feel. Though this moment was all but a fleeting moment and it dawned upon him near instantaneously that he shall need to send this all to the National Superior Health Service and call Shannon McLean to confirm this and get his aunties treatment underway.

The Tech-Night 1.0

"Well Devonte, good doing business with you!" Jarred replied.

"Good to do business with you too Mister Lane Johnson sir," replied Devonte Lacy with a wide grin on his face to match Jarred's wide grin. They both felt a sense of euphoria at the exchange of money on their respective Dala Devices.

The two of them shook hands. To Devonte in this moment, it felt like a deal with the devil somewhat for his knew this deal would lead to his imprisonment. Though it was a deal he had to make so that he could keep his auntie alive and get her the treatment that she needed. Family was everything for him.

"Now Devonte, do I need to worry about the smell? I understand it's a large amount of weed and if I transport it, I might arouse the suspicion of police and perhaps trigger the Marijuana Smell Detection Sensors?" asked Jarred.

"No sir. That sh*t be sealed shut inside your Mega-Terrarium. And it's perfectly fine to smoke inside the Mega-Terrarium. The filtration system means the plants will be aite and ain't no smell gone come out. Ain't no one gonna smell it or see the smoke from outside and plus it be your private property. Inside the container with all the weed, I got some smaller smell-proof containers as well. I would just be careful where you be smoking that sh*t cos as you said, if you smoke that in public, you could attract the attention of the police and you might set off an MSDS, which you ain't wanna do – trust me on that one. But they only be there in specific places. You should be aite in some private property like car parks and sh*t; placed that ain't so boujee. But to be honest I don't think you gone be hanging there anyways."

"No Devonte, we likely won't be anywhere near these sorts of establishments. It'll just be for transport between my place and locations of my associates. But yes, private property so I am sure we will be fine. But what is a MSDS?"

"MSDS is the Marijuana Smoke Detection Sensors you was referring to. And yeah you should be aite then. Just put them in the smell proof containers I was telling you about. I'll show you them before I go anyways. But do you mind if I quickly make a phone call?"

"Of course. MSDS is the abbreviated format. And fine, no problem at all Devonte. Come find me in my Cigar room," said Jarred on as he looked down at his phone and walked off.

Devonte Lacy waited for Jarred Lane Johnson to leave, before falling to the ground and sitting with his knees up and taking in deep breaths to calm himself down. He liked to calm his breathing and meditate if possible when making a purchase or sale using his Dala Device ever since The Tech-Night of just a few days prior. Since then, whenever he made a purchase, he experienced flashbacks on a minor level, and he never wanted to depend on the feeling and satisfaction the Dala Device gave him ever again; *that sh*t had control of me man*. He knew some people who had already fallen back into the trap and had lost consciousness of what it was doing to their minds every time they used it – but not Devonte. He did not know what it was that was happening to his brain when he was using it. Though on the infamous Tech-Night when he could not use his Dala Device, he realised his dependency on it and the reaction he had to not being able to use it. Using the Dala Device came him a rush of some sort, unlike anything else he had taken before – the closest thing Devonte could think of was valium which he had taken in his university days, a deeply addictive drug.

Devonte calmed his breathing and tried to counter the high that the Dala Device had given him, but knew it was likely to no avail. It was impossible to fight, for everything depended on this. He could not live without buying things or selling things. No one could. Not since the UK went completely paperless with money.

And so, Devonte Lacy prepared himself to use his Dala Device once more, though this time he did not care for the fake joy he would get from the purchase. He did not care that the Dala Device would alter his mind when he made the purchase and that it would leave him in a sense of elation. For this elation was one he would feel anyhow, and he wanted to feel this elation exacerbated. He was slyly craving the ecstasy and euphoria that came with it … it truly was a drug. He searched through his contacts now somewhat frantically and found the number for Shannon McClean of the National Superior Health Service. He was to make a call that was going to provide his auntie with a licence to live. It was all worth it for this.

Saturday 14th November 2065, 09:02: The Basement /
The War Room in The League of Shottas HQ

And so, Devonte Lacy once again walked down the narrow stairs leading to the War Room, with Samson the Eerie Shadow of the Door following behind him. He had been with the League of Shottas for less than a month and had already been to the War Room more times than one of their Global Ambassadors, his dear friend Bixente Lemaire. He had not had a chance to speak to Bix since he had made the sale to Jarred Lane Johnson yesterday and did not have the chance to message him and warn him in the morning either. Frankly, he did not want to. He felt as though it was likely Bix was to be called to this meeting, if he was available to attend the meeting. However, Bixente was a busy and famous man; he frequently found himself travelling and away from home. A part of him wanted Bix to be present at the meeting, in case he could make a plea for him and ask for a favour from Mike da Silva, and allow Devonte to walk free. Conversely, he did not want him there for he feared he would be ashamed of his friend, for ruining his carefully curated reputation and relationship he had with the League of Shottas and their executives; Bixente Lemaire had vouched for him.

Samson clapped his hands and the door was unlocked from the other side. Once again Devonte Lacy walked into a room with all eyes locked onto him instantaneously. Though this time there was no blood on the floor. There was no dying man. And Bixente Lemaire was indeed present in the room. And he did not have his trademark smile plastered across his face. Instead it was a solemn Bixente Lemaire, for he looked close to bursting into tears. Devonte and Bix exchanged a look and Devonte felt shame; he had let his friend down. Devonte sat in the chair purposefully placed in the middle of the room.

"Now let's just get straight to business. It's early, especially for a Saturday, and we have a lot on the agenda. Unfortunately, we begin the day with a transgression and a disciplinary. Now. I don't like to hear about this first thing in the morning. But when these things occur, I must hear about it first thing in the morning because its important. This should not be going on. It should not be occurring. The Compass of Commandments of the League of Shottas are simple and there are not many commandments on there and so when one is broken, it is a transgression that cannot be ignored. The transgression I refer to today is one committed by Mister Devonte Lacy Junior and the act in question is a not paying his taxes. Hah. Not paying his taxes. And for context to anyone who may not know Mister Devonte Lacy Junior. This is his first sale with the League of Shottas. He was inducted into the League of Shottas by the Head Honcho himself, Mike 'The Black Tiger' Da Silva. And he was brought in on merit by a Global Ambassador of ours, Bixente Lemaire. And so this transgression, on the face of the matter, is completely, and utterly stupid. I mean I find myself looking at the facts here and I turn to Mister Devonte Lacy Junior and I just think what a f**king idiot you are. What is this kid doing? The sale you made was for £8000 Mister Devonte Lacy Junior. That's only £3200 in taxes. And in all honesty, I commend you for making a £8000 sale for your first sale. That is big money and that tells me you have some good connections and had the potential to make a lot of money. That is no ordinary sale and it's one that caught our attention, straight away young man. You have earning potential that is for certain. But we here at the League of Shottas. All of the executives, are disappointed and quite frankly a, vexed, that you've decided to break a Commandment of the Compass, especially with your very first sale and in your first month of being with us. It is not a good start. Not a good start at all. However, you had things in your favour Mr Devonte Lacy Junior. Now

I am just the speaker here. This is how disciplinaries operate here. Two people speak. The one who has committed the transgression and the one who deals with the transgressor. Now today that responsibility is bestowed upon me. But before you were here. We spoke, all together. Including your friend Bixente Lemaire. He offered his thoughts also. And you are lucky you are friends with Bixente Lemaire. He speaks highly of you and once again he has vouched for you. But anyhow. As I was saying. You have things in your favour Mr Devonte Lacy Junior. You are liked by Mike da Silva. You know Bixente Lemaire. And you made a sale of £8000 in your first sale as a Shotta under our books. So you know the right people. And you have the potential to make a lot of money for yourself and for this Organisation. And so, we have come to an agreement, which was near unanimous. Some people did not agree but they accepted the majority's decision. And ultimately the fact that Mike da Silva likes you, helped your cause more than you know. But it is the verdict of the Executives of the League of Shottas, that if you pay your taxes now, then you will not face punishment for your transgression and you shall walk away a free man and able to conduct further business as a Shotta on our books, albeit with a watchful eye on you. So when you are ready, let me know and we can put the sale through Devonte Lacy Junior. You are a lucky man," said Jamal Pitcher as he paced back and forth in his £2000 bespoke tailored suit.

"Yessir I hear all you be saying. And my name be Devonte Lacy, ain't no Junior, but it's aite. Anyway man, thank all of y'all for your time. I'm sorry to bring y'all out here so early. But I'm afraid I can't pay that now," replied Devonte.

"Devonte don't make this difficult. You're being given a lifeline. You can't or you won't?" replied Jamal Pitcher.

"I can't."

"So you've already spent it?"

"Yessir."

"Here we go. Alright so you're telling me that in less than a day you have spent £8000?"

"Yessir," replied Devonte stoically.

"What did you spend it on?" replied Jamal Pitcher.

"That ain't none of your business," replied Devonte.

"It is when it's money of the League of Shottas you're spending Mr Devonte Lacy Junior."

"Well I'm a grown ass man I don't feel like disclosing that. That be my own business. I hope you can respect that," replied Devonte.

"Fine, I understand. Let the record state I do not respect your right to withhold this information from us, as this is a disciplinary and full transparency is advised – but fine. Considering the position you find yourself in now Mr Devonte Lacy Junior. Do you regret your actions? Do you regret spending our money?" asked Jamal Pitcher.

Devonte hesitated for a moment for he knew that he could lie very easily. This question felt as though it were to determine his fate and he could easily say he did. But he did not regret his actions and did not regret spending the money – Devonte was a proud man and an honest man. This was the first time he was speaking aloud about spending money on his aunties cancer treatment. He did not want to talk negatively about it on his first moment speaking about it. And so he spoke his truth, however it was going to be taken.

"No Sir I do not. I would do my actions again if I had to and I would still spend the money. I know that ain't the answer y'all looking for, or probably even expecting but that be my truth and I'm an honest man. So y'all do what you gotta do. I accept my fate and I respect whatever decision y'all come to. I didn't mean to cause no disrespect to y'all. I can pay that money back in time. But right now; I ain't got that there. So do what you gotta do. I did what I had to and I don't regret that sh*t at all I aint even finna cap to y'all since we being honest and imma accept the consequences to my actions. Standing on business you feel me. So yeah man let's get on widdit."

"Samson, please see Mr Devonte Lacy Junior out of the room for a brief moment whilst we deliberate on the matter. Thank you for your testimony Devonte," said Jamal Pitcher as he Samson escorted Devonte out of the room.

· · ·   · · ·   · · ·

The Executives of the League of Shottas spoke together on the fate of Devonte Lacy. It seemed the group now somewhat unanimously agreed that they ought to punish Bixente Lemaire's friend for his action. For he did not seem to have any remorse over his actions and this was not a good sign. Now it did not matter whether or not he was favoured by Mike da Silva. For being remorselessness of Devonte showed the executives that Devonte did not respect the rules of the League of Shottas. And so, Bixente Lemaire pleaded with them. He pledged to instantly pay the taxes that Devonte owed. They told Bixente that Devonte needed to pay for his sins now regardless of whether the money was paid; his defiance meant he had to pay his dues. Though Bixente Lemaire was adamant and very convincing to the group. He pleaded shamelessly. Devonte did not know it, but he was a lucky that Bixente had not called in a favour from the League of Shottas as of yet in all of his time being a Shotta for them.

The Executives wished for Devonte Lacy Junior to be sentenced to face three years of jail for his offence; for he had broken the Compass of Commandments instantly, there was a large amount of tax that he had now paid, and most importantly he had no guilt and alas had to be punished accordingly. However, Bixente Lemaire pulled his influence and convinced the Executives to give his dear friend Devonte Lacy a reduced sentence of just three months, which would potentially equate to only six weeks months with good behaviour. The meeting is concluded and Jamal Pitcher summons Devonte Lacy back into the room. It is time for his sentencing.

· · ·   · · ·   · · ·

Devonte Lacy walks back into the room and sits back on the chair placed in the middle of the room. He locks eyes with Bixente Lemaire once more, sweat drips down his face. Bixent looks down to the floor.

"Mister Devonte Lacy Junior. Thank you for joining us once more. We have come to a verdict. You are sentenced to three months of jail time for your transgressions against the League of Shottas. You will be a Headline Arrest and so if you service this well and accept this well, as I feel you will do – we would be more than happy to accept you back here. You are, in a weird way, still serving the bigger picture here at the League of Shottas and fulfilling a duty for us. We can take care of you inside. You will be moved to jail within the next few hours, once our team finalise the paperwork with our judge on call. And so, you will be in jail by the end of the day. I hope you know Mister Devonte Lacy Junior, that you are a very lucky man. Had it not been for your friend Mr Bixente Lemaire, you would have found yourself sentenced to jail for no less than three years. His contributions and loyalty to this organisation is the only thing that has brought your sentence down to a mere three months. You could have walked away today with no jail time. Even considering you could not pay what you stole from the League of Shottas. However, you show no remorse or guilt over your actions and so we could not let you leave here without any punishment. I hope you realise how lucky you are. Mr Bixente Lemaire is paying back what you owe in full and so once you have done your time in jail, you will be able to sell under the League of Shottas again though you will be on probation for twelve months. Now do you accept your sentence Mister Devonte Lacy Junior. Well you have no choice but to accept, but I have to say it," said Jamal Pitcher.

"Yessir I accept the time. It is what it is. I know what I done. And let it be known I'm grateful for Bix. He my dawg for life and please don't look down on him for how I conduct myself. I know Bix vouched for me and put hisself on the line for me and I'm grateful for it. But please don't be judging him for what I done. I'm responsible for myself and how I conduct my business is my own business and it ain't got nothing to do with Bix. He told he how it be here and I f**ked up and that's on me. That's all I gotta say. So yeah it is what it is. Please just tell my auntie I love her, that's all. If you can get that message through to her somehow, I'd be grateful. And just tell her that imma see her when I get out, God willing. I know she gone be aite now and that's all that matters," said Devonte as he remained stoic, despite the fact that he found the gravity of what was about to happen, begin to hit him.

"Thank you for your words Devonte. Let it be known that our opinion on Mr Bixente Lemaire has not changed despite his connection to you and despite the fact he brought you to this organisation. Mr Bixente Lemaire is a valued part of this organisation and will continue to be so for as long as he wants to be a valued part of this organisation. Regarding your auntie – we will pass your message on. Now if you would like, you can speak to Mr Bixente Lemaire for a minute before you are put into solitary confinement here at The Warehouse, and then taken to prison once your documentation is sorted. Now do you have any questions?"

"Yessir I'd like to Bix and no I ain't got no questions. Thank you again for your time and for being kind to me. I appreciate it more than y'all know and imma get y'all back for sure. Y'all inviting me and accepting me has helped me out big time. Just know I didn't f**k this up on purpose. It ain't personal or cos I ain't respect y'all and your organisation. I did what I had to do is all. That's it."

"You're welcome Devonte. You have two minutes with Mr Lemaire," replied Jamal Pitcher as he tilted his head down with acknowledgement to Devonte. He gestured for Bixente to approach Devonte, who jumped up and skipped over to his friend. The two embraced with a dap before hugging. They had never hugged like this. But neither of them had ever faced the proposition of jail time before.

"Devonte man. What the f**k man? I tried to do what I could bruh but you f**ked it when you told them you didn't regret it. Why you do that man," said Bix as he looked up to his friend in confusion.

"Bix man, it is what it is. As I done said man, I did what I had to do bruh. Ain't no other way it could've gone down. For real though I apologise if I put you in a sticky situation. That weren't my intention but I can see how I could've f**ked you up, and I'm sorry for that. Word to my mother bruh I ain't mean to put you in a bad spot like that," replied Devonte.

"Its good bruh I'm just glad they didn't go crazy on your ass. You lucky as f**k you know. I ain't even gone lie. I saved your ass bruh," replied Bix as he let out a slight smile for the first time, though this quickly dissipated as he remembered the situation his friend found himself in. "I gotta ask though. Why the f**k did you not just pay the taxes? What the hell you need £8000 for?"

"It was for my auntie bruh."

"What do you mean? She good?"

"She is now. She's in surgery now. She got cancer bruh. And the damn NEHS ain't give her the treatment she need man so I had to pay for that sh*t with the NSHS. Damn privatisation man. It is what it is man. As I done said, I had to do what I had to do and paying that sh*t for my auntie was worth it man. Even if it mean I gotta go jail. My father and my grandfather done been to jail so it's just another Lacy going jail you feel me. It ain't nothing my ancestors ain't seen before and well it is what it is you feel me? Sh*t had to be done bruh, I ain't regret it. But I can't lie, I had mad guilt man. I was feeling hella guilty. When I was planning all this sh*t it felt like I was using you man and you know you're my dawg. I ain't ever want you to be feeling like I done used you man. So I'm sorry to you bruh. I'm sorry. But man I don't regret none of this man, I had to do what I had to do. Sh*t played out as it had to," said Devonte as him and Bix embraced again.

"Devonte man I'm sorry bruh. I didn't even know man. Why the f**k you didn't tell me? Stupid ass. Bruh I would've paid that sh*t for you man. I already paid now anyways. You wouldn't need to be here man. F**k sake man. Devonte man. You stupid mother*****r."

"Cos Bix man. I ain't always wanna rely on you bruh. It ain't nothing personal but I'm a grown ass man you feel me. Some sh*t we gotta do ourselves. And respectfully bruh it ain't your business to be worrying about. It ain't your family. It's my auntie and I had to handle my business. Sh*t was time sensitive too man. It needed to happen asap. If I didn't have the money or couldn't find a way to geddit of course I would've asked you. But I was able to make that money so I did. An opportunity presented itself to me with my employer and so I took that opportunity. And plus Bix I wanted to pay that sh*t off myself you know. I just felt like I had to you know. Don't take it personal bruh you always done been there for me and loaned me money when I needed that sh*t but this time I had to do it myself. No matter the consequences. You my brother man. I love you bro and imma see you soon bruh," said Devonte as he dapped up his friend one more time before Samson took him away. He turned back one more time as he looked back at his friend who stood in the same spot.

"I'll see you soon man," Bix shouted out. He wished things went another way as he now knew what had transpired. He understood Devonte's actions but still could not help but wonder if things could have gone differently. *If only I knew wagwan*, he thought to himself. *I wish that mother*****r told me man f**k,* he thought. For Bixente Lemaire £8,000 was a drop in the ocean. He would have paid it in an instant.

And Bixente Lemaire realised in this moment, and felt it truly for the first time, that no matter how much money and success he had in this life and in this world – there were still things out of his control and his money could not solve all his problems; he could not stop bad things happening to people he loved – this was the nature of life. He wished he had never brought Devonte Lacy to the League of Shottas, and then he had rejected his friend. *He would've found a way anyway though man; Devonte a stubborn mother*****r man. Ain't nothing we could do.* He wiped his tears away as he watched his friend be taken away.

*20:51: Cell 219 in a London Prison, secretly owned
by League of Shottas*

Devonte Lacy sat down on his bed in his lifeless clothing, surrounded by cold and plain walls. And so, within the space of just 24 hours, he was officially a convict and was in a jail cell. His job taken away, his freedom taken away, his future taken away; but the future of his auntie had been secured. And for that, it was worth it. Rather maniacally, he began to laugh to himself as he put his head in his hands and pondered on the proposition of being stuck in this jail for the next three months.

How the f**k I done found myself here man, he thought. *What other choice did I have? I had to turn to crime to save my family, but was there another way? It is what it is man, I had to do what I had to do. If they don't know me they would probably judge me – but they don't know what I done been through.*

And then, the laughter slowly turned into sobbing. This sobbing went on for a little while, in what was pure catharsis and a release of angst for Devonte Lacy; he had been very stressed. Then soon the sobbing turned into tears of not sadness or regret, but rather of joy and relief. He had helped save his auntie's life, and so his prison time was worth it for this. And so strangely, he felt content and at peace.

BOOK 14

MALABAR JONES

Thursday 12th, Friday 13th, and Saturday 14th November 2065

Thursday 12th November 2065, 20:22: The SSSA provided Home
for SSSA4 Malabar Jones, Knightsbridge, London

Malabar Jones cut into his fourth chicken steak as he looked at his phone expectantly waiting for a call from the SSSA; they had ignored his calls ever since The Dala Electricity Hub of London had been switched off by Brian Harrison to incite the, now infamous and mysterious, Tech-Night. The SSSA had used their leverage to get him out of jail, but they had not contacted him. He used this opportunity to rest, but Malabar could not lie to himself. He feared the worst. He knew how the SSSA operated and he feared he would be blacklisted and have his special privileges and his licences to operate revoked. He knew it was not unlike the SSSA to blacklist an agent in lieu of a major failure. And Malabar Jones knew that he had failed on a major scale.

Does this mean the SSSA1, the Yonige-Ya, will be sent to terminate me?

He had over thirty successful cases as SSSA4 and had protected his country on numerous occasions. But this did not matter now. The success and the peace he had previously secured for the nation did not matter now. For the weight of importance and the stakes involved with his missions as a SSSA4, meant that it only took one failed mission for potential termination as a SSSA. He was the countries last line of defence with terrorism. And in this job, one was only as good as their last mission – he was a failure now, and a liability to the SSSA.

AAJ

Malabar Jones knew the Board were likely weighing up their options with regards to his conduct and his role. There was national crisis created as a result of his failure, and he wanted to clean his mess up, to tie up loose ends of his case. He felt as though there were now many questions and much mystery surrounding the Dala Device, that he and the SSSA were not aware of. The aftermath of the Tech-Night, that this eventful night was now being called, was not something that they could have anticipated. This worked in his favour; he was adequately placed to investigate further into this considering it was his case, and that he was so close to apprehending his target.

The phone rang and he did not hesitate to answer the call.

"Malabar Jones, SSSA4. This is a pre-recorded message from the SSSA on an encrypted line, from 1Honcho. Do you wish to proceed? Respond with Yes or No to proceed," said the automated message.

Malabar Jones took in a gulp as he heard the word '1Honcho'. For 1Honcho to want to speak to him and leave him a message – meant that this message was directly from the top of the food chain of the SSSA. 1Honcho was the top dog and decision maker – the 1Honcho was the direct contact with the Royal Office. It was typically not good if 1Honcho was getting involved directly with the agents. He had never heard the voice of 1Honcho, did not know who 1Honcho was, or how they looked – this was top secret, a strictly need-to-know basis.

"Yes," replied Malabar as he stood up.

"Thank you for confirming. The call will automatically end once the message has been played – please do not end the call on your end, unless it is necessary to do so. Your pre-recorded message will read out in T-minus fifteen seconds. Thank you."

He paced up and down his marble floored kitchen before leaning over the kitchen counter, as he expectantly waited to hear the message.

"Malabar Jones, the current SSSA4 appointed by his Royal Highness in servitude of this United Kingdom. This is 1Honcho. We have never spoken before and you do not know who I am, but I know who you are. Unfortunately, you have failed in your most recent mission to apprehend Mister Brian Harrison, and as a result national security has been compromised on a mass scale. You are therefore blacklisted, and your special privileges as a SSSA4 are to be revoked. You failed, and your failure has cost this country greatly. I see on the notes from your mission that you believe yourself to have seen the first SSSA4, Fergus-Sundar. We know that Fergus-Sundar is an agent who went missing in 2025, and thus we are also uncertain as to the mental state you find yourself in. From the notes, it is established that you temporarily abandoned your mission to chase this man who you claim to be Fergus-Sundar. This delusion is not one I can explain, and looking through your file and the missions you were previously on, I do not quite understand how or why you would abandon your sworn duty. And so, it is of the belief of the Board of the SSSA – that we will give you another chance to correct this failure of your mission. There is no explanation for your conduct and so we want you to see this out. The terrorist Brian Harrison has been taken by the police and he is no longer of concern to us here at the SSSA. Now if you give us something we can use, some concrete information and more clarity on this f**king mess with the Dala Device – then your special privileges as a SSSA4 will not be revoked, and you will not be terminated. You have a week SSSA4, a week. Give me something. Fix this f**king mess. Check in with Keyshawn Braun if you have any information, but note he will not be on hand to help you along the mission. You will fix this f**king mess yourself. Do not let us down again. Or else I will have to call in the Yonige-Ya, the SSSA1. Good luck Malabar Jones," said 1Honcho as the call ended. Her tone was firm, he could tell that there was no leeway on what she had said – he had to salvage this case.

*Friday 13th November 2065, 22:20: The Dala Device
Electricity Hub, London*

Malabar Jones scanned the fake ID he had created and entered The Dala
Device Electricity Hub of London from the top floor of the building. He
had climbed round the back side of the building from where the bins were
collected. He clicked a button on his TechSuit and the weatherproof gloves
and shoe covering disappeared from his outfit, and with that so did the
snow on his clothing.

He activated the flashlight embedded within the palms of his TechSuit,
dimmed the light, and activated sneak mode – removing the sound of his
feet smacking the floor, enabling him to move through the Hub stealthily
and silently.

Malabar Jones did not know exactly what he was looking for but knew
that he needed to look around the facility properly and look into the documentation in the main offices. He located the offices on the fifth floor
and began to make his way there. Then he saw a group of five security
guard's, armed with guns, congregating outside the staircase. He had no
choice but to confront them. However, he did not want them to trigger the
alarm system, and so he would need to systematically break them down and
split them apart. He reached into his pocket and found a packet of chocolate covered nuts – his favourite snack. He took out three of the chocolate
covered nuts and threw two of the nuts into the opposite direction to the
security guards.

"Did you boys hear that?" said security guard one.

"Hear what mate? It's f**king silent," replied security guard two.

"Go check it out," replied security guard four.

"Why? There was no sound. Billy's just lost his f**king marbles is all.
His missus been driving him up the f**king wall at home, so the poor fellas
losing his f**king mind. Hearing noises and sh*t," replied security guard
two as he nudged security guard one.

"I heard a noise Grant. It weren't a loud noise, but I f**king heard something mate. Ain't got nothing to do with the missus you c**t," said security guard one as he looked around, gun in his hand.

"I heard it too. It was faint but I heard it. It's probably a mouse or something," said security guard three.

"Listen stop f**king around and go check it out. We're here 'cos of what went down earlier this week. We know they're on high alert right now. No point us all standing here anyways. Billy and Grant go check it out. I ain't gonna f**king ask again. Come on lads; we're here to work," replied security guard four.

"Alright Jerome, chill out mate. Me and grant will go check it out now. Let's go," replied security guard one.

Malabar sat with his back against the wall and knees pressed up to his chest, and peered round the corner of the boulder as two of the five security guards marched down the hallway and out of sight. There were now only three of them that he had to get past.

"Jerome, you want me to do a sweep of the stairs one time?" said security guard five.

"Yeah, go on then mate. Take Ali with you. I want you to go upstairs Mo, and Ali you go downstairs alright," said security guard four.

"Yes boss. You good here by yourself?" said security guard three.

"What do you think Ali? Look at the f**king size of me! Meet me in the lunch hall in an hour alright," said security guard four as he outstretched his arms and let his gun hang by his waist, so as to show Ali his large frame. Security guard four was built like a linebacker.

"Say no more boss. Catch you in a bit innit. Shout us if you need anything yeah," replied security guard five as he departed into the staircase with security guard three.

"Billy, Grant – we'll rendezvous in the lunch hall in an hour. Copy," said security guard four as he spoke into his walkie talkie.

Malabar smiled to himself as there was now only one security guard to get past, but now there were two security guards on the staircase who he would have to deal with. Whilst he would have liked to have to fight the big man and humble him, he would have to approach the situation differently; it seemed the noise carried over easily in this building – and so he would have to subdue him without making noise.

He waited for security guard four to turn his back before running at him, sliding on his knees as he approached the big man, and in a dirty and disrespectful move – with his full force and torque generated, he threw his right arm between the legs of the behemoth of a man and up into the man's private parts. As the weight quickly went out of the man's legs, in a swift motion, Malabar took a mouth silencer out of his TechSuit and threw this into the mouth of security guard four – who was now on his knees and holding his balls. He saw his opportunity and quickly jumped on the back of the behemoth and sunk in a rear naked choke and squeezed tight. And as the man quickly tapped on the arm of Malabar Jones, Malabar continued to squeeze and waited till the thudding taps he felt on his arm could no longer be felt and the man's arm went limp. Malabar had choked him unconscious and quietly removed his legs from the body lock that he had on security guard four and let the security guard four's face slowly drop onto the concrete floor. He took out a pair of handcuffs from his TechSuit and applied one to the right hand of the man and to the left ankle of the man, behind his back. *He won't be a problem anymore.* He took the guard's walkie-talkie and entered the staircase.

The SSSA4 knew he needed to go down the stairs to get to the fifth floor, but he did not want to have to deal with two security guards and alert one of them by them not responding to the other. The smart play seemed to take them both out. And so, he checked his TechSuit to ensure that sneak mode was still activated. Once he saw that it was still activated, he sprinted up the staircase, galloping like a horse, making sure to take long strides and he leapt up three steps at a time, covering the distance in no time. He soon found security guard five, with his headphones activated and listening to rap music, slowly plodding up the staircase and bopping his head to the beat of the music.

He was conscious of the fact that any noise would likely be heard by security guard three. And so, without hesitation he threw another mouth silencer into the mouth of security guard five and this time threw the head of security guard five against the wall, as though he were attempting to crack open a coconut. He caught him before he fell to the ground. Another security guard was downed, and Malabar tied him up also. Again he thought, *Yeah he won't be a problem anymore.*

He proceeded to descend the stairs and was surprised to see security guard three quickly approach him on the staircase. He saw the size of the man and considered the fact that the guard was also nimble on his feet – this man was an athlete, and so Malabar knew he would not be able to take him front on like this, he was not prepared. And so, Malabar jumped up and grabbed onto the bottom of the staircase above him, pulled himself up in a pull-up motion and ensured to secure his grip, before bringing his body parallel with the staircase, activating his core strength in an extraordinary feat of calisthenic strength.

As security guard three made his way up the stairs, Malabar Jones waited until the man was directly under him before dropping down, catching the man's head and neck between his legs, and creating momentum to swing him around and throw him down a flight of stairs. Security guard three was now somewhat weakened and as he slowly made his way back to his feet, Malabar threw a vicious teep kick at the knee of the man – forcing his knee to hyperextend backwards, before then releasing another leg kick to the exterior of the same knee. Though whilst this clearly weakened the man, it did not stop him and he managed to propel himself forward and utilise his long reach to grab a hold of Malabar by the neck and fling his wiry frame into the wall. If it were not for the TechSuit providing him some protection, the impact from the wall would have kept him downed for longer than it did. He quickly got back up and rolled under a leaping check left hook that the man threw his way. And it was good for him that his reflexes and fight IQ allowed him to see the telegraphed punch by the strong man; if it had landed, he would have been knocked out cold.

But as the man threw his full power into the left hook and overextended on the punch, Malabar Jones rolled under and stepped towards the man before quickly turning him by shuffling his feet like a ballerina and threw three consecutive left hooks to the face of the man, who had his back towards Malabar. However, the man was trained in boxing and instinctively tucked his left elbow in and raised his left hand up to the side of his head. He took this opportunity and secured a double under hook body lock on the man. The big man again did well to defend the wrestling position as he lowered his body and attempted to fight the hands of Malabar Jones, but to no avail for he had a snake like grip developed through his commitment to calisthenics. *This is a good little scrap, but stop f**king around Malabar, finish him*, he thought. He quickly readjusted his grip on the body lock and hooked his left foot on the inside of the man's left foot and used his momentum against him to secure an inside trip. And then within moments, Malabar had the man's back and secured a rear naked choke.

"You've fought well my friend. Very well. But stop this. It's inevitable at this point. Let it happen. Don't be ashamed. I do this for a living. So don't fight it anymore. This is above your pay grade. It's not personal, you're just in my way."

"F**k you mother*****r," said security guard three as he breathed heavily with spit coming from his mouth as he spoke, and he threw his head backwards in an attempt to headbutt Malabar, but sadly hitting his own head on the floor.

You wanna play dirty? Malabar found the attempted headbutt to be disrespectful, and riskily let go of the rear naked choke and reversed the position to move towards full mount, before readjusting to side control. He unleashed a series of vicious, piercing elbows with the point of his left elbow, slicing the man open. Security guard three valiantly attempted to get up and get a single leg on Malabar Jones. But Malabar Jones read the now lethargic movements of the larger man and quickly sprawled before grabbing the vulnerable neck of the bloodied, outstretched and desperate but brave man in front of him. He took his opportunity to end the fight and secured a D'Arce choke. He did not feel or see the man tap out and smiled to himself as he dropped the limp body to the floor. The man was brave and he had put up a good fight and it gave joy to conquer a game opponent like this. He had been on a losing streak in lieu of his fights with Fergus-Sundar – he needed this victory. He secured the man: he put a mouth silencer in place, secured his ankle and wrist together with cuffs, and went about his way.

As he proceeded to the offices on the fifth floor and noticed that the radiation detector on his TechSuit had gone off. Amidst the hubbub and adrenaline rushing through him, he had not realised the radiation detector had gone off. There was an abnormally large amount of radiation inside of The Dala Device Electricity Hub London. *That's peculiar? Something strange is going on here.* He looked down at his watch and figured it was likely that the downed security guards would be awake soon – he ought to move swiftly.

Malabar entered the office of the Site Manager and quickly hacked into the account. He was surprised to see the systems were somewhat primitive in terms of technological advancement – he expected better considering this was a government building. He was in but could find little information that was useful. It seemed that there was nothing here at The Dala Device Electricity Hub London, in terms of legal documentation that was of interest to him or the SSSA; there was nothing here that he could not see from online or from his computer at home. However, Malabar Jones found that the building and systems of The Dala Device Electricity Hub London were directly linked to The Facial Recognition Scanning Centre London and to The Amy Dala Factory. He continued to scour through the systems and found those restricted documents – but it seemed he could only access this directly at the source location, which was The Amy Dala Factory in Croydon.

And so, he knew he would have to go to The Amy Dala Factory in Croydon to uncover more behind the Dala Device.

He did not have any experience using the Dala Device as he everything was provided to him by the SSSA and so he had never had to use the device that everyone else in the UK depended on; he had a fake device himself. The reaction people had to not using the Dala Device during the Tech-Night was extreme, and so Malabar figured it would be useful to see the factory where they were made, distributed from, and repaired at. On site, he could look into the restricted documentation also. And so it was decided, he was to go to the Amy Dala Factory in Croydon tomorrow night. As he was about to exit the office, security guard one and security guard two walked in.

"Well, well, well Grant, look what we have here," said security guard one. "Here we are coming in here to grab the bosses' bottle of whiskey and we come across this f**ker. Who the f**k are you?"

"Don't worry about who I am. It's above your paygrade fellas," replied Malabar Jones. He knew saying something like this would be cause the two men to get enraged – it was a comment directly aimed at their ego, and it seemed to work; the subtle facial twitches activated on their faces upon hearing the words 'above your paygrade' gave them away.

"You hear that Billy? Above our paygrade. Boss will love to hear this. Eh boss do you copy. We got a little fella here inside Angela's office right now," said security guard two.

"Your colleagues won't responding to your call."

"Oh yeah and why's that?" replied security guard one.

"Well because they've been incapacitated."

"In-f**king-capacitated. What the f**k? Let me get this straight. You took out Ali, Mo and Jerome? Bullsh*t mate," said security guard two.

"Yes, didn't take long. Now why don't you boys step aside. I've got things to do. No need for me to rearrange your faces as well."

"Hah. Funny little fella ain't he," replied security guard one. "So Mister Incapacitated, I could shoot you right now, and I would be well within my right to do so. But I think Grant and I are both a little bored to be honest. These nights are f**king long mate. There's no f**king action. So shooting you would deprive me and Grant of a good little beatdown. So what do you say Grant? Fancy a little fight with the little man? We can go one at a time and sub each other in if you like? Like a good old fashioned tag team match," said security guard one as he took his gun off his waist and took off his heavy jacket.

"Yeah why not? You ain't gotta ask me twice Billy. Beats having a f**king drink," said security guard two.

"Well, we can have a drink once we're done with this one," security guard one said with a beaming smile, and guffaw to follow.

"Who's first then?" replied Malabar Jones. His plan had worked, and the two men's ego had been successfully challenged, and so they had dropped their guns and the threat he had initially faced had dissipated. *Perfect. They don't know what they're in for.*

Security guard one stepped forward and approached Malabar in a squarish sumo-like stance, and he figured he should not waste any time and disrespect his own ability by playing around with the man. And so, he threw out the most disrespectful strike he could think of, with violent intentions, the front kick to the face. And as the front kick to the face landed perfectly on the untucked chin of the man, he saw his eyes roll back, his incisor fly out of his mouth, and the man faceplant on the floor. He was out cold.

Malabar looked up at security guard two and saw his jaw drop to the floor and his eyes look up and directly into his own eyes.

"F**king c**t. Alright, let's f**king go then. You think imma go out like that mate you got another f**king thing coming. C**t! Let's f**king go!" the man screamed out to Malabar Jones as he attempted to intimidate him. However, Malabar smiled back at the man as he noticed security guard two circling around him and bouncing up and down on his toes, in a style akin to a classic karate or taekwondo style fighter. Malabar cracked his neck. *Let's have some fun.* He had incapacitated all the other guards, and he had the information he needed from this place, and so it was indeed time to have some fun.

He mimicked the man in front of him and bounced around in an orthodox stance with karate like movement, before switching stance to Southpaw seamlessly like Willie Pep, utilizing a V-Step and leaping with a straight left hand. However, the man smartly stepped back out of range and threw a counter straight right hand down the pipe which landed cleanly on the temple of Malabar, and resulted in Malabar dropping to the floor – the perfect counter for from an orthodox stance to a southpaw fighter. He laughed to himself. He could indeed have some fun with this opponent; he was skilled, and he could step up his own game and use some different techniques – the risk and competition made it more enjoyable.

Malabar knew now he could not be sloppy; his opponent was strong and skilled, and evidently had good timing and a gauge of distance. He quickly rose to his feet and threw out a lead right kick from the southpaw stance to the left leg of his opponent, and quickly doubled this up. He threw the kick again but found this time the man checked his kick and threw out a counter check left hook, which Malabar cleanly avoided by stepping back out of range. The man stepped in with a jab and threw a lead left switch head kick from the orthodox stance to create a beautiful combination, which Malabar felt despite bringing his right hand up to block the kick. Malabar nodded and made a face of acknowledge, he recognised the skill involved with throwing an untelegraphed combination as the man had done. The spy threw out a left teep kick towards the gut of the man, which the man backed away from as he slid backwards out of range. The SSSA4 then decided to revert to his boxing and again utilised the V-Step, and found himself switch stance to orthodox and stepped into close quarters with his opponents; he had to fight inside. He started an offence with a blistering combination of punches – a range-finding jab and right uppercut, followed by a left uppercut, and then a jab and a straight right hand down the middle. The man had felt those punches as he reverted into a tight high guard after his head had been knocked back by the punches. Malabar now had his respect and the man knew that his punches had pop behind them – he couldn't take too many of them.

Malabar this time stepped in with a stiff left jab, Mexican style with his hand facing twelve-to-size, piercing through the high guard of the man. He followed this up with two Mexican style jabs which again pierced through the guard of his opponent, and landed cleanly on his nose, causing blood to rush out of his nose. However, the man had heart and threw a thunderous a right kick to the midsection of Malabar Jones, which he certainly felt. Malabar backed away and found his hands drop slightly. The man took advantage of his momentum shift and released a barrage of punches – a jab, straight right, jab and another straight right, and followed this up with a right head kick which Malabar managed to just about lean away from.

"Nice! Come on then kid! Let's see what you got. Hit me b**ch," said Malabar Jones as he took control of the situation. He knew if he egged the man on, he would open up and an opportunity would present itself. He wanted to bait the man and let him think he was taking control of the fight; he just wanted to see how he would throw his strikes, so that he could gather the fight data and counter accordingly.

The man nodded his head and spat out blood onto the floor. He threw out a left kick at Malabar's opposing lead left leg which moved him and took his balance away. The man waited for him to regain his balance before throwing the left leg kick at Malabar's calf again, but this time following it up with a straight right hand which Malabar managed to shrug off as he quickly brought his left shoulder up to misguide the shot which was destined for his chin. The man again went to throw his left leg kick which Malabar could see was coming his way – however, unexpectedly, he changed the direction of the kick and threw a lead question mark kick which landed nicely on the side of Malabar's head and threw his equilibrium off. Malabar Jones had gotten too cocky and was rocked and in serious danger. He felt himself go off balance and sway from side to side. The man leapt into a flying knee with his right knee as Malabar slightly ducked. Thankfully for him, the knee missed slightly and the SSSA4 grabbed a single leg on the man and pushed him up against the wall. The man defended the single leg and managed to get an underhook on him and turn him against the wall. He had Malabar pinned against the wall and threw a couple of hooks which landed cleanly on his now bloodied face. He backed away from the bloodied Malabar who was leant against the wall, and landed a couple of staggered jabs before throwing a straight right hand which the spy managed to parry away. He fired back with his own straight right, but the man slipped this nicely and landed his own counter straight right hand on Malabar's chin, but luckily for him it was a shot without power and this moment allowed him to regain his composure.

The man was now in control of the fight and Malabar realised he needed to end this quickly. He was playing with his prey and got caught. He did not have the liberty to do so and realised he needed to end the fight, or attempt to do so as soon as possible. Malabar Jones leant back on the wall and moved his upper body up and down from the waist like the great fighters of old school pugilism, Henry Armstrong and Joe Louis, and evaded the barrage of punches that security guard two was throwing at him. And then Malabar Jones saw his opening. He noticed amidst the onslaught of punches coming his way, that the man tended to drop his right hand slightly when throwing his left hook.

And so, Malabar waited patiently and launched a sharp counter check left hook in the pocket when the man threw his own left hook, and the spy saw the legs of the man go and he dropped to the floor. He had landed his shot right on the button. The man was dazed badly. However, instead of jumping on top of him and ending the fight, Malabar gave the man a 10 count and the opportunity to stand back up – he was enjoying the fight, and this gave Malabar a chance also to regain his breath. He knew he ought to end the fight as quick as possible, but he was enjoying the fight – he couldn't help himself.

The man staggered back to his feet and valiantly moved forward with his hands up. Malabar threw another Mexican style jab which pierced through his defence and rocked his head back. However, this was simply a set up. He then feinted with the left jab, the man flinched, and he threw a straight right hand down the pipe which landed cleanly and sent the man flying backwards. He lay on the floor, his eyes barely open and looked up at Malabar as he attempted to get up.

"Great fight man. F**k. You did well. You were better than I thought. I swear you almost got me. But yeah, it's over. Tell the other boys I said bye. I won't tie you up; you can help them when you're back to your senses alright. But seriously good fight kid – you should do that instead of security," he said as he wiped the blood away from his face and made ways to the door, once again.

"You ain't gonna get away with this. There's cameras everywhere," said security guard two as he lay on his side, wincing with pain.

"Kid. I disabled all the cameras before I even got here," said Malabar Jones as he shut the door of the office of the Site Manager with both security guards bloodied and on the floor.

His work was done for the day.

Saturday 14th November 2065, 22:27:
The Amy Dala Factory, Croydon

As Malabar entered the Head Office of The Amy Dala Factory in Croydon, he noticed blood on his shoes. He took a handkerchief from his left pocket and wiped the blood away. He sat down at any computer he could find and hacked into the system.

Once he was in the system, he felt that before he delved into the top-secret files and restricted access files that he was here for – he ought to know more about the Dala Device itself.

And so, he watched the instruction and tutorial videos which were sent out to all factory workers and attempted to process and piece together just exactly what made up the composition of the Dala Device. Malabar was a fast learner and so he picked this up quickly: if he were tasked to creating a Dala Device with the components it was made from – he was certain he would be able to do so. He found a Dala Device on the desk he was seated at, and decided to put his newfound knowledge to the test and began to take the Dala Device apart.

The Dala Device was like any other technological device, similar to the mobile smartphones which were inseparable from human beings from 2000s to 2030s – people could not function without them, they had become an extension of the human being – a precursor to the bionic human. However, as he deconstructed the Dala Device, he found a strange and mysterious element which looked as though it did not belong inside of a technological device. This strange and mysterious element was directly connected with the Retinal Verification Scanner inside of the Dala Device – a process which had to be activated and used every time a transaction involving monetary payment was completed in the UK by a person, using their Dala Device.

Malabar Jones picked up this element and noticed that within small element – was a powdered substance which was enclosed and had a filter and release system integrated within it which seemed to convert this powdered substance into a vapour or gaseous format of some sort. He was not quite sure what exactly this was and was left somewhat perplexed looking at it. His mind wandered as he looked upon this mysterious element, and as his mind wandered and drew up numerous different conclusions – he reverted to the same conclusion each time but did not want to believe it. Thus, he broke the small but tough element by breaking the strong tempered glass and emptied the powdered substance onto the table. He dipped his pinkie in the powdered substance, ensuring to take a large amount so that he could quickly determine what this substance was, and wiped it on his gums.

Whilst waiting for the powered substance to impact him, decided to delve into the restricted files now. As he looked into the restricted files, he found a breakdown of the elements which comprised the Dala Device and found the orders for these parts. And as Malabar was looking into this, he found himself feeling very relaxed. Unusually so, and he knew instantaneously what type of substance this was. The powdered substance integrated within, and seemingly released upon usage of the Dala Device, was certainly a Benzodiazepines – a drug similar to that of Diazepam and Alprazolam. Before even reading the restricted files, he knew what the functionality of this substance was in the device. However, he would have the answer in front of him, through physical and concrete evidence with these files and so he attempted to not allow his mind to wander to foregone conclusions no matter how obvious it felt to him. He could not allow his emotions get the better of him – but he was disturbed at what he thought he had discovered. *Surely not?*

And as Malabar looked into the order list for the parts that comprised the Dala Device, his outrage continued to grow at the discoveries. The strange and mysterious element he had stumbled upon was the registered as a Brain Signal Exchanger, with the company it was supplied by and bought from, listed as GHEE. Malabar put his hand to his head as he scrolled through the documentation. This meant that Elisabeth Cervantes and GHEE were directly involved with the creation of the Dala Device. He had experiences with Elisabeth and GHEE previously, but had never managed to pin anything to them – however, this time he now had evidence of their involvement with potentially nefarious activities. However, he knew that the Dala Device was a mandatory technological device that people had to use, as decreed and provided for by the Government of the UK – the UK used a paperless monetary system, with the Dala Device being the technological device which processed all financial transactions.

He looked further into the restricted documentation on the Brain Signal Exchanger and discovered that the Benzodiazepine-like substance was released every time a person made a payment – thus causing one to receive the sensation of the drug every time they bought something. Therefore, causing its user's to become both addicted to the Benzodiazepine-like substance within the Dala Device, causing it's users to be in a somewhat constant altered state of mind, and also addicted to spending. And as Malabar Jones attempted to fathom what this meant for the people of the UK, it all made sense. Ever since the Dala Device had been introduced and became a mandatory piece of equipment for the average UK citizen, since the Isolationism Act – the UK had been voted the Happiest Country in the World every year, and the economy and spending had skyrocketed. The Dala Device altered the mind of its users and acted as an anxiety relief, inadvertently also causing an addiction to the effects of the device and the act which allowed them to receive the effects – spending their money.

This explains why when Brian Harrison and his terrorist group shutdown The Dala Electricity Hubs across the UK, and caused the Tech-Night, – as it's being called by the media – that people suffered extreme withdrawal effects from using the Dala Device that caused people to have mental breakdowns, and resulted in psychedelic-like experiences – which are being called Dala Realisations. It all makes sense. GHEE made this Dala Device and they and the government are releasing anti-anxiety drugs into everyone on a daily basis to give them a spending addiction, and to alter their minds and distract them from reality.

He was in disbelief at what he had discovered. It was a scandal, a complete scandal and at the heart of it were the Government and GHEE; GHEE were in cahoots with the Government. And so, he now felt somewhat comforted by the fact that he could not previously apprehend Elisabeth and GHEE when he had a case on them; they were backed and supported by the Government. The whole system was flawed and those at the top were feeding the nefarious technology mogul that was Elisabeth Cervantes and GHEE.

The people were effectively using technology like a drug, and they did not even know it – the government and the companies and people they admired, moguls like Elisabeth Cervantes were feeding their addiction.

However, as he sat at the desk with all this information running through his head, questions began to through his mind. He had never used the Dala Device. He had never had to use one. He was told this was being they did not, and could not, have his personal details be on the main systems of Government – for this would leave him and the SSSA susceptible to hacking and could leave them compromised on their missions. He would not be able to be an agent of the shadows this way. Though what if the SSSA knew of what was behind the Dala Device? *Does the SSSA know about this?* Was this why he was tasked with foiling Brian Harrison's terrorist plot? So that this would all not be exposed? Were they compliant? Did they support this all? Or did they want Brian Harrison stopped just because of the financial turmoil that would be caused by a day of no spending in the UK? To Malabar Jones, the latter was certainly one of the reasons, he just did not know what the SSSA's awareness was on the Dala Device. He did not know if anyone else in the SSSA used the Dala Device either; he was not permitted to keep friendly relationships with others in the SSSA.

I understand what Brian Harrison meant now. He must have known about this. But how I wonder? Why would he know about this?

There was much to uncover still, and this was all far too much for Malabar Jones to process in this moment. And so, he made note of this information and proceeded to look into the restricted documentation on the Dala Device. What he discovered shocked him and, for a brief moment, wished he had not known all of this.

He stumbled upon the lie at the heart of the Dala Device. The Dala Device had been named after the creator of the device, who was thought to be Amy Dala, a technology genius who had served in World War Water and was declared to have passed away from stage four pancreatic cancer just before the Dala Device was brought into usage in the UK. This was all a lie. Amy Dala was a fake moniker created as part of the backstory – a way to get the British people to empathise with her and the Dala Device – a wicked ruse. There was never a person called Amy Dala. This fake moniker was called Amy Dala; named after the Amygdala. The Dala Device, primarily the Brain Signal Exchanger inside of the device, was designed to target the Amygdala – a part of the brain which could be understood to somewhat be the fear centre of the brain. This device, with the Brain Signal Exchanger and Retinal Verification Scanner intact, was apparently created by Elisabeth Cervantes and GHEE for the Government to help soldiers struggling with post-traumatic-stress-disorder and suffering from the extreme withdrawal symptoms of drug dependency that they had from war. The device was created as a way to provide these solders with anxiety relief. Malabar Jones continued to read into the documentation and discovered that this was scrapped upon testing it on soldiers, as it seemed that soldiers very quickly became addicted and dependent on the device for anxiety relief.

As Malabar continued to read, he continued to grow frustrated and vexed at how deep the deceit ran. The Government, with advice from various panels which included Elisabeth Cervantes and other Board Members at GHEE – determined that in lieu of the UK's Isolationism Act and the disruption caused from the Psychedelic riots of the late 2040s, they would need to boost their economy and regain control of the people. Thus, it was determined they would integrate this device, with the Brain Singal Exchanger and Benzodiazepine-like substance and the Retinal Verification Scanner, into a device that would be used for their new paperless monetary system. Consequently, resulting in people to be addicted to spending, receiving anxiety relief and increasing their happiness, whilst also boosting the economy. The introduction of the Dala Device allowed the government to introduce something new and revolutionary that was positive – the paperless monetary system and Dala Device – in lieu of the massive change the UK was experiencing by employing Isolationism as a government and geo-political policy.

He transferred the restricted documentation to his personal device, closed the computer, eradicated any evidence that he had been on the Dala Factor's system, and sat back in the office chair for a while as he attempted to process all the information. It was too much for one man. *How can I fix this? What can I even do? The whole system is f**ked*, he thought. He was defeated once again, though this time it was knowledge and awareness of things going on in the world which had defeated him – the knowledge of truth. He stood up from the chair, grabbed the computer screen and flung it across the room before screaming out.

However, Malabar calmed down as he made ways out of the Amy Dala Factory, as he remembered that he could not allow all the negativity going on in the world and the injustice, get to him. He had to care about it all, he had no choice but to – he was only human and even though he tried not to get emotional on his missions and not be too empathetic, there were some things which could not be overlooked.

Though he recognised in this moment also that he himself was just a man, and was just one man amongst billions, and there were billions which had come before him, and billions which would come after him. His impact on the world, in reality, was little and so he could not get overwhelmed by negative things which were rooted in society by the involvement of many people and for many years.

Though he would do what he could and all that was in his power. But he was now even more apprehensive and sceptical of everything and everyone. He did not even trust the SSSA anymore either. He knew that the SSSA were in employment and servitude to the Crown and not to the Government. And so, there was a possibility that the SSSA may not have been aware of the nuances behind the Dala Device. And so, he decided he would need to find out more information about this all before he would give them the information he had. He would finish this once and for all. Malabar Jones decided he had to apprehend Elisabeth Cervantes and question her. He was to take matters into his own hands.

No more instructions. I can't trust anybody right now, not even the SSSA. Not right now. It's time to pay Elisabeth Cervantes and GHEE a visit.

BOOK 15
FERGUS-SUNDAR

Saturday 14th November 2065

*13:14: The Global Hub of Extraterrestrial Exploration
(GHEE) HQ, Hampstead, London*

"One minute please they/them," the security guard said as he entered.

"Huh? What's they/them?" replied Fergus-Sundar. He was confused at the term; he was from a different time.

"I said one minute please. I need to check your ID card before I can let you in. I'm scanning it now alright," the guard replied as she took his card and placed it under the scanner. For a brief moment, he felt the nerves overcome his body; he had just printed this identification card yesterday via the machine provided to him by the SSSA over forty years ago – he did not know if it still worked and if the technology would hold till this day.

"Alright you can go through now Ferguson Sri ... Srinivas. Is that correct? Ferguson Srinivas, Professor of Quantum Physics at UCL?"

"Yes, that is correct," replied Fergus-Sundar.

"Miss Cervantes has left a note saying she will come and meet you in the reception area. She will be here in a few minutes, she's never late. Have a seat please Mister Srinivas," the security guard said as Fergus-Sundar nodded in acknowledgment and went to have a seat. He had used the alias Francis Srinivas before back in 2020, and so now posed as the son of this Francis Srinivas – Ferguson Srinivas with a Master's degree in Quantum Physics.

Fergus-Sundar composed himself and took in a few deep breaths before closing his eyes. Elisabeth Cervantes was to arrive at any moment, and he had to ensure that he did not let anything slip. If his research and the character analysis he conducted were accurate, then she would be highly astute and would pick up on anything he said which had holes in it.

And then, in walked Elisabeth Cervantes, and Fergus-Sundar stood up instantly and felt as though a gust of wind had come into the room. He was taken aback by her beauty and as she outstretched her hand, waiting for him to meet her hand with his own, he stood in front of her and was almost stuck standing where he was with his mouth ajar.

"Hello Professor Srinivas, it's a pleasure to welcome you to our facility. Welcome to the Global Hub of Extra-Terrestrial Exploration, otherwise known as GHEE. My name is Elisabeth Cervantes, and I am the founder and CEO of GHEE," she said., "Firstly thank you for making the time to visit, we appreciate your time. Though I must say I am uncertain to what this meeting is about; it was only confirmed on my diary last night. An oversight from my personal assistant."

"Hello Ms Cervantes. It's a pleasure to ma…" he started.

"Please. Call me Elisabeth, or Elisa if you would prefer. Follow me Professor. Let's walk and talk," said Elisabeth as she led the way out of the vast reception area and began walking briskly through the facility – she nodded her head seemingly at every person who they walked past.

"Elisabeth. It's a pleasure to make your acquaintance," he said as he awkwardly reached out his hand once again as they walked side-by-side, even though he had only just shook her hand. He found himself sweating. "Yes, apologies. It was not a mistake on the part of your PA. The university only informed me of the meeting yesterday also. Though I have long been intrigued by the work of your organisation."

"Oh really. What exactly is your specialty Professor? I must be frank and say I've actually never heard of you before. I didn't know your university even had a Professor in Quantum Physics. Have you just recently come to your post?"

"Yes, just within the last year. It is a small department though and a very small team, I don't have a large class. But this does have its benefits, it allows me to spend more time on my research, which is why I am here actually. And please call me Ferguson, no need for all the formalities," said Fergus-Sundar. The two continued to talk and walk.

Some time had now passed, and they now found themselves in the office of Elisabeth Cervantes. It was isolated from the main GHEE building, but her offices were still in the grounds of GHEE's vast HQ. She had private quarters; if she wanted to stay on the complex.

"So, the focus of your work is to create a formula for Interdimensional Travel? And you hypothesise that this is possible through Wormholes, which might I add is a theory that is not proven to exist. And further to this, you believe that these Wormholes are situated within Primordial Black Holes? Which again, is not explicitly proven to exist?"

"Well to put it simply, yes this is the focus of my work and that is my theory. I believe there are Wormholes which are situated within Primordial Black Holes. If only we could travel to one of these Primordial Black Holes, I believe it would show that they do exist."

"This is still just a theory Ferguson. Until we see it and until there is a formula which proves this hypothesis as being feasible, then I am afraid it is quite simply fiction. Though ultimately, I do respect your perspective and I can see how something like this could very well exist. We have come to similar potential, and I stress the word *potential*, conclusions ourselves here at GHEE. But again, these formulas have all been close though ultimately not been finalised. Plus, the technology does not exist. We here at GHEE have travelled into space on many an occasion. We have been to the Moon. We have been to Mars; on many an occasion. But to travel through a wormhole … this is just not possible. Now. Let's just say for the sake of the argument, or debate I should say, that these Primordial Black Holes do exist and that they do hold Wormholes which link two dimensions to one another – how does one pass through this? How does anything pass through this? I know you are aware of Event Horizons and that if an object were to hypothetically pass through this, it would be ripped apart by the edges of this Event Horizon. Do you also have a theory for this?"

"Well, regarding Event Horizons and passing through this. I do not have a formula for this as of yet. Though I know it is possible to pass through the Event Horizon and come through unscathed," said Fergus-Sundar, holding back his smile. He knew it was possible to pass through an Event Horizon for he had done it himself, but as Elisabeth Cervantes was pointing out, he had no reason or real explanation for all of this – right now it seemed to be magic. "Yes, in theory one would get ripped apart due to gravity and the different rules that govern a Black Hole – but truthfully we do not know all of the true rules which govern a Black Hole. We know that our normal laws of physics do not apply in a Black Hole, but we do not really know what laws of physics *do* apply. We know of a few and that is all. But there are many unanswered questions that pertain and plague our understanding and validity to the rules that we know to be true in Quantum Physics."

"And what is that Ferguson?" said Elisabeth, leaning back in her chair and looking at who she thought was Professor Ferguson Srinivas with a look of perplexion and ultimately, curiosity. He had her attention before, though this was due to her professionalism – now it seemed to be her unbridled attention.

"Well, the fact that we can currently only account for around five-percent of matter. What of this sixty-eight-percent of Dark Energy and this twenty-seven-percent of Dark Matter? What is the functionality of this matter and energy? We know that this simply cannot exist without there being a use for it. The unanswered questions we have regarding this dark energy and dark matter goes to show that perhaps, in these unanswered questions, lies the answer to our unanswered questions regarding many other scientific mysteries."

"A fair point you make Ferguson, but what question do you think dark matter and dark energy answer in the context of Black Holes and Wormholes and Event Horizons. Are you proposing that with this can pose the secret for passing through an Event Horizon?"

"The question is, why not? We know not what this respective sixty-eight-percent and twenty-seven-percent of Dark Energy and Dark Matter is. Certainly all of this respective Energy and Matter is not exactly one and the same. So why can a fragment of this unknown, amalgamate with that which we already know – to make something a possibility? Do we not always discover something new about quantum physics decade by decade, century by century, millennia by millennia?"

"This is true. Though I am not sure. I am a woman of science and so you cannot expect me to accept your hypothesis based on one singular conversation, that which is also not backed by any tangible evidence at that," replied Elisabeth as she now smiled and flashed her pearly whites at Fergus-Sundar, who smiled back and felt himself blush behind his brown cheeks. *Wow she is beautiful.*

"Well that I can appreciate. But do you agree that there is scope that this could be a possibility?"

"Anything is possible. Yes. Anything. I'll give you that. You still did not tell me what question you think Dark Matter and Dark Energy answers, in relation to making it possible to pass through the Event Horizon. I don't understand the relevancy?"

"I don't know exactly. Therein lies the problem and that is why I am here today Miss Cervantes. I hope to combine my research with that of yours and GHEE, in hopes of figuring it out. Though it is of my belief, from my deductions based on that which I already know to be true and that which could be a possibility – that if an object, or being, were to laced with Dark Energy and Dark Matter within its existing composition, that this could allow for Negative Gravity to exist within the object or being, which could in theory prevent this object or being from being ripped apart by the Event Horizon."

"Ah Professor Srinivas. Now you're talking my language. This is something that has scope. Our team here at GHEE have long been looking at Dark Matter and we have found that there must be Negative Gravity existing within this Dark Matter. And so yes, in theory I see where your theory has some validity to it, or at least I can see why you would think it would enable one to pass through an Event Horizon. As in theory this would allow for an object or being to be ripped apart by the Event Horizon. But this potential solution creates another problem altogether. How then can anyone or anything from this Earth ever pass through an Event Horizon? For if a person or thing were to contain this Dark Energy and Dark Matter, then this would not agree with the laws of physics that we know to be true on this Green and Blue Earth. So, if anyone or anything can pass through a Wormhole and Event Horizon, with this Dark Matter and Dark Energy within them – then they cannot be from this Earth. And that is a fact."

Fergus-Sundar had no response. For he agreed that his hypothesis in relation to Dark Matter and Dark Energy, would go against the laws of physics of Earth. *How did I do it then?*

"I agree with you on that. The truth is I don't know. Again, that is why I am here Miss Cervantes. I wish to figure out that which I don't know by combining what I know, with that which you know. Considering this, would it be possible for me to speak with some of the people employed here and to have a look around the facility?"

"Yes. Yes, you are more than welcome to. This has been a very interesting conversation Ferguson. I think we could sit and talk all day about this. But alas, I do have more meetings to attend concerning less interesting topics. Though consider the facility yours. You have access to all our research and facilities. Oh and, if you should like, you are welcome to stay in our guest quarters for the week. I don't know what your schedule looks like with university, but yes, we will happily accommodate you. We regularly host academics such as yourself from all around the world as they conduct their research here at our facility."

Fergus-Sundar could not say no to this offer; he was without a place to stay for the time being, without access to money or this Dala Device which seemed to be the only means of using money in this time, and he was not on the government register. It would allow him the opportunity to investigate into GHEE and Elisabeth Cervantes; he could look around GHEE at night and begin the real detective work.

"That is most generous of you Miss Cervantes. I think I will take you up on that offer. I'm grateful. I will make good use of this opportunity."

"I'm sure you will Ferguson. But I have just one question. Now correct me if I misheard you, but I think you said you did not have a formula for passing through an Event Horizon. Does this mean you do have a formula for Interdimensional Travel through Primordial Black Holes containing Wormholes? Now that is a mouthful isn't it! But yes, do you?" she asked him, ensuring to look directly into his eyes, searching for the truth.

She had held onto that single line from long ago in their conversation, whilst talking about other complex ideas; nothing went past her. And so Fergus-Sundar would be careful now with what he said. She was quietly intuitive and highly intelligent. He understood why she was on the radar of the SSSA. There was likely much at play here at GHEE, though Fergus-Sundar could not judge the situation at this stage – he would be coming to an early conclusion without any tangible evidence of their involvement with nefarious activities.

"No, I don't have a formula. But it's something I'm working on. I wish I could tell you I had one!" he said. He did not mean to say the truth when he told her he wished he could tell her. It simply came out of his mouth. Though considering the context of what he was saying, it would not be cause for any doubt. It was the truth wrapped in a lie and thus her suspicion would not be aroused. Fergus-Sundar then felt his newfound apprehension towards her doubled. *Does she know?*

"Ahh a shame. Now that truly would be groundbreaking. But anyhow. Dinner is at 21:00. I must go Ferguson. I'll see you later."

"Good day Miss Cervantes. Thank you again," said Fergus-Sundar as he shook her hand again and found himself for a brief moment, forgetting where he was. In the midst of his conversation with Elisabeth Cervantes, he felt a serenity which he never known in his adult life. *Is this because of her or because of my altered senses from passing through the wormhole?* He watched as she walked out of the door, and then stared a distracted stare as a guard of GHEE escorted him to his quarters – his mind was not present; his was mind elsewhere – on Elisabeth Cervantes. *Focus Fergus-Sundar, focus.*

He sat on the edge of his bed and went into a series of push-up variations and did this for the better part of twenty minutes. He had to regain a presence of mind, succeeding with this act of exercise. But, he could not deny that which had happened, no matter whether he tried to push it to the back of his mind; he had never experienced that feeling before. So long had he been focused on his career, never before did he have the liberty of even allowing his guard to be down to notice the little intricacies of life or to admire the beauty of women. Though he thought to himself and realised again this was a lie he was telling himself. He had been acquainted with women before, though this was different for he felt something as soon as he was in her presence and had been touched by her energy. This perhaps though was due to that which Fergus-Sundar had been through in the Wormhole-Maze. For since his return to Earth, he had felt everything more intensely. In one sense he was more attuned with his senses and emotions and could see things more clearly. But also, he was more distracted as his mind would latch onto these things more – before his was undisturbed by the reality of life, there was a bliss and blessing to being ignorant. It dawned upon him that the gift of knowledge and truth seemed to be balanced out by the curse of knowledge and truth, for there was nowhere to hide – once it is known, it cannot be unknown. The truth was, much like with GHEE, he did not know what to think of the situation, and so he would let the situation play out as it is before coming to a conclusion. This seemed to the nature of his life ever since he went to sleep on his fortieth birthday back in 2024 – every moment ahead was unknown.

Perhaps this was the first time he had ever truly been aware that every moment in his life was technically unknown territory – he lay back on the bed in the luxurious and spacious room offered to him by Elisabeth and GHEE, and continued to ponder this.

AAJ

21:12: *The Dining Room of Elisabeth Cervantes' Mansion in GHEE HQ*

"How is the food?" she asked as she cut into a thick slab of the finest Argentinian beef steak on the market.

"It's lovely. Probably the best steak I have had for years," said Fergus-Sundar – once again he did not lie about this, he had not eaten a steak in what seemed like forever. He had demolished his food, hoovering it up like Henry, much faster than he would have liked to. He had not properly eaten since he landed in 2065.

"I'm glad to hear it. We have plenty more if you would like. I can request for more to be made?" she asked.

"No its's no trouble. But thank you," he replied. He did want more but did not want to showcase his hunger more than he already had. "I'm curious to know more about you though Elisa. How did you come to this position you find yourself in now? I had read that you founded GHEE at just twenty-one years old and now you are worth billions. That is quite some story."

"Well, how long do you have!" she said, breaking into laughter. *For you, I have all night,* he thought. "So I don't know how much you read Ferguson. But I am an orphan. And it's okay, don't say you're sorry or anything please, and don't feel sorry for me. I came to terms with what's happened in my life a long time ago. My parents and my brother died back when I lived in Guyana. There were mass floods, because of climate change and rising sea levels; anyone living on the coast pretty much died. Thousands died. I don't know how I survived to be honest. All I know is that it was by the grace of God. It was God's plan. And that trauma drove me and brought me to the place I am now. Then I moved to Miami as an orphan at aged ten, and by the time I was twenty-one, I founded the Global Hub of Extraterrestrial Exploration whilst I was at MIT. And in the following years, some of my inventions have of course become very successful and pivotal to this most recent age of technology, with the satellites and my development of Web3.0. So yes,

I suppose that is how I came to be where I am now," she said, squinted slightly whilst looking at Fergus-Sundar.

"Wow that is some story. I know you said not to comment on it, but I do commend you. I am sorry for the trauma you experienced. I too am an orphan and so I can empathise with your struggle. But I haven't been as successful in my endeavours as you have in yours."

"Thank you Professor, but that's not entirely true is it? You are a very successful and exceptional man yourself. Not everyone can become a Professor," she replied, tilting her head and raising her eyebrows.

Fergus-Sundar smiled; he did not know if she was teasing him or holding back information. It seemed she was testing him.

"Well thank you. May I ask though, what are your companies objectives? What is it you see for the future? I ask just because it seems as though your company are involved in many different avenues. I'm curious to know what your personal vision is for the future?"

"That is a good question Fergus," Elisabeth Cervantes began. He felt the hairs on the back of his neck stand up.

Was that a slip of the tongue or is she dropping a hint to me? Has she known who I am all along? Is it me getting played?

She continued, "I know my own personal vision for the company, but I also know what our strengths are and where we make the majority of our money. And there is somewhat of a disconnect with this. As I have told you, I come from a country which was devasted by the impacts of Climate Change and I have personally seen first-hand the unjust and unforgiving devastation it can cause. It literally ends lives. Yet in more economically developed countries, such as the one we find ourselves in, I feel this is not truly understood by people. We talk about Climate Change as though this were an abstract concept, but in reality it is a real thing with real impacts on people, many thousands of miles away. We do not truly feel it here, despite the fact we contribute most to it. We feel Climate Change on a somewhat superficial level, with erratic weather. But ultimately we contribute most to

Climate Change because we have the financial means to do so in this country, and this is because our society has developed as such. It is precisely because we are economically developed countries. And now that other countries are striving towards a developed society themselves, they follow the tried and tested method of economically developed countries of the west, and it contributes even more to Climate Change – and countries such as mine, Guyana, and our people suffer as a result, while they barely contribute to Climate Change. And so, my vision for GHEE is to use more of our budget towards technologies that can help capture carbon in the atmosphere, and that can offer sustainable uses of energy. It seemed for a while that our society was going towards a more sustainable society with investment going in this direction. But for the last twenty-to-thirty years, with World War Water and the dawn of the Petroleum Rights Federation, and countries choosing to negate the fight against rising emissions – it has been hard to push towards investment into sustainable based technology. Here at GHEE, it seems where we have had the most success has been with Government based projects, such as the City Terrarium Carbon Capture project, or with the AirPol masks, or the Facial Recognition Scanning Centre. These are all our technologies created by GHEE and we supply these to the UK government and we are proud of this for sure. It has certainly made us a lot of money and we have had good impact on the enhanced digitalisation of our society here. But yes, I would like to work towards sustainable technology and to tackle issues such as water scarcity. We did a lot in the aftermath of World War Water; we managed to provide a lot of countries with some good infrastructure for reusing the water they already had. This felt good on a personal level. However, I know we can do more if only we put more of our budget towards such causes. And then of course, to continue with space exploration, with the hope of one day encountering extraterrestrials," said Elisabeth.

She let out a deep sigh and looked at Fergus-Sundar. She was surprised she had let out so much to him. She felt comfortable enough with him to speak openly and honestly. She had much going on and for her to be so open and honest like this, was not entirely good for business. *Put your guard back up Elisabeth, change the conversation. Enough flirtation now, get down to business. It's time,* she thought.

"But anyhow Professor Ferguson Srinivas. Tell me more about yourself? How is it you came to be a Professor? It was not so long ago that you were just … well … just Fergus-Sundar?" she asked and again looked at him with an unflinching stare. He could not hide his state of perplexation. He had been played.

"Don't be alarmed. And please, don't make any sudden movements. You're not in any danger – fret not, Fergus-Sundar. If I wanted to cause harm to you – you would already be harmed. But if you do react in the wrong way … well then you would be dealt with accordingly. Now I can see you are dazed and confused. How do I know who you are? Because it is my business to know who you are. Did you think my team would not recognise that you hacked into my diary? Did you think I would not notice? That I would not look up Professor Ferguson Srinivas? You did a stellar job hacking into the system and you did cover your tracks with the fake identity well. But you don't understand, that to dupe me, and to dupe GHEE – it would have to be an extraordinary effort. And you are extraordinary …," she stopped speaking for a moment to look down at her DigiPad, "Fergus-Sundar, but your efforts this time around were not extraordinary. In fact, it was a bit lazy and I think you know that. You popped up on the Facial Recognition Scanner. As you now know, our company provide this technology for the government. Now you came up as unregistered on the system. Non-identifiable. And so, you were flagged. Technically we should not cross-reference and look at the data ourselves. The technology is there so that the government may cross-reference the data, they have available, and decipher this themselves. But our system flags certain things and we can see things if we choose to do so. Now you are an interesting one. It says you disappeared forty years ago, almost to the day in fact. Just a week later. But here you prop up forty years later, and unless you were a baby forty years ago, you are the same age it seems. Forty years later. Now that is curious. So, tell me Fergus-Sundar, who are you? I have my own suspicions though. I think you are a SSSA," she said.

"Well. I'm lost for words and I guess backed into a corner. I feel trapped but I did walk myself into this spot. I am Fergus-Sundar – that is true. And it is a long story. I know not where to begin in all honesty. And yes it is smart how you came to know who I am. I overlooked that. It didn't cross my mind. But before I begin to explain myself, what is a SSSA?" he replied.

"Don't play dumb with me. Don't to be a smartass. And don't play games with me. You know what the SSSA is."

"I do not," he lied with a poker face. This he was good at, for he had sworn an oath and long done whatever was required to uphold that oath, no matter the circumstance. "What is a SSSA?"

"Fine. I'll entertain this. The SSSA is the Secret-Special-Service Agency. An underground, technically non-existent, monarchy funded spy agency, a task force you could say, dedicated to the protection of the United Kingdom, with spies appointed and in service to the King or Queen. Now are you a SSSA, Fergus-Sundar? I am being respectful and open with you. Show me that courtesy in my own home. My patience will wane very quickly if you do not."

"Why do you know this information? This is my last question to you and then you have my word, I will speak," he said as he needed to know what her thoughts were and to know the story of her interaction with the SSSA, from her perspective. This was a technique he long employed when he was in his service, if a target he was tracking knew of the SSSA or of who he was; to obtain the information without giving away more than what they already knew.

"I have had previous encounters with the SSSA. We had an agent by the name of Malabar Jones, a SSSA4 agent seemingly focused and specialised with science and technology, whilst also being athletically adept, who harassed me and my company on numerous occasions. He stalked me and meddled into my personal affairs. He used to follow me home. It was really strange. It seemed like he wanted access to our research and the scientific developments we were making. We do groundbreaking stuff here at GHEE and so it seemed like he was trying to obtain that information for the SSSA. But I don't know that for sure. It's just what it seemed like. And so yes, that's how I know of the SSSA. Are you also a SSSA4? You are certainly knowledgeable with Quantum Computing and Web3.0, and considering your knowledge of Quantum Physics – I believe you are a SSSA4 also. Talk to me Fergus-Sundar."

She knows way too much, and she is smart. He was impressed and knew he should not be; he technically should be loyal still to the SSSA. He had sworn an oath to them and to this country. But the SSSA were trying to kill him, it seemed and things were different now; he had travelled to another dimension and so was his oath still valid? Had he not technically died? He knew a part of him died as soon as he entered that wormhole, but another part of him was also born? Elisabeth Cervantes' testimony of Malabar Jones also did well to cessate his angst regarding her, for he knew not whether to believe her or not. It was true all that she had said of the SSSA and of SSSA4's. Was Malabar Jones simply doing his job or was he being overly intrusive, with no good reason for him to do so? These were still questions unanswered and ones that Fergus-Sundar could not base solely on his conversation with her; he needed to delve deeper into the work and the things going on behind the scenes here at GHEE. Thus, he knew he ought to play along to the tune she was playing and to let this situation play out. He would scope the facility at night. However, from his own experience with the SSSA4, he knew that he was not so discreet in his movements and was brash. *Could it be that the SSSA has lost their way?*

"Well Elisabeth. You've told me what you know. So it is only fair that I tell you the truth now also. I was once a SSSA4, this is true. But I am no longer a SSSA4 – we're no longer associated," said Fergus-Sundar.

"I thought so. But how are you here? What are you? You must tell me now. I told you, you're not in any danger. I am just curios. Are you a clone of Fergus-Sundar? If you are a clone, then you are the greatest clone I have ever seen and I need to know more. You are so real – there is no tell that you are a clone."

Fergus-Sundar laughed out loud at the thought of him being a clone. It was a feasible conclusion to someone who did not know of how he arrived in 2065 from the year 2025.

"No I am not a clone. I am Fergus-Sundar, the one and only," he said with a smile on his face. It comforted him to own his identity and say his name aloud. He had not been honest like this in many years and he felt his cheeks grow warmer with every passing moment, the hairs standing on his arms – he felt a rush of dopamine as he spoke with her.

"So how are you here? Your face has not shown on the Facial Recognition Scanner ever before, and our system has been in place worldwide for years. So don't lie to me. You cannot lie. Tell me how you're here, and how you look as you are unaged in appearance. Have you travelled in time? Or between dimensions?"

She had hit the nail on the head and again had cornered him with facts that he could not deny. He was on her radar now and he had walked himself into this position. There was nowhere to hide. And frankly, Fergus-Sundar did not want to hide anymore. He felt to trust Elisabeth Cervantes with the truth of his story and journey. He did not know why exactly but he felt to trust this feeling. Never before would he rely on feelings and intuition, instead he would always go with logic and undeniable facts that he would find through his own investigations. Though he was no longer a SSSA4, and he was no longer the Fergus-Sundar of old. He wanted to change and wanted a new life. *I have changed. Maybe this is the new start, the new life.* This is what he sought out, and here it was before him. The opportunity to be truthful.

Fergus-Sundar pushed his chair back slightly with his feet propelling him, sat back in his chair and crossed his right leg over his left knee with the outside of his right ankle delicately resting over his left knee.

"It's a long story," he said as he began to tell Elisabeth Cervantes of his story from 2025, to the Wormhole-Maze, to 2065. There was no going back now, he had chosen to trust Elisabeth Cervantes.

23:15: Guest Room 14 in GHEE HQ

Fergus-Sundar crossed his legs over as he lay back on his bed and found his mind racing from one thought to the other without any discernible pattern involved. His head was scrambled, yet it felt clear. He felt somewhat distracted and without focus, yet somewhat contented with where he was at this present moment. He felt a freedom. And undoubtedly, he knew this was because he was able to share the reality of his story with another person. And sharing such thoughts and truths was not something he was used to. There was a catharsis in it and for once, Fergus-Sundar thought of a different future for himself – one doused in human connection. This is what he sought and if he were to be stuck in this dimension, this is what he would continue to seek. He felt himself confounded by the fact that he had spoken so much to her. At times during his confession to her, it felt as though he had spoken uninterrupted for so long, something he was not accustomed to doing.

Thought despite this, he knew not to be completely trusting of her; he trusted no one – life had taught him this for he had been betrayed and duped before. Though he had already shared more than he ought to have. However, he had shared information as Fergus-Sundar, the man. Not as Fergus-Sundar the SSSA4. *I'm no longer Fergus-Sundar the SSSA4.*

Regardless, he decided he would have a quick nap before going about his business – the real reason he was here at GHEE. He would break into the office of Elisabeth Cervantes and try to observe more about GHEE and herself. He would scout the facility too. Despite the fact he was no longer a SSSA4, he kept the skills of a SSSA4 and the gadgets of a SSSA4 with him. He had a case to investigate.

23:23: *The Bedroom of Elisabeth Cervantes in her Mansion in GHEE HQ*

"I was right Jarred. You should know that when I have a feeling about these sorts of things … I'm always right," said Elisabeth Cervantes, wiping makeup off her face in front of the mirror.

"That's good honey," replied Jarred Lane Johnson as he stared at his DigiPad whilst lying on the bed in his silk pyjamas.

"Are you even listening?" she asked him. She knew he was not but wanted the clarification.

"Huh what did you say?" he replied.

"You never f**king listen. No point anyway you don't even know what I'm on about," she said.

"I'm sorry honey. My head's a bit spaced out right now. I smoked quite a few joints today with some of my associates who came over from the states. You know the ones I told you about?" he shouted out to her.

She walked into the main bedroom in her own silk pyjamas and looked at him in a confused manner from the edge of the bed.

"You smoked weed today? Jarred you know what that sh*t does to your head. Eats away your brain cells is all it does. Where did you even get it from?" she enquired.

"I know but these guys wanted to smoke some and I've got very, very, important business with them – I had to entertain them," he replied.

"Okay fine but Jarred – where did you get it from? You're the CEO of Johnson Pharmaceuticals for God's sake. You need to be careful. What about our companies business together?"

Jarred started chuckling to himself at the question she had asked him, and in response she instinctively folded her arms.

"It's not funny J. You seriously need to be careful. If you get caught with this kinda thing, and if it comes back to me – it will not look good. Now, answer the question – where'd you get it from?"

"Alright, alright, I hear you love. I got it from the Terrarium gardener guy. You know that black kid who does my MegaTerrarium's. You know the kid from the states, Devonte."

"Okay well can you trust him? He'll keep his mouth shut?" she asked as she kept her eyes lasered in on him.

"Yes, he will. If he doesn't then he'll lose his job. I can ruin him if I need to. He's nothing Elisa. He's a little fish in the big ocean and I'm the f**king shark. He's a Mega-Terrarium Executive for the City of London, and so if he gets caught being involved with the weed industry, well then he won't need me to lose his job – they'll fire him themselves. There's nothing to worry about okay. And plus, I saw him on this streamer's video on the Dark Web – so I've got evidence on him being involved in these activities. He won't say anything."

"Cool. Make sure you save that video. Just in case," she replied as she let out a sigh of relief. She knew he would have his back covered, but she had to make sure; she left no stone unturned. "Well I'm coming to bed in just a minute, I'm just going to go and make a call quickly to Bridger quickly. I'm going on the balcony."

"Bridger? Why are you calling Bridger at this time? It's late," he said, as he now sat up in his bed.

"Relax J. It's business. I won't be long," she said.

Elisabeth briskly walked out of her bedroom and out onto her balcony. She looked up at the ArtificiaSky that her company had installed, and smiled as she saw the fake stars shine brightly despite the air pollution and light pollution, which clouded the skies of London. She took out her phone and called her right hand man, Bridger Falcon.

"Bridger. Hey its Elisa. Listen, so update. He knows that I know that he is Fergus-Sundar, and that I know about the SSSA, and Malabar Jones. But he doesn't know about the Dala Device plot. He does not know our role and we keep it as that. And he does not know we saw him and Malabar Jones together. And he does not know that we've been tracking him since, and that we have his SSSA4 profile. I played the dumb, honest, sweet girl and it has worked of course. He is vulnerable right now. Now he's staying in Guest Room 14 and we'll be entertaining him for the coming week. We will see what comes of this relationship. I believe much good considering the information I have at my disposal. Considering all this, sorry I know I'm throwing a lot at you but this is important and I need you to know this so I hope you're paying attention Bridger. So when you meet him – you act oblivious of course yes. Now, he will likely be looking around the facility at night and try to find some dirt on us I image. Let him. Tell security to ease off. Let him access where he chooses to go. Let him think he's got one over us. I've got him there right now and we're in control of the situation. I have him where I want and so let's keep it that way for now. So yeah. Got all that. Please confirm and as you know, ask me if anything is unclear," she said, pacing as she talked.

"I got it all Elisa. I'll get the team on that MO (modus operandi) right away. Save this number?" he replied.

"Good. Yes that's the one for this week. Now tell me. What have you got for me on the Malabar Jones' situation please. It's been a few days since we've spoken," she asked.

"Alrighty, so a few days ago we had located at his home and we know he previously was at the Dala Electricity Hub London after all the Brian Harrison stuff. But just now, like literally thirty minutes ago, I found out he's at The Amy Dala Factory just outside of London. So it's likely that the SSSA4 now knows of our involvement. He's probably gonna be making ways over here now in the coming few days," he replied.

"Okay good. Well keep an eye on him and you get a new sim and you text me on this number with updates. We'll speak soon Bridger. Have a good night," she replied.

"Yes Elisa. Will do. You too," he said as she hung up the call.

And so, as Elisabeth Cervantes leant over her balcony and looked over the City of London, finally allowing her mind to quieten and embrace the stillness of the present moment for the first time in her day, the following thought entered her mind – *London is mine, still mine.*

BOOK 16

HOMO ILLUMINATUS

Sunday 15th November 2065, the Early Hours of the Morning

The Narrator

And so, the pivotal moment had arrived. For after the morning of the 15th November of 2065, the lives of those mentioned in this story, changed forever. What had transpired could not be undone, and it was decreed by a force greater and more mysterious than they could possibly fathom. That which happened to these selected people, could not be understood by logic alone – there were supernatural forces at play, bigger than themselves and bigger than that which Fergus-Sundar had encountered; it was of another world, and thus adhered to rules outside of the confines of what was possibly on a metaphysical level known on Earth. For energy from another world had entered this dimension, and thus altered the course of this Earth, and of the lives and DNA of a select few. This Dark Energy interacted with things whose DNA just so happened to be compatible with it; a perfect fit.

And so, in the early hours of the morning of Sunday the 15th of November in 2065, Doctor Luftana Amara, Shackleton Nair, Mike da Silva, Devonte Lacy, Fergus-Sundar, Oticus the Dog and four-hundred-and-fifteen humans experienced something unfathomable. A total of 420 Homo Sapiens, along with Oticus the Dog, experienced an Illumination of some of the Dark DNA which lay in their bodies, as this Dark DNA fused with the Dark Matter brought into this dimension in the aftermath of Fergus-Sundar's arrival.

This is the tale of how these Homo Sapiens, underwent an overnight evolutionary fast-track and changed to become Homo Illuminatus.

AAJ

Doctor Luftana Amara

Luftana Amara put her head back onto the pillow of the hospital bed; it was the first time she had been horizontal for near 24 hours now – sleep was needed. Ever since the 'Tech-Night', as the news were calling it, and the subsequent Dala Realisations that people experienced – she had been inundated with work. Many of her nurses and doctors had called in sick, citing mental health reasons and post-traumatic stress disorder as the reason. These doctors and nurses claimed to be suffering with extreme anxiety and, or, hallucinations. Luftana knew that this may very well have been accurate for some of these claimants, as she suffered from the same issues and had patients who were also suffering from these ailments. Though she was also aware that this was the perfect excuse for people to get out of work, and that some would certainly milk this. She did not blame them for if she had a family, she would certainly do the same.

Though Luftana did not have a family, and as she closed her eyes, she thought of her family in Palestine and wished they were here with her. She wished they were alive. Luftana then could not help but hear the screaming voices she had seen and heard. And for a moment, she did not know whether the memory of screaming voices came from the suffering of her fellow Palestinian people from when she was just a child and stuck under the rubble, or whether it was from the screams of people of London, suffering from extreme withdrawal effects of not being able to use their Dala Device during the 'Tech-Night'.

Despite the fact her mind was racing with these thoughts and the memories of her trauma – she was soon fast asleep. For that amount of sleep deprivation, meant she conked out nearly instantly. Once Luftana Amara had entered a deep state of sleep, and was in the fourth stage of REM sleep – it happened. The Illumination of her DNA took place, and her body glowed and levitated at the same time. She let out a scream as she felt an unimaginable pain – it was the second time this week she had felt a pain like this, the first being during her Dala Realisation. Upon hearing the scream her fellow doctors in A&E ran into the room and almost as quickly as they had run into the room, they came to a standstill and felt their jaws drop.

"Oh my God! What the … what's happening!" Joan the A&E doctor shouted with a look of desperation on her face.

"I don't know. What do we do? Is she possessed or something? She's glowing. And levitating," Sunil the A&E doctor replied.

"Do something Sunil."

"I'm not touching her. Not like that, are you mad?" Sunil replied.

"We can't leave her like this. She's in pain," Joan replied. Joan approached Luftana, not knowing exactly what she was going to do. But once Joan got within two feet of Luftana Amara, she could not approach anymore, for she came into contact with an invisible wall of some sort. Luftana Amara had an energy around her which could not be penetrated. That which was occurring had to occur, and would occur at all costs. The fusion of Luftana Amara's Dark DNA and the Dark Matter brought in by Fergus-Sundar, had created an impenetrable energy bubble around her, as it did to all those who experienced the Illumination of the DNA.

And so, Sunil and Joan stood back as they watched Luftana Amara wince in her sleep, amidst her Illumination. Though the Illumination was short, and soon enough Luftana Amara stopped glowing and her body dropped onto the bed. And then she awoke.

"Woah, what happened? Joan are you okay? Oh my God, Joan? Come here. What's happening? I am tripping?" Luftana Amara said as she sat up in bed, looking completely unphased and surprisingly very fresh. Though she did not have the glow permeating all around her body as it had done amidst the Illumination of her DNA, her face had a natural glow still – she had become even more beautiful.

"Me? Am I okay? Are you okay! Babe what the hell! You were glowing, like literally. And you screamed and then you were mid-air, like levitating. I tried to come close to you, but then were like a block of some sort, almost like you were in a cocoon or something," replied Joan as she now slowly began to approach Luftana Amara, with Sunil hesitantly following behind.

"I mean I feel great. I feel really, really good actually. But Joan come here. I can see stuff. I don't know what happened. God knows what happened. But this must be the work of God. I can see stuff now Joan. Joan, please come here. I don't know how to put this. But I'm just gonna say it straight babe. I can see you have something wrong with you. Come here please. Hold my hand."

"Luftana you're not making any sense. You're scaring me."

"Luftana we need to get you checked out as soon as possible. That was not normal what just happened," replied Sunil.

"Sunil, its Joan who needs to be checked out, ASAP. And I mean ASAP. But yeah of course, I'll get checked out too. Joan, please just come here," replied Luftana, now with a sense of urgency and sadness underpinning her voice.

Joan came towards Luftana now and they held hands, and Luftana closed her eyes and saw everything. She found herself deep inside of Joan Pearson. And Luftana had a tear as she had her eyes closed. She could see that Joan was not in good health. Prior to Joan touching her, she could see that Joan was not of good health and that she had an illness – it was almost like a meter showed her this, like a car displaying that there is not much fuel left in the tank. Joan's meter showed that she had a terminal illness, and now Luftana touched Joan's hands and connected with her – she could see inside of Joan's body and directly at where the ailment was. Joan had stage three pancreatic cancer.

"Joan, do you know?"

"Do I know what?"

"I can see it Joan. It's okay," said Luftana as she did not want to disclose her medical history. For if Joan already knew, then she likely would have been keeping it private purposefully, and she would be entitled to keep it private.

"What can you see? Are you okay?"

"I'm fine Joan. But I can see it. I can see it now; I can't explain it. But I can see inside of you. I can see the, you know the thing."

"Huh? What? Luftana you're scaring me," Joan said.

"Sunil give us the room for a moment please," Luftana said. Sunil nodded and promptly departed the room, though did so with some hesitation as he almost stopped and turned whilst walking away.

"I'm sorry to say it like this, but I have to say it. I have a duty of care. You have stage three pancreatic cancer Joan. I can see it inside of you. Before I touched you, I could see there was something wrong, almost like there was a dial showing me. Then when we touched, my mind was transported to inside of you and I can visually see it. I'm so sorry Joan. You need to get checked up immediately."

"Luftana what the hell. Who have you been speaking to?"

"No one Joan. I didn't know till now. I can't explain it, but whatever just happened changed me. I'm so sorry Joan. Did you know?"

"I know Luftana. I haven't told anyone yet. I just found out last week. How can you tell? How can you see it? I don't understand. Oh my God I'm getting hot. I need to sit down. What the f**k is going on?" Luftana helped Joan have a seat next to her as Joan sunk her head into Luftana's chest as tears rolled down her face uncontrollably now.

"I don't understand either Joan."

And so, this was how Luftana Amara had undergone her Illumination of the DNA. She was had changed. She had the ability to recognise people's illness and it's relative extremity, their current state of health upon seeing them – though could not identify exactly what this illness or ailment was until she touched then. And if she touched a person, she could instantly determine what illness they had.

And thus, Luftana Amara was no longer a Homo Sapien, but rather a Homo Illuminatus.

AAJ

Shackleton Nair

Shackleton Nair brushed his teeth as he showered alone; he had asked his wife, Claudia, to join him – but she refused. They had not been on good terms ever since the Dala Realisation they both experienced; at this stage, he was worried. She had known of his infidelity and the relationship seemed near unsalvageable at this point. He longed for things to go back to the way, and he wished he had not gone to that Mycology Conference. And so, he left the shower and made his way into their bedroom.

"I've set the sofa up for you Shack. Pillows there as well," she said.

"Claudia please. Can I not just …"

"No Shack. Please. I just need some time and space. I already told you this. Can you please just understand where I'm coming from and be considerate. For once in your f**king life."

"Alright. I understand. Claudia I really am …"

"Shack. Respectfully, I don't wanna hear it now. We've already spoken about this. I told you I just need some space right now. Please can you just go downstairs. I just can't right now," she replied.

Before he made his way downstairs, he entered the room of his son Charles. He looked at his son as he slept for a brief moment. This was all that was keeping him and Claudia together, and the most precious thing in his life.

He made his way downstairs, and struggled to fall asleep on the sofa, tossing and turning for near an hour as he pondered whether he could ever find his way back with his wife of twelve years. Soon enough, he fell asleep. And once he entered a deep state of sleep, and was in the fourth stage of REM sleep – it happened. Shackleton Nair screamed in his sleep, unaware he was screaming, as the Illumination of his Dark DNA occurred. The fusion of his Dark DNA and Dark Matter occurred, and Shackleton Nair's body began to glow, much like the Bioluminescent Fungi he had recently discovered.

"Pappa! Pappa! Mummy come quickly. Something's happening to Pappa," Charles cried out to his mother, as the young boy looked on as his father's body levitated and glowed.

Claudia entered the room and screamed at the sight. She grabbed her son and held him close to her. Her motherly instincts kicked in.

"Shack! Shack! Wake up!" she shouted out to him.

"Mummy help him. Something's happening to Pappa. I'm scared," Charles said as held on close to his mother, whilst attempting to look away from his father – though he could not help but look at his father as he underwent his Illumination.

"Stand back Charles. Mummy's going to go help Pappa okay," Claudia replied as she knelt and looked deep into her son's eyes, tears rolling down both of their faces. "Don't worry okay, Pappa will be okay. He's just having a fit okay, he'll be fine soon."

Claudia approached Shackleton Nair.

"Shack wake up! Please Shack," she said as she approached him. Though as she approached him and got within two feet of him, she could not go further; for she came into contact with an invisible wall of some sort. Shackleton Nair had an energy around him which could not be penetrated. That which was occurring had to occur, and would occur at all costs. The fusion of Shackleton Nair's Dark DNA and the Dark Matter brought in by Fergus-Sundar, had created an impenetrable energy bubble around him, as it did to all those who experienced the Illumination of the DNA. Nothing could stop this.

A few minutes later, as Claudia called and waited for the ambulance to arrive. Shackleton's Illumination ended and the man awoke, though no longer as Shackleton Nair, the Homo Sapien.

He was now Shackleton Nair, the Homo Illuminatus.

Claudia and Charles looked on at their husband and father respectively, as he got up from his sleep as looked around. They looked on at him with fear. Shackleton had not spoken yet. Shackleton knew something was different instantly. For his vision was distorted. He looked upon his son and his wife and no longer could he only see his son and wife – but instead now he could see remnants of mycelium and particles emanated from mycelium on his body son's hands and his wife's. Shackleton Nair realised that he could see mycelium now in the air. He could see it all around him.

"Charles, Claudia are you okay? Don't worry I'm okay. Pappa's okay. Come here son," Shackleton said.

"Wait Charles. Shack what just happened? You were in the air Shack. And you were glowing. I can't let him come to you. I don't know what's going on," replied Claudia as she held her son close.

"It's fine. I think something magical just happened Claudia. Something special just happened. I can't explain it … but I think it's to do with that strand of Bioluminescent Fungi I found on the Tech-Night. The one with the Dark Matter. I can feel it. I can see it. I can see mycelium everywhere. Even on your hands. I can see the roots even. I can see the mycorrhizae. I can actually see the networks beneath your feet even. It's like an X-Ray scan but for fungi. I – I can't quite explain it Claudia. Wow. This is amazing. I wish you could see as I see. Something special has happened. I can see fungi residue on everything. I can see it Claudia," he said as he looked around the room.

"Charles run to your room," she said.

"But I wanna …"

"Charles listen to me. Go to your room right now. Pappa's not well."

"Claudia what are you …"

"Charles. Go to your room. Now," she said.

"Claudia I'm fine. It's a miracle," Shackleton replied.

"Shack you've gone crazy. I don't know what's happening. You've lost your mind. I need you out of here tonight,"

"Claudia what? Please let me explain …" he said as he approached her.

"Don't touch me! Get away! Please Shack. I can't. You don't understand what I just saw happen to you. I think you've gone insane."

"Claudia?"

"Get out!" she screamed in fear as she began to weep. It pained her to be so afraid of the man she loved. And it pained him. The distance between them grew even more, irreparably, and the Illumination of Shackleton Nair was the final straw, cementing their separation.

And so, if Shackleton Nair had not experienced the Illumination of his Dark DNA in this moment, he would have been more sad at the ending of his marriage which had just occurred. But instead he made his way outside and looked over his fields, and looked on in wonder. He could see the mycelium in everything. He could see the underground networks which connected nature together, the mycorrhizal networks which connected everything and shared nutrients and information between nature – the wood wide web. He had changed. Tears of joy rolled down his face as he considered the abilities he had at his disposal now. Shackleton knew that this could not be the extent of his powers and instantly tested its limits. A thought crossed his mind and he opened his palm and found a mushroom in his hand. He placed the mushroom in his pocket; so he could run tests on the mushroom later on. Again he closed his eyes and tested his newfound power. A small leather wallet made of mycelium appeared in his palms. He could harness his powers to make anything that could be made from fungi and mycelium. This was not the extent of his newfound powers; in time he would come to develop and further understand his powers.

And thus, Shackleton Nair was no longer a Homo Sapien, rather a Homo Illuminatus.

Mike da Silva

Mike da Silva put his legs up as he looked upon his ninety-six inch TV and sipped on a cocktail from a diamond-embossed glass. His friends sat on the sofa on the other side of the large living room. The marble glistened from the glare of the TV despite the darkness in the room – the diamonds embedded within the exterior coat of the marble glistened. The diamonds from his ring glistened as he again sipped from his drink. However, his diamond-embedded sunglasses blocked the glistening and shimmering.

He fell asleep quickly after the drink, as a woman massaged him. His friends watched on whilst he slept. He was out cold and soon enough the snoring begun. He snored like a big cat, fitting for a man nicknamed the Black Tiger. As he snored, the woman remained cuddled up to him.

Soon enough, Mike da Silva entered a deep state of sleep, and entered the fourth stage of REM sleep – it had begun. He screamed out in pain, in what felt like a roar as he slept. The Illumination of his Dark DNA was taking place. Dark Matter was fusing with the Dark DNA in Mike da Silva; it was a perfect match. The inevitable had occurred.

And so, Mike da Silva began to glow, his body floating in the air as he remained in the same position in which he fell asleep. The woman shrieked and quickly backed away, though was given a push by the Impenetrable Energy Bubble that grew around Mike amidst his Illumination. His friends woke up. They themselves had fallen asleep, but they did not have an Illumination of the Dark DNA. It was only Mike da Silva, and to them it was fitting that it was Mike; for he was extraordinary. He was the reason they were living as they were living.

'The boys' though did not react with exasperation or anything of the sort. Despite the Abnormal nature of what was transpiring in front of them – they did not appear to be in shock. The boys seemed to be somewhat accustomed to seeing things which were out of the ordinary it would seem – as they seemed to be more curious and in awe of what they could see. To them this was just another Abnormal event before them; Mike da Silva – their boy – was levitating in the air, and his dark brownskin body was somehow glowing despite it being really dark – which seemed to intrigue them. They were used to the Abnormal being in Mike's inner circle.

"Bruh, y'all seeing this sh*t. Am I tripping or y'all seeing this too?" said Bix as he got up from his seat, zoot in his hand.

"Yo Mike is shining bruv. He's f**king glowing. Chill out girl, it's cool.

He's aite. Yo this is some spiritual sh*t I'm telling you man. Some supernatural sh*t. Watch it man. Embrace that sh*t. You're witnessing something great here. I can feel it. Take it in man," said his friend, the former fighter Edgar 'Dinamita' Reyes. "Man this is beautiful," he continued as tears of joy rolled down his face.

To Edgar Reyes, Bixente Lemaire, Samson Smithson, and eventually to the women in the room who the three had only met tonight – what they were witnessing was a miracle, something extraordinary and unlike anything they had ever seen before. It was something divine or dark and mystical that they were witnessing.

They all stood back in awe as they watched the process in wonder. And soon enough, Mike da Silva stopped levitating and fell back into the same position where he had been sat before, no longer glowing.

"Bix don't post this. Not yet. I hope you stopped the streaming," replied Edgar Reyes as he continued to puff the zoot in his hand. Bixente Lemaire switched off the stream. He had been recording till now and everything that had transpired, was captured on stream. Thus, millions saw the Illumination of the DNA of Mike da Silva. The point from which his life changed forever, from which he changed forever. And fitting it was that it was caught on camera, for it was in front of the camera, fighting, that Mike da Silva had gained his fame, and earned his millions. However, what occurred next was not caught on camera and was not on stream. He awoke from his sleep and looked upon the faces looking at him, as they looked at him in wonder.

"Yo stop looking at me like that. Youse know I hate when people stare like that. Anyways, something weird happened innit? I blacked out. But sh*t that wasn't like a normal blackout or anything. It weren't like sleeping or getting knocked out. It was different. Man it felt like some spiritual sh*t I can't lie. I feel good. I feel f**king good right now. I think I just had a trip. Sh*t felt like when I had DMT or something like that. What happened man? Did one of youse put some sh*t in my drink? Be honest" said Mike

da Silva as he buzzed around the place. "I feel so f**king alive. I feel like I've
been reborn or some sh*t. Stop staring though, real talk."

"Mike. Bruh. No one drugged you let's just get that straight gangy.
But if you saw what we. What your ass was doing when you was knocked
the f**k out and screaming at the same damn time. Then you'd know why
I'm looking at you like that mother*****r. You was f**king glowing bruh.
Word to my mother you were glowing bruh. It was some crazy sh*t and
I done seen a lot of crazy f**king sh*t man. Y'all know that," replied Bix as
he backstrapped his zoot.

"Mike you were Illuminating man. You're damn right it was some trippy
sh*t man. It was beautiful man I ain't even gonna lie. Had me crying man.
You were like levitating too. I'm telling you man we just saw something
special. You're chosen Mike. You been blessed or something. I dunno if it's
God or what man. But something just happened. It was something divine
I'm telling you," replied Edgar Reyes. Samson Smithson stood quieter, but
still looked upon Mike da Silva with awe and an element of fear.

"I mean I feel good. I feel different though. I'm different now. Edgar
bro. Let's roll. Let's wrestle or box or something. I need to test something
man. I feel heightened man. Like my senses and everything. The reactions
man. I can see everything man. I can see heat," Mike laughed, "I'm not even
joking cos I know that probably sounds crazy but I can see the heat radiation.
I can smell everything. And I feel heavy right now. Like I've put on weight.
Let's spar Edgar," said Mike da Silva as he walked over rapidly out of the
living room and towards the gym in the house. The crew followed behind
him swiftly.

"Mike baby you sure you okay to fight now?" the woman who had been
with him prior to his Illumination asked him.

""I am always okay to fight. Put some respect on my name please," he
said laughing, his ego hurt in this moment. If there was one thing he could
do, and one that that came as naturally to him as breathing – it was fighting
and all the facets involved in this.

"Let's go then," said Edgar, who needed absolutely no convincing; he was a competition junkie like Mike da Silva, and a combat athlete who had succeeded at the highest level.

The two began to sprawl and wrestle, and within moments it seemed extremely evident who had the upper hand, and who had so in a freakish manner. He had not been wrong; he was faster, physically stronger and his bones were denser. His reactions were better and his senses were indeed heightened. His newfound changes made him even more of a predator. And within moments, Mike da Silva had gotten the back of Edgar Reyes and performed a suplex on him, throwing him back as though he weighed only ten kilograms in a move which nearly took his life. Mike da Silva had almost thrown him out of the ring completely – an extraordinary feat of power. Mike da Silva was now the strongest man in the world, and likely the fastest. He was no longer just an extraordinary human being. He was now extraordinary in a different sense; he was a Homo Illuminatus.

Later in the evening, Mike da Silva was discovered another ability. He had grown hungry as he tested his newfound abilities with his friends in his gym through extraordinary athletic feats of strength and agility. As he grew hungry, he quickly grew hangry. And he very, very quickly reached these respective stages of hungriness. And when Mike da Silva's hunger was not satiated, the anger took over and his hunger reached another stage never seen before in humanity.

He became a beast. Mike da Silva's hunger turned him into the Black Tiger. Once a nickname for him, now it was reality. The man shapeshifted and became an actual Black Tiger. Though now his friends smiled not. Instead they screamed, and screamed for their lives. They fled, the majority successfully. However, one was caught. The woman who had been with him prior to his Illumination was caught in the predatorial rage of the Black Tiger; she had tried to reason with him. And so she became dinner for the Black Tiger. It became the first human the Black Tiger would eat, and the last. For once he awoke again, and metamorphosised back into Mike da

Silva – he sat in his house alone, his friends having fled in fear, as he looked upon the blood around him and at the devastation that the Black Tiger had caused. He told himself he would never again do this and that he would need to learn to control this part of himself. For although Mike da Silva had killed before, never had he killed an innocent civilian like this – someone who didn't ask for it, deserve it, or enter combat with him. He had slaughtered this time, and without control, and eaten his prey.

What am I? What have I done? Is this who I am? Nah, I can't do this again.

The Boys would return after being called by Mike, and the League of Shottas cleanup team would deal with mess and remains of the Black Tiger's lunch; they were a resourceful and meticulous team.

And so, Mike da Silva had undergone the Illumination of the DNA. He had changed forever. The Dark Matter had found a match in him, and fused with his Dark DNA.

And thus, no longer was Mike da Silva a Homo Sapien; he was now a Homo Illuminatus.

Oticus the Dog

And so, Oticus the Dog tugged on his lead as he took his owners on a walk; they were so slow. He was in a rush for he wanted to reach the park ahead of him as soon as possible. Oticus had not been to the park in some time now and so he was desperate at this point; there was so much grass and mud for him to rub his thick white and cream coat of fur on. He was feeling very clean at the moment, and this made him uneasy. He hated being brushed and washed, but his owners seemed to be obsessed with maintaining his aesthetic, much to his chagrin.

The walk was fruitful for Oticus the Dog as he successfully rubbed himself on the dirty grass and smelt many pees and poos in the park, and ensured his emptied his bladder till it was completely empty – he did a wee on every lamppost and bin and tree and bench he could see. As Oticus arrived home finally, he drank some fresh water which his owner knew to get for him. For Oticus the Dog was a boujee dog; the other water in his bowl had been put there hours before – this was beneath him; he wanted fresh water. This enthralled his owners as they made what he considered weird noises whilst he drank.

Oticus made the most of his owner's enthrallment with him and sat down like a good dog and faced them, as they faced the TV. Again the weird noses came out from these humans and they gave him some chicken. Oticus had done this before and he would do it again. He continued to sit down like a good dog and even offered his paw on a few occasions, and the food kept on coming his way. He had practically had a third meal now, and Oticus was tired. He fell into a deep sleep and dreamt about his walk in the park, and thought of his human owners giving him food.

However, his sleep was quickly rudely interrupted as someone walked past his house, causing the house's alarm system to notify his human owners "Motion detected at the front door". Though Oticus knew what this sound meant too. Though he did not understand English, he knew what this weird noise signified. And so, Oticus wriggled his body up and jumped out of his bed and desperately galloped to the front door before letting out a ferocious bark. He barked, and barked, and barked. Oticus was the sworn guardian dog of his house. This was his territory. His house. No one would pass without him letting them know that they were not welcome, and that they should not enter his territory. Despite the fact he was only small, a mixed breed of a miniature poodle and west highland terrier, his bark a full grown rottweiler's. He continued to bark and bark before his owners pleaded for him to stop; the humans grew tired of his barking. For Oticus, this was his duty, and he would do his duty whenever it needed to be done. The humans shouted out the word 'chicken' and he desperately galloped back. Once again, he sat like a good dog and he ate the chicken within seconds despite the fact that he ought to be full. He did not understand the meaning or feeling of satiety; he would eat till he died.

His favourite out of his human owners called him out to join her by his side, and Oticus did so instantly. He loved his human mother and sat on her lap as she placed her hand on his hair body and watched the TV. Oticus this time faced the TV also and his serenity alongside his human mother was soon interrupted as something caused him to be irate once more, another potential threat to his home. Oticus the Dog did not quite understand what a TV was, or a hoover or suitcase for that matter. And so, he let out one bark at this animal on the TV, before quickly stopping. His owners continued to make weird noises as it seemed Oticus was be enthralled by this animal on the TV.

Never before had Oticus the Dog looked on in wonder, perplexed at the beast he saw on the TV. Horses, lions, rats, cats, hippos – it did not matter what animal it was; he would bark at them if they dared show themselves on his TV in his house. However, he found himself looking on in wonder at this beast. It was large in sizer, the size of a house, and this animal burned everything in front of it as fire left its mouth, before flying off into the sky. Oticus the Dog has seen a Dragon for the first time and he was captivated. This was something he could not compete with. A lion or tiger on TV he felt he could conquer for they were just cats, though this Dragon he knew was something different and out of his league. He wished he could fly off as this Dragon had done. And now Oticus turned back to the humans as they watched the TV and also looked in wonder. He craved this for himself, to be respected and feared, and to have this power that the Dragon did.

Eventually Oticus the Dog found himself in a deep state of sleep. And then it began, he began to howl in his sleep as he was hoisted into the air by the invisible and impenetrable energy bubble – the Illumination of his Dark DNA was occurring. The Dark Matter brought into this dimension by Fergus-Sundar, which had infused with the mycorrhizae of this Earth, was now fusing with his Dark DNA. His human parents cried out and looked on in wonder and fear as they could not comfort him or touch him. They cried as Oticus cried and whilst in this state of panic, they called the emergency vet on call, who ushered them to bring him to them as a matter of urgency.

In time, the Illumination of DNA for Oticus the Dog had stopped and the impenetrable energy bubble dissipated. His human father grabbed him as Oticus was weak; the Illumination of DNA had knocked him out. He could not stand even, his breathing grew heavy, and he panted profusely. The body of the dog was far smaller and weaker than that of the Homo Sapiens who had experienced the Illumination of DNA, and thus the impact on Oticus was tough. He was holding onto life.

His human mother held him as the human father of Oticus the Dog drove dangerously to the emergency vet. Whilst Oticus was a dog, he was like a child to this young human couple and they were desperate to ease his pain and discover what was wrong with him.

They were now in the emergency vet's room and the vet could not determine what was wrong with him. The human parents of Oticus, could not explain adequately with their words of what they had seen occur to him; it was unbelievable. He continued to pant and yelp in pain. And then it occurred once more. Oticus the Dog found himself hoisted into the air once more, and began to yelp and bark in pain. The vet and the human parents of Oticus stepped back in fear and looked on in confusion at what they were seeing. However, this time was different – the effect on his body was different. The impenetrable energy bubble formed around Oticus the Dog, and this time his physical body changed as the Dark DNA infused with the Dark Matter.

The Illumination of his DNA was now taking place completely and Oticus the Dog began his metamorphosis. His skin toughened. His body hardened. His bones grew denser. His organs grew larger. His tail elongated. And his bones and body grew in size, to that of a horse. His fur remained, though underneath this he developed scaly and reptilian-like skin. Then his skin tore on his back as he bones expanded and changed shape – wings grew from his spine, like branches on a tree. He barked and yelped in pain.

And then his neck grew hot, as hot as lava from a volcano. And so, the metamorphosis of Oticus the Dog due to the Illumination of his DNA, had occurred. He was no longer then same, he had changed. And now the impenetrable energy bubble was gone once more. His owners looked on at him with both fear and sadness in their eyes as they felt his pain as though it were their own.

"What the f**k," the man said, his black face turned white.

"Be careful. I dunno what's happened," said the human mother of Oticus, as tears rolled down her face. "Oticus, my baby. Is he okay? Oh my God, is he breathing?"

"Oti, are you okay baby?" the human father asked, approaching him.

He opened his eyes to see his human parents, but found his vision had changed. He felt the pain no more, but knew he was different. He saw his human owners in front of him. They spoke to him, and he attempted to speak back to them, in the only way he knew how to – though barking. Though as he barked – no longer was it a bark. Fire came from his mouth as he attempted to bark. He breathed fire

And so, Oticus was no longer Oticus the Dog.

He had metamorphosis was complete.

He was now, Oticus the Dragon-Dog.

He grew afraid as he suddenly realised, in what was perhaps his first moment of experiencing autonoetic consciousness, what and who he was. And fear took over him. He reverted to habit, and tried to bark in confusion and fear to his owners; he was scared. Though what happened, would be something that would alter the life of Oticus the Dragon-Dog forever.

He opened his mouth once more and watched his humans be set alight on fire. He again reverted to habit, and out of fear he yelped and went to bark in sadness and pain; he did not want this, he did not want to see this, he did not want to hurt them. But once more, as he opened his mouth fire continued to descend his mouth, and then his owners and the vet and the entire room was on fire. Oticus continued to cry and attempted to lift his paw onto the now dead and burnt corpse of his human parents, again through habitual action. Though as he pawed on them, his now sharp nails and thicker and denser paws cut through their charred bodies, and they crumbled before his own eyes.

Oticus the Dragon-Dog had killed three people, and he did not know how he had done it; for he had not adjusted to his metamorphosis.. He did not know what had happened. He was afraid. Oticus the Dragon-Dog attempted to run away in fear and blasted through the wall in front of him and heard the cries and screams of the people. He looked on as the humans and animals around him looked on at him in fear. With his newfound autonoetic consciousness, Oticus the Dragon-Dog thought to the moment he saw the Dragon on his TV and had wished to be feared as the Dragon had. However, he had killed the only thing that truly mattered to him; his human owners. He turned and looked upon the destruction he had caused. He looked once more at the faces and at the energies radiated from the humans in front of him. And then in another moment of Oticus exhibiting his newfound autonoetic consciousness; Oticus thought of himself and what he had done before, what he was seeing in front of himself now, and what future he wanted to avoid; he didn't want to repeat his mistakes.

And so, he began to think, with an understanding and awareness of himself and his past and his present and his future. He felt and saw the wings on his back and recognised they were not there before. Then he thought of the Dragon he had seen on the TV, and he remembered what those wings did.

Alas, he put his wings into his practice and flew through the roof of the veterinary clinic. And in a display of purposeful aggression, he cried out in the skies of London knowing that fire would erupt from his mouth – tales and footage of this event would go viral. The Illumination of the DNA had changed Oticus into the Dragon-Dog. He would retreat to lonely locations across the world over the years, residing in abandoned caves and mountains; inaccessible to man.

Though this was not the last time he would interact with humans. A time would come again when he would return to society. Oticus the Dragon-Dog would not be seen by another human till the year 2070. His role in the Tech-Night epoch had only just begun.

Devonte Lacy

The cell doors slammed shut as Devonte Lacy took a seat on his bunk bed. His cell mate, Larry Schmidt, jumped onto the top bunk.

"Devonte … Devonte. Another day in the mad house," said Larry.

"Another day man. Just another day. It is what it is. I'm tired as f**k now I ain't even gone lie. That mother*****r really went for it. F**ked my whole damn stomach up bruh," replied Devonte tho winced as he touched his lower abdomen. He had been caught with a clean knee to his stomach before being slammed onto the table.

"Hey man. It's your fault for getting into that scrap," Larry replied.

"F**k you mean bruh? What the f**k I done bruh? The mother*****r disrespecting me like I'm some b**ch ass mother*****n. I ain't no b**ch. I ain't let no man disrespect me like that bruh. Don't matter where we is. On god. That can't run," Devonte replied.

"Well you got his respect innit. Seems like he knows wagwan now," Larry replied.

"Damn straight bruh. All of them know now. Y'all aint gonna f**k me with me like that. I ain't no b**ch ass," replied Devonte.

"Chill out bro. You already won the fight so why you stressing?"

"Stressing? Bruh I ain't stressed bout this sh*t."

"Shutup man. You know what I mean. Cool though, long as you good. I said it before. And damn right I'm gonna say it again. What's happened, has happened. Forgive and forget bro. Enjoy your …"

"Aite bro I got you. You done told me this sh*t time and time again bruh. I only known you like three days or some sh*t and you already told me this same sh*t again and again bruh. Doing my f**king head in bruh. How about you chill?" replied Devonte.

"Hey man. If it's the truth, it's the truth. The truth frees you. It brings me peace. You need to take up meditation. Man I'm telling you, that sh*t will change your life. One time we need to …"

"Aite bruh that's my cue to sleep I think bro. Imma meditate my ass to sleep now. Night bruh. Keep your snoring ass down."

Soon enough, they both fell asleep. Devonte was knocked out cold, and as the night went on he found himself enter a deep sleep and went into the 4th stage of REM sleep. And then it happened. Still asleep, he began to scream in pain as the Illumination of his Dark DNA occurred. The fusion of his Dark DNA and the Dark Matter brought into the atmosphere by Fergus-Sundar, was occurring. And like the others who experienced this same Illumination, Devonte Lacy's body was lifted into the air and levitated as a glow grew around his body.

"Jesus Christ," said Larry as he watched Devonte from the edge of the room. "Guard! Oi guard! Guard! He's having a fit I think! I dunno what to do. Help! Someone f**king help! Guard!" he shouted out.

Larry approached Devonte but found he could not place his hands on him. He was covered by the impenetrable energy bubble, that had been formed from this fusion of Dark DNA and Dark Matter. Nothing could break or enter this energy bubble. Larry noticed his hand unable to get through this air, for seemingly no reason. And so he continued to fight his hand past this point to no avail. He grew frustrated and threw himself into this impenetrable energy bubble, which caused him to bounce off the bubble and slam into the wall.

Devonte continued to scream out in pain as he hovered in the air, with his eyes remaining closed. He looked to be possessed.

"Shut the f**k up!" an inmate shouted.

"Devonte you f**k! I'm gonna kill you tomorrow!"

The ruckus quickly woke the majority of this section of the prison, and inmates angrily shouted out. A commotion was caused.

"Oi he's f**king glowing bruv," another inmate shouted out.

"Yo wtf," another shouted out.

"It's a miracle. God has his soul now," another shouted.

Soon enough people were scrambling to see Devonte from their own cell. What had started off as frustration from the inmates, soon turned to wonder and excited murmurs. A few guards eventually made their way to the cell of Devonte and Larry – it was the early hours of the morning, and so they moved relatively lethargically to the cell despite the ruckus. They attempted to subdue Devonte Lacy, though they too found themselves unable to make their way towards him, as nothing could come within two-feet of him while the Illumination of his Dark DNA was occurring. Though Devonte Lacy had stopped the screaming now and began to shine bright.

"I see you shining," an inmate shouted out. This began to be shouted out versions of this phrase around the prison as inmates looked at the near blinding light emitting from the body of Devonte Lacy, out into the night of the prison halls. They were gassed.

The inmates and now even the prison guards felt as though they were witnessing the miracle. One of the guards even stopped to make a prayer, with tears rolling down his face as he prayed. Soon enough, Devonte Lacy's body dropped back slowly to his bed, in the position he had been in before, and the blinding light was no longer there. Though that feeling and moment, would stay with all that witnessed the Illumination of Devonte Lacy in the prison that day; for it was something beautiful they could hold onto, and that too, in the darkest of places – hope was always there for all, no matter how dire a situation.

"Rah. What the f**k? I can hear them all. Larry, I can hear it all," he said as he sat up. He heard screams coming from the courtyard of the prison, and felt it's pain.

Those around him spoke to him, but Devonte Lacy could not hear them. Not right now. His ears, or rather an intuition deep within the previously inaccessible recesses of his brain – were focused elsewhere at this moment. For he was blind before to this part of life and reality, and it was as though he was experiencing sight of this part of life and reality for the first time, truly. He heard the leaves fly around in the air and felt the solitary, isolated tree in the courtyard cry out. Devonte Lacy could hear nature, like never before, and he felt it cry. The trees silently crying, at frequencies and wavelengths not audible to the human ear. And Devonte Lacy found it hard to think straight, to focus on the present moment. *It's alone and isolates – that tree can't share its knowledge and nutrients with none other; f**k its lonely man, the tree is lonely.*

Faintly, he heard his friend Larry tell him to 'breathe', and so he began to breathe consciously. Larry had mentioned meditating to him just hours before, and it would seem be that meditation would have to become a part of Devonte's life now; his senses had become acutely hyperaware of the different elements and truths of life – he heard and saw nature, as it truly was occurring. Devonte Lacy remained quiet and attempted to keep to himself, despite the hubbub surrounding him. Thus, he was transferred to solitary confinement for the night, and told it was 'for the protection of the other inmates'.

Devonte sat and meditated through the night as he tried to quieten the noises he now heard. And in time, he reached a state of mind whereby he could control his thoughts and choose to hear the nature. He sat cross-legged, looked upon his hands and felt something within him, deep within, that he knew was powerful yet somewhat unfathomable.

However, what was occurring to him was already unbelievable. And so, he chose to follow this thought. He held his palm out and cleared his mind once more. He thought of what had brought him here to this prison, to the thing which had saved the life of his aunty. And then two grams of the Knightsbridge OZ strain of weed, appeared in the palm of his hands. He had made the weed out of nothing from the palms of his hands. He began to chuckle, and what started as a chuckle, quickly ascended into what became raucous laughter.

And so, this was the tale of the Illumination of Devonte Lacy. He had changed forever and what had occurred, could never be undone. He had the ability to hear the thoughts and feel the feelings of nature, and could make weed from the palms of his hands. Though his powers extended beyond this; he was yet to unlock the full potential of his powers – but he would in time.

No longer was Devonte Lacy Homo Sapien; he was Homo Illuminatus.

Fergus-Sundar

What was intended to be a quick nap, had turned into a deep and dream filled sleep for Fergus-Sundar. He had not intended to sleep for long, but he could not help himself. He was destined to enter a deep state of sleep on this night, for this was the night the Dark Matter would infuse with the Dark DNA of things on Earth. He had to be in a deep state of sleep on this night; for as he brought the Dark Matter into this reality, the condition of him being in this fourth stage of REM sleep was required by the Dark Matter, in order for it to infuse with the Dark DNA of things on Earth. The Dark Matter in the atmosphere induced an exacerbation of the naturally occurring adenosine in his body, thus resulting in him feeling more sleepy.

And so, as Fergus-Sundar entered this deep state of sleep and was in the fourth stage of REM sleep –the Illumination of his Dark DNA occurred, it had happened to him as well. The Dark DNA within Fergus-Sundar, interacted and formed in a perfect symbiosis with the Dark Matter and thus the process of Illumination occurred.

Unlike the rest of those who underwent this Illumination, Fergus-Sundar fittingly was alone as he underwent this process, without anyone else there to witness this extraordinary event or support him through it. It was much like his journey into this dimension itself. Whilst the Impenetrable Energy Bubble formed around him, his body levitated in the air and a glow emerged around his body. But he did not scream. The Dark Matter was already within him and so it's fusion with the Dark DNA was not painful. The sound-proof rooms in GHEE HQ meant that no one heard the deafening silence in Guest Room fourteen as the ex-spy DNA underwent an evolutionary fast-track.

Soon enough the process was completed and Fergus-Sundar now was no longer a Homo Sapien, he was a Homo Illuminatus. Though in the case of Fergus-Sundar, it could be understood that he was perhaps never a Homo Sapien. For the reason Fergus-Sundar was able to pass through the Wormhole-Maze which was situated in the Primordial Black Hole, was because of the Dark Matter which seemed to be embedded within his very being, prior to him entering the Wormhole-Maze; the was the only thing which allowed him to pass through the Event Horizon of the Primordial Black Hole, without being completely ripped and obliterated.

Thus, this evolution of Fergus-Sundar from Homo Sapien to a Homo Illuminatus was unlike the others, for he had Dark Matter within his very being already. Though it was unknown at this time how Fergus-Sundar exactly had this Dark Matter within him. This would be revealed to Fergus-Sundar in his own chronological future, though paradoxically it would actually technically be being revealed to him in the past in terms of the linear chronological timestamp of the universe or time as we perceive it.

Though he was aware of none of this at this stage, for it was not yet important to his story; it was his present moment and this current epoch of his life that was of importance, not his future. It would reveal itself at the right moment in time, when it was destined to unfold.

And so, Fergus-Sundar sat on the end of his bed as his mind raced. He now had the ability to visually see and feel the unique vibrations of every Homo Sapien and Homo Illuminatus, and could see the purest part of their essence. He received the power of hyper-empathy, which in this moment pained him, as he felt and saw an influx of vibrational patterns and energy given out by people – even though these people were in different rooms of the building.

However, he could not control this power at this moment, and this is what he would spend the rest of the night doing – for his mind was cluttered with the thoughts of others and it would be on him to control this and bring his focus to the present moment, and to tune out that which was not necessary for him to feel.

And as Fergus-Sundar trained this power of his, it would lead him in the future to uncover the rest of his powers. In due course, Fergus-Sundar would discover that when he connected physically with any person – he could directly hear and feel their thoughts. And when entering focused meditation with them whilst maintaining physical contact, they could transcend their current location and state of consciousness and would be transported to their memories, viewing this concurrently.

And so, this was the tale of the Illumination of Fergus-Sundar the Dimension Travelling Spy, the first Homo Illuminatus.

The Narrator

On this globe-defining morning, there were a total of 420 Homo Sapiens who had undergone the Illumination and become the first of Homo Illuminatus. Though, it must be known that the Illumination did not have the most magnificent of effects on the entirety of the Homo Sapiens who became Homo Illuminatus. For some, it resulted in a large degree of ostracization from society; they had become something undesirable and frightening to those around them. And some became a danger to the society in which they lived in. For the impact the Illumination of the DNA had, was dependent on the traits, interests and intrinsic calling of those impacted by the Illumination – it accessed something deep within these people, and thus it was not always good.

When the Illumination occurred and the world quickly came to know of this extraordinary event, and news broke – of course, the GHEE were called to take hold of the situation. They had a vested interest themselves, but their reputation also determined that people around the world called for these Homo Illuminatus – as the scientists would end up calling them – to go to GHEE and be tested upon.

For the reaction had been mixed; fear was rife. Elisabeth Cervantes, the CEO of GHEE invited all 420 of those who had experienced an Illumination of their DNA to their facility in London, and ensured to send out private jets to every single one of them. She recognised the unique nature of what had transpired and saw the opportunity before her. She was being given the power and opportunity to take control of the situation. Elisabeth Cervantes would bring them all together and unite them under GHEE. She sent private jets around the world, to the homes of all Homo Illuminatus and would brought them to the GHEE facility in London. Though before inviting all 420 of Homo Illuminatus, Elisabeth Cervantes invited one of Homo Illuminatus to arrive before the other 419 Homo Illuminatus.

She called for Doctor Luftana Amara to come to the GHEE HQ.

BOOK 17

LUFTANA AMARA

Sunday 15ᵗʰ and Monday 16ᵗʰ November 2065

Sunday 15ᵗʰ November 2065, 14:36: The Home of Luftana Amara, in Wapping, London

And so, Luftana Amara sat on her sofa as she sipped on her cup of Earl Grey– the only tea she drank – as she contemplated again on the events which transpired and the situation she found herself in. She could not switch off her mind from this. Her thoughts raced, like a cheetah hunting its prey. Though this was not uncommon for her; she was a workaholic and her thoughts were always be focused upon work, the only difference now being that her thoughts raced upon the fact she would not be at work for an unspecified amount of time.

Near immediately after her Illumination, she had been contacted by GHEE, to be brought in for questioning and tests. They were a globally known company and Luftana herself had long wanted to meet the founder of the company, Elisabeth Cervantes; for GHEE had created some of the most groundbreaking medical technology in the world – something she had somewhat fangirled over in the her formative years in medical school. Though she could not help but wish this invitation had come at another time. She knew that what had happened to her was extraordinary and that the changes this Illumination had on her, was extraordinary and truly unique.

She herself did not understand what it was and could not even begin to fathom or hypothesise on what had happened to her. She knew it was reasonable that they would want to conduct tests on her, for she herself wanted to understand what had occurred – but she felt bad. Luftana Amara pondered upon the events of the last week and thought of how inundated her A&E ward had been in the aftermath of the Tech-Night. Whence the Dala Realisations occurred on that night, it left her fellow colleagues helpless and patients suffered as a result. They were so behind in A&E that she felt bad going away at this time. And thus, she was utterly conflicted. *This is a gift Luftana, take this opportunity – it may not come again*, she thought to herself as she replied to the hologram message sent by Elisabeth Cervantes who had personally invited her to the GHEE HQ.

And so, Luftana accepted the invitation from Elisabeth and would become the first of Homo Illuminatus to be welcomed into the GHEE HQ, excluding Fergus-Sundar who was already present.

* * *   * * *   * * *

Then she heard the noise, which likely was heard from every flat around her. She recognised the sound. *It that a helicopter?* She recognised the sound from the movies. She looked upon her phone and saw the message which told her they were outside. Luftana Amara gathered her overnight bag as Elisabeth had requested, and left. She could see Elisabeth's mode of transport from the fourth floor and could not stop the smile appearing on her face. She had never seen a helicopter before.

"Doctor Amara. It is an honour to meet you my love. Elisabeth," Elisabeth said as she attempted to shout over the helicopter while outstretching her hand. "I hope you are doing well?"

"Hey, it's good to meet you too. Wow, I didn't know you were coming in a helicopter. I've never seen one before," she replied nervously as she went to shake Elisabeth's hand. And as she did she could not help but see the medical status of Elisabeth. She was in near perfect health apart from the fact that she was pre-diabetic and this was because she had a family history of diabetes.

"Yes it's a MiniCopter. I use it to travel around the City. The roads are too congested to drive through – it would've taken me two to three hours to get to you from Hampstead. And I can't be taking public transport. I'd be swarmed in all honesty," replied Elisabeth.

"It's beautiful. It's the perfect size. It's like a …"

"Mini Helicopter!" they both said in unison.

They both got into the MiniCopter as it rapidly ascended into the cloudy sky of London.

"Wow, I've never seen London from up here before. Well I've never been in a helicopter before."

"Ah you get used to it my love, trust me. But yes beautiful isn't it. The city of lights," replied Elisabeth.

"Yeah but I never realised how many buildings there are. It's so …"

"Congested. Yes it is. But it's understandable; there are fifteen million people in this city. Theres not much room for anything but housing and buildings to be honest. We need the housing for all the people, and the buildings host businesses which in turn provide people with jobs and the means to financially sustain itself. It's a self-sustaining society we have, and it's the happiest one in the world. It's not for no reason the UK been ranked as having the happiest people in the world. And the capital, London, as a result is the best city. The epitome of metropolis. Be carefully considered, balanced, and beautiful design," Elisabeth replied as she proudly looked upon the City of London.

"The sky looks a bit different from up here though, it's a lot cloudier and well, foggier than I'd have thought."

"Well yes darling, that would be the air pollution and light pollution. The sky you see from below is not the true sky. We have had ArtificiaSky in place in London for over a decade now. What you see if in essence a digitally rendered 3-D integrated holographic that my AI system enables. ArtificiaSky essentially produces the image of the sky as it would be if we could see it without all the light pollution and air pollution hindering our image.

It provides our people with an increased synchronicity to our circadian rhythms. The sky helps provide this to us, without vision of it, we are lost. So yes it does look different from up here. It was a project we helped the government with here in the UK. We being GHEE. ArtificiaSky is in place in thirty countries around the world and we hope to help more nations with this problem that we face in light of the continuing climate crisis."

"Wow that's, that's amazing. I have to say I'm very happy to meet you. Some of the technologies you've created are, are just amazing. You and GHEE, you've really revolutionized the medical industry lightyears. I used your technologies in medical school and some of them I still use daily in A&E," Doctor Luftana Amara replied.

"Thank you Luftana that means so much. Yes the medical technology sector is one we are heavily invested in and one that is an integral part of our operations at GHEE. I always look to try and bring in new technologies which can make our world a better place. No matter what the cost," replied Elisabeth.

"Yeah I mean, it's amazing. You're doing a great job. So is medical tech something you're passionate about? Like is that your passion?" Luftana asked with great curiosity.

"Well my love, it's certainly close to my heart. But I would say my first passion is climate technology. But of course medical technology is another passion of mine. I lost my family when I was just ten in the floods on the coast of Guyana due to rising sea levels. And I suppose that moment started my journey and brought me to where I am now. It made me want to stop climate change and the resultant impacts from it, or at least help us as people deal and adjust to the changing world we live in. The only way I saw fit to do that with my skillset, was well to create technologies and systems that could help either mitigate these issues or eradicate them as issues for us. And I mean, seeing my parents die due to drowning, well that inspired me to create the WaterExtractor device which is now used by millions, and I hope has saved many people's lives – as I am sure you're aware," replied Elisabeth.

"Wow that's fascinating. And yeah I've had to use the WaterExtractor once. It's amazing honestly and it did help me save the patient's life. But wow yeah. I never knew you were an orphan, I'm an orphan too," replied Luftana.

"Ah I'm sorry to hear that. I didn't know that," replied Elisabeth Cervantes who lied through her teeth. She was meticulous and paid attention to every detail available to her; she read Luftana Amara's file prior to reaching out to her.

"It's okay. That's just life isn't it. It's all God's plan, who am I to fret and think I know better than God. Life is tough but there's always goodness in the world. Losing my parents and seeing my loved ones pass when I was young brought me to where I am today, and it has made me stronger undoubtedly. God has blessed me to be here today despite all I saw as a child in Palestine. Seeing all I saw and going through what I did, I guess like you, brought me to this place in my life and inspired me to become a doctor. I would always think as a child – when I saw my friends and their families and my own family, in the rubble, suffering from their injuries, left all alone and without help or respite for their pain – that I wished I could help them. I wished I could help them. And now I know, again in hindsight, that God gave me this suffering to make me stronger and I find myself now able to help people. God willing I will never see suffering like that again, and no other child, no matter their religion or race, will know pain like this. However, I am aware of the nature of humanity; whilst change is constant in this life, and the Earth was different a thousand years ago, one constant that remains and has remained, is that war is entrenched within human nature, for people always go to war for power or for principle. But my heart hurts when I think of that time. Even now. All these years later. I can't unsee the suffering and the waste of those lives. For what? Such a waste. God willing it gets better. But anyway. I'm getting emotional now. Let me stop talking about this. I don't even know how I got here, gosh. One minute I'm talking about medical tech and the next I am crying about my past. Gosh I didn't want to even talk about this right now. But here I am. Anyways," replied

Luftana Amara as she found tears roll down her eyes as she looked out of the MiniCopter and looked over the sky of London.

"That is a sad, sad story and I'm sorry you had to go through that. Thank you for sharing Luftana. You are a wonderful person. I'm glad I've had the opportunity to meet you today. What happened to those kids in Gaza, well to yourself as well, was unimaginable and pure unjust suffering. I hope as well that we never see a war like this again. I hope we don't lose sight of our shared humanity like that again. But, I'm sorry to be bleak and negative about this, I am not sure if that is realistic as you've alluded to. I've studied human history over our thousands of years of existence as a species. And whether you subscribe to the knowledge of science, or if you subscribe to the realm of religion and God as it seems you do – one thing that is unchanging in people despite the evolution of society and people, is that violence and war seem to be embedded within our nature. There is no age whereby war has not taken place. And this is sad. But this is the nature of human beings. We are violent beings it seems, destined to continually seek to self-destruct in one way or another. But yes as you said earlier. Even in these darker moments and darker parts of ourselves, there is always hope. And there are always shining lights. And this persistent hope and shining light embedded within humanity, despite the predilection to darkness and violence, seems to keep us as a species going. People like yourself Luftana. You are a shining light. Quite literally now too. You are one of the Illuminated ones!"

"I'm not special Elisabeth. Truth be told I don't know what is going on. I don't quite understand what has happened to me. My colleagues explained it to me, they saw what happened. And I saw the reports on the news of how it happened to other people too. I don't want to be called Illuminated or an Illuminated being. It's blasphemous. It's scaring me to be honest. I don't know why this has happened or what exactly has happened to me. I know my physiology is different, I can feel it. And that which I can see and feel, is, is not normal. So I'm torn. Because on one hand I know that this is not normal, but it is special. On one hand it feels like a gift, to be able to instantly accurately diagnose an illness that someone has, to physically see it. But then I wonder, is this some dark magic? Is this the devils work? Or is this a blessing given to me by God. I don't know. I find my faith wavering in this moment, and so forgive me God. My faith is important to me, it's an integral part of who I am and how I see the world and conduct myself. So it's just tough. Whatever this power is, I know it is unique. And I don't want to take it for granted or overuse it or abuse it. I don't know if there are any side effects either. Or if it is moral. I. I just don't know Elisabeth. But yeah it is what it is. It's God's it seems, and I'll see it out till the end. I suppose I just feel guilty as well for leaving my colleagues and patients behind in this time. Especially because of everything with the Tech-Night and the Dala Realisations. We're so backlogged as a result in A&E and understaffed like crazy."

"Well Luftana. Fine. I understand what you are saying. And for your sake, I won't call you one of the Illuminated ones. But I am warning you, whether you like it or not, that others will call you this. Because the people will know you and all 420 of you, have undergone this process of Illumination as you levitated in the air and your physiology changed. Whether you like it or not, you are special. Now I don't know anything about the moral and ethical or religious side of this gift or power or whatever it is that you have. But I know it's a great power. Now what I can help you with. And this is why I called for you. Is to help understand what has changed, and what has happened on a physiological level. We have all the facilities and latest technologies available at the GHEE HQ and that's why I wanted to bring you to the facility. So we can get you tested and we can find out what's going on. And to perhaps help you with this. It's an extraordinary thing that's happened to you and to the others. You are alone in this. That I will be frank about. Because no one, from what we know about this Illumination as they're calling it, has the same power or adaptation. And some people let's be honest, will be scared of you and the rest of these people who went through this Illumination. Because you're different now and you have abilities that other human beings don't have. And so I hope that us at GHEE can perhaps offer you a haven of some sort and maybe we can help guide you with how you navigate and use these powers. Because you do have an extraordinary gift Luftana, and you could do a lot of good in this world. Just know that we here at GHEE are here to help you in whatever capacity we can. We're here for you. And I mean, I came to you first Luftana. All 420 of you who underwent this Illumination – you were the first person I contacted and the only one I've personally come to see and bring the facility. You'll be the first to arrive, the rest are scheduled to arrive on Monday. Your gift is just so special, we had to bring you in as soon as possible. Thank you for your time. I know you are busy and I know how committed you are to your work. I saw your interview on the news in the aftermath of the Tech-Night, from when you were helping people on the street. Heroic. Truly heroic. But yes, you can go back whenever you please. We just ask that you might stay with us at GHEE till at least Tuesday so we can run some extensive tests and so that you can meet with the other Illuminated. And maybe we can convince you to stay with us for longer, considering your newfound powers and all the good we can do. But that's a conversation for later."

Luftana took in that which Elisabeth said and pondered upon it. The two sat in silence for the rest of the journey, soon to arrive at their destination, the famous, self-sustaining HQ of GHEE.

18:12: The Medical Ward of GHEE HQ

As the doctor unplugged Luftana Amara from the machines, she smiled for she had been undergoing tests for near two hours now and grew tired of it. She was pleased that the testing was done for now and that she could browse the facility as Elisabeth had promised. She had promised Luftana that she could explore the facility, and this was what she was most excited for this weekend.

18:55: The Prototype Room of the GHEE HQ

Luftana Amara spent the next couple of hours exploring the Prototype Room in the GHEE HQ, where she could see the design drafts and the prototype devices GHEE had created. And she was lost for a few hours, managing to forget the trauma and pain that was on her mind earlier in the day. It was a wonderous few hours for Luftana Amara and she was glad she was here.

Soon she was joined by Elisabeth who divulged into the finer details behind the technology and the two enjoyed their conversation. However, Elisabeth left Luftana nearly as whence she had first joined her in the Prototype Room, as she took a phone call which seemed to grab her attention, like endless scrolling on a phone or a red coloured notification alert on the phone to the human brain.

21:15: The Corridor outside of The Prototype Room in GHEE HQ

"Yes, so what's the update? How do the results look?" asked Elisabeth as she raised her eyebrows with intense curiosity.

"It can be done," the doctor on the phone replied.

"Are you sure? One-hundred percent certain?"

"I can't give you a one-hundred percent guarantee Elisa Nothing is one-hundred percent certain."

"Listen Alexis. We cannot risk this. It can't be for nothing. If we can successfully extract and harness it, then we proceed. So I'm going to ask you again. Can it be done successfully?"

"Yes Elisa, it can be done, and it can be done successfully," replied Doctor Alexis.

"Good. That's what I want to hear. So, what do you need to do this?"

"We need all of it. The essence and core of the power seems to be situated within her DNA and in the blood. Unfortunately, I will need all of it to extract and harness this into a device. It seems to be a unique fusion between the previously Dark DNA in her blood, and a matter which could very well be Dark Matter, that has caused the Dark DNA to be illuminated and resulted in her being one of the Illuminated. Technically she may not be human anymore. She seems to have evolved. But yes we can extract and harness this into a device, as long as I get all of her blood – so that I can condense this and extract the pure essence of this fused Dark DNA and Dark Matter within her, and convert this into a source of power or element of some sort. I won't explain the exact science behind it and bore you with the details. But once this has been extracted, condensed and converted into this element or power source, I will be able to put this into a device and we will certainly be able to replicate this. It will take a lot of power though. Likely when I initiate this process, we will lose power in the building for up to ten minutes," Doctor Alexis said in an unflinching manner, showcasing the unwavering commitment and passion to the project.

"Okay great. I'll bring her to you as soon as possible."

"I need an hour. Bring her to Room Twenty-Seven."

"I'll see you in an hour Doc. Thank you. Bye now," said Elisabeth as she ended the call. She took a seat on the rich cocoa brown sofa in the corridor and put her head to her hands as she took in a deep breath. She pondered upon that which the Doctor had told her and she shook her head. *Is this too much?* Elisabeth looked at the door and back again at the floor in front of her and repeated this process on a few occasions as she wrestled her nerves and angst regarding the course of action she was about to take.

She is so nice. Gosh she's so nice. She is a good person, she thought. *Can I do this? It is for the greatest good. It has to be done. This device could change the world. And we need her power in order for it to work. It's a sacrifice for the greater good. The cost doesn't matter. If we can do it, it'll be worth it. And we can do it. She must die. Luftana Amara must die. There is no choice. I've come this far. I cannot be afraid at this point. It will be all for nothing now, it will all be in vain unless we go ahead now. We must do this, for the greater good. No matter the cost.*

22:26: Room 27 in GHEE HQ

"And that's it. So now just relax, I've synched up your MeMusic playlist so whilst we undergo the tests you can relax and enjoy yourself. It shouldn't take too long. You should fall asleep within the first ten minutes and the music should ease you into your sleep. But beware that you might feel a tingling sensation through your body before you go to sleep. At which point you can click on the button that's in your hands if it is too painful and we can always stop the process. Is that clear?"

"Yeah, all clear. I'm assuming that's why you've got me strapped down like this? Because of the pain?" said Luftana.

"Yes, it's just a precaution for your safety and for ours of course. We're still learning about the nature of this Illumination that you went through. And I am not sure if you will have an adverse reaction to the tests, including on your mental state," Doctor Alexis said as he looked to and from Elisabeth and Luftana.

"I understand. I am safe though right? Right Elisa?" said Luftana as she worriedly looked at Elisabeth for reassurance.

"Yes Luftana. Doctor Alexis is the best doctor we have here, and he would never do something to compromise your safety. It's just a precaution is all. It'll all be fine, don't worry," she replied.

"Okay. Thank you, Elisa. For everything. It's ended up being a great day actually. One of the best I've had in a long time. I got to switch off for once. I haven't had a rest in so long and taken some time to actually enjoy myself."

"Please don't thank me Luftana. I've done nothing. Thank you for coming to see us today and for undergoing all these tests. You really are contributing to science here and we're finding out some groundbreaking stuff here which could prove pivotal to the development of the medical field in the years to come and it's all because of you. Be proud of yourself and know this is all for the greater good," Elisa replied.

"That's all I want honestly. It's been a pleasure to be here and to help in any way that I can. I have to say though, I don't know how I feel about that term you called me earlier. Makes me feel uneasy. God forgive me," Luftana replied as she looked up at the bright light in front of her, with a solitary tear rolling down from her eye.

"Which term?"

"Homo Illuminatus. I'm still human. I still feel human. I know I'm different now. But I'm still a human being. I was born a Homo Sapien."

"Well, there has to be some differentiation and I have to say that you simply are not a Homo Sapien anymore. You might not want to hear it, but it's the truth. You are a Homo Illuminatus now. You're distinctly different from say Doctor Alexis and myself. But this doesn't mean that you're not a human being. Of course you are. You're different now; you're special. You're an evolved version of a human being. You have quite literally fast-tracked, potentially, thousands or hundreds of thousands of years of evolution in a single night. It's quite extraordinary. You should feel special. And I'm sure when we run tests on the others, they will show to be Homo Illuminatus. You're not alone in this Luftana, I'm here for you," said Elisabeth Cervantes as she grabbed the hand of Luftana Amara and held it tightly as they looked directly at one another.

"Thank you Elisa. Ahh it doesn't feel so special. It feels strange. God forgive me. Ahh I'm a mess. I don't know why I'm getting emotional now. I guess it's just been a long day and a long week. But it's all come full circle now. I feel blessed to be here. Thank God for everything. Thank God. Whatever it is that has happened to me, it was part of God's plan. It is what God has willed. And God willing I can help people with this gift. Even if it does make me feel like an Abnormal being," said Luftana Amara.

Abnormal being; interesting way of saying it, Elisabeth thought.

"There, there now. It's okay, don't cry. You've gone through a lot Luftana. But it'll all be over soon now. You just lay back and try to relax. This will be the final test we need from you. You've been very brave. Sleep and rest well now. I'm grateful to you Luftana Amara and I appreciate you."

"Ahh stop. You're gonna make me cry again. Gosh why am I getting emotional again. Why does this feel like a goodbye?"

Elisabeth laughed, "Well goodbye for now is all. We'll see you soon. I think the Doctor is ready to begin the process now."

"Right yeah of course. Okay I'm ready too. But one thing Elisa, I hadn't told you yet because I guess I'm still trying to work out where it's acceptable to just say what I see and feel; this power is a lot of responsibility in a weird way. It's only the first day of having this power. But I'm not sure if you know. But when we first touched hands earlier today, I could see that you were pre-diabetic. Did you know?" she said to Elisabeth as she held onto her hands.

She smiled at this, "I didn't know that actually, but I do now. Thank you for that. Wow. What a gift you have Dr Luftana Amara. You'll do so much good in this world, I know it."

And so, Elisabeth Cervantes let go of Luftana Amara's hand, and the platform that Luftana was laying on, slowly fully retreated into the cave like machine that somewhat resembled an MRI machine. At first, Luftana Amara felt no pain, though this was because the machine was not on full power. And as Doctor Alexis slowly increased the power on the machine, the Blood and Energy of Luftana Amara was drained and sucked out, like a mosquito drawing the blood of a human. And Luftana did feel that tingling sensation through her body, though it was not a slight pain, but rather an excruciating pain of the highest order, an ineffable type of pain that one could only know if they themselves had experienced it. Luftana pressed the button frantically and repeatedly and instinctively, to the point whereby her right thumb broke the button and the plastic pierced through the skin on her thumb. And soon enough, she did indeed fall into a sleep.

Though it was not a temporary sleep as the Doctor and Elisabeth had promised it would be. She had unfortunately entered a permanent sleep that she could not recover from and the only silver lining in this, was that her pain and suffering had ceased. Luftana Amara had died and the unique energy created from the fusion of her Dark DNA and the Dark Matter, which had once upon a time given her the power to identify medical ailments upon first contact with another human, had been captured and converted into an element or power source. Doctor Alexis put this into the Device and his face lit up, much like the Device itself and as Luftana Amara had done when she became Illuminated. The Doctor looked to Elisabeth who had tears on her face that she frantically wiped away; she did not like to show weakness or emotional vulnerability, especially in front of those who worked for her.

"It is successful. The energy has been captured successfully and converted into this matter or source of power. We have done it," said Doctor Alexis.

"Not we Alexis. She did it. This is her success not our own. She has not died for nothing. Let's see if it actually works now."

Doctor Alexis placed the device on Elisabeth Cervantes and a reading came up which listed the details of her pre-diabetic condition, and the Doctor then placed this upon himself and it successfully showed the fact that he had stage three lung cancer.

"It works Elisa. It works! This will revolutionise medicine forever."

"Yes Doctor it's a miracle. Congratulations. You will be a rich man from this, I will make sure of it."

"What will we call it? This device?"

"I will call it the DMT. Diagnosis Medical Tech."

And so, this marked the end of Doctor Luftana Amara. She had been killed by Elisabeth Cervantes and Doctor Alexis for GHEE, and she became the first of Homo Illuminatus to meet their end. And in her case, it was all too premature.

The Global Hub of Extra-Terrestrial Exploration, near immediately, would announce, in a press statement released by Elisabeth Cervantes, the death of Doctor Luftana Amara, stating complications from her change from Homo Sapien to Homo Illuminatus as the cause of death; her body was unable to adjust to her evolution from Homo Sapien to Homo Illuminatus.

AAJ

Doctor Luftana Amara had died for the creation of the DMT device and GHEE had killed her. No one would know of the truth. Her end was a tragedy, and she died alone The only positive being that she would join her family in the afterlife, and she would finally find peace, a peace transcendent to that available on earth.

In her final moments, *thank God for everything*, is what she thought.

BOOK 18
MALABAR JONES

Sunday 15th November 2065

21:46: The Waste Disposal Exit of GHEE HQ

And so, Malabar Jones looked around for yet another time as he tried to establish whether anyone had seen him sneak over the tall gates. He had ensured to use his tech to block out the camera prior to his arrival. The loop would play for at least fifteen minutes as he entered the building. The coast was clear and so he began to test his all-access accreditation pass. He scanned the pass and found that the heavy door opened automatically, like the boot of a luxury car. He ensured to check the corridor was clear and made his way into the building. His heat sensor embedded within his DigiLense told him that there was no one ahead of him and in the nearest rooms and corridors which connected to this entrance and exit point.

"This is SSSA4 Malabar Jones checking in. I am inside of GHEE HQ. I am here to apprehend Elisabeth Cervantes for further questioning. I repeat. I am in the GHEE HQ. I am here to apprehend Elisabeth Cervantes for further questioning. Confirm you have received this message. Over," Malabar whispered into the phone embedded within his TechSuit. However, he received no response. He checked the signal and found he that the 69G mobile connection embedded within his TechSuit was fully connected and enabled. This was the 69th generation of wireless cellular technology, which utilised Web3.0 and Quantum computing compatibility – it never failed if was connected and enabled. Malabar Jones knew what this meant for him, but he proceeded to reach out to the SSSA once again.

"Repeat. This is SSSA4 Malabar Jones checking in once more. I am at the GHEE HQ and am here to apprehend Elisabeth Cervantes of GHEE in relation to threats to the National Security of the United Kingdom. I repeat, this is SSSA4 checking in to confirm I am at the GHEE HQ and will be apprehending Elisabeth Cervantes of GHEE for further questioning in relation to threats to the National Security of the United Kingdom. Please confirm you have received this message. Requesting ground support," said Malabar. Again, there was no response. When he was on missions, if he reached out to the SSSA, they would always respond, without fail. Unless they had been hacked or taken over from within the SSSA – they would not ignore him.

"SSSA please confirm if you are receiving this message. Requesting ground support. I have successfully entered GHEE HQ. This is a prime opportunity to apprehend Elisabeth Cervantes for further questioning," he continued.

He waited for a few moments more before finally conceding defeat and realising that he was not going to hear from the SSSA. He was left alone without ground support – he was entering blind. They had told him they would not be helping him, but he did not think it would be so literal, and would extend to a circumstance like this. He had never before made it into the GHEE HQ successfully. He tried to break in a few times prior when he was previously investigating them, but to no avail. And so, despite the fact that he was without ground support from the SSSA, he knew he would have to proceed with his mission; he may not get this opportunity again.

If he completed his mission and successfully detained or was able to question Elisabeth Cervantes and bring back tangible information to the SSSA – he would be pardoned for his previous failure with the Brian Harrison terrorist plot and his transgression for abandoning his mission in pursuit of Fergus-Sundar. All would be forgiven. Though he knew he had to act quick, for he knew the SSSA well. *The Yonige-Ya, SSSA1, is likely on his way to make me 'disappear into the night'. I must give him reason not to. I must move quickly.*

And so, Malabar Jones proceeded with his mission.

The Tech-Night 1.0

Malabar Jones successfully bypassed and evaded the numerous security inside of the GHEE HQ with relative ease. He ensured to actively loop the security cameras as he made his way through the GHEE HQ and using the Heat Sensor embedded within his DigiLense, he could see when there were security guards in close proximity to him. He loved a good little scrap but ensured that he did not partake in any fights for he knew, with the amount of security on patrol, that the others would be alerted if he engaged with any of them. And so, he kept a low profile and, quickly, managed to find his way to Elisabeth Cervantes, who he located through the SONAR Echolocation setting inside of his TechSuit, to be in Room 27 of the GHEE HQ. Though as Malabar Jones found himself outside of the room, and seeing that which was occurring inside of the room through the SONAR Echolocation inside of the TechSuit – he witnessed something that would stay in his mind for years to come.

He looked on at the image that he was seeing in his DigiLense with disbelief as he saw a woman strapped down to bed, who essentially was unconscious and having a fit of some sort. The woman seemed to be in excruciating pain from the jerky moments she was making and Malabar then knew that which was occurring. He watched as Elisabeth Cervantes and the Doctor watched the woman pass away from whatever it is that was occurring to her.

The woman eventually passed away and he could not believe that which he had just witnessed. He wanted to run into the room whilst this was going on, however, he knew it would not be wise to do so; he needed to catch her when she was alone so that he could question her and have the best chance of taking her away. If he could not apprehend Elisabeth for her involvement in the deception and mind control and mind alteration of the citizens of the United Kingdom, then he could certainly now get her for involvement in the murder of this woman.

Malabar Jones waited for them both before entering the room. He wanted to identify the woman before he proceeded to apprehend her. He entered the room and looked upon the face of the woman who had just witnessed being murdered. The woman's ID came up on his DigiLense as being the UK citizen, Doctor Luftana Amara of Palestinian origin. However, he recognised the name Luftana Amara and was sad that he did; he had seen the name just today on the news. It took him less than a minute to research and find that she was one of the 420 human beings who had undergone this supernatural process of what was being described as an evolutionary fast-track and 'Illumination'. And there she was now in front of him, lying dead at the hands of GHEE. He knew that these Illuminated beings were all scheduled to make their way to GHEE for extensive tests upon themselves. *Is this what they're going to do to them all?* But then he saw on the news report that they were all scheduled to arrive at the GHEE HQ on Monday 16th November 2065, not on the Sunday.

Is she the only one here? Why did she come a day earlier? Many questions were running his mind at this moment. Other than the fact that there was a dead woman in front of him in the headquarters of a multi-billion dollar valued company – he knew something was awry here and it was up to him to figure out what. For it seemed there was no one else who was conscious that suspicious and nefarious activities were going on at GHEE; Elisabeth Cervantes was a loved public figure, and GHEE had released technology which people loved and relied upon.

Let's go question this b**ch. She ain't getting away this time.

22:41: The Balcony of Bedroom of Elisabeth Cervantes in her Mansion in GHEE HQ

Malabar looked at the Heat Sensor on his DigiLense and waited for Elisabeth to enter her bathroom and close the door, before beginning his climb up the back of her mansion. He threw an electronic rope up and over the balcony, and heard the rope auto-lock onto the railing of the balcony. He rapidly ascended up the rope and stealthily pulled himself over the railing, and returned the rope into its slot on his TechSuit. Elisabeth entered the room once again but Malabar ensured to hang around on the balcony. He peered into the room to find that she had dropped her silk robe which had diamonds embedded within it, like a Ric Flair robe. He averted his glaze out of respect as he saw her naked body from behind, but found himself struggling to do so as he saw her wide hips and slender waist. He waited till she slipped on her silk pyjamas before making his move.

"Malabar Jones I know you're there. I'm changed now so you can come on in now. No need to be coy," she shouted out to him. She had known he was there all along. He was taken aback, he did not expect her to call him out like this. He entered the room with one hand on the waist of his TechSuit; he had his gadgets at the ready to apprehend her.

"How did you …" he began.

"Oh come on now. You think I didn't know you were there. Or that you were here at GHEE? Malabar baby come on now. Do you have no respect for me? I knew as soon as you stepped foot on our facility. I let you in. You really think I wouldn't know? Now what can I do for you? What's up?" she said nonchalantly. She did not seem phased at all about the fact that he had stalked his way into her room.

"Elisabeth Cervantes, I am hereby seizing you in the name of, and for the protection of, the Crown and its People – as a serious threat to National Security. Note that anything you do say, may well be used against you in the future should you pose or continue to pose a threat to the security of this nation and of its people. Do you understand? You are being seized as a major threat to National Security. Do you accept the charges?"

"Malabar, have a seat," she replied.

"Did you hear what I just said? You are hereby being seized in the name of, and for the protection of, the Crown and its People – as a serious threat to Nationa …"

"Yes, yes, National Security. I heard you the first time. Have a seat Malabar. Let's stop this nonsense."

"Elisabeth Cervantes …"

"Please call me Elisa."

He looked at her blankly. She was vexing him with her blatant disregard for what he was saying.

"I'm going to put handcuffs on you now and I will be escorting you to the SSSA for further questioning …"

"Oh you naughty boy. Of course you brought your handcuffs with you. Is that what this is? You want to f**k me is it? That explains it all. It's a bit creepy you know. Stalking a girl and watching her take her clothes off in her room. But I've got it say I find it kinda hot that you went to so much effort for me. Green flag Malabar Jones, green flag. I didn't think I'd be turned on by you but here we are. You like what you see?" she teased him as she slowly unbuttoned her silk pyjamas to expose the expansive cleavage on her tight caramel skinned body.

"Stop it! I'm not f**king around here! Enough!," Malabar exploded.

"Woah. Easy tiger. We can f**k around if you want. You are. You look like you have abs too. Do you have abs?"

"Fine. I'm going to have to forcibly take you for questioning if you are not going to comply."

"You think that's smart Malabar Jones? SSSA4 – Mr Spy. How about we rewind this situation a little bit and really assess the situation? You've entered my property without my consent or a warrant. Right? Because I know you SSSA operate underground , and so I know there is no legal warrant. And then you've watched me strip naked from my balcony and you've stared at my bum and my boobs, and actually you're still looking at my boobs now – don't think I can't see where your eyes are going. It might be dark in here but I can still see your eyes. Those green eyes. Whoops it seems like I'm getting distracted now. Anyways. Where was I? Oh yeah. So you've entered my room, without my consent, watched me change, and now you've threatened to take my forcibly against my will? So how do you think that's going to go down? Not too well is it? If I call my security and tell them there's a strange man in my room with handcuffs and some weapons; I'm assuming you have weapons in that TechSuit of yours," she said to him as she leant back on the end of her extravagant bed with her legs crossed and shirt now completely unbuttoned. "And so I'm going to ask you again, to please have a seat."

Malabar looked at her in her eyes and squinted and shook his head slightly; she had him at checkmate. He sat on the chair at her desk.

"Good," she began. "So, what do you want to know? You might as well do your questioning here, or begin it here. I'll play along with your spy 'I'm taking you in for questioning' little game," she said as she mocked him.

"Fine. Let's do it like this then. It is your house we're in. Firstly, I am sorry that I came in when you were changing, it was not my intention to see you like that and so on a personal level I'd like to apologise to you," he began.

"Oh stop. You wanted to see me like this don't lie. I can see you looking. We're all grown here aren't we. We're not virgins. Wait are you a virgin? A forty year old virgin? Does the SSSA allow you to have romantic relations?" she interrupted.

"Right, anyway. I have evidence of your involvement with the Dala Device, and I know what is inside it. I know what you've done. What this government have done. You've drugged this country for years. That's why people went through the Dala Realisation. You caused havoc in this nation and controlled the minds of millions of people against their will. You will go down for this. I've got all the evidence."

"Where's the evidence?"

"It's all in my TechSuit."

"Ah cool. So it's on your person. It's not with the SSSA?"

Malabar stopped for half a second, he did not anticipate being caught, and what this would mean for the incriminating files he had of Elisabeth Cervantes and GHEE. "Yes, it's on me."

"And the SSSA can't access it can they?" she asked. She knew the answer but she wanted to see the confusion and thoughts process on Malabar's face as he realised that due to the encryption on his TechSuit – he would have to load the files he had directly into the SSSA database. "Don't worry, you don't have to reply. I know the answer." Again, she had him at checkmate. "So there's no evidence unless you upload the evidence. But please carry on."

Malabar felt himself somewhat at a loss for words. It seemed she pre-empted his answers with her questioning before he spoke.

"Why? Why did you do it? Do you not feel bad? You're controlling people against their will?

"Against their will. Oh give me a break. You think the people don't know what it does to them? People like the feeling they get when they use their Dala Device to buy things. You think they don't know the feeling? Of course they do. Why do you think they keep going back for more? Why do you think they abuse it? Why are they still using it despite these Dala Realisation's they've all gone through? Because they like the feeling. They are not ignorant and they are not dumb; they are complicit. It makes them happy. Think about coffee or alcohol. People know it changes them when they use it. Those things are drugs. So why can they not get a feeling of joy, drug induced or not, when they buy things? If it brings them joy? Who are you to deny them? And also give me a f**king break. I worked with the government to bring this about. It was not me alone. It was not GHEE alone. It was the Government and GHEE. Me. I created this yes. It's my invention. But I am not the sole one in charge here. I just have the power to implement this. And there have been several benefits Malabar Jones. Since the Isolationism Act whereby we, the UK, separated from other countries on a political level since World War Water – we were essentially stranded, granted a decision we made, but still we were stranded. We have to fend for ourselves. Like Japan back in the 18th and 19th century when they underwent Isolationism, we had to see our nation grow from within. And I've helped this nation grow financially because of this. People receive happiness when they buy things because of me, because of the Dala Device. The people have experienced happiness and the economy is thriving as a result. So what's the catch? Spoiler alert Malabar Jones, there isn't one. That's the answer and truth of the matter."

"Yes, but it's not real. It's fake. It's all a lie."

"Well what's the difference between fake happiness and real happiness? With fake success and real success? Is there a difference? Happiness is happiness and success is success. Who are you to say otherwise? What is real? What is fake?"

"You've changed their minds against their will. They didn't choose to use the Dala Device. The people have to use it. This is the only way they can pay and buy things. This is our monetary system. They have to use it. Now they're hooked. So it ain't their choice is it?"

"The Government implemented this scheme. Not me. I made the Device. That's all."

"I know. I can't take them in yet. But rest assured Elisabeth, I'm going to expose this all. You will not get away with this, and neither will they. Once they see the documents on what this Dala Device really is, and they see the origins of the device – they won't be on your side anymore. The people will turn on you and so will the government."

"Listen Malabar. It's all happened already now. And there's nothing you can do to undo this. What's happened has happened. I recommend you move on with your life. Because you will not be taking me in. I've been one step ahead of you since the start Malabar Jones. I was tracking you, as you tracked Brian Harrison. I wanted you to stop that man. Because I knew if he succeeded that this all would be revealed. And it's only because I was a step ahead of you, that I stumbled upon Fergus-Sundar. Yes, I know about him. He is here at GHEE right now. And thank God he arrived in this time. He holds the key. He's the key to this Dark Matter that's in this world now. He brought it into this world and because of that we have these superhumans, these Homo Illuminatus. And because of him, you were distracted. And because of that we might be able to find the missing key to global exploration. He travelled between dimensions. I can travel between dimensions once I harness his power, how I harnessed the power of Luftana Amara."

"So you admit it? You killed her?"

"I didn't kill her. She sacrificed her life for a greater cause. Her sacrifice will save millions of lives."

"What did you do to her?"

"Her power to detect medical ailments perfectly in other people, and accurate diagnose them to the most specific detail – has been harnessed and her energy has been captured and transformed to become a power source to power my new device. The Diagnosis Medical Technology Device (DMT device). How could I not seize this opportunity? Never before have we seen a power like this in human history. I had to do what I had to do. And this is for the better of mankind."

"You killed her for this. You didn't even give her a chance to use the power. You killed her in cold blood. And you will pay for your sins Elisabeth Cervantes. Enough of this malarkey. I'm not playing around anymore. I'm hereby seizing you in the name of, and for the protection of, the Crown and its People – as a serious threat to National Security."

"You naïve little man. I told you already. I am one step ahead of you. Actually, I'm three steps ahead of you. I have security waiting outside the building right now as we speak. There is no way you are leaving this building with me in cuffs. And no way you are leaving here a free man. You are mine now Malabar Jones. I am not under arrest. You're in my home. This is my facility. You seriously thought you could walk into my home and take me in my own home?. You're a fool Malabar Jones. Your desperation to catch me and close this case made you sloppy; I honestly expected better. Your downfall is sad to see. You had the evidence you needed, and you walked straight into my hands. You were the only one who was onto me. And you walked straight into my hands and brought the evidence you gathered straight to me. I must thank you. You've made my life incredibly easy. Now that I have you here at GHEE, I have nothing stopping me. No one to stop me. You have failed Malabar Jones," she said. "Guards!"

Elisabeth Cervantes stood tall over him as he remained slumped in his seat with his shoulders down and stared down at the ground below in shame. She did the buttons up on her pyjamas back as the GHEE security swarmed the room with their guns raised up at a defeated SSSA4, who did not move as they ran up to him and shouted profanities. A guard smacked the butt of their gun into his mouth, as another pulled him down to the ground. They swarmed him and began to kick the downed man, who did not fight back. He lost the will to fight, and accepted his beating – and blood dripped from his mouth.

Malabar Jones faced the final defeat in his downfall. He had failed and there was no coming back. Elisabeth Cervantes and GHEE had defeated him, and he was now their prisoner.

And so, his time as a SSSA4 had come and it was due to GHEE.

BOOK 19

ELISABETH CERVANTES & HOMO ILLUMINATUS

Monday 16th November 2065

14:19: The Events Hall in GHEE HQ

Elisabeth Cervantes

"Barry, check the lighting once more please. And Bill make sure sound is all good to go," Elisabeth asked as she spoke into her mic once more. This was her third time checking. They reported back that they were good to go and that all checks had been successfully completed. And so, she gave herself a pep talk as she was about to walk onto the stage.

Come on now Elisa you got this. Get your sh*t together girl! No reason or need to be feeling nervous. Don't doubt yourself girl. You've done this before plenty of times. We're just delivering a speech and making sure this networking event goes smoothly. And note to self, the main purpose of this event is to put together a team of Homo Illuminatus, to unite them and have them work for GHEE Don't lose sight of this Elisa. This is a means to an end. And it's gotta be done. So get your sh*t together girl. You're the superstar here. You're Elisabeth Cervantes and you can rouse up a crowd of ten thousand, let alone a group of 419 frightened Abnormal people. It's your time to shine Elisabeth. Make them remember what they're here for, who they've come to see and why they're here. Get it together woman.

And almost instantly, she walked onto the stage and felt the heat from the bright lights shining on her. She was ready for this. She had delivered speeches to crowds before on plenty on occasion. Nerves were only natural.

"Good afternoon and thank you all for gathering here today at the Global Hub of Extra-Terrestrial Exploration Headquarters here in Hampstead, London. I hope you all enjoyed your journey into our facility and trust that the private jets and helicopters were to your liking. I'll tell you for free that they were not to the liking of my bank account!" she started as the crowd of Homo Illuminatus laughed raucously at her quip. "Now I think we all know why we are gathered here today. We are gathered here today because of an extraordinary event which occurred in the early hours of yesterday morning. You are all different now. You are changed. You are special. You are Illuminated. And thus, you are now no longer Homo Sapiens, but rather Homo Illuminatus. I am being told that this is what we are calling you. And if you feel like I am singling you out and isolating you somewhat. Saying you are different than regular human beings. It is because this is the truth. And I think you should come to terms with it and accept it. I'm sure some of you already have. And be prepared for what's to come. Because yes you are special now and you have powers. But with this comes envy and responsibility. With this comes attention. People will look at you and wish that they have what you have. People are afraid of what they do not understand. They are afraid of things and people that are different to them. And you all are different now. Know it. Embrace it. Be prepared for what's to come. They will heckle you. They will swarm you and bombard you with disinformation and fake news. You will be targeted. And that is why we are here today. I gathered you here today because here at the GHEE we are not afraid of the extraordinary. We are not afraid of those who are different. Instead we embrace them. I think you can probably tell that from the name of this organisation. And I believe the world knew that too. This is why leaders of countries from around the world personally requested that I reach out to you all and gather you under my roof. Because they and I, know that right now, at arguably your highest moment in life, whereby you have evolved beyond the confines of what is possible in the eyes of our conventional understanding of what it means to be a human being, you have developed supernatural superpowers, abilities – you are the most alone. Because there are so few of you. From what we understand, there are only 420 Homo Sapiens who have become Homo Illuminatus. And considering that there are over eleven billion people in the world, you really are in an extremely unique spot. You are alone. It's likely that no one else will have the abilities you have. You are gifted and you have been blessed. But you are alone. I don't understand you. I can get some tests done to ensure that we know exactly what powers you have, and to see how your physiology and DNA has changed. But ultimately I still do not understand you or not what it is like to be you. I do not know what you have undergone when you were Illuminated. No one out of the eleven billion people who are alive and living on this Earth, and the billions of Homo Sapiens who have come before us – none will know what it is like to have gone through what you have gone through. You are all alone in this. You are the first of this species. Of Homo Illuminatus. Alas, you have weight on your shoulders, and a responsibility that I cannot fully comprehend. But this is one area where I can help you a bit; because I too have a ton of responsibility – it's not easy being the founder and CEO of a multi-billion dollar company. And it's for all these reasons that I have brought you here. That the GHEE has brought you here. Because as alone as you are. Ultimately all human beings are alone in this world. We come into this world alone as we are born as an infant. And we are supported by our family and friends as we grow to become adults, and then we commit our time and energy in this life to a job, to our friends and family and the duty and responsibility that comes with it, to making new memories and experiences, to developing skills, and of course, to love. But then at the end of this we are all too. For just as we entered this world alone, we leave this world as we die alone too. And whether you believe we simply die and go into nothingness, or whether you believe there is a heaven and hell. We are alone when we die. We go through life alone. But we share. We experience this aloneness together. And so, I implore you today, to network with those around you. Take a look to your left, and to your right. To the person in front of you, and to the person behind you. For they are alone too. But you can share with them. You can experience and live with them. You are alone, but you don't have to go through this alone. And just as your fellow Homo Illuminatus are here for you to share with. So too are we here at the GHEE. We are here for you now, and always," she finished as the crowd of Homo Illuminatus begun what seemed to be a never-ending applause. The clapping reverberating and echoing in the hall, resulting in a slight vibration in the hall.

"Thank you, I am overwhelmed and honoured by your reception. It is an honour for me to be able to host you here at the GHEE. Now I want you all to network with one another. Speak to each other openly and honestly. Be yourself and be kind. There will be drinks and canapes served through-out the afternoon, complimentary of course. So please do tuck in and fill your belly's, but please remember that if you have a problem with alcohol consumption, to be considerate of this and take it easy. I have to say that, I'm sorry. I know personally I'm going to be sinking the champers back. Wait am I allowed to say that?" she said as the crowd guffawed slightly at this comment. "Okay so once we've conversed for a few hours, you will all have some health checks. Just to ensure everything is okay with your vitals and all of the health malarkey. Because even though you are now special and powered. You are still human. I hope you know that. You are not immortal. And we sadly saw this for ourselves here at the GHEE just yesterday. Some of you may be aware that we lost one of our own yesterday in Doctor Luftana Amara. She was struggling ever since her Illumination and so we brought her into the GHEE HQ yesterday a day before you all. And unfortunately, she passed away as a result of her body not being able to acclimatise to the changes as a result of her becoming a Homo Illuminatus. She will forever be remembered, for she was a great human being before she became Homo Illuminatus. So there is now only 419 of you Homo Illuminatus. And so please, if any of you do feel unwell now, then please come find me or a member of staff here at GHEE who you will see in the

Black pinstripe suits with brown shirts and a black tie. Let us know and we'll get you looked at straight away. This is of paramount importance. We don't want to lose any of you. But anyhow. Let's get on with it; I've been talking for far too long now and I can see some of you are getting distracted. Yes, yes you; I can see you!", she laughed. "Anyhow everyone. Enjoy. Get talking! I'm going to make my way around the room as well. Thank you everyone for listening! I'll speak to you all soon!" said Elisabeth Cervantes as her speech was met with another bout of wild applause and a deafening noise from the claps. And then she looked around the room and realised that the deafening noise was also due to a particular few of the 419 Homo Illuminatus, who were now blessed with an extraordinarily unnatural amount of power.

As she stepped off the stage and went backstage, she was met by Bridger Falcon.

"Perfect Elisa. That was perfect," said Bridger.

"Thank you Bridger, but it wasn't exactly perfect. Nothing is perfect. There's always room for improvement," she replied.

"Sure, but I mean it was good still. I think you covered all your bases," he replied.

"Yes I did. Now it's up to them to converse. I'm gonna go and work the room. Remember to keep an eye out. Watch what's going on. The mics and cameras are all set. And please. Ensure security are on high alert still. They are in good spirits now Bridger, but there are still dangerous people. If any of them want to, they can do some serious damage to us and to this facility. Do we have the backup plan in place?"

"Yes Elisa, understood. We've got the backup plan in place and security are all in position if needs be."

"Fantastic. Now let's hope we don't need them. Time to work the magic. I'll speak to you later. Text me if you have or need any info for me. And please remember to keep track of the situation with our spy and the girl. Update me when you receive updates.

"Yes Elisa. Will do. You let me know if you need anything."

"I need you to do what I just told you, nothing else. Text me with updates please if you can," she said as she nodded at him before departing on her way to go and get to know some of the Homo Illuminatus in the room. It was her goal to speak to all of them.

Go time Elisa. Work your magic girl, work the room.

Homo Illuminatus
Devonte Lacy and Mike da Silva

Devonte Lacy awkwardly held his glass of champagne, obtaining a full grip over the top of the glass; he felt out of place. He did not really know what was going on. Devonte knew that he was exactly where he was meant to be, and yet he still did not feel at home. There were many new faces in front of him, some which were quite extraordinary and abnormal – Wayne de Vale the French playboy owner of the largest croissant empire in the world, who had metamorphosed into an actual croissant, with a croissant for a head, could make croissants out of thin air and had croissant textured skin, was one Homo Illuminatus that he found his eyes constantly reverting to; he was hungry. came to mind as Devonte could not help but look at him. Another was Mr BurgerFace, a man who had grown a Burger on his face as a result of his Illumination – a phenomenon which had been inadvertently foreseen by artist Abhinav Akali Jayanth in 2014, with his painting, known as BurgerFace. Devonte turned to his left and was near blown away by a man's burp; it was an extraordinary, an abnormal, burp; for the burp that came out of this man's mouth was one that went up to a speed of 30mph – the man's name was Lance Dratner, who would become known as SuperBurp. Devonte walked around through the crowd and was pleased by the fact that he saw people of all races in the crowd – it seemed that the Illumination did not discriminate on race. He knew he had powers, but he did not feel like a superhero of any kind. *All I can do is make weed man,* he thought to himself as he watched Sheila Wonka hoist a man over her shoulders in a standing shoulder press. And then he heard someone call his name. He turned.

"Devonte? What the f**k you doing here? Ain't you meant to be in jail? We jailed your ass? You Homo Illuminatus too? Who would've thought? I knew there was something different about you kid. Come here kid show me some love," said Mike da Silva as he walked towards Devonte Lacy with open arms.

"Mike. Damn dawg it's good to see you bruh. Sh*t man, you here too? F**k me bruh. This sh*t crazy as hell bruh. This sh*t got me tripping man. It been a wild couple days I ain't even gone cap," replied Devonte.

Mike da Silva cut him off, "How the f**k you get outta jail? We sent your ass to jail – I know that. And I hope you didn't take it personal young man. The Compass is the Compass and there isn't a lot of stuff on there. I read it out to you personally. You received your dues from the Head Honcho, and you still done f**ked up, and you done f**ked up on your first sale boy. So it is what it is. You had to go down. But listen, I saw Bix after your hearing. And your boy managed to convince me to shorten your sentence. Now that's only cos of Bix; he pleaded your case and he told about your situation. And I can empathise. But how the f**k you get out of jail?" said Mike da Silva. His demeanour had changed, Devonte could see a red tinge in his pupils, something he had never before seen in a man – this was not something that Mike da Silva had prior to his Illumination.

"Sh*t man. Listen I didn't break out of jail or nothing if that be what you thinking. The warden just came to my cell and told me that I can go. And then next thing you know, I was on my way here. I don't now who authorised this sh*t, or what happens with regards go the bureaucracy and all of that sh*t, but I is assuming it's cos of all this Illumination stuff. I mean f**k, they done brought every single one of these Homo Illuminatus people here. Now I'm here it's obviously cos of GHEE. They brought us all here dawg. I don't know sh*t. Now regarding the situation that brought me to jail. It is what it is man. Like I done said in the meeting, I did what I had to do and I ain't regret it. Cos my family come first, no disrespect to you. I didn't mean to disrespect you like that. Y'all trusted me and I'm sorry I had to violate that trust. But as I done said, I had to do what I had to do for my family. I ain't got nothing else to say on that. Again, I'm sorry if you feel like I done disrespected you; I just wanna reiterate that I didn't do that sh*t with no bad intentions you feel?" said Devonte Lacy. He felt no need to lie, even if the truth might've caused Mike to become irate.

"I understand. But why didn't you ask Bix? Why didn't you tell us? Hell we would've loaned you the damn money kid. We could've deduced that amount from your future sales. Why didn't you speak up boy?" said Mike as he looked at Devonte in a state of perplexion.

"To be honest. I don't know. Bix done said the same thing to me. But I guess I wanted to sort that sh*t out myself. Bix done helped me out plenty times before and I ain't no b**ch ass. I don't wanna be taking handouts from nobody. And I'm a grown ass man. And that's my family. So it was time for me to step up and be a man and support my family. I ain't tryna let no one else sort out my sh*t for me. I done that enough times now so I had to do what I had to do for my family. Some things we gotta handle ourselves in life."

"I respect your honesty and I respect what you done. I know how it is to lose family and there's one thing that's more important to me than anything in the damn world and that's motherf****ng family. But know kid, you can always speak to someone. When you struggling or whatever it is. Reach out to your friends, speak to people. Cos you do not know what the other man or woman in front of you is feeling. You do not know. They might be going through the same damn thing. We all human beings at the end of the day. Everyone got a family they care for you know. Anyway. As you said. It's done. And I guess us putting you in jail didn't f**king matter anyway. You're here now. Respect to you kid – you got a bright future," said Mike da Silva as he outstretched his hand to receive a handshake from Devonte

Lacy. "Look at us now. Both Illuminated or whatever it is they be calling it. I call it motherf****ng superpowers cos that's what it f**king is."

"I appreciate it man. You cool as hell Mike. I'll be real you was scary as f**k the first time we met man. You damn killed the g …"

"Shut your damn mouth fool. Speaking my business out here."

"Mike everyone know you killed people before bruh. You Mike da Silva, the Black Tiger, Khan of the Kumite?"

"Boy shut your damn mouth. How you know these fools done seen all that sh*t? This a new venue. New me. And plus. I'm a motherf****ng superhero now. I ain't about with none of that killing sh*t no more; I'm a changed man. I was a dangerous mother*****r back then, but I'm even more dangerous now. I'm too dangerous now. And that Illumination, it was trippy as hell. Sh*t was spiritual you know. It changed me. And I saw what can happen if I don't control myself and my rage and I am not trying to let that part control me. I am a beast now, a pure beast. And I can't let the rage or the hunger for violence kill the real me and take over. What if the hunger takes over and I can't change back? I gotta control it. Cos Devonte I'm telling you it ain't fair no more. Even just me as Mike da Silva; all my senses are heightened, my reactions is better, my vision is better, I'm stronger now, I'm faster now. Fighting ain't fair no more. I can't fight any other normal man no more. I'm evolved. And so it's time to be a new version of me."

"Mike what you talking about bruh. What you mean you if you can't change back?"

"You know that nickname I got – The Black Tiger? So that's cos I'm half Tamil and half black, and cos I'm ferocious in combat. Well that name isn't just a metaphor anymore. I turn into an actual Black Tiger now. And I done some sh*t I already regret but it is what it is you know. Like I said, I gotta control myself now," said Mike da Silva.

"Huh? What the f**k you saying? Like an actual Black Tiger?"

"An actual Black Tiger, like imagine a panther. Like a Black Panther. But instead I'm a Black Tiger. Full on tiger."

"Bruh. On God, that's the most gangster sh*t I heard. Course you got that power. What it be like? What did you do that you done regre …"

"Kid. I'm not talking about that. I'm not talking anymore okay. Enough about me. Everyone always wanna talk about me. I'm bored. I'm done talking about me. What's your power? What can you do?"

"Well it ain't nothing half as cool as your sh*t. But I can like hear nature. Like I can hear it talking. I can feel it's feelings and sh*t."

"Damn that's kind lit. Good for you. I mean you is a gardener right?"

"Mega-Terrarium Executive but yeah I'm basically a gardener."

"So that it? Damn you got a sh*t one but it's cool. You cool still. Girls will f**king love that sh*t. At least you got that sh*t on your side."

"I can make weed from my hands. I can make it in my hands."

"Bullsh*t. I don't believe you. Show me."

And then in a split second, Devonte had a nug of weed in his hands, and Mike da Silva's eyes lit up. He grabbed the weed and smelt it.

"Wedding Cake?" asked Mike da Silva.

"Yep. I thought of Wedding Cake and it came in my hands. It's cool but what am I gonna do with this sh*t man?"

"Listen, we're gonna do business together. You gonna be rich. Don't worry about what you gone do. I got a plan," said Mike da Silva as he grabbed Devonte Lacy by the shoulder and excitedly shook him.

Fergus-Sundar and Shackleton Nair

"Oh my God. It's you," said Shackleton Nair as he stopped in disbelief as to what he was seeing before him. "You're him? You, you are full of it. It's all over you. Sorry, I should introduce myself. The name's Shackleton, Shackleton Nair. What's your name? It is an absolute pleasure to make your acquaintance."

"Pleased to meet you too. The name's Fergus-Sundar. I can sense your shock and confusion? What's the matter Shackleton?" he replied.. He figured he no longer needed to hide his name. He felt safe here with GHEE and Elisabeth Cervantes.

"You're full of it? It's you. Sorry I'm just going to say it straight. my name is Shackleton Nair. Crap I've already told you my name. Anyhow. I'm a mycologist; I study mushrooms and everything to do with this essentially. And recently I discovered a new type of bioluminescent mycorrhizae – meaning that it was glowing, and for reference, this is not completely uncommon in nature. But this mycorrhizae I discovered was levitating, much how we all did when we were Illuminated, and it is my hypothesis that this type of mycorrhizae consists of what could only really be determined to be Dark Matter, for I did not know what else it could be. We do not know what Dark Matter is and everything is just off with these mushrooms, the weight, the energy, the vibrations, everything. It has something else in it. So this brings me here. Since the Illumination, I have developed the ability to see mycorrhizae particles in the air, as well as to see the mycelium everywhere in this world – I can see the residue even in front of me now on the floor. And I'm sorry for my excitement at having seen you – but you are full of this mycorrhizal residue, that is akin to that of the one I recently discovered in lieu of the Tech-Night. Everyone here in fact has some of this within them, but you are completely filled with it – when I look at you it seems to be within every shed of you. I think this strange of fungi is the cause, or at least a catalyst behind this Illumination that we have all undergone. And I did not know where it came from. This strand of fungi has appeared seemingly out of nowhere. But now that I see you, and I can see that it is within your very being – it looks to make up your DNA even if my vision of the residue is not deceiving me. And so I think it is you. I think you have caused this. Who are you really Fergus-Sundar? You are not from here are you. Are you from another planet? Perhaps you are genetically modified."

Fergus-Sundar was at a loss for words. The man had within moments deciphered that he was not from this world, and he could not even deny it, for this man in front of him had even brought up Dark Matter, which he knew to be within him. He had his curiosity.

"Well that's a lot of information to process. It sounds like you have quite a unique talent Shackleton. But no I am not from another planet; I am from Earth. I am a person, like you."

"You cannot be. You have brought this Dark Matter with you. I am certain of it. The more I look at you, the more it seems the fungi residue I see in you, is the mother fungi, the original of this kind. You can't be from Earth, Fergus-Sundar. Are you an alien?"

"I am a human being, or Homo Illuminatus now I guess. And I am from Earth Shackleton. Though I come from another time. It is not easy to explain. I am telling you this because I know what you can see and so there is no point me denying this. Yes, I do have Dark Matter within me – I do not know how it got there or within me, but I knew upon my arrival here that I had this within me, for I would not have made it here without it. But I did not know that this Dark Matter had fused with the fungi on this Earth. We have much to discuss it seems Shackleton Nair, and I think we can help each other."

"Yes we do Fergus-Sundar. We will keep in touch," said Shackleton Nair as he tipped his hat at Fergus-Sundar, a courteous sign of respect.

And so, this was the first encounter of the Shackleton Nair and Fergus-Sundar, the first of many.

Fergus-Sundar and Mike da Silva

Mike da Silva took a swig of his drink and due to his large frame, bumped into a comparatively small man, spilling the drink on him.

"Rah I'm sorry. My bad mate. Hope I didn't mess up your suit," said Mike as he looked at the man.

"Oh don't worry. My suits have seen worse. It's rented anyways!!" replied Fergus-Sundar with a chuckle. He was having fun and had now loosened up. "I'm Fergus, Fergus-Sundar. What's your name?"

"Mike da Silva if we're going by full name. You can call me Mike though. You uh, you ain't from around innit?"

"Nice to meet you, Mike. What do you mean by that?"

"Nothing mate. Just most people tend to know who I am, it's rare these days that someone doesn't know me but I like that."

"Oh right, fair play. What're you famous for?"

"Mixed Martial Arts. I'm an MMA fighter.," Mike replied.

Fergus-Sundar looked at Mike da Silva up and down, and could see the man's muscles bulging through his suit even. He was a behemoth.

"That's cool man. I've had a few amateur boxing fights myself but I don't really keep up to date with fighting sports. I don't have the time unfortunately," said Fergus-Sundar as he kept his own fighting history to himself – he knew if he divulged into his own boxing pedigree, Mike da Silva would question how he does not know who he is.

"Nice. So, what do you do?"

"I work just a standard boring government job man. Nothing special to be honest."

"It's good to be boring man. I wish I had a boring life sometimes. But here I am," said Mike da Silva as he let out a sigh.

Fergus-Sundar did not need his newfound superpower of hearing the thoughts of others, to decipher that Mike had guilt within him.

"Why is that?" replied Fergus-Sundar.

"You see sh*t man. You see bad motherf****ng sh*t in this world, that's why. And you do bad sh*t. If I was boring, I'd be a good man. I wouldn't have done none of this sh*t I done or seen none of this shit."

"Well just because you've done bad stuff before in you life, doesn't mean you're a bad person necessarily. We live, and we learn. You don't have to let your past mistakes define you, you have time Mike. So an ability I've developed, post-Illumination, is that I can see people's true essence, the pure and individual energy that one radiates. And from what I can see, no matter what you've done in your past – you seem to be a good person to me at your core. Take that for what you will. But don't overthink it. If you have done bad stuff, as long as you're working on it and your intentions are good and you're trying to change – I'd say you are good. But what do I know? I'm just a man. We don't know very much. I've learned recently, it's best not to judge where you can. Most seem to be on the periphery of being either good or bad, and it's minor things and our intentions which take us to one side or the other. Sometimes it can be decisions which take us on either path. But there is always a path back to the light. I'd say if you're conscious of the things you've done, and of how your actions lie in the face of morality, however you deem that – you're on the good side. Because if you were a purely bad person, you wouldn't even know you're doing wrong, or you wouldn't care. That's just how I see things. So don't stress. Or perhaps keep stressing."

"Man. Thank you man. You got a good energy bout you Fergus-Sundar. You a cool mother*****r I ain't gone lie. I'm glad we met. All God's plan. This sh*t has been on my mind the last couple days. Ever since I got these powers, I just been thinking about life different. I wanna change man. But when you done the sh*t I done, and you seen the sh*t I seen, you dunno if it's possible. I'm an old mother*****r Fergus. I'm an old dog. And you know what they say about old dogs. You can't teach them new tricks. But I feel good now man. Maybe we can still learn as we get older; just gotta have an open mind you feel? You cool though. If ever you want some weed, hit me up – no charge."

"Thank you Mike, you're cool too. And it's okay; I don't smoke weed. My job don't let me," replied Fergus-Sundar who then realised he no longer worked for the SSSA. He was no longer a SSSA4. The world was his oyster now, he was unburdened by duty. "However, I guess I don't work for the government anymore; I'm in between jobs at the moment, so I suppose I can smoke. Would be good to try it out. Let's do it sometime."

"Why not right? And if that ain't your cup of tea, maybe we can enjoy a cigar together. But yeah, imma go work the room a bit. I see a leng ting over there, so imma go introduce myself. You can come too if you want;

she got a nice friend, we can double team that. But if not, stay in touch my man. Give me your number," said Mike da Silva as he took finished his glass of champagne and eyed up the woman across the room, who was also consciously making eye contact with Mike.

"I'll leave you to it Mike, it's been a pleasure to meet you. I'm afraid I don't have a number at the moment; I'm between contracts."

"Damn. Aite say no more. Take my business card. Drop me a message when you get that number," said Mike as he shook the hand of Fergus-Sundar before adjusting his suit and making his way over to the woman across the room.

He watched on as he watched Mike walked away. He had a good feeling about the man, despite the fact that Mike da Silva had done bad things in his life; despite how it might've looked from the outside, Fergus-Sundar felt and saw, using his newfound powers, that intrinsically he was good and kind at heart.

Shackleton Nair and Devonte Lacy

"You," called out Shackleton Nair. "What's your name?"

"You? Bruh who the f**k is you?" replied Devonte Lacy as he turned. Respect was of paramount importance to him and he felt disrespected at the way the man had called out to him.

"Shackleton Nair is my name. I apologise if I came across as rude. Do forgive me. What's your name young man?"

"Devonte. What's up?" he abruptly replied. His shoulders were tense. He looked Shackleton up and down, judging his outfit from the get go.

"Erm not much to be honest Devonte. I'm enjoying the evening's festivities. It's just exhilarating to be surrounded by such extraordinary people. I'm honoured to be here and to make your acquaintance. May I enquire as to what it is that you do?"

"Yeah, you can enquire. I'm a Mega-Terrarium Executive. What you do Mister Nair?"

"Ah! Fascinating. I thought as such. Well I did not quite know you were a Mega-Terrarium Executive but I knew you must have been around a Terrarium recently. There's no other reason why you would have such a high level of fungi residue on you. Please though, call me Shackleton."

"It's cool. Mister Nair is fine. What is you talking about bruh? Fungi residue? I hope you know that you a weird ass dude. Yeah, I work with Terrariums. I see to all the nature inside of them, so yeah I got my hands and clothes and shoes in mycelium and all that on the regular. What it is you do?" replied Devonte.

"Well, I'm a mycologist and I am a Professor also. I have a PhD. Though I tend to be doing independent research these days."

"Wait. Is you that Shackleton Nair? Oh sh*t it is you. The Dark Matter guy? You found that bioluminescent strain right. You said that sh*t come from outside this Earth. Damn they tryna cancel you for that too. I thought I recognised you. F**k. Small world man. If it's any consolation I read your paper and I liked it. Some interesting sh*t for real and personally I think you was onto some sh*t. And I guess with everything that happened with the Illumination and all that, I guess that sh*t you said ain't so controversial now is it. They gonna uncancel you now sir. It's good to meet you Professor."

"Ah yes. Thank you. I am glad to hear you've read it. Yes some of the papers and journals I've published, as well as my blog – tends to receive a lot of negative press from some of the more close-minded people in the industry. Though whenever I do meet people who have actually read my work, in person they tend to be very friendly. So yes I'm glad to hear you like it. Anyhow, may I enquire as to what it is that your power is? What has the Illumination done to you young man?"

"I can hear nature. I know that might not make sense. But I can like sense they feelings and sh*t. I can see it too, like I can see the vibrations and sh*t and feel what they be feeling. It don't make sense really but I guess none of this does if imma keep it a buck. I can make weed too man. It sounds funny as hell, I know, but I can make that it from my hand. It some useless ass sh*t other than the fact I can make some good money from it maybe, but yeah bruh that's it. What's yo power?"

"That is interesting. Very interesting. It seems we both have developed abilities to do with nature. Perhaps a result of the fact we both are educated, work in, and well are evidently passionate about nature. My ability is that I can see fungi residue in the atmosphere and just about anywhere to be honest. That is why I called out to you Devonte – I could see a lot of residue on you and that is not very common. As you know, nowadays there is not much nature that is around us, especially here in London – our climate doesn't allow for them to thrive due to the high amounts of pollution. And well I can physically see the mycorrhizal roots with my own eyes, even through physical elements such as concrete or wood. I would compare this vision to x-ray vision but for fungi and mycorrhizae. And much like you, I can create fungi based things from the palms of my hand," replied Shackleton, who then opened his palm and out came a little cardholder. He gave it to Devonte who held the cardholder, which felt like leather to him.

"That sh*t cool as f**k, I ain't even gone cap," said Devonte as he chuckled to himself. "You making my sh*t look weak as f**k though I ain't gone lie. This a mycelium based leather wallet right?"

"Yes. A gift to you. But fret not Devonte. I believe our abilities we have now are not completely developed yet. I am certain that with time your abilities shall expand, you just need to tap into it. Have faith."

"Let's see man. Right now I'm just tryna control that sh*t bruh. Hearing all these extra voices of nature and sh*t. That sh*t be tiring as f**k bruh, but it is what it is."

"Well it's a blessing, is it not? I know that me and you alike, both are aware of the beauty and complexity of the natural world, of nature. However, you are now experiencing first hand, the true complexity of nature, that others would not be able to fathom or believe to be possible. So you hear nature?"

"Yeah bruh. I can hear their cries. Even right now. I can hear that sh*t. When that sh*t first happened to me. The Illumination that is. My head was f**king ringing bruh. It was killing me, hearing all that sh*t. The trees is lonely bruh. They sad I'm telling you. I knew this sh*t before. We ain't got enough nature in the city man. All the trees when you walk down the road. They all be by themselves. Like they isolated. People think that just cos it be nature, like they ain't got feelings and sh*t. But I know, and I know you know since you a professor in mycology and sh*t. That trees and nature suffer isolation and sh*t too. They share nutrients and information and communicate with each other through the wood wide network, through underground mycelium networks, through the roots. But here in the big cities man, where these trees all alone, and separated from each other, chilling out on their ones – they sad bruh. They can't share information with one another. They all alone. But I can hear it all now and it's been killing me for real."

"Yes, this is nature's world. They came before us. We have taken over the world us, human beings. And we have pillaged this land of its green and beauty. And we have killed nature; so we can live in the masses."

"Well I ain't think it's their world. It's God's world bruh, we just living in it. But God put us here on this world too. We gotta share this world with nature. I done think we lost our balance man. We lost the value of nature man. We became technology obsessed man."

"I do not know if it's God's world. I believe it's natures world and we're just living in it. However, I certainly understand your sentiment. We have lost sight of the value of nature. I hope one day we realise it. We owe it to them. This is the impact of climate change is so severe. We've pillage the land and Earth, and it fights back in the form of natural disasters, to seek balance."

"I hear you bruh. We just gotta get the balance bruh. In time man, God willing. We gotta share the Earth with nature; it ain't just for us."

"Yes well I believe it's nature's world. Nature always fights back and wins eventually. That's how and why human civilisations always fall. Because we think it's ours but it's not. Nature will always strike back."

"I feel you bruh, but I still got people over nature man. We gotta just realise the value of nature before that sh*t gets too late. Anyway though gangy, good to speak with you for sure. Imma go for a piss real quick. We gone keep in touch though for sure. Imma come find you."

"Well we can agree to disagree, but I understand and respect your viewpoint. We will certainly keep in touch. It's been an absolute pleasure to meet you Devonte. I'll see you around," replied Shackleton as he watched the young man walk away with a spring in his step. *Impressive,* Shackleton thought to himself as he thought of Devonte.

And so this was the first encounter between Shackleton Nair and Devonte Lacy, and it would be the first of many.

Elisabeth Cervantes

Elisabeth looked at the message pop up on the BioniPhone screen which was embedded in her skin on the back of her hand. She took another big gulp out of her champagne glass: it was the her fifth glass of the night. She received updates from Doctor Alexis who continued to work on the DMT Device, and received updates from Bridger Falcon as he dealt with the Luftana Amara situation. So much had occurred in just twenty-four hours. It was not common for her to be stressed, however she felt so in this moment. There was much at stake, and she had three situations occurring simultaneously that she was at the centre of, not including her work commitments with GHEE and other organisations she was affiliated with. She had to oversee these 419 Homo Illuminatus who had gathered at her facility, and who collectively most certainly had the power to completely destroy her billion-dollar facility and cause serious harm to herself and others – if they chose to do so.

The responsibility was on her and if things went wrong then she would be the one who would be held accountable; they gathered here under her instructions, and with her money as those from around the world were brought via her horde of private jets. Further to this, there was the situation with Malabar Jones' capture and his imprisonment at the GHEE HQ. And lastly, there was the DMT device which they had just created, and she had to ensure that Bridger Falcon correctly disposed of Luftana Amara. She had complete trust in him and her team; this was not their first rodeo. There were too many hazardous plates spinning around at the GHEE HQ at the moment for her liking – it explained why she was drinking so much. Then her BioniPhone, embedded in her skin on the back of her hand, buzzed once more. She read the name on the message alert and read it to be Bridger Falcon. She swiped the message open, about to read it, before feeling a tap on her shoulder. She turned to see Fergus-Sundar standing in front of her.

"Fergus-Sundar hello. How are you doing? I'm so sorry I've not had a chance to speak to you all day, or even yesterday. I understand you were somewhat troubled in the morning after your Illumination and so I thought it would be best if I left you to your devices," she said as they looked at one another, crossing her legs as she stood, delicately placing one leg in front of the other.

"Elisabeth. It's so good to see you. Yes, I am sorry if barked at you from inside the room yesterday. It was just … just a lot to adjust to. My mind was racing like crazy. I couldn't control all the thoughts. They were racing like crazy. I just could not control them. It was driving me crazy. There were so many thoughts fluttering around in my head and they were just coming from all angles. And none were my own, and so I couldn't hear myself amongst all the excess. To be honest it took me about a day to actually get a grip of it. I feel like myself once more. Well my new self I suppose. I still have all of these thoughts swarming my head. But I can control it now. I've learned to harness it and activate it as of when I need it. However, some are still slipping through what I guess you could call my defence. But I think this is a good thing if I'm being objective. It's only natural right to have some intrusive thoughts every now and then. How we manage them is what's important."

"Ah I'm sorry to hear it's been tough, but I'm glad you're feeling better. Remind me again though please – what is your power? Sorry, it's been a long day."

"Don't worry. Well I'm still discovering and unlocking all of these powers. But long story short, I can see the unique vibrations that people radiate and I can see the pure essence or energy of people upon looking at them. And I think when I connect with them, physically, I can hear their thoughts and feel their emotions. That's why yesterday it was just a lot to process and manage. It's tough enough dealing with one's own emotions, let alone be hyperaware of everyone else's. It put me in a state of anxiety, but it seems I am destined to be in a constant state of angst now I suppose. But that is part and parcel of this gift that this Illumination has given me. And it is a gift. I think maybe this is why I've landed here in this reality you know. I didn't know why before, but maybe this is why," he said, losing himself in conversation, forgetting others were around.

"Anyhow I'm talking too much and taking too much of your time. You've got other people to and entertain and here I am rambling on. I guess I just find it easy to talk to you. I know I had my apprehensions about you before, and that my arrival here at the GHEE HQ was under false pretences, but I do trust you Elisabeth Cervantes and I believe in you and I see the good in you. Now I have this power, I have no doubt that you are good. And I want you to know that you have me. I'll be with you and the GHEE whilst I'm stuck here in this reality. And I do want to stay here for a while longer. I think I am finding my purpose now," he said as he spoke honestly and openly to her. Gone was the Fergus-Sundar who was reserved by nature, constantly sceptical. He had an open heart now, and sought peace and goodness in life – though with this came naivety and blindness.

"What's the matter?" he continued. "I can sense sadness and guilt in you now. And now the tears that are beginning to well up in your eyes. Look at me Elisa." Elisabeth Cervantes lifted her head and raised her gaze to meet the eyes of Fergus-Sundar.

"You don't even know me Fergus-Sundar. How can you say this about me? How can you know this?"

"I see you Elisa. I told you, I can see your core essence. The purest part of your energy. And I know you are good and that you have a kind heart. Even now without my powers. I look into your eyes, and I see kindness deep within you. But, I think it's best I stop looking you're your eyes, those big blue eyes. I fear every time I look into them, that I'm getting more and more lost in them, and that scares me Elisa."

"Oh God. Fergus," she started as she took a step back from him, looked away and took in a deep breath to regain her composure. Thoughts were flying in her mind and she had to remember where she was. "I'm humbled. You are so kind. But you don't know me Fergus. I'm not as good as you think I am. I've done bad things."

"Wanna do some more?" he replied cheekily; he was referring to a different type of bad thing, to the ones she was reminiscing upon.

"Fergus-Sundar. Stop it," she said while smiling. "I appreciate your kind words. You've touched my heart today. Thank you. And I'm sorry. You are very handsome, but I have a boyfriend."

"You're very welcome. And hey no need to apologise. I just thought I'd shoot my shot you know. I thought maybe you felt that connection between us too."

"I think it's just platonic Fergus. I don't see you that way. But really I am flattered," she said as she lied to herself. She felt a connection with him, but she was too was frightened of her feelings. It was a feeling she had not felt before with anyone else. To be seen for the purest parts of herself. She felt vulnerable around him and able to simply relax and loosen her guard. And this frightened her, for she was used to keeping her guard up, for when she had let her guard down before, she was hurt. And she did not want to experience that again. She thought of Jarred Lane Johnson and felt bad, for she had never connected with him on an emotional level like this.

Further, Elisabeth was afraid that if Fergus-Sundar got closer to her, that he would see the worser parts of herself, and he would not like what he saw. She did not want to anyone to see parts of her; she knew no one could love her for this. She knew, she could hold this part of herself back with other people – but something inside her told her that with Fergus-Sundar she would not be able to. He would see her for her, and her true self would come out – perhaps regardless of his power, and so she was afraid of what this might entail. There was a vulnerability that seemed to ignite when they were together.

"Anyhow," she continued. "I've gotta go make my way to the podium now. Think it's time we wrap this up. We'll speak very soon Fergus-Sundar. Don't stray too far now."

"Bye Elisabeth. Sorry for troubling you and if I made it weird."

"Ah you're fine don't worry. Enjoy yourself, have some champagne before it runs out!" she said as she hurried off.

He watched her walk away and felt something he had not felt before, and he did not truly understand it at this stage. It was love that was beginning to blossom for Elisabeth Cervantes, and his love that grew for her was pure and from the deepest and purest recesses of his soul; he wished to see her to be the best woman she could be. Fergus-Sundar wished stop the sadness that he could see in her eyes, and wished to be able to offer her comfort through the trials and tribulations in life, that all people encounter, that she would inevitably come across. Never before had Fergus-Sundar felt like this or had thoughts like this. She had, in a few brief moments, captured his imagination and opened a part of his soul he had never before known. And thus, Fergus-Sundar once more was with a mission; exploring love was his mission now. Love was not allowed as a SSSA4, and so from this moment on, his time as a spy had truly ended –the final piece of his metamorphosis.

•••   •••   •••

As she walked away, she felt herself becoming somewhat overwhelmed by emotions; her memories of her actions yesterday was creating guilt within her. Her crassness with how she had dealt with the SSSA4 Malabar Jones, and the heinous act she was involved with in Luftana Amara – brought terrible shame to her in this moment. This was lingering in the back of her mind, and Fergus-Sundar complimenting her as he did, and seeing the good in her, despite the fact she had acted as she had acted in the last twenty-four hours – was too much for her to process. She then remembered where she was, and carried on about her business and glided through the sea of Homo Illuminatus who continued to converse with one another. She calmed herself, took in a deep breath, and walked onto the stage – it was time for her to perform.

She delivered a rousing speech to the 419 Homo Illuminatus who had gathered in the room. In a laconic yet punchy manner, she informed them of their importance to the future as she reaffirmed that they were the future of human history. She pledged to always support them, and that the GHEE would always be there for them – whatever they needed. Finally, she promised these Homo Illuminatus that they would receive free lifetime healthcare from the GHEE, and would be provided with a full health check prior to their departure from the facility today in lieu of their recent Illumination; the unfortunate death of Luftana Amara and her side effects from the Illumination, meant they all had to be conscious and cautious of side effects. The speech was met with raucous applause from Homo Illuminatus who were guided out of the hall and to their respective health checks.

· · ·   · · ·   · · ·

Some time passed and all Homo Illuminatus had departed the hall and were all respectively getting their health checks. Elisabeth Cervantes was sat on the stage in the hall with Doctor Alexis, Bridger Falcon, and a woman named Sabrina Xavier, who did not like Elisabeth. Images of Homo Illuminatus popped up on the screen in front of them; it was decision time.

"Okay so we know who is a definite no go. We've cut it down to just ninety-eight now, which considering we started with 419, is pretty good. So we know who we do not want, or need – the useless ones. Now who do we actually like out of those remaining? Think about how they can be useful for this team, to us. Think about their powers, the skillset. Yeah? It's all important. Let's isolate those we like for this team. And I reckon we then create a sub-section of these people we like into two groups – those we can control, and those who are likely to be hard to control, the livewires. Sound good? We'll spend another fifteen minutes brainstorming and then we'll go through the options. The Illuminated we all agree on, whether we like them or do not like them – we move ahead on and either they go through to the next round, or we disregard them. Because we cannot select too many. If it's too many they'll be hard to control, and it can reduce their value in their role. Remember we want them to feel important still, and that spaces are limited and so if they want to be able to act and utilise their powers with freedom, and for them to have potentially significant impacts on the world – then they will need to be compliant to us, and remain special and useful. Therefore, we can't have too many of them, and it can't be too few. Now there is someone who others here disregard as being valuable, but you believe would be good to keep on the team, be prepared to fight for them – have your argument ready. And conversely, if there is someone who you firmly believe should not be a part of the team, then speak up. Right. Hope that is all clear. Let's get to work now people. Fifteen minutes. Let's do it," Elisabeth said.

18:55: Meeting Room 69 of GHEE HQ

After some deliberation, the line-up had been selected. It seemed to be the case that some of Homo Illuminatus had been selected and the decision to include them was certainly unanimous. And there were some, whose inclusion was fought over and debated. One of these being Mike da Silva, the Black Tiger. Lauded for his power and speed and fighting ability, and self-evident leadership skills. Though feared for his penchant and commitment to violence, and for the fact that he could turn into a Black Tiger at any moment and kill them all. Another whose inclusion was debated, was

Devonte Lacy. For he was young and had yet to unlock all of his skills. It seemed to the group that he was not yet ready to have such power. Though Elisabeth herself seemed to fight for his inclusion as she saw potential in him and liked his fiery nature and self-assuredness; he was mentally tough, and she felt this was needed in the group, as well as his budding ability to understand and manipulate nature.

The list of Homo Illuminatus, selected for this group, was as follows: Mike da Silva, Devonte Lacy, Fergus-Sundar, Shackleton Nair, Judge Hana Usman, Kwesi Ofori, Yacine Edouard, Elijah Quintrell, Officer Juliette Palmer. They had all been summoned once more by Elisabeth Cervantes. They stood around the room somewhat awkwardly and hesitantly looked at one another. Though a few had already been acquainted, and it seemed as though two sub-groups had already been established somewhat from the get go, naturally as human beings tended to do, whether they were Homo Sapien or Homo Illuminatus. The groups seemed to be as follows: (1) Devonte Lacy, Mike da Silva, Kwesi Ofori and Yacine Edouard, (2) Shackleton Nair, Elijah Quintrell, Hana Usman and Juliette Palmer. Fergus-Sundar did not seem to exactly fit in one another and was aptly stood in the middle of the room, with his eyes fixed on Elisabeth Cervantes as she was about to begin her speech.

"I hope you all have enjoyed your day here at the Global Hub of Extra-Terrestrial Exploration Headquarters. Now it is time for the main call of business. You are probably confused as to what this main call of business is. But fear not. I'm about to tell you. You all have powers now. You could call yourselves superheroes. I mean that's what your powers would suggest you could become right. But you cannot be a superhero if you do not do extraordinary things for the public. You are all special. For some reason you have been bestowed with these powers. Some of you might believe this is a chance, whilst some may believe this is God given. You can believe what you want, it doesn't bother me, and it ain't none of my damn business quite frankly. Each to their own you know, it don't matter to me. But the fact remains. You are special. And you do have powers. And what does matter to me, and what is my damn business, is this world. That's been my business for some time now. We got several issues around the globe. I know that and I know you know that. This world is real and the problems are real. And now you've all got these powers, and I have the resources to give you the liberty to act, legally and with permission from governments around the world, to better the world and tackle these problems. I think together we can make this world a better place for people, and end suffering. In theory, there are enough resources already in the world to support every human being, but that's not how life works is it. Politics and religion and greed for power and money gets in the way, our histories get in the way. It's Abnormal quite frankly. The fact the world operates as it does, considering all we have here, and there is still suffering and inequality and injustice on a wide scale, visible to all – it's abnormal. And so this brings me to my final point. I think as a team we can tackle these Abnormal issues. If you agree to join this team, you would use your unique skills on a potentially global basis to tackle inequalities and injustices around the world. Now you'd all have your own individual sectors and industries you'd be working in, and you'd have a team around you to help you with this. But the choice is yours whether you want to be a part of this team or not. I don't know what is going to happen to you Homo Illuminatus and I don't know how the world is going to react to your powers and you using this on your day to day. But I know if you work with me and GHEE, you would have freedom to use your powers. The public will be scared of you, I guarantee that. Because people always fear that which they do not understand and in theory, some will say you are a threat to mankind. For you an evolved version of Homo Sapiens. You too are Abnormal now in the world. I want you to join me. Become an Abnormal for GHEE. I would unite you and form the team as The Abnormals of GHEE. Own the narrative, and we can do good together to make this world a better place. There are 419 Homo Illuminatus but there's only nine of you here in the room. Think about that. You have been chosen especially because of your skill set, experience, your personalities, and because of the potential we see in you. And if some of you have not met yet, I'm just going to say what powers you have you know so we can see what extraordinary and amazing gifts you have here. Kwesi Ofori. The man is a supremely talented artist and a boxer. If he draws something on paper, it comes to life. It comes to f**king life. So if you need a well, the man can draw a well into the terrain he sees in front of him and it comes to life. That is f**king wild and it's an amazing gift. Yacine Edouard is a man who you wouldn't think would be here, but here he is. An ex-convict, I hope you don't mind me saying – for armed robbery and breaking and entering. Yacine has since turned his life around and now he can travel through walls and objects, and if he's in a car, he can even take a car through the wall just because he's in it. That is amazing. And then you've got the famous Elijah Quintrell. The electric race car driver. One of the best in the world. He's a five-time world champion and I've personally seen him race before in Monaco and Seoul. The man has the power now to create electricity with his bare hands – is that not amazing and supremely useful. Then you've got Judge Hana Usman, who has presided over some of the most high profile court cases in the last ten years and has never been afraid to make a decision for true justice. It's said that she can bring any person to tell the truth now by uttering a specific phrase – though I don't want to expose this without her prior permission. Then we have Office Juliette Palmer, who recently delivered a rousing speech here in London in lieu of the riots after the Tech-Night and calmed people down and has seriously changed the attitudes of the police for the better. She can do something similar to Hana and it's said she can make something come true by simply saying it too. And then we've got Shackleton Nair who can create mycelium from the palms of his hands. I could go on and on. But you all are extraordinary and there is so much potential here for you all to do good. We must work together. And don't worry about money – you'll all be millionaires within a year for having to quit your jobs and take on this new venture. But let's not waste this. This is a once in a lifetime opportunity. This is greater than us. I know I've been rambling on for some time now and I'm sorry but I have truly been speaking from the heart. Now what do you say?" finished Elisabeth Cervantes as they all kind of looked up and down from the floor back up to Elisabeth. There was tension in the air. It was palpable. No one seemed to want to talk.

Mike da Silva slowly stood up, and everyone watched as he stood up – for he was easily the biggest and most intimidating presence in the room. "I'm in. F**k it why not. I'm ready to do some good sh*t with my life. People think I'm a bad man. But I ain't. I've done bad stuff. But I wanna do good stuff too. Count me in. And youse all better be f**king in with this sh*t too. The woman's speaking f**king sense. Why wouldn't we use these powers? Don't b**ch out," said Mike da Silva, whose deep voice resonated and created an echo of some sort.

Devonte Lacy stood up. "Y'all can count me in."

"Yes, why not. Count me in too," said Shackleton Nair.

"I will join this team. I believe God give me this power. I will use this for good. I want to help make this world better. You tell me how I can help, and I will help," said Yacine Edouard.

"I'm in Elisabeth. Thank you for the opportunity. I ain't gone let you down," said Kwesi.

"Yes Elisabeth. Thank you for the opportunity and consideration but I have a career that I am committed to and passionate about. I cannot just chop and change like that. I'll have to take some time to think about all of this," said Judge Hana Usman.

"I'll second Hana's sentiment. I have a career too and a family; I can't just leave like that. I have commitments and people who rely on me," said Officer Juliette Palmer.

"I understand Hana and Juliette. Completely. So of course take your time to think about this opportunity. You can work with us on a part-time basis as well. There's still a lot to discuss with regards to the projects and time commitments and all of that. However, just be conscious as well. Considering that for both of you, your voice is your power. Do you think you will be able to continue with your jobs as a Judge and Police Office respectively, just as normal? Just like before?" said Elisabeth Cervantes. She could visibly see the confusion go through both Hana Usman's and Juliette Palmer's minds. It seemed to be a thought which had gone over their head's. Hana Usman could make anyone tell the truth even if they did not want to by simply speaking in a certain way, and Juliette Palmer could make something happen or become real by simply saying it in a certain way. "You are both women in very high positions of power. Do you think that you can really continue on with your jobs considering this?"

"I'll be honest. I did not think of that before and you raise a valid point. I think I'll have to discuss this in further with my people and the bar. So regardless I will have to get back to you on this Elisabeth. But yes fine, preliminarily consider me in on certain conditions, which we'll have to discuss later on."

"Again, I'll second what Hana said. Sorry to jump on what you're saying again," said Juliette as Hana and her smiled at one another. "I'm in though."

And then soon enough, everyone had agreed to join the team. Elisabeth Cervantes could not contain her excitement. The group began to converse with one another and unlikely combinations of people began to speak to one another. From Juliette Palmer and Yacine Edouard, to Hana Usman and Devonte Lacy, to Elijah Quintrell and Kwesi Ofori. Elisabeth watched on excitedly, and then saw Fergus-Sundar approach her.

"Well don't you look happy," said Fergus-Sundar.

"I'm so happy right now. I can't control it. This feels very strange. I feel exposed. I'm usually so stoic," she replied.

"No please, keep it up; it's great," he replied.

She looked at his eyes before looking down at his lips. He was doing the exact same thing.

"Stop it Fergus, I know what you're doing."

"I'm not doing anything."

"Hmm really? You know what you're doing."

"Maybe I do. Can you blame me?"

"Hmm no not really. I know what I look like today."

"I don't think it's just a today thing Elisa."

"Okay now stop," she replied.

"Alright, my bad lol. Anyway I just want to say. Thank you for this. I've been lost Elisa. Ever since I've arrived. But now I am found. I know myself and I think I know why I landed here now. This is my purpose now. I'm glad to be a part of this team. I don't know what I can do, but I'm here. And I'm on your team Elisa. Whatever comes ahead," he said as he spoke from the heart.

"I'm happy to hear that Fergus. I'm glad you are here too. This wouldn't be possible with you. And don't worry. We'll find something for you. Welcome to the team. You are one of the Abnormals of GHEE now. But please. do excuse me; I need to make a phone call real quick. One moment," said Elisabeth Cervantes. Fergus-Sundar nodded his head and made a gentleman like gesture, showing her the way whilst slightly bowing. She left the room and clicked on the number for Bridger Falcon. He answered instantly.

"Bridger, I saw your message. What's the update?"

"Hi. Well the clean-up is done with the Luftana situation. We're in contact with the family now. All traces of interference from us has been cleared so we're good to go on that front," said Bridger.

"Fantastic. And the other thing?" said Elisabeth.

"He's fine. Well he's not fine, but he's under control is what I mean. The situation is under control."

"Okay. But what does that mean. Specifics Bridger," she said.

"Are you sure you want me to say this over the phone?"

"It's a clean line. New number. Hit me with it."

"He's in the chamber now. They're torturing him now as we speak. I'm outside the chamber."

"Good. Anything? Has he said anything?"

"No Elisa. I think he's been trained to resist this. It seems like he's gone through something similar before."

"Yes but he's not had it from us before. And he's ours now. He's not leaving here anytime soon. Get me the SSSA's location."

• • • • • • • • •

And so, this was the story of how Elisabeth Cervantes brought together this team of Homo Illuminatus to unite under the GHEE as a group that would come to be known as The Abnormals.

Malabar Jones was in captivity and being tortured by the GHEE, and the truth behind Elisabeth's involvement with the conspiracy of the Dala Device was unknown still to the world.

Fergus-Sundar now was integrated into this new reality, into the Tech-Night World and into the year 2065. Though he was no longer a SSSA4. For Fergus-Sundar was now a Homo Illuminatus, and the once sceptical man was sceptical no more, instead he was now blinded by love; his love for Elisabeth Cervantes.

And so, Elisabeth and the GHEE had control of The Abnormals, and the liberty from governments and monarchies around the world, to move forward with this squadron of Homo Illuminatus, who in essence were now Superheroes, to tackle some of the world's most pressing issues. This would begin immediately on from this point onwards, and thus Elisabeth Cervantes was the most powerful woman in the world; the world and it's most gifted individuals, in her control.

BOOK 20

SSSA1, YONIGE-YA

Monday 16th November 2065

. . . .

SSSA1:
The Yonige-Ya of the SSSA:
Tasked with vanishing agents – otherwise known as, Termination.
This applies to: Rogue Agents, Former Agents, and Failed Agents.
The SSSA1 is the Hitman of the SSSA.
But the Yonige-Ya has No Name. The name is the title.
The SSSA1 is the Yonige-Ya.

. . . .

20:25: The Security Centre of GHEE HQ

The six foot plus man with a wide frame, walked into the room with his wavy brown hair showing behind the back of his ear and behind the tiger mask that covered his face – he took out his jet black gun with a silencer affixed to the end of it; and shot a solitary shot at each of the heads of the three security guards in the room. They each dropped to the floor, like bowling pins, as the man casually strolled through the room – however, ensuring to close the eyelids of the men as blood rolled down from the gunshots and to the floor.

The man in question was the Yonige-Ya of the SSSA; SSSA1. He checked the room to check for cameras and realised there were two in the room. He again took his gun from his holster and shot once at each of the cameras. Now that the cameras were out, the Yonige-Ya took off his mask and could relax a little.

He twirled the ends of his moustache as he scrummaged through the various different camera feeds which were dotted around the GHEE HQ. And then the Yonige-Ya saw the man whom he had been looking for. He watched the screen as he saw Malabar Jones – the SSSA4 he had been sent to terminate and move into his final night – being whipped on his back relentlessly. He saw the blood run from the torn skin on his back, and he realised then that the SSSA4 was unequivocally failed in his mission, a failed agent, but also a captured one who was being tortured and thus a potential risk to the SSSA. He did not need to terminate the SSSA4. *I will obtain the data from his TechSuit before I depart.*

Though the Yonige-Ya wanted more context to the situation, and so he continued to search through the security footage. And very quickly he saw another face which he recognised – Elisabeth Cervantes, a woman who was perpetually on the watchlist of the SSSA. But it was who was with her that caught the curiosity of the SSSA1, Yonige-Ya. *He did not lie – Malabar did not lie; it's Fergus-Sundar.* And thus, he knew then that the SSSA4 of 2025 had indeed been found, but forty years later and he was in cahoots with the enemy and thus was now officially an enemy to the SSSA and to the nation. He realised then that Malabar Jones' failure had perhaps more to do with the unique circumstances of this case, rather than madness and incompetency – which is what the SSSA had initially thought upon hearing his feedback to them.

He checked his TechSuit and realised that as Malabar was within a one mile radius to him, he could indeed retrieve the data from his TechSuit; the SSSA had given him the access codes to do this. Thus, allowing him to have access to the files which were encrypted and securely stored on the TechSuit of the SSSA4.

And alas, two SSSA's had now infiltrated the GHEE HQ. However, where Malabar Jones' entry into the facility was known by GHEE; the Yonige-Ya's presence was not known. His presence in the GHEE HQ would be known after his departure from his facility, as the trail of bodies would eventually be found. But the SSSA1 had obtained the data from the TechSuit of the SSSA4.

And thus, the true nature of the Dala Device and the Tech-Night of 2065 would become known to the SSSA1. And the Yonige-Ya now was on the case of GHEE, and nothing would get in his way, for morality and a value for human life was not something that he had – *win at all costs, no matter the cost.*

IN MEDIAS RES

EPILOGUE

And so, this was the tale of The Tech-Night 1.0.

Fergus-Sundar's arrival had altered the course of humanity irrevocably.

Though this was simply the beginning.

The Tech-Night Epoch has just begun.

Fergus-Sundar and the rest of Homo Illuminatus will return.

The story would pick up again in The Tech-Night 2.0.

In the year 2070.